*the*
# AMISH
# COWBOY'S
# HOMECOMING

*the*
# AMISH
# COWBOY'S
# HOMECOMING

*USA TODAY* BESTSELLING AUTHOR
# OPHELIA
# LONDON

Entangled Publishing, LLC
10940 S Parker Road
Suite 327
Parker, CO 80134
Visit our website at www.entangledpublishing.com.

Amara is an imprint of Entangled Publishing, LLC.

Edited by Stacy Abrams
Cover design by Elizabeth Turner Stokes
Cover art by Photographer Tom Hallman,
kudla/shutterstock and nuchstockphoto/shutterstock
Interior design by Toni Kerr

Print ISBN 978-1-68281-571-7
ebook ISBN 978-1-68281-593-9

Manufactured in the United States of America

First Edition May 2021

AMARA

## ALSO BY OPHELIA LONDON

# GLOSSARY OF AMISH TERMS

*auf wiedersehen* – goodbye
*bobbeil* – baby
*bruder* – brother
*daadi hous* – grandpa's house
*daed* – father
*danke* – thank you
*dochder* – daughter
*fraa* – wife
*gaul* – horse
*Gott* – God
*Grossdaadi* – grandfather
*Grossmammi* – grandmother
*guder daag* – good day
*guder mariye* – good morning
*guder owed* – good evening
*gut* – good
*guti nacht* – good night
*hör mir zu* – listen to me
*jah* – yes
*kapp* – hat/bonnet
*kinnahs* – children
*Liebchen* – sweetheart
*maam* – mother
*mach's gut* – goodbye ("make good")
*meine liebling dochter* – my very special daughter
*nichts* – good night
*nummidaag* – afternoon
*Rumspringa* – Amish "running around" period
*Wie geht's* – How are you?
*Wunderbar* – wonderful

# NOTE FROM THE AUTHOR

Ten years ago, my sister moved to Hershey, Pennsylvania, a thirty-minute drive to Lancaster County. Ever since my first visit to Amish Country, I've lived in awe and admiration of the "plain" culture and its unique lifestyle. In researching for the Honey Brook series, I spoke with a woman named Mary Garver, who grew up near an Amish village and still has many close friends who are Amish. Along with some hilarious stories—one about her being one of four people named Mary sitting at a dinner table of five people—she gave me wonderful insights about that particular community's *Ordnung*, along with other rules and traditions specific to them. For example: individuals reading from the Bible aloud, "hands off" courtships, and the use of electricity for business purposes. From that, I learned that Amish congregations/communities can vary greatly in their unique customs and practices— which are often unwritten and not taught in church. This fascinated me further, yet what I did see in all the different groups was a love and devotion to God, family, and hard work. I've grown to love the Amish people and their desires to live good lives full of service and fortitude. The Honey Brook series is dedicated to them.

*To my Covid bubble: Kevin, Ashlee, & Puppy.*

# CHAPTER ONE

Isaac King slowly ran his finger down the center of her nose, ever so gently.

"Morning, sweetheart."

He felt her take in a breath, responding to his simple touch.

When she made a sound, he stepped closer, placing a hand on the side of her face. "I know, I know," he whispered, looking into her eyes. "I hate to leave, but it's something I have to do." With both hands now, he gently caressed all the way down her neck. Then, when there was nothing more to say, he touched his forehead to hers, taking in a deep breath. She smelled of earth and energy but mostly like…oats and molasses.

"Easy there, girl." Isaac laughed as the surefooted, petite Haflinger horse shook her head. "You know I could never leave you for long. It's just a day or two, and then we'll see what happens—probably nothing." He exhaled, trying to stay optimistic. He looked up into the blue-sky morning, feeling a slight flutter in his stomach.

*This could be it*, he thought, though not wanting to get his hopes up too high. *This could be my way out. Our way out.* With a lump in his throat, he glanced toward the house. No one was awake yet. That was good. He'd said his goodbyes to Sadie last night before he tucked her in bed. That had been hard enough—he didn't want to go through it again.

After giving his *gaul*—the one he'd had since he was just a boy—one more stroke down her nose, he knew it was time to stop procrastinating. Sunny wouldn't be coming with him on this trip, though she'd accompanied him everywhere else he'd ever gone. She was getting on in age, and this time, he wouldn't be needing a horse to just pull a buggy. Scout would be his travel mate.

From just thinking the fella's name, he heard the deep *neigh* coming from two stalls over.

Isaac grabbed his saddle, reins, and the rest of the tack off the back of the gate. "*Jah, jah,*" he said while approaching his white mount. "You excited, boy?" He laughed, patting his strongest, hardest-working horse—the one he could always count on. The one who would see him through what might be the most important moments of his life.

After leading Scout out of the barn, Isaac gave him a few extra minutes of brushing. Yes, he was stalling again. "Okay, time to go." He threw another glance toward the house. If he didn't hurry, his in-laws would be waking up soon and maybe try to talk him out of this. The buggy was already packed for an overnight stay if needed, and he had a fresh change of clothes on a sturdy wooden hanger in the way back of the carriage. He smoothed the front of his hair down and slid on his favorite straw hat. The one shaped more like an Englisher "cowboy" hat than a traditional Amish one, with the round brim.

He easily recalled when that hat had been given to him as a gift. As he clicked his tongue, prompting Scout to walk, he pulled down the front brim, ready for business. He could've had one of his Mennonite friends drive him the thirty miles in a car, but the four-hour buggy ride would give him time to think, more time to mentally prepare.

He'd been over every angle dozens of times. He'd

sought counsel from his brother and good friends, but mostly he'd prayed his heart out. This route, this very road he was on right now, was the path that felt right. This brought a certain amount of peace to his heart, though potentially taking his little family away from home might be the hardest thing he'd ever have to do.

The early-morning spring sunshine shone down an hour or so later—time to give Scout a break, and Isaac needed to stretch his legs. Maybe do some jumping jacks, try to pop that tight area on his lower back. He might've worked the new draft horse too hard yesterday. If Isaac himself was sore, Nelly would be, too. His stomach dropped slightly, always regretting when he overworked a horse—he cared so much about the animals, especially the ones that had come to him from rescue situations. Those were always extra special to Isaac.

He gave Scout a few additional rubs and scratches down his neck. When the retired racer had first been brought to him, the poor horse had been worked nearly to death. Even though violence had never been a part of his personality, Isaac would've loved five minutes alone with the person who'd done that to a helpless *gaul*.

All these thoughts were still going through his mind when he arrived in Honey Brook. Following the careful directions given to him, he took the last stretch down a long, winding road past several well-kept dairy farms. While at the top of the hill, Isaac easily saw the horse ranch—the large telltale pasture ring in the front of the property giving it away. As he drew near, he noticed someone was in that ring with a horse. Probably John Zook, the owner of the property and the man who just might be his future boss.

Wanting to quietly observe the man's technique—

wondering how well it would match up with his own—Isaac slowed the buggy, then tied Scout to a nearby hitch. The closer he got, the more he noticed how tall the horse was. The caramel-colored gelding looked to be about twenty hands high. A giant.

Isaac neared the white fence, his curiosity getting the better of him. But now, the closer he got, he noticed it wasn't that the horse was tall; it was that John Zook was short. Very short and quite slim, more like a teenage boy than a grown man. Isaac tilted his head. Was John Zook wearing a…dress? That was definitely a blue top with a long black apron. The skirt of the dress, however, was hiked up, tied in the back. And were those pants underneath?

Isaac felt a smile slowly spread across his face when he realized it wasn't a grown man or a boy working with the horse but a young woman, though she was petite and probably no more than nineteen years old at most.

"Good day," he said, using the Englisher greeting instead of "*Guder daag*," the traditional Amish phrase, though he was pretty sure she was Amish. She dropped the long stick she was holding and spun around. He hadn't meant to startle her. Even her horse let out a little whinny.

"Oh," she said, sounding out of breath while pushing back loose strands of hair that had fallen out of her *kapp*. "Morning." She looked at him for another moment then began dusting off the layer of dirt from the front of her dress. After probably realizing it was no use, she lowered her chin and smiled—but it seemed that smile hadn't been meant for Isaac. By the way she was looking off to the side, she was smiling at something personal. A private memory?

For some reason, this intrigued Isaac.

Without speaking again, she returned to her task, working the pretty gelding to trot in a circle.

Isaac leaned an elbow on the top rung of the fence and watched, a bit captivated now, for she seemed to know what she was doing. Though the stick never touched the horse, she kept it right at his peripheral vision, so he would know it was there but receiving no harm.

"This the Zook's Horse Training Farm?" Isaac asked.

"Aye," the woman said without looking at him. The ties of her black prayer *kapp* were caught in a breeze as more of her hair came spilling out. It was brown, reminding Isaac of someone else in his life—someone who used to be in his life. "If you're looking for John Zook," she added, "he's in the house."

She switched the stick to her left hand so she was holding the lead rope in her right. Without missing a beat, the obedient horse did an elegant turn, his hoofs keeping perfect time, trotting in the other direction, steps high.

Isaac was taken aback. He hadn't known many Amish who preferred the English style of riding over the more common Western, especially if all you needed was a strong horse to pull a plow or an obedient one to lead a buggy.

"Impressive," he couldn't help saying. "How did this *gaul* come to you?"

"Pardon?" she said, tossing back her skirt in a manner that seemed unexpectedly feminine.

Isaac stepped onto the bottom rung of the fence so he could observe her more closely. "Where did you get this horse?"

Before replying, the woman began slowing the

gelding's speed, gently pulling in the lead one inch at a time. When he was close to her, she leaned in and whispered something Isaac couldn't hear.

"Honey Pot came as a new foal," she finally answered, leading the horse toward the fence.

Isaac couldn't help lifting his brows. "Honey Pot?"

The woman was close enough now that when she smiled again, he noted a dimple in her right cheek, making her look...maybe not younger but much more innocent...and rather pretty, despite her tomboy exterior.

Even simply noticing that another woman was attractive caused an illogical knot of guilt to form in Isaac's stomach.

"I think it fits him quite well," she replied, turning to the horse, running a hand down his neck. "Though I didn't name him."

"So he didn't come like that?"

"Like what?"

He was about to say "so well trained" but didn't. "Nothing," he said instead, not wanting to insult her if she'd helped train him in the English style. But how likely was that? Isaac knew very few—if any!—Amish women who took more than a passing interest in horse training.

*Martha didn't*, he couldn't help thinking, that misplaced guilt returning. But then he forced a smile, thinking of Sadie. There wasn't a bigger horse lover than her, and she was always very interested in what he did.

"What's the joke?"

He looked over at the woman. She was shading her eyes from the bright afternoon sun. "Joke?" he asked.

"*Jah*." She patted Honey Pot. "The way you're

smiling, like you're thinking of something funny."

"Not funny exactly," he replied, noticing that the loose strands of her hair had flashes of red. And her eyes were blue. What was the sudden impulse he felt to wipe the streak of dirt off her cheek?

Not wanting to reveal what he was thinking, he blurted, "Yes, I was remembering a joke."

She turned to face him squarely, one corner of her mouth lifting. "*Jah*?"

"Uh." Isaac dusted off his hands, stalling. "Ever heard the one about the Mennonite and his favorite cow?"

After a short pause, the woman lifted her chin and started laughing. It was loud but also purely female, maybe because her voice was a lovely soprano, high like a bell. "Oh gracious!" she said between laughs. "You sound like my brother." She waved a hand in the air. "And all his friends." She cleared her throat and dusted off one shoulder. "Aye, I know all about the Mennonite and his cow."

While watching her, Isaac grew even more intrigued. Who was this woman? And how could she be both feminine *and* act like one of the guys?

"Anyway," she said when the silence stretched on for too long. "Best be getting back to work."

Isaac nodded. He needed to pull his thoughts together so he would be prepared for his meeting with John Zook. Last thing he needed was to be preoccupied by a dimple and a pair of captivating blue eyes.

The woman clicked her tongue, causing Honey Pot to stand at attention. She then clicked another three times, and the horse began to trot in the same circle as before, front knees high, chin tucked. Despite how he needed to focus elsewhere, Isaac couldn't stop watching.

She lifted the stick, reached it out, and tapped at the horse's chest. Suddenly, the *gaul* reared up. The woman stepped toward it boldly, tapping at its chest again. "*Hör mir zu*," she said in a strong, commanding voice, though the horse continued to rear.

Just as she lifted the stick again, Isaac leaped over the fence and grabbed the stick from her. "What are you doing?"

She whirled around to him, those blue eyes flashing. "What do you think *you're* doing? Give me that."

Isaac held the stick away from her. "Not if you're going to be cruel."

"Cruel?" She pointed her chin toward the horse. "You consider that cruel?"

"I do."

"Then you don't know the first thing about training horses."

Isaac almost laughed, but seeing how angry she was, he quickly handed back the stick. "They respond better to positive reinforcement, you know. Just like people."

"No one asked you."

Surprised at her brashness, Isaac took a full step back. Was she always so loud and bold? Well, never mind—his business was with John Zook, and not some ornery woman using the man's ring to beat down a horse. Though knowing any animal was being mistreated caused his hands to clench into fists. Maybe after his meeting, he'd talk to her.

Looking her in the eyes, he tipped down the front of his straw hat. "You said John Zook is in the house?"

"*Jah*," she replied, petting the horse's nose. "That way."

"*Danke*," he said simply, then walked back to his

buggy, giving Scout a few tender pats. "She's a lunatic," he couldn't help saying under his breath, though he immediately felt shamed for it. His parents hadn't raised him to be unkind. After all, he knew nothing about her.

And a woman like that? He never would.

He parked the buggy in front of the house and led Scout to the water trough. It was a fine house, plain whitewash with a big porch, two stories. Modest flower beds in the front. Just as he made it up the front steps, a tall man opened the screen door.

"Isaac King?" he said in a low voice. He had dark hair and an even darker beard, though there were evident flecks of gray along his temples.

"*Jah*." Isaac felt momentarily intimidated by the large man with a striking presence. "And you're John Zook."

"Since the day I was born." The man grinned and stuck out his hand for Isaac to shake. The polite gesture made Isaac feel calm again. "Nice *gaul*," he continued, walking toward Scout. "Arabian?"

"Good eye," Isaac replied.

"Racer?"

"*Jah*." Isaac followed him to his horse.

"Criminal what they do to them, ain't so?"

"*Jah*," Isaac repeated, grateful he'd found a kindred spirit in John Zook. Not enough of his Amish friends felt that way. Then he couldn't help thinking of the young woman he'd just met and that stick she insisted on using.

"Well," John Zook said as he gave Scout a friendly stroke, "I'm glad you were able to find the place."

"Oh, it wasn't difficult."

"And I see you met my daughter."

"Daughter?"

"Aye." John Zook pointed toward the woman with the dimple—the one Isaac had just scolded and then insulted to her face.

His stomach hit the ground like a rock.

# CHAPTER TWO

Grace Zook usually let insults roll off her back. With two brothers and a slew of cousins, she had grown up with thick skin. But never had a total stranger derailed her like that.

"How dare he?" she muttered under her breath as she glanced over her shoulder, watching as her father welcomed the rude visitor into their house. "What could *Daed* possibly want with someone like him?" Well, this was a horse training farm and, since the man was obviously Amish, except for that strange straw hat he wore, he probably just needed their services. This should've been good news—though *Daed* hadn't mentioned it, she knew they needed the money.

They always needed money. Now with that new doctor at the Hershey Medical Center, maybe *Maam* could finally get the surgery she needed.

She checked the time on her slim wristwatch. Time to go sit with her mother. During the heat of the day, it was the best opportunity for both of them. Grace noticed the dirt under her fingernails and wondered if the stranger had noticed, too. But why should she care if he had? He was nothing more than a slight annoyance to her otherwise pleasant day.

Honey Pot's training was going exceptionally well. Grace was in competition with herself only, but she was getting faster all the time, and her training skills improved with every new horse that came to the farm. For the last few years, her father had been giving more and more of the difficult horses to her. Grace thrived on the challenge.

In fact, deep in her heart, what she wished for most in this world was to take over the family business when *Daed* decided to retire. Her brothers were barely interested in horses, except when they weren't pulling their buggies fast enough. And besides, Adam was more interested in working at the Stolzenfus's dairy farm on the other side of town. Probably because her younger brother had had a crush on Charity Stolzenfus since before he could talk.

Still, Grace couldn't help it. She knew she would be the very best person to take over for her father. She also knew how rare it was in her village for a woman to run her own business. There were plenty of Mennonites and New Order Beachy Amish females in Honey Brook who did. And last Sunday at church, didn't the bishop say that times were changing, and we all needed to prepare?

Just remembering that reminded her that there was nothing she couldn't do if she put her mind to it.

"Come on, boy," she said, leading Honey Pot toward the stables. "Good boy, you did so well today." The gelding whinnied. "Okay, okay, one sugar cube for your good behavior, but don't get used to it."

Again, she glanced toward the house. The rude stranger had been in there a while now. Maybe he needed more than one horse trained. That would be marvelous news for them. Okay, okay, so maybe he hadn't been so bad. After all, Grace shouldn't have tapped Honey Pot like that, but earlier they'd been working on his high trot, and she knew he could do even better with just the slightest of extra encouragement. And besides, she could tell the stranger had been watching, and maybe she'd wanted to show off.

It wasn't very pious of her, and not gracious at all. He did have strong hands, though. Which she couldn't help noticing when he'd grabbed the stick from her. And nice eyes, too. They were a light hazel, which she'd always preferred, and heavy lidded. More than once, she'd heard her sister Mary refer to such as "bedroom eyes."

The stranger also had a beard, though very short. In her community, that meant he was married.

Didn't make a difference either way to Grace. She wasn't interested in men at the moment. If she did want a date, there was always faithful Collin Chupp, who'd been asking her out since the day she'd turned sixteen and had been free to socialize more freely.

Well, all right then. She forgave the stranger for his abrasive correction of her training style. He did know what he was talking about, and Grace would never dream of being "cruel" to any *gaul*. The thought made her stomach turn.

"Good boy," she said, giving Honey Pot one last scratch behind the ears. "Yes, I hear you, Pluto," she said when the horse in the next stall began stomping around. He came to the gate, hooking his chin over the top. "You're a good boy, too." Grace's heart filled with joy, expanding with every horse she greeted. Being in the stables with all the horsey smells and noises made her happier than even preaching Sundays.

As was her habit, she stopped by the gate of each horse stall as she headed out of the stables, which took a while. By the time she was finished, her father was standing on the front porch. "Hallo, *Daed*," she said hesitantly, wondering if the stranger would suddenly step out of the house and confront her again. But his buggy was gone. Though she'd barely even given it a glance as she'd led Honey Pot to the stables.

"Grace, my girl. I was just looking for you." Her father was wearing a big, easy grin. This had become rare ever since her mother's accident. The world seemed to weigh heavily on her father's shoulders these days.

"*Jah*?" she replied, mirroring his grin.

"I have good news."

"More horses?"

Her *daed* nodded.

So Grace had been right. The rude—no, the *handsome* (though married) stranger had come to bring them business. Lots of business, by the way her father was smiling.

"How many?" Automatically, she started thinking of all she needed to do to accommodate multiple horses. Two of the stalls would be freed up at the end of the week, and she didn't think they were reserved for anyone new yet.

"One."

Grace felt her body sag. "One?" she asked, feeling deflated. What was the big fuss, then?

*Daed* nodded in agreement, but then his smile grew. "Do you remember the Kirkpatrick Farm that we toured last year?"

Of course she did. Kirkpatrick's was the biggest non-Amish horse training company within a hundred miles.

"Let's sit down." *Daed* motioned to their porch swing, and they both sat. "A man came to me last week, saying he heard Brian Kirkpatrick is moving to California. They're closing."

"What?" The sudden rush of adrenaline nearly

lifted her off her seat.

"The fellow went on to say that he has a horse-breeding business and he's heavily relied on Kirkpatrick's. With them gone, he'll be looking for a new training farm—in fact, a lot of Englishers around here will be looking."

"Okay." Grace nodded eagerly when her father took a pause. Butterflies filled her stomach as she considered that they might be getting business from Kirkpatrick's. Were the Zooks about to have all the work they could ever hope for?

"Thing is, a lot of Englishers don't trust us plain folks, don't realize we can train just as well—or even better sometimes, praise to *Gott*."

"But folks come to us from all over," Grace said, frowning. "These Englishers can ask anybody for a referral. More than likely they'll say we're just as good as anywhere."

"That's the point." Her *daed* stared straight ahead. "That Englisher who came to me last week, he's got a horse. And he likes us Amish folks. Says it's unfair that most of his breeder colleagues shy away from us. He wants to help."

"As in, if we train his horse well, he'll tell his friends?" Grace was getting the point now. More butterflies zoomed around inside her stomach at the thought.

"Exactly." *Daed* was grinning again. "Says he's always felt like he wanted to give a hand up to us—though I don't like that it sounds like charity." He leaned back and laughed. "But I'll take his money for services rendered. I'll take any Englisher's money."

Grace laughed, too. Though in most cases, her Amish community tended to take care of themselves, not involving English outsiders. Because their village was near a highway, they did tend to get a lot of tourists. Her sister-in-law's sister, Esther, had a pretty lucrative business of homemade soap; her products flew off the shelves the minute a group of out-of-towners came through. And Esther was one of the most honest and pious people Grace knew.

"What kind of horse is it?" she asked her *daed*.

"Four-year-old Morgan," he replied. Then paused for effect. "A thoroughbred."

"He wants us to train a four-year-old? That's kind of late in the game."

"They want us to train *and* break him. Train to show."

"Golly. A show horse." Grace drummed her fingers together in excitement, already thinking three steps ahead. "He's been gelded?"

"Just," *Daed* said. "And apparently the procedure hasn't done much for his disposition."

Grace smiled, knowing a new challenge was on the horizon. "Energetic, is he?"

"I believe he was referred to as 'mean as the devil.'" *Daed* shook his head with a laugh. "This horse is the foal of Grand Prix champions, two generations. My understanding is he's been sitting in a stall all this time."

"That breaks my heart," Grace said, wrapping her arms around herself in a hug. "A horse they value so highly should've been treated better." She promised herself then and there that she would give him oodles of love the moment he arrived. "What type of competition?" she asked. "Dressage? Endurance running? Morgans are built for that."

"Jumping," her *daed* said. "The owner wants him shown at the Speed Class and Classics at the WEF."

She sat up straight. "*This* year's Winter Equestrian

Festival? Will we have time?"

Her father lifted a slow smile. "That's why he came to us."

Grace's mouth went bone dry—with both excitement and a feeling of tackling something beyond her talent. Though if ever there was a time for her to step up and show her father just how good she was…it was now! Then he would have no choice but to let her run the family business.

"I can see it in your eyes," he said. "You think we should do it."

"Of course we should! This could mean more business for us than we ever dreamed. *Daed*, this is incredible. What a blessing!"

"I think so, too." He stood up, brushing his palms together. "That's why I hired a professional trainer."

*A wh-what?* Grace blinked, at a complete loss for words.

"This is too important to not have outside help," *Daed* added.

"But…we don't need… *I* don't—"

"Gracie." He took her hand and helped her stand. "You don't have the experience yet. A horse like this, and in so little time?"

"And you assume this *professional* does?" She immediately felt ashamed of her tone and the sassy way she'd spoken back to her father. "I'm sorry, *Daed*. But I know I can do it. I'll learn along the way."

"You can help, sure," he said, a bit hesitantly, "but I believe I made the right choice."

Grace's heart sank to the floor as she pressed her hands to her temples. How would she ever prove to her father that she was just as good a trainer as anyone if he wouldn't give her a chance?

"He'll be here in a week."

"The Morgan?" Grace asked, tears of frustration building behind her eyes.

"The trainer," her *daed* said. "His name is Isaac King. In fact, you met him earlier when you were out in the ring."

Grace blinked hard, trying to understand who he meant. Then she froze mid-heartbeat, wondering if she was about to faint.

# CHAPTER THREE

"It's so unfair. I don't mean to sound"—she was about to say *cruel*—"unkind, but why doesn't this *professional* find his own job?"

"I think that's exactly what happened."

Grace turned to her older sister, about ready to question why she wasn't automatically on her side. But she managed to harness her temper just in time. "Mary, that's not the point."

"Okay, then what's the point?" Mary was gently patting the back of her *bobbeil*, fresh from heaven only three months ago. Rose was such a blessing, such a good baby that sometimes Grace wondered if she would ever feel the ache to start that part of her life: wife and mother. But then she remembered the very reason she was there, the reason she'd barely sat with *Maam* at all but practically raced out of the house and straight to her sister.

"What does he look like?" Hannah chimed in before Grace could reply. She'd been Grace's bosom friend since the afternoon Hannah had asked to walk home from the big schoolhouse with her when they were barely six.

"Who?"

"The *professional*," Hannah said with a twinkle in her eyes. "Is he tall?"

Grace couldn't help picturing him. He was tall, all right, and those hazel eyes… Then there was that oddly shaped hat, though. How strange. "I hardly noticed him," she fibbed.

"Uh-huh." Hannah tossed a handful of flour

Grace's way.

"And who cares? He's stealing my job!" Grace winced when she saw the baby stir.

"Can you knead this batch for me?" Hannah asked.

Grace looked down, noticing the ball of bread dough she hadn't touched. She'd been so preoccupied with griping that she'd forgotten that Mary and Hannah needed her help. It was more than convenient that her older sister married Hannah's brother and that they all lived together in Mary's husband's family home. There was always something going on…always something delicious cooking or a game happening at the big wooden table, or a tag competition happening in their oversize backyard. And now with little Rose, the sounds of a heavenly baby.

"Of course," Grace said, pushing up her sleeves and beginning to knead the dough. It smelled fresh and delicious. "How many loaves are you making today?"

"Twenty, we hope," Mary replied, switching to hold sleeping Rose against her chest.

"That's a lot," Grace said.

"Not really," Hannah added. "Making the dough is no problem; it's the baking that will take the longest."

Mary began humming while rocking her baby. "I have nowhere else to be. I can take bread pans in and out of the oven all day."

For a moment, Grace felt almost envious of her sister and her simple life. All she really had to do right now was be a loving wife to her husband and a strong mother of their baby. Everything else around her seemed to be taken care of. Grace hadn't felt like she'd had a day off in years. Not that she was complaining—she loved working outside in the sunshine. Even in the winter, there was always something to do in the stalls or barn.

"Will these loaves go to the same store?" Grace asked as her wrists and arm muscles began to ache. She was not the best bread maker in Honey Brook.

"*Jah*." Hannah smiled, dusting her floury hands across her black apron. "The bakery across from the mercantile. The family is ever so kind to allow us to sell there, even though it's only a few loaves a week." She sighed. "But Leah Yoder says they sell awful well. I think it's the name."

Grace eyed the roll of stickers with the bright logo and swirly lettering. "The Sweetest Amish Friendship Bread," she read. "Englisher tourists think that's special?"

"Because it is. Every batch comes from the same starter—it's kind of darling."

Grace bit down on the cuff of her sleeve and yanked it above her elbow. "What do you mean?"

"Gracie," Hannah said, "you and I made friendship bread all the time when we were in school. You don't remember?"

Grace tried to think. So much of her life now revolved around horses that she sometimes had little memory of anything else. Moments like right now, she halfway wondered if her life should've been more diversified. "I guess not," she finally admitted.

Hannah lifted a kindhearted smile. "Each batch we make can be split, so a little bit of the original batch is part of every new batch. You see?"

Grace scratched her cheek. "Oh! You mean like keeping the pure bloodline of a thoroughbred?"

Both women stared at her. "Um, sure," Mary uttered, then covered her smiling mouth with the back of a hand.

"You still haven't told me," Hannah broke in. "What does this new fellow look like? You said he's tall."

"I didn't say that," Grace pointed out, enthusiastically kneading the dough. She might've been frustrated by the subject jump but, since it was about the handsome stranger, she didn't mind picturing him.

"Aye, but when I asked you earlier, I could tell by the look in your eyes that he is."

"What look?"

"I don't know, your gaze just kind of went all soft."

She felt the strangest impulse to hide her telltale eyes behind her floury hands. "They did not."

"So he's young?"

Grace turned away and sniffed. "Think so."

"Good-looking?"

Grace pushed out a breath. "I don't know. I suppose."

Why did any of this matter? Did they not understand that this...this *outsider* would be standing in the way of her future?

"Wait." Hannah grabbed her arm. "You're saying a young, tall, good-looking, single man is moving to Honey Brook?"

"I have no idea if he's single." She shut her eyes tight, trying, unsuccessfully, to not envision him. "He had a beard—well, a short one."

"Where is he from?"

"*Daed* said Silver Springs."

Hannah pressed her lips into a line, then began rubbing them together. "They have a different bishop and different Ordnung, and I'm pretty sure they're New Order."

"So?" Grace asked, wishing for another subject change.

"*Jah*, but the beard might not mean anything. Some communities in Ohio, boys start growing beards at sixteen before they're even close to marriage."

"Okay," Grace said. "For all I know, he could be single, but it doesn't matter to me. This is the man who's taking away my dream."

Mary turned to her sister. "Training this one horse is your dream?"

"Aye!" Grace had to slow her breathing. Would Mary or Hannah ever understand? "I've been Papa's right hand on the farm since I was a girl. I know just as much as he does now…maybe even more," she couldn't help adding. "After all, he can't break a horse as fast as I can these days, and doesn't Abraham Lambright always ask especially for me when he brings over a new pony?"

"I don't know how you can spend so many hours a day covered in dirt," Hannah said, washing her hands at the sink.

Grace sighed again. She often wondered the same thing, why she was so different from the other women in the village. "It's where I feel the most at home. And I'm awful good at it. It comes almost…easy."

"But how much longer can you keep it up?" Mary asked.

Hannah placed her hands on her hips. "All I know is—married or not—having another strong young man in Honey Brook is a benefit," she said. "And maybe he has a single brother who'll come for a visit."

Grace and Mary both looked at Hannah. "You've always been boy crazy," Grace said, leaning her hip against the kitchen counter. "You still haven't told us why you stopped writing to Noah from Ohio."

Hannah dropped her chin. "It...fizzled out."

"He stopped writing to her weeks ago," Mary interjected.

Grace turned to her. "How do you know?" Then she glanced at Hannah, whose cheeks were red. "You told Mary before you told me?"

Hannah shrugged then looked down at her feet. "You've been busy, I suppose. And Mary, you know, lives here."

Mary lifted an innocent grin. "Factual, sister," she said. "Location is everything."

Grace felt a knot form in her stomach as she shook her head, taking it all in. Had she become so wrapped up in the horses that she'd forgotten her best friend and sister?

"Let's get back to the basics, though," Mary said, stepping in gracefully before things might get tense. "You are going to be working side by side with a handsome stranger from out of town? You'll be shoulder to shoulder, sweating together, sometimes holding the same rope, sometimes touching by accident—or maybe on purpose—your skin hot and—"

"Mary!" Grace cut her off before she started to blush. "You mustn't..."

"I'm just pointing out the obvious." Mary kissed the top of Rose's sweet head.

"I don't think I've ever been so jealous of you, Grace Zook," Hannah said, her voice sounding pouty but jokey.

"You just said I spend too much time in the dirt."

"Well, maybe this...this *professional* will be someone special to you." She clasped her fingers together under her chin and stared into space.

"Maybe your future husband!"

Grace blew out a long breath, closed her eyes, and shook her head, remembering the way he'd spoken to her, his exact words, calling her *cruel*. "Not in this lifetime," she muttered.

# CHAPTER FOUR

Isaac felt more comfortable in his brother's home than just about anywhere. Simply being with his family gave him peace.

"When do you start?" asked his brother Daniel. He had more gray in his hair than the last time Isaac had seen him—which was less than a month ago. Still, Daniel was bigger and stronger than anyone he knew, even though he was fifteen years older than Isaac. Practically a father figure, since their own father had gone to live with the Lord nearly ten years ago.

"Three days," Isaac said, buttering a piece of bread. "Thank you, Fern," he added to his niece. She had to be close to sixteen years old now. Almost ready to attend youth group activities and game nights.

"Will you be ready?" asked Daniel as he helped his daughter carry a large pot to their stove top.

"I'll have to be." Isaac ran a hand over his face and exhaled, mentally running through his to-do list. "There's a lot to prepare. And a lot to plan for, in case this turns into something more long-term."

"Uncle Isaac," said Fern, "I thought you were hired to train just one horse."

"True enough," Isaac replied. "But there might be a lot of publicity with training just this one horse. Do you know what publicity means?"

His niece pressed a hand to her forehead and frowned in thought. "Is that like when Miss Annie Sutter puts a sign up in her store window about candy tarts being half price?"

"Exactly," Isaac said, then grinned over at his

brother. With only a few years of formal education, his children—all seven of them—were right smart. "The horse John Zook has hired me to train in Honey Brook is owned by a very important Englisher."

Fern frowned again then humphed under her breath. "Englishers think they're so important."

"Fern," Daniel said in a low, though patient, fatherly voice. "We talked about this just last week when we caught you kicking dirt at the nice man's car."

Fern folded her arms. "How do you know he was nice?"

"How do you know he wasn't?"

When Fern didn't reply to her father, Daniel turned to Isaac and shook his head. "Teenagers."

The two brothers laughed. Isaac didn't listen to the horror stories; he couldn't wait to have a teenager.

"Don't act so smug," Daniel said, pointing at him. "Happens to the best of us. Fern, go help your mother with the washing; your uncle Isaac and I will finish cleaning up."

When Isaac formed his brows into a curious arch, Daniel shrugged. "I'm not such an ogre; things have changed. We're trying to be more enlightened, and isn't that an important part of being New Order? It's not like when we were kids and *Daed* never spent time with us. Catherine and I talk to the kids—we're in their lives." He paused to sigh. "Well, unless they're about to turn sixteen and believe they know everything about life already."

"Is she thinking about *Rumspringa*?"

Daniel turned his gaze toward the doorway where his daughter had just disappeared. "Solomon really enjoyed his out in Florida with the Sweitzer cousins. I reckon Fern will want to go there, too. Well, there's the man of the hour," Daniel added, clasping a hand over the shoulder of his oldest child. "What do you think, son? Will your sister take *Rumspringa*?"

"Ack, I don't know, Pa. Fern only talks to her friends. I try not to pay attention."

Isaac so loved the healthy banter that always went on in his brother's home. He hoped to have the same someday.

"Sit down." Isaac pushed out a chair with his foot for his nephew to join them. "Your father told you I'm moving away for a while?"

Solomon nodded. "Training some fancy Englisher's horse, *jah*?"

Isaac definitely heard the same tone in his voice as had been in his niece's. "Something happen between your kids and someone from town?" he couldn't help asking his brother.

"Heaven knows," Daniel said. "But my eldest was taught that we are to be kind to every living creature. Even if they ain't like us. *Especially* if they ain't."

"*Aren't*," Sol corrected, elbowing his father. "*You're* the one made me learn grammar when I wanted to be manning a plow."

Daniel laughed, sounding exactly like their father. Rest his soul.

"To answer your question, Sol," Isaac said, "yes, it's for a man from Harrisburg who owns a horse breeding business."

Sol's hazel eyes brightened. "You're going all the way to Harrisburg?" Then he turned to his father. "That's the capitol of Pennsylvania, Papa."

"Very funny." Daniel reached out to pretend to choke his son.

"Nay." Isaac answered, feeling that excited flutter in his stomach return. This really could be his big chance to start over. "Only as far as Honey Brook. That's where I'll be doing the training."

"Honey Brook." Sol sat up straight and tossed the front of his hair out of his eyes. "They have the prettiest girls there." He shrugged, keeping his shoulder raised. "I mean, so Moses Shetler says—he's got ten cousins out that way, been to visit every summer." He blew out a breath and crossed his arms. "But how would I know? *Daed* never lets me go."

*The prettiest girls, huh?* Isaac couldn't help thinking. Well, he hadn't seen all the girls in the village, but one sure did stick out to him, and Sol was right—one of the prettiest girls he'd ever seen. *Though so far off-limits that I shouldn't even be thinking about her.*

"Anyway," Isaac said, "that's where I'll be living."

"With the folks you'll be working for?"

Isaac shook his head. "Nay. A family a few farms over had a sign in the front yard for a lodger—Amish only." He paused to grin good-naturedly. "I already made the arrangements."

"Place you're working," Daniel said. "Does a family live there?"

Isaac bit the inside of his cheek, stalling while he, again, saw the woman with the dark, flyaway hair in his mind's eye. "I met the husband—my boss—and one of his sons, though I reckon there's more. Fella said his wife was upstairs and I'd meet her later. I didn't know it at first, but he's also got a…" Isaac couldn't help trailing off when he visualized her face close up. The dimple and blue eyes.

"A what?" Daniel asked, shaking him awake.

"A…" He shifted in his seat and cleared his throat. "A daughter."

"She pretty?" asked Sol.

"I…" Isaac didn't know how to reply.

"Lord sakes, Sol," Daniel said to his son.

"What? I bet she is. Moses is always right about that kinda thing."

"Solomon." Daniel stood up. "Don't those chickens need feeding?"

"Probably, but that's for the girls."

"Okay, the pigs then."

Solomon stood. "*Jah*, Pa. Good luck, Uncle Isaac, with the new job, if I don't see you before you leave."

"*Danke*, Sol." They shook hands. "You're a good man. Be easy on your father, *jah*?"

Daniel chuckled as Solomon stomped out of the room. "So…?" his brother began again, his voice low. "Is she?"

Isaac looked up. "Is who what?"

Daniel sighed. "Is she pretty? The daughter."

Isaac didn't mean to, but suddenly he saw her perfectly, head to toe. First from afar when he'd been watching her with the horse, how her body moved gracefully yet with confidence. You had to have confidence when training an animal that powerful. And then when he neared her…the color of her eyes, how they brightened as she laughed and teased him about his bad joke. And that dimple. Isaac felt himself smile; it was complete impulse.

"You old fox." Daniel laughed out loud. The sound shook Isaac awake. "She's *beautiful*, I take it from that sloppy look on your face."

"Okay," Isaac admitted. "She's…attractive. Nothing special, I mean, but you know how some people just look a certain way. It's a gift from *Gott*."

"Sounds like it's a gift to *you*, brother," Daniel said.

Isaac looked at him. "What do you mean?"

Daniel leaned forward, crossing his arms and putting them on the table. "It's okay, you know," he said, tenderness in his voice. "It's okay to feel that way. Whenever you're ready."

Isaac could've played along, not wanting to address the subject, but what was the use? "No, I know. I know it is." He stared forward, fighting back the feeling that used to cripple him at times. He thought he was over that.

"Especially ain't no sin thinking a woman is attractive, even beautiful."

"You're the one who said beautiful, not me."

"What does she look like, then?"

Isaac laughed under his breath—he couldn't help it. "I said she was attractive, but that wasn't what… *interested* me." It was difficult to utter that word aloud, though Isaac knew there was nothing improper about it. "There she was, out in the middle of the pasture, working a horse in a circle." He chuckled softly. "I thought she was a boy at first, her form was so good. But then I got closer and… *Jah*, she's beautiful."

"Well, okay, then." Daniel punched his brother's arm. "Things are looking up."

Isaac sighed, that crippling feeling sweeping over him again. He had to take a few deep breaths to push it out. "You know I'd never do anything about it, Daniel. What about Sadie?"

His brother scratched his beard. "She's going with you?"

Isaac straightened his posture. "Of course. You know I can't leave her with those…" Again, he had to force himself to take in a few deep breaths to calm down. "Our living situation isn't the best for either of us," he finally replied. Though he did have a lot more he could have said, such as he didn't want to be living with his in-laws anymore. Their home was stifling, and they could be overbearing, even for plain folk. And that was another thing. They could sometimes be… disobedient. He didn't want to live in that atmosphere any longer than he had to.

*Which is why this chance to move to Honey Brook, if even for a while, is a special gift from* Gott. One that he would not squander.

"Things have gotten worse over there?" Daniel asked.

Isaac stood, not wanting to speak ill of anyone, even privately to his brother. "This is a good opportunity for me…for *us*." He smiled, pulling forward his natural optimism. "It'll all work out."

*And it better*, he couldn't help adding to himself. He didn't like to admit it, but he desperately needed a lucky break—for things to turn his way. He couldn't go on how he was going; he would be miserable. *If this doesn't work out*—no, he couldn't even think that way.

Success was much too important. To him and his family.

# CHAPTER FIVE

For the last two days, Grace had been busy outside from sunup to sundown. With all her regular chores plus the six horses she was working with, she also had to prepare for the Morgan's arrival. She wasn't about to leave anything out or leave anything to chance, not if she wanted to show her father that she didn't need any help.

The new horse would be arriving late this afternoon. As well as Silver Springs' so-called "Amish Cowboy."

Yes, Grace had done some research on Isaac King. Even though she and her father worked mostly with horses owned by plain folk, they did receive colts and geldings from Englisher neighbors—which really helped supplement their income. Not to mention the retired racers who needed to be trained to pull a buggy. Therefore, a few years ago, her father deemed it necessary to be "connected." A cell phone sat in a drawer in his office just inside the stables. Grace had had no reason to touch it…until now.

Two days ago, when Hannah had been over, she'd shown Grace how to do an online name search. Seemed as though Isaac King did have quite a reputation as a competent horse trainer in Lancaster County. He even had his own website and business phone number. Which must mean he had his own personal phone.

Grace tried to force that fact to bother her. But since so many of the dairy farmers in Honey Brook were allowed to use power generators to keep the milk refrigerated— not to mention her own father's technology—she couldn't really begrudge Isaac King a phone.

On the website, there was a short article about that cowboy-hat–shaped straw hat he wore. It had been given to him as a gift, and even though it was slightly different from the indistinguishable wide-brimmed straw hats worn by all the other men in his community, the leaders in his church had given him special sanction to wear it. This, along with the fact that he preferred to travel on horseback rather than in a buggy, left Isaac Zook with the nickname of the "Amish Cowboy."

All of this left Grace more puzzled than ever. Weren't her people not supposed to draw attention to themselves? How could Isaac King conform while wearing a hat like that? How progressive was this man?

"*Jah*, and hello to you, too," Grace said with a smile as she passed by the last stall, giving the spotted Indian pony a scratch behind the ears. The stall next to her was the biggest one, with the tallest walls, and it was currently vacant. Grace paused to give it one more once-over. Everything looked in place and ready to receive their new guest. Grace had even buffed all the tack, so it looked shiny and new. She took in a deep breath, smelling the freshly lain straw.

As she was climbing the porch stairs to go inside and wash up, she overheard her father's voice from around the corner. "*Jah, jah*," he was saying, speaking quickly in Pennsylvania Dutch, obviously on the phone. She paused when she heard her own name mentioned. But the call ended too soon after that for Grace to make out what her father was discussing, or with whom.

"Ah, Gracie. We were just talking about you." He held up his cell.

"Aye?" Grace replied breezily, as if she hadn't overheard. "Anything important?"

Her father adjusted his straw hat. "Isaac called me along the way—he's fancy with his phone. Says he's nearly here."

"Hmm." Grace tried not to care, to at least sound disinterested. But then she turned to her father. "You can still tell him not to come, ya know."

"Why in heaven's name would I do that?"

Grace took in a deep breath, prepared to say what she'd been holding back for days. "Because...because *I* can do it, *Daed*. All by myself. You know I can. Why don't you trust me?" She was frustrated when she heard the quiver in her voice. She wanted to sound strong and sure, not weak.

"Now, Gracie. I thought we already talked about this."

"*Nay*, *you* talked." She instantly felt ashamed of her tone. This was not the conversation she had envisioned having. "What I mean is, you decided without talking to me." She lowered her chin in humility. "I know you're in charge here, but I thought we were more of a partnership. After all, I do most of the training now, and all of the heeding."

"You do have a very special touch with the younger horses," her father said. "But this one, well, he's very important to our future."

"I know. Believe me, I understand what it could mean for our business, and for..." She let her voice trail off when she glanced over her shoulder to the house, toward where her mother sat on the couch.

"Honestly, Gracie, I believe you could break and train this horse. If you had enough time, maybe. But

Isaac King has the experience."

"Has he trained an aggressive Morgan for the Grand Prix?"

John Zook opened his mouth to reply, but then didn't speak.

"Papa, he hasn't?"

"Not exactly, but he worked with stallions one summer a few years back. He knows how they are, the temperament and complications. You know well enough yourself, Grace, that we've had only a handful over the years. And believe me, they are very different."

"What all horses need is love," she said under her breath. "They need someone to look into their eyes, to pay attention to them. They always respond positively to that. But they also have to know who is boss." She leveled her chin. "I'm the boss."

Her father chuckled. "Looks like you had a good teacher."

Grace smiled. "The best," she said, the frustration and anger toward her father softening.

"Oh, I don't know, I'm getting on in years and can't keep this up forever."

"Keep what up?"

He raised a hand, gesturing toward the front pasture and ring. "All of this. I'll be selling some land soon—I can't keep up this much property, especially when I retire someday. I'd like to know whoever takes over, it will be in good hands." He looked Grace directly in the eyes.

Grace's heart lifted. They hadn't yet had a proper discussion about it but, since none of her brothers were interested in taking over the family business, she was sure her father would want her to.

"Oh, *jah*, you can be sure of that!" She grinned

when her father's eyes twinkled.

"A lot of work, you know."

"Like you said, I had a good teacher."

John Zook took in a deep breath, then blew it out. "Thing is, Grace, it's not that simple. Not in this county and not in this church. I know our congregation isn't as modern as some around here, but at least we're not in the dark ages like the Old Order Swartzentruber sects. Even so, it's rare, Grace—mighty rare for a woman to own a business of this size."

"Is that in our Ordnung?"

"No," her father replied.

"Would Bishop Turner be against it?"

Her father didn't answer immediately. "I don't know for sure," he admitted. "But we would require permission from the leadership of the church, that's for certain."

"The brethren love you, Papa. You all grew up together. Preaching Sunday is this week; can we talk to them then?"

"Slow down, Grace. Let's not get ahead of ourselves. I haven't decided anything. Barely crossed my mind, actually."

At his words, Grace's heart sank. It wasn't that she wanted her father to retire right now, she simply wanted to get on with her future, plan the next part of her life. And that was being confident that she would be taking over the training farm when it was time. She felt it as surely as knowing *Gott* had made all living creatures.

"You know I never enjoyed being in the kitchen," she said, her voice quiet. "Mary did most of the cooking with *Maam* before she got married and moved out. By that time, I'd found my place with the horses. It's what I'm good at."

"Aye, Grace. Don't think I haven't noticed that over the years. And don't think it hasn't pained me some."

Grace felt a sharp stab in her stomach. "Pained you?"

"You're hard to explain sometimes, my girl. See, most other young ladies your age are married, or engaged at the least. Your sister was married at twenty-one. That's two years younger than you are." He turned to look at her, his blue eyes in earnest. "Whatever happened to Samuel Chupp's boy?"

Grace sighed in frustration. Definitely not the way she'd hoped the conversation would go. "Collin? Oh, he's still around. Would probably marry me next wedding season if I showed the slightest interest."

"But you feel nothing for him? Seems like a capable young man."

"*Daed*, please. If I wanted advice about dating, I would talk to *Maam*, or Mary…or anyone besides you."

He chuckled and scratched his beard. "All I'm saying is it's a mite strange that you're always in a dirty dress with your brother's trousers underneath."

"I'm on the back of a horse most hours of the day. Wouldn't be proper without pants."

"Grace, I think for a man of my position in the community, I've allowed a lot when it comes to you. And with this Morgan business, you'll just have to trust that I know what I'm doing. This is too important to not do perfectly."

Grace opened her mouth to say *she* could train perfectly, *too*, if given the chance. But she knew it would end in another argument, and she respected her father too much to go against him.

"I think you'll like working with Isaac," he

continued. "You'll be a good apprentice."

Ack, that word. Grace wasn't sure if it was *apprentice* or *Isaac* that annoyed her more.

"Sure, *Daed*."

"Speaking of the Chupps, that's where he's staying."

She stared at him. "With Collin's family?"

He nodded. "Got that big empty room on the second floor since his daughter moved back east." He wiped his brow. "Should be enough space," he added as he walked toward the side yard, leaving Grace on the porch. "It's just him and, er…Sadie, I think is her name." He turned back to Grace. "Tell your mother I'll pick her those peaches she asked for."

*Sadie?* Grace thought. *So he is married.*

Well, that was fine with her. Why shouldn't he be? And sure, fine, he was quite handsome, now that she thought about it. And wasn't it okay to think that now when he was completely off-limits? In fact, she could be as friendly with him as she wanted to be.

Though maybe if she was slightly *overly* friendly, it would make him so uncomfortable, he'd quit his job and go back to Silver Springs. Gah! Grace shouldn't be so unkind to a perfect stranger. She promised herself that she would not, while also promising that she'd also be extra patient with her sister-in-law, Sarah, tonight, helping her with dinner.

Just as she smiled at the new plan and dusted some dirt off her apron, she noticed a buggy arriving, No, it wasn't a buggy but a man on horseback. And was he wearing a cowboy hat?

# CHAPTER SIX

Isaac saw her on the porch. As he neared, he noticed she was in another dirty dress, a pair of men's trousers and work boots that came nearly to her knees. The moment before he could have waved a long-distance hello, she whirled around so her back was to him.

Mercy, did she despise him so much already? Her father had mentioned to him last week that his daughter was a key member of their training team, and that she would be something of an apprentice to him with the Morgan, if Isaac wanted.

Suddenly, she whipped around to face him. Her hair was now tucked neatly inside her *kapp*, no flyaways like last time. But hadn't that added to her appeal?

No, no appeal. He mustn't think that way about his boss's daughter. Having that discussion with Daniel had put her square in the front of his mind for a few hours—where she didn't belong.

"You're early," she said, her expression unreadable, though her voice sounded accusatory.

Having nothing to say to that, he climbed off Scout and led him to the water. "Mighty nice day," he offered, walking toward her.

"I said, you're early," she repeated in that same tone. She walked to the front of the porch, while Isaac stood at the bottom of the stairs, not sure he was welcome any farther.

"I spoke to your—er, John Zook a little while ago, told him I'd be here shortly."

She didn't reply for a moment, then her hostile

posture untensed a bit. "Heard you're staying at the Chupps' across the way."

"*Jah*. I just came from there. It's real nice. Nice folks."

"Hmph," she grunted, crossed her arms, then looked away.

He took a step closer. "Why do you ask?"

"No reason."

For just a moment, he couldn't help examining her to see if she'd be pretty enough to pass his nephew Sol's definition. Blue eyes, pink lips, long neck, and he could tell she had a narrow waist under all those layers of dress, apron, and pants.

"What are you staring at?" she asked.

Isaac blinked himself awake. "Nothing." He couldn't help that his smile was turning into a crooked grin. "I think I like *this* place, too. I was impressed when I visited before. You must work hard to keep it up so nice."

Again, her shoulders lowered another few inches. Perhaps he could get her on his side by being charming. He'd been told more than once in his life that he could charm a skunk out of its own smell. Not that he would use his gift manipulatively. For he knew it was from *Gott*, being able to persuade people to like him when they didn't at first.

Would it work on John Zook's daughter?

"*Danke*," she replied, folding her hands together. "Um, would you like a drink from inside? Sarah, my sister-in-law, made fresh strawberry lemonade this morning."

"I would love some." Neither of them moved for a moment, and Isaac wasn't sure if she'd invited him into the house or not.

"I'll be right back." She turned and disappeared

through the door.

*I guess that answers my question: not invited in.*

He came up onto the porch, wondering how she would react when she saw him there. He smiled to himself, already enjoying this private little game of his. She came out a few minutes later, pausing briefly when she noticed that he'd stepped onto the porch, leaving less distance between them now. She was carrying a tall glass of a pink drink, ice cubes clinking together. It looked delicious.

"Nothing for you?" he asked when she handed it to him.

She took in a feminine breath, then let it out. "Nay, this one's for you."

Isaac thanked her again, then took a long drink.

*Ack!* Either this sister-in-law of hers didn't know the first thing about lemonade, or John Zook's daughter had put something in it, something like... salt?

"You like it?" she asked with a sticky-sweet smile that Isaac saw right through...answering his other question.

"Mmm. Tasty," he said, taking another, much smaller sip. "Unique. Never had anything quite like it." He'd had some bad food in his life, but this topped the list.

"Well, then." She tilted her head. "I'll tell Sarah she has a fan."

He cleared his throat, the sharp salt burning his windpipe. "P-Please do."

"Sure is a hot day," she said. As she stood, smiling eagerly at him, Isaac suspected she was going to wait right there until he drank it all. He was completely prepared to call her bluff.

"Good thing I have this, then," he replied. He

downed the rest of the foul liquid in one big gulp, straight-faced, doing his best not to gag. "Mmm-mmm," he said, wiping his mouth with the back of his hand, staring her dead in the eyes.

Her gaze narrowed as he handed back the glass. "Refill?" she asked in a sweet tone.

"Oh, gosh, no thanks." He held up his hands, palms out. "That was the perfect amount. I wouldn't want to be rude by drinking more—which I could, by the way." Isaac was hoping she wasn't about to drag out the entire pitcher.

He could tell by looking at her that she was chewing on the inside of her cheeks, probably trying to figure him out. He was trying to do the same.

"Would you mind showing me the stables?" he asked by way of escape, taking off his hat.

"Didn't Papa show you the other day?"

Isaac swallowed, trying to get the nasty taste out of his mouth. "*Jah*, he did, but I'd like to see where the Morgan will go."

After another moment of chewing the inside of her cheek, she nodded, then came down the stairs. Isaac followed, not too closely, so he could spit the rest of that salty swill into the bushes. Maybe hearing the noise, she glanced quickly over her shoulder at him, a little smirk on those pink lips.

"Second stall on the right," she said, allowing him to enter first.

The stables were pristine, as tidy and organized as any he'd seen, even when he'd worked with rich Englishers who had the best of the best. "Is this tack yours?" he asked. When she didn't reply, Isaac turned around, finding her before the stall next to him, standing on a little stool, nuzzling a pretty Indian pony. He could barely hear what she was cooing to him, but the cadence sounded like a Bible verse.

"Who teaches us more than the beasts of the earth and makes us wiser than the birds of the heavens?" she recited.

"Job?" Isaac said.

She blinked and looked at him. "Chapter thirty-three."

"Verse eleven," he finished for her. And for a moment, they stared at each other. Isaac wasn't sure why he found it odd that she was quoting scripture to a horse. But then, why not?

"*Jah*," she said, stepping off the stool while running her fingertips down the front of the pony's nose. "That tack is ours. Why?" She turned to him. "Is it not good enough?"

"No, no, it's fine. It's very nice, actually. I just wondered if they'd sent any supplies ahead of time."

"Oh." She dipped her chin. "Nay, not that I know of."

"Did you prepare the stall? It's perfect," he added before she could ask again if it wasn't good enough.

"*Jah*," she said, her voice sounding a bit more pleasant, less suspicious, her expression, too, like when he'd first met her out in the ring. "The straw is our best, but I might order a different kind next time I'm in town. There's one that is supposed to be good for aggressive horses."

He felt his eyebrows lift. "Do you think our *gaul* is going to be aggressive?"

She shrugged. "My father seemed to get that impression. I was trying to prepare for anything."

"That's very smart." He put his hat back on. "Well then, I suppose there's not much more I need to do here. You've taken care of everything. Thank you very much, uh…" He paused, feeling foolish. "I beg your pardon, but I can't remember if your father told me your name."

"Oh." She lifted a smile, a real one this time. At least, Isaac hoped it was, because her whole face changed, brightened, lightened. *Definitely pretty*. "Grace. I'm Grace."

*Yes, you are*, he couldn't help thinking.

"Grace Zook, I am very pleased to meet you officially."

"You too…Isaac King." She dipped her chin, and when she slowly lifted it again, her cheeks were pink, and did her eyelashes just flutter?

Isaac hadn't felt hot under the collar like that since…forever. "Well, uh…seeing how well you were training that horse the other day, I know you're going to make a fine apprentice."

He wasn't sure what he'd said wrong, but Grace Zook suddenly sent him a steely glare that he felt all the way through to the back of his head. Next second, she was marching out of the stables. Isaac had no other choice than to follow.

"Apprentice?" she said through clenched teeth as she glanced at him. Even though she looked like she was about to kill him, darn it if Grace Zook didn't *still* look pretty. "Is that what my father told you I was?"

"Well, *jah*. He said I…that we…" Well, shoot, had he just ruined everything? They'd finally been getting along.

"My father," she said, her voice firm, "doesn't understand everything. He's…very set in his ways, and I tried to show him…I mean, I show him every day that I'm good enough to—"

"Looks like we're both about to see who's good enough," Isaac said, not meaning to cut her off, but while she'd been talking, a big silver truck pulling a horse trailer was driving up the path, past the front pasture. Even at that distance, he could hear snorting and kicking coming from inside the trailer.

"Mercy," he heard Grace whisper. "What in heaven's—" They both jumped when the truck came to a stop and whatever was inside nearly kicked the back off the trailer.

Isaac couldn't help looking at Grace, for help, maybe? Or advice? Maybe even to share a nervous laugh? He wasn't sure. But his confidence certainly didn't increase when she turned to glance at him, her blue eyes wide as two dinner plates.

# CHAPTER SEVEN

Grace was trying to read the expression in Isaac King's eyes. But all she saw was a mirror of her own reflecting back. A moment later, her father came onto the porch. As he stared, slack-jawed toward the trailer, she read pure distress on his face.

"Afternoon," a man said as he climbed out of the shiny truck. He wore sunglasses and a baseball cap. "You John Zook?"

"Jah," her father said, walking down the porch steps, eyes still fixed on the trailer. "Mr. Carlson?"

"Yes, sir, but please, call me Travis," the man said. Just then, another person joined him; he was quite a bit younger. Seventeen or eighteen, at most. "This is Wade, my son," Travis added. "Good to meet ya."

All of their attentions were pulled toward the trailer…as it began to rock. Grace had no idea what the horse was doing inside there to make the whole thing shake like that, but suddenly, she felt a chill run up her back. For the first time, she wondered, was she really ready for this?

"How many you got in there?" her *daed* asked.

Travis chuckled under his breath. "Just one. That's our Cincinnati."

"But we call him Sin." When Wade laughed, it sounded a little…sinister. The menacing expression on the young man's face made Grace wrap her arms around her body and stare at the trailer again.

"Named for the city?"

Grace's heart jumped when she realized Isaac had left her and was walking toward the three men. She should've been first to approach! *Wake up, Grace!*

"Naw," Travis said. "After Ulysses S. Grant's horse." He took off his sunglasses. "He was a soldier in the Civil War, but I suppose folks like you don't know much about that."

"He was a three-star general," Isaac said. "Commander over the entire Union Army, then became the eighteenth president. Hi, I'm Isaac." He put out his hand for the man to shake.

"Oh." Travis chuckled again. "Well, now, it's nice to meet you. My apologies."

Isaac lifted an easy smile. It humbled her to see he was obviously more used to doing business with Englishers than she was. Something she now needed to work on.

"Travis, this is Isaac King, he'll be training Cincinnati." Grace couldn't help but elbow her father. "Ack, sorry, along with my daughter. This is Grace."

"Seriously?" Wade said, his eyes moving to Grace. Even at that distance, she felt uneasy as his gaze slid up and down her body.

"Wade," Travis hissed under his breath as he gave him a stern stare. "Check yourself, boy. I think what my son meant," he added to the group, "is that there will be two trainers?"

Grace held her breath, not sure what to say.

"That's how we've always done it here," her father said, making Grace exhale in relief. "At least the last five years or so. We haven't had any issues."

"And I've worked with multiple trainers before," Isaac said. "Never a problem." He shot a quick glance to Grace. Was he attempting to make her feel better? Or just trying to keep Travis from worrying? Grace couldn't tell yet, didn't know his character.

*He's a good sport, at least*, she thought to herself.

*That disgusting glass of Sarah's "lemonade" barely fazed him.*

Travis pointed at Isaac. "You don't work here normally?"

"I hired him for this specific job," her father said. "You have the best of the best."

Travis looked confused, and Grace suddenly feared that he was about to get in his truck and drive away.

"Tell me about your horse," Isaac said, perhaps thinking the same thing as Grace.

"When was he gelded?" she broke in, stepping up, not wanting to be left out of the conversation any longer. Usually, when they received a new horse to train, both she and her father got the instructions from the owners. Even if she was slightly intimidated, this time should be no different.

"Last month."

"Was he this…aggressive before?"

"Why do you think we call him *Sin*?" Wade said, his lips curled into a crooked sneer.

Travis seemed like a respectable man, but there was something off about his son. Grace was grateful she wouldn't be having to work with him.

Travis removed his baseball cap. "He's never had much attention—the horse, I mean. We have racers, good ones, and our show horses are champions. After he was weaned, I suppose he was a bit neglected."

"Has he been heeded, at least?" Grace asked, making mental notes about how best to start.

"Nah," Travis said. "He didn't get along with the other horses, so we kept him in a stall most of the time."

Grace felt her blood grow hot in her body. Why did people insist on having multiple *gauls* if they didn't treat them right? She'd seen too many cases when it was almost too late to get a horse to trust her.

"That's fine," Isaac said. "I have a special method that I use with troubled horses. We'll get him calmed down quick enough." There was a new firmness to his voice, like he was suddenly in charge of everything, yet he was composed, as if attempting to get everyone to trust him.

"*I* have my own method," Grace inserted. "It's what we've always used here at Zook Farms." For some reason, both Isaac and her father looked at her as if she'd just spouted the worst nonsense in the world.

"Like I said," *Daed* added, chuckling like the situation was nothing out of the ordinary, "the best of the best."

"You were telling us about Cincinnati," Isaac said, using that trust-invoking tone again. "He's a Morgan, four years old, and you'd like to see if he can compete in jumping."

"Not *see if*," Travis said. "He needs to compete. At the highest level. His pedigree goes way back; he was born to be a show horse."

*Then why have you been ignoring him all these years?* Grace wanted to ask.

"Currently, we have one horse down. Sin will fill that slot this winter."

"That's mighty fast," Grace couldn't help saying.

"Well, if you're as good as he says you are"— Travis nodded at her *daed*—"shouldn't be a problem."

"That's right," Isaac said.

"Exactly," Grace chimed in. For a quick moment, she and Isaac shared a look. "I think it's time we meet our new friend."

The racket and snorting coming from inside the

trailer increased the closer they got to the back. In fact, one powerful kick actually bowed the side of the trailer, exposing the galvanized steel underneath, chipping off the white paint.

Grace wasn't worried—of course not.

Still, she couldn't help glancing at Isaac. His expression seemed laser focused, though she did notice his motions were slow and cautious.

"Do you want him free in the pasture first, or straight to his stall?"

"Pasture!" Grace and Isaac said at the same time. At least they were in sync about that. Hadn't the poor thing been isolated long enough?

The moment Travis released the lever of the tailgate, it turned dead silent inside the trailer, causing another chill to race up Grace's spine.

Then, like a wild bronco ready to break loose, the snorting began. Was it possible that Grace felt the aggression and power flowing off the horse and wrapping around her? Warning her? She looked through one of the tiny holes in the trailer.

Even just standing there, snorting, he was magnificent.

At first, she noticed the basic Morgan build: tall but compact, muscular hindquarters, broad forehead, and that beautifully arched neck. Yes, he was born to show. Suddenly, he turned his backside to the gate and kicked, hitting it so hard that the lower hinge snapped off. Grace heard the metal parts skipping across the dirt. All four men leaped at the tailgate, keeping the doors closed.

For some reason, this made Grace break into a fit of laughter.

"Something...er...funny about this?" Isaac grunted, leaning a shoulder hard against the gate, his cowboy hat sliding off his head.

"Nay," she said after containing her laugh. "He's gorgeous." She took another look inside the trailer. "He's a rusty red with three white socks. Coal black mane and tail with the sweetest white patch on his nose." Smiling almost to the point of tears, she looked at her father. "You should see him, Papa."

"About time we *all* see him," Isaac said. "Everyone to the sides, out of the way. I'm opening the doors."

# CHAPTER EIGHT

It hadn't been what Isaac had expected. But of course, he'd seen worse.

Or had he?

"I mean it," he said to the other men. "Cincinnati must see me, the sooner the better, and we need to get him out of there before he tears it apart."

"Be my guest." Wade stepped aside, raising his hands in the air. "He's all yours."

"You sure?" John Zook said, brows furrowed in concern, face red from effort.

"Yeah," Isaac said, reaching down to pick up his hat. After he slid it on, he motioned for both John and Travis to move out of his way.

Right before he opened the tailgate, he felt the need to look at Grace, for something strange had come over her when she'd looked inside the trailer at the horse. It had been like she'd seen an angel in there, intriguing Isaac to no end. Honestly, now he was dying to get a look at the *gaul*, too.

He'd also been taken aback by how Grace had inserted herself into the discussion, asking questions he hadn't thought to, and adding to the conversation about Cincinnati. Maybe she really was up to the task, though it was still difficult for Isaac to imagine. Even back in his own New Order congregation, a woman stepping into a man's role like that was uncommon, despite their capability.

"He's tied up here?" Isaac asked Travis, pointing in the direction of the door on the side of the trailer. Usually, a horse was led in via the tailgate, got situated, tied to the side hooks, then the trainer exited through the side door, not the back.

"Yeah," Travis answered. "About halfway up."

Isaac nodded, adjusting his hat again, sending one more glance toward Grace. Her blue eyes were fixed on him now, hands gripped in double fists, waiting to see his next move. Seeing her attention focused on him made him feel strong and able…confident. Like he could do anything.

He *could* do anything.

Taking in a deep breath first, he undid the lock, slid out the arm, and slowly opened the first door. It was dark inside, only streams of sunlight coming in through the tiny holes in the trailer. He heard Cincinnati before he got a good look at him. In the shadows, the animal was breathing hard and fast again, but he was not going to kick or buck—not under Isaac's watch.

He ran his eyes over the left side of the wall, where the lead rope should have been. It was there, all right, but only a foot of it was left hanging.

*My word, he must've broken free from it*, Isaac thought. *How strong is this thing?*

The rest of the short rope was hanging slack from the harness at one side of the horse's head.

"Lead broke," he said, just loudly enough for the others to hear. "John," he continued, speaking calmly, "do you have a rope with a hook nearby?"

"Be right back," he heard John say. Only moments later, he was at the tailgate. "Here."

Isaac reached back and took it, holding the hook in one hand. He would need to approach the horse now, get close enough to hook one side of his harness. He felt a bead of sweat roll down his spine. But he wasn't afraid. He was never afraid.

At the thought, something flashed through his mind. That one time he was afraid, terribly afraid, so afraid that it made him freeze in place now.

*Please, no. Not now. Lord, please help me. Not now.* He would have closed his eyes to pray, but Cincinnati was looking straight at him, and Isaac was not about to break eye contact.

He took a slow breath in through his nose, out through his mouth, sending more pleading prayers heavenward. At the same time, his training kicked in. He could do this without thinking…

Isaac kept his gaze fixed on the pair of huge brown eyes, not blinking. His steps were steady as he walked straight up to the horse, reaching out and attaching the hook. Cincinnati didn't move at first, then he shook his head in defiance, blowing puffs of air out his nose.

*And that's how it's done.* Isaac stayed at the horse's side, standing tall and confident, though feeling the beats of his heart. A second later, the animal started to turn, trying to get his backside to face Isaac. The *gaul* was scared and uncomfortable, and his normal reaction to that was a finely placed kick.

"No," Isaac said firmly, tugging at the lead, not allowing the horse to move much at all.

"Do you have him?" Isaac's focus was momentarily pulled when he heard Grace's voice.

"Jah—*ack!*" Cincinnati suddenly swung his big head, pulling the lead right out of Isaac's hands. Isaac didn't waste a second, he stepped up to the horse and grabbed the rope. "Shhh," he hissed through his teeth. "You're coming with me. You're mine."

He looped the rope around a hook near the back of the trailer, then stepped out. Sin wasn't going anywhere this time. "He's uh, mighty riled up."

"Let me lead him out then," Grace said, walking toward the tailgate, as brazen as any man he'd seen.

"I don't think he's going to let anyone lead him just yet." He wiped his forehead with the back of his hand. "It's about ten yards to the gate?" he asked John, pointing toward the pasture.

*A long ten yards without a lead.*

"If you're thinking of guiding him there," Grace said, "I have an idea."

"Yeah?" Frankly, Isaac was willing to listen to anything.

"See?" Grace gestured to the tall bales of straw stacked to the left flank. "He won't go that way. We just have to keep him in the center. He'll lead himself."

"What about to the right?" Isaac said, beginning to see her plan. "There's nothing there to divert him at all."

"*I'll* divert him," she said. "*I'll* be the noxious stimulus."

Again, Isaac was taken aback. Where did a plain Amish woman learn a phrase like that? Before he could speak, Grace flew behind the straw stacks, then came out with two long pieces of wood nailed together like a T, probably something she'd pulled off a crate. "Just add this…" To his shock, she untied then tore off her black apron, hooking the neck strap to the top of the wood.

Isaac wasn't sure where to look, and he felt warmth gush through his chest, probably coloring his ears bright red. Without the apron, Grace Zook wasn't dressed properly—some might even say immodestly. Though…she was wearing pants underneath her dress—which wasn't all that proper to begin with.

"It's a scarecrow," Wade said, sounding amazed.

Isaac was pretty impressed himself.

"See, I'll stand behind it and hold it up like this." Grace lifted the…"noxious stimulus" so it was as tall as she was, then shook it side to side. Isaac almost laughed. The thing might be noxious enough to divert even him.

"It's an excellent idea," Isaac offered, "but someone else should hold it. John—"

"He certainly will not," Grace said. "I'm as capable as anyone." She moved into place, directly blocking the spot where Cincinnati would be tempted to make his escape. With a loud huff, she held up the scarecrow. "Do it now. I'm ready. Open the gate."

Isaac glanced at John, who didn't look worried in the least. Apparently, he had absolute trust in his daughter. "Would you open the pasture gate, John?"

Isaac moved to the tailgate, ready to open both doors. But first, he couldn't help sending one more look Grace's way.

"Oh heavenly days!" she called out to him. "I'm *fine*!" The exasperation in her voice made him chuckle under his breath. "You're overthinking it."

She was right again. *Huh*. This whole scene had been completely overthought and taken way too long. So he opened the doors and stepped inside. It took only two clicks of his tongue to give Cincinnati a clear signal to follow the light out the back.

And he was gone.

Isaac heard a few "woot-woots" and "this way!" But by the time he'd made his way out of the trailer, the horse was safely inside the pasture, running the fence. He looked at Grace, who was smiling brightly at him.

Without thinking, he ran to her side. "How did it go?"

She tipped her chin to look up at him, her blue eyes squinting into the sunlight. "Only took one shake. The good boy went right in." She exhaled and turned to look toward the pasture. But Isaac kept his eyes on her.

They'd only just begun their training together; he barely even knew her. But he liked her. He was… interested in her. Where did she get such confidence and bravery? Creativity? He looked at her profile, at her long neck and dimple.

*If it was six years ago…*

He cut off the unwelcome thought that had crept into his brain. It was ridiculous, no use to think that way. The past was the past, and the present—*this very moment*—was more important than just about anything in his life.

Grace Zook, even though they had to work together, despite the eyes and womanly figure, would not be a distraction.

# CHAPTER NINE

Grace stood close to the fence. She didn't know Cincinnati yet, couldn't recognize a pattern in his behavior. All she knew was, he wanted to run. It had been nearly an hour since that silver truck and its dented trailer had driven away, and the Morgan hadn't stopped. For a while, her father had stood with her, watching the horse continue to run the perimeter of the pasture, over and over, until he finally went to tend to the other livestock.

Isaac was on the opposite side of the ring, about as far away from Grace as he could be. She wondered why. Hadn't they had a moment earlier? *She'd* felt connected to him, at least—connected as in a good partnership, not connected like…anything else.

It was foolish to keep apart like that. She at least needed to know his thoughts about the horse. Once Cincinnati was at the far end of the pasture, Grace began walking across toward Isaac, who was leaning one shoulder against a fence post, the brim of his hat low over his eyes.

Okay, so he did look pretty cute like that. She could report back to Hannah that he was definitely handsome, and charming…at least when he wanted something.

*But Sadie.*

Yes, and with a wife, he was positively off-limits.

As Grace continued her way across the pasture, she couldn't help noticing that the second Isaac saw her nearing where he stood, his posture straightened, hands dropping to his sides, gaze sharply focused on hcr as if *she* were the wild horse.

His attention so fixated on her made her stomach do a little backflip. By the time she was ten yards away, he'd actually taken a few steps forward to meet her.

"Hey," she called out, offering a friendly smile.

"Hey." That riveted expression on his face was still there, and when he turned away, she noticed his corded neck, muscles, and the veins straining against his forearms.

Right then, Grace also noticed that Cincinnati was barreling straight toward her at a full gallop. She picked up her pace, making it to the fence and Isaac's side a little faster than she'd intended.

"Whoa," she said, easily getting out of the horse's way in time. "He's got so much energy. That was close."

"That was *thoughtless*," he said.

A little out of breath from her quick trot, she stared at him, feeling like a block of ice was suddenly dropped in her stomach. "Pardon?"

Isaac lifted a hand, massaging one of his shoulders. "Shouldn't you have used the other side of the fence?"

"Why?"

"Because it's safer." He blew out a breath. "Because he could've killed you."

Grace put her hands on her hips, that coldness turning to an annoyed heat. "Look here, Isaac King, this is where I grew up. I've lived here twenty-three years, and I've dealt with twice that many horses." When he tried to sigh and glance away, she moved into his line of vision. "It might surprise you that I know more about training a horse—any horse—than even my father, and he has more experience than anyone in twenty miles." When he didn't reply, she added, "Did you hear me?"

Isaac was staring down at the ground. "*Jah*," he finally said, softly.

She cocked her head. "And I'm not about to be treated like a helpless creature who can't handle herself with a horse." She took a step toward him. "I know what I'm doing."

"I see that." When he glanced up, his hazel eyes softened. "Sorry. I shouldn't have said that to you; I was…concerned for your safety."

"Okay, then." Grace wasn't sure what to do next. She couldn't just stand there forever with her hands on her hips like a scolding mother. "As long as we've got that straight." She blew out a breath then moved to his side. "And I'm sorry about the lemonade."

He sent her a sideways glance, a small smile tugging at his lips. "What did you put in that?"

"Nothing," she said, leaning against the fence. "That's how Sarah makes it. She's a terrible cook but, since I'm outside all day, most of the housekeeping tasks fall on her. I don't think she minds, but she really needs lessons."

"What about your mother?" Isaac asked.

Grace's heart froze inside her chest. Was he trying to be funny or mean? "My mother doesn't cook anymore. She can't."

Isaac turned to her, his brows furrowed. "Can't?"

Grace shook her head. "Not for the past five years."

"Why?"

Evidently her father hadn't said anything to Isaac about *Maam*'s situation. It wasn't a secret; how could it be? But still, Grace felt it would be a betrayal, talking about her behind her back to someone she barely knew.

"It's a long story," she simply stated.

And when she didn't go on, Isaac said, "Okay," and they both set their focus on Cincinnati as he galloped by. "What do you think about him?" Isaac asked.

Grace paid close attention to the horse's legs as he ran across the field. "Surprisingly good gait," she said. "Probably a natural jumper."

"I was thinking the same thing," Isaac said. "He's rhythmic. I wonder if there's any dressage experience in his bloodline. If he's got any brains in him, he'd probably catch right on."

"We're training him to jump."

"We can train him to do anything." He paused. "At least *I* can."

Grace stared at him, wondering if he was attempting to tease her, because hadn't she just explained to him that she was the best around? When his expression didn't change, she felt her teeth grind. "I don't know about you, but I intend to stay focused." She turned away from him. "You obviously don't understand how important this job is."

"Believe me, I understand plenty." When he looked at her, his hazel eyes flashed, giving him an intensity that she hadn't noticed, even when he'd been about to walk into Cincinnati's trailer alone.

Well, she could be just as intense.

"All I'm saying is my father may have hired you, but that doesn't mean you're calling the shots." She made herself stand as tall and confident as possible. "This is my home—my training farm. My father may trust you right off the bat, but that doesn't mean I do."

"Who said—" Isaac suddenly cut himself off, then looked down at the ground. Whatever he'd been about to say, he suddenly thought better of it. Grace was no mind reader, but she could've made a good guess.

"Trust is earned," she added, softening the firmness in her voice.

"Just like with a horse."

Grace blinked. "Exactly." For a moment, they shared a gaze. How would she ever learn to really trust this man? This man who'd come to take her job? Her future? The only future she'd ever wanted?

"Well, it's been a long day for me," he said while rubbing the back of his neck.

Grace suddenly remembered that he'd traveled all the way from Silver Springs today, or at least halfway. Then stopped at the Chupp's before coming here. He must be exhausted.

"I'll corral him," she said.

Isaac opened his mouth, probably ready to tell her *he* would do it, but then, surprisingly, he nodded. "Mind if I watch?"

# CHAPTER TEN

It was like muscle memory—the way Isaac could jump in and help with the evening milking. He'd been working with horses for so long that a lot of the basic farm duties were left to the others around him. But he wasn't about to not pitch in, even though he was paying for room and board.

"Last one?" Samuel Chupp asked while taking a long drink of water from an old milk jug.

"Aye," Isaac said, feeling good about his day's work, but also mighty exhausted. Not only because of the long ride from Silver Springs, or even from the sun beating down on his head and body all day. No, he figured most of it was mental exhaustion.

*That…Sin*, he thought as he followed Samuel over to an outdoor sink to wash up. *Never seen anything like him. He's strong and mighty, energetic as a racer, and I know he'll be a magnificent show horse, if only he had the slightest interest in interacting with humans.*

He chuckled inside, remembering Grace's attempt to corral him. It took nearly an hour, and the ornery woman's pretty face was glowing with heat and effort, long strands of her dark hair hanging loose from her *kapp*, by the time she was done.

Not that Isaac could've done much better on his own.

Cincinnati's nickname was sure appropriate.

He knew he was smiling as he recalled when Grace finally shut the wooden gate, the panting horse safely on the other side, in his new home for the first time.

"Piece of cake," she'd said, making Isaac almost laugh. The brightness of her eyes and complexion—that was what Isaac was picturing most clearly now. Her happy smile. She was a mighty hard worker, never giving up, never asking for help. Not that Isaac wouldn't have offered any. He'd been interested to see how she would do. And again, he'd walked away more than impressed with Grace Zook.

"Have you seen Sadie?" he asked Samuel as they walked toward the house, needing to clear his mind of his boss's daughter.

"Most likely with Eliza and Emma in the garden. They'll stay out there until the last flicker of daylight. We take our boots off here," Samuel added as they reached a door on the side of the house, a sort of side porch with numerous pairs of muddy boots in a variety of sizes.

Entering the house in his stocking feet, behind his host, he saw the kitchen was bright and noisy with several women, both young and old bustling around. Isaac half expected to see Martha. Then he blinked and searched the room for Sadie.

"Anything I can help with?" Isaac asked Samuel. "Looks like a lot's going on."

"I wouldn't step foot in there, if I were you," he replied with a smile. "There's an order to their chaos, though I will look to see if the trash needs to be taken out. That's about all I'm good for in these situations. Feel free to sit on the couch until supper or rest up in your room. Wherever you're comfortable."

"*Danke*," Isaac said. He chose to stay in the big family room, admiring the energy and rhythm coming from the kitchen, reminding him of his own upbringing. He and Daniel had been the only boys born to their parents, along with four daughters. He smiled inside, thinking of his sister's blackberry pies.

A knot formed in his gut, one that he'd been living with the past few years. Had he simply gotten used to it, or had it returned at the sight of a big, happy family? Something he didn't have anymore, but desperately wanted.

"Someone's messing with the chicken coops again," said a young man who came in through the front door. He looked to be in his early twenties. "I used a stapler to fix it this time."

"Good idea," Samuel said. "How long you expect it to hold?"

The young man shrugged and removed his hat. "Not long. I'll replace it soon as I can." Then he disappeared up the stairs.

"We're eating soon, son!" Samuel called up the stairs, getting only an inaudible grunt in reply.

"More than soon," added Dorothy Chupp, Samuel's wife. She was short and plump with the cheeriest disposition. When they'd met last week, Isaac had instantly liked her. "Would you call in the girls from the gard—"

Cutting her off mid-sentence, the front door flew open and two little girls came running inside. "Emma," Dorothy continued, "take your little sister upstairs to wash up." Without a word, they, too, disappeared to the second floor.

"Daddy!" Isaac's heart welled up when he turned back to the front door.

"Sadie!" he couldn't help calling out as his daughter came running toward him, the hem of her little dress brown with dirt. Isaac didn't care. He caught her in a big hug. "Oh, *meine liebling dochder*," he whispered, kissing the top of her head, pulling her onto his lap. "What kind of mischief did you get into today?"

She giggled, making Isaac's heart swell. "*Nichts*, Papa," she said, smiling up at him, her eyes matching her mother's to a T, causing that knot in his gut to tighten once again. Would it ever go away?

"Do you know where to wash your hands?" he asked, his gaze pointing toward the staircase.

"*Jah*, Papa." Her big eyes brightened.

Isaac cocked his head. "Quickly, then. We don't want to hold up dinner, do we?" With that, Sadie ran to the stairs, nearly as fast as Cincinnati.

"She's adorable," Dorothy Chupp said. "Perfectly beautiful."

Isaac relaxed into a smile. "She looks like her mother."

"Nay," one of the older girls said. "I think she looks like you."

"Aye," another of the daughters chimed in, pressing her lips together. "Exactly like you."

Isaac was beginning to feel warm with embarrassment as so many female eyes were suddenly fixed on him.

"Ahem." Dorothy cleared her throat after a moment of silence that seemed to stretch on forever. "Dinnertime."

Isaac let out a sigh of relief when Samuel Chupp's *dochders* went back to their kitchen duties. He escaped up the stairs to find Sadie in their bedroom changing her dress.

"I got dirty," she said, pulling it over her head.

"I see that." He crouched down to help her. "You had fun, though, I think?"

"Oh, *jah—I* can do that, *Daed*," she said, brushing his hand away when he went to help with the hooks inside the side pleats of her clean dress. "Emma taught me this morning."

Isaac balanced back on his heels. "I see. Very *gut*, indeed." She was growing up so fast. Wasn't it just yesterday that she learned to walk, said her first words, chased the newborn chicks around the yard?

Why, then, did it feel like a thousand years ago since he'd carried his then-four-year-old daughter home, alone in their house for the first time…just the two of them?

"I'm ready," Sadie said, attempting to tie the strings of her bonnet under her chin.

"You can leave those loose if you want," he said, "like the bigger girls do."

Sadie thought for a moment, then nodded. "*Ewkey, Daed*," she said in a singsong voice, sounding much too grown up.

Most of the family was gathered at the table by the time they made it downstairs.

"You can sit next to me," one of the older daughters said, pointing at the empty chair at her side. Isaac swallowed, trying to ignore her all-too-welcoming smile. He'd never had an issue with the Amish tradition of marrying young, but she couldn't have been more than seventeen—a ten-year age gap.

"I made a special place for Isaac and Sadie right here," Dorothy said, pulling out a long bench on the other side of the table.

"*Danke*," Isaac said, while Sadie ran to take her place.

"We're waiting for you, Collin," Samuel called out. A moment later, his son came stomping down the stairs. He'd washed up and wore a clean white shirt.

After the blessing on the food, Isaac was immediately passed the bowl of roasted potatoes. First, he dished some up for Sadie and for himself, then passed it on. Before long, his plate was full of delicious-smelling food.

"I heard you say something to your *daed* about the chicken coop?" Dorothy asked Collin. "Does it look like the same damage as over at the Kings'?"

Collin's mouth was full, so he nodded. "Pretty sure someone messed with it," he finally said.

"A group of kids from a few towns over," Samuel said, leaning closer to Isaac. "They've been vandalizing some folks' property."

"Not just vandalizing, *Daed*," Collin said, his lips set in a snarl. "They set a fire over near the feedstore. And they're always lighting off those Englisher sparkler things in the middle of the night, even when the grass is dry."

Samuel sighed. "We can only hope their parents keep a better eye on them."

"I'd love to get my hands on just one of 'em," Collin said with half of his mouth full. Something about the kid's boldness made Isaac want to chuckle.

"How was it out at the Zooks' place today?" Samuel asked as he scooped up a large spoonful of green peas.

"The *gaul* came just as I arrived," Isaac replied while helping Sadie cut her slice of roast beef. "He's a big one, powerful, years of pent-up energy, if I had to guess. Might take all my patience, but I've got help. John's daughter."

"You talking about Grace?" Collin asked, lowering his fork. "John Zook's Grace?"

"*Jah*," Isaac said, wondering why the kid suddenly looked so interested. No, not interested—intense. "She's good with the horse, corralled him herself, even though he seemed dead set on killing her."

Collin slammed down his fist, shaking the table. "I told her to stop that, but she won't listen."

"Girl's got a mind of her own," Dorothy said after taking a drink of milk. "Been like that since she was knee-high."

"Stop what?" Isaac couldn't help asking.

Collin groaned loudly. "She's had her fun with the *gauls*, but it's high time she goes inside. Learn to cook and clean and…take care of a man." Collin turned his gaze to rest on Isaac. "She's my girl, ya see. We'll get married someday."

"Ah," Isaac said. "That's…" His voice faded, not knowing what to say. True, he'd been around Grace for only a few hours, but could a woman like her really be interested in…

Again, he cut off his thoughts. None of his business.

"Maybe *this* wedding season, even," Collin continued. He wasn't smiling like a happy husband-to-be but instead wore an expression of almost… obsession on his face. How odd.

And how odd was it that Isaac felt a rush of protection toward Grace? His throat got tight, and he could feel his heart beating hard. He took a long look at Collin Chupp, protection turning to defensiveness.

But why should that be? He hardly knew either of them. He'd basically stepped into their lives from out of nowhere. Perhaps he didn't know Grace's character at all. Or maybe there was something more to Collin.

"If only she'd go out with me," Collin added, his voice dropping from forceful to almost sulky.

One of the sisters started to laugh, nudging the other. "You've been asking to court her for a hundred years." They broke into giggles.

"Not *officially*," Collin said, rubbing the back of his hand across his chin.

Finally, that alarm pushing through Isaac's blood

died down. *Grace won't even go on a date with him…* He covered his mouth with a hand, hiding a smile.

"*You're* not interested in her, are you?" Collin continued, looking straight at Isaac.

Isaac lowered his hand. For the life of him, he didn't know how to respond.

"Of course he isn't," Samuel practically jumped in, letting Isaac off the hook. Though Samuel's resolved tone made Isaac want to frown. "She's his boss's daughter. There's a firm line there, son."

"Oh," Collin said, though still looking incredulous.

"And being from Silver Springs," one of the daughters added, "the girls in your community are more traditional than Grace Zook. That's the kind of woman you'll want to marry, *jah*?"

*I will?* Isaac couldn't help thinking. It was true: his New Order congregation was a bit more liberal when it came to technology and worship services, but the rules about women's roles were nearly as old-fashioned as the Swiss Amish in Nebraska.

"That so?" Collin said, staring at him hard now, all that intensity returning.

This wasn't a topic Isaac wanted to discuss—it was personal. Plus, he wasn't anywhere close to thinking about getting married.

"*Jah*," he finally said, tired of feeling the weight of all the eyes in the room on him. "I'm definitely traditional." He'd spoken the tiny fib mostly to pacify Collin, and with the hopes of moving on to another subject. "And I would never overstep my place. Your father's right—he's my boss."

He looked at Collin again, who was back to shoveling food into his mouth. Isaac breathed out the last of that unexpected, overreactive protection for Grace, turning his full attention back to Sadie.

# CHAPTER ELEVEN

"I need that bowl—no, Amos, not that one, *that* one."

"Sorry. There are five bowls where you pointed."

Sarah exhaled in a loud huff and stared at her husband. "Maybe if you spent more time helping me and less time at the sawmill…"

"Here," Grace said quietly, handing the correct blue mixing bowl to her older brother. "She needs it to make the pancakes."

"*Danke*," Amos said, rushing over to his wife.

"He *works* at the sawmill," Grace pointed out, then instantly regretted butting in.

"Don't defend him, Grace," Sarah said, planting her hands on her hips as she stood near the stove. "And don't get in the middle of it. It's not your place."

*Then why do you always ask my opinion about why Amos works so much, or why he still hasn't fixed your rocking chair, or why can't he be a better husband?*

Grace loved her brother, and she'd even liked Sarah Miller fine enough when Amos started courting her three years ago. But a few months after their wedding day, it was as if nothing her brother did satisfied his new bride. And, since Sarah had decided it was best that the newlyweds move in with Amos's family instead of the tradition of moving in with Sarah's, Grace was too often front row to their arguments.

In addition to making the worst lemonade in Lancaster County, Sarah was grumpy all the time and constantly yelling at her husband, then demanding Grace take her side.

"I'm not in the middle of it," Grace said, smoothing down the front of her apron. "All I did was hand him a bowl."

Sarah sighed again. "You'll understand when you're married. Or maybe you'll find a husband who actually cares about you."

A fist squeezed around Grace's heart as she looked at her brother, his chin lowered. Amos didn't deserve this. But Sarah was right; it wasn't Grace's business to interfere in someone else's relationship. Even though she'd been holding her tongue for years.

"I gotta go," Amos said.

"Of course you do," said Sarah.

Amos exhaled, his shoulders slumping. "I gotta go to *work*," he said. "I'm nearly late."

"Then go," Sarah howled. Her harsh tone made Grace's heart ache for her brother again, and also wonder if she'd awaken the whole house at this early hour.

"I'll be back for supper," he added, putting on his straw hat while walking to the door, not even attempting to kiss her goodbye. Grace would sooner try to kiss Cincinnati...

"Of course you will," Sarah muttered. "*Auf wiedersehen*," she added, turning her back to him after offering a quick and stiff goodbye.

"*Mach's gut*," Grace said, smiling lightly at her *bruder*, hoping to convey her purest of sympathy to him. But really, what was she supposed to do?

Since she couldn't say anything, she simply sent Sarah a look she knew she'd understand.

"Your brother can take care of himself," Sarah replied, rolling her eyes.

"And you could be easier on him," Grace said, then held her breath.

Sarah stared at her, closed her eyes, and shook her head. "Are you eating breakfast with us?"

"Can't," Grace said. "I've got to get out to the new horse. Training starts today."

"Don't know how you can stay out there for so many hours."

*Having you in the house all day makes it easier*, Grace wanted to say, but didn't. She silently apologized to the Lord for even thinking it.

The sky above was still a dark purple, but bright lines of orange and yellow settled along the horizon. In just a few minutes, she would see the first sunbeams.

*Danke, kind Heavenly Father, for this beautiful day.* She continued her prayer from earlier. *Danke for Maam and Daed, and all my family.* She smiled. *Even Sarah. Please bless me with patience and kindness, and with a heart that wants to serve thee better. And please help me to find my way, dear Gott, that I may do my duty to—*

She suddenly cut off, hearing a noise coming from the stables. A sound that wasn't equestrian.

"*Guder mariye!*"

Grace was shocked to see Isaac at Cincinnati's stall, handfeeding him a carrot. "*Guder mariye*," she echoed, but with way less enthusiasm. "When did you get here?"

"Oh, 'bout fifteen minutes ago."

He was wearing clean black pants and an olive green shirt with short sleeves, brown suspenders, and boots. Plus his "cowboy" hat. Grace envied how well-rested he looked, even after such a long day yesterday.

She bit her bottom lip, loathing that he'd beaten her to work. "You didn't have to," she said, walking toward him. "I planned on brushing him out first thing."

Isaac shrugged. "I'm an early riser."

"Hmm." Grace exhaled, taking note. "The brush is right there."

"I'll get it."

"No, I—" Suddenly, Isaac had the horse brush in his hand and was holding it behind his back. When she took a step toward him, he took a step back, one side of his mouth tipped up. "This isn't a game."

Isaac frowned and looked to the side. "It isn't?"

"It's serious."

He held the brush out in front of him. "*This* is serious?"

Grace grabbed the brush, hearing him snicker as she turned her back to him. "What are you so happy about at this hour?" she couldn't help asking.

Isaac tipped back the front of his hat. "Woke up in a good mood, I reckon."

Grace blew out a breath in exasperation. She'd woken in a good mood, too. But him beating her to Cincinnati made her competitiveness flare up.

"I have a very specific way of grooming a new horse," she said. "It leads into my heeding routine."

"I have my own techniques, for which I was hired." His voice was calm and level, which made Grace want to stomp her foot. "But your father says we're a team—so, we're a team, or did you forget that?"

He was playing his charming card again. Okay, if this was all a game to him, Grace could play her own card.

"I was only teasing you," she said with a lilt to her voice. "You're so touchy this morning. Loosen up, Isaac King." She purposefully fluttered her lashes as she passed him, noticing that he didn't break eye contact as she'd expected.

As a married man, shouldn't he be ignoring her friendliness?

"You're a curious woman, Grace Zook," he said, pulling down the front of his hat.

Grace swung around, holding out the sides of her skirts. "And you haven't even seen my heeding skills."

Isaac chuckled. Even though he was completely off-limits and basically out to steal her future, something in the sound made Grace want to join him.

*What a lucky woman Sadie is to be the wife of a strong, cheerful, talented man*, she thought as she stood beside him, both of them reaching into the stall, getting Cincinnati used to their smells. *I hope she appreciates him, takes good care of him.*

She couldn't help thinking about Sarah and Amos. How much longer could Grace be expected to live in the same house as Sarah? Her sister-in-law caused so much tension.

"I'm going in," Isaac said, breaking into her thoughts. He was already opening the small gate before she could make a move. She wanted to object, to say *she* was going into the stall with the horse first. But that was selfish. And hadn't he let her corral Cincinnati on her own last night?

"Good boy," Isaac said, his voice calm and soothing as he offered the back of his hand. The horse was tentative at first, but then he moved up to Isaac, smelling his hand, his palm. A stab of jealousy hit Grace when Isaac reached up and ran a knuckle down the front of the horse's nose. "Good boy," he repeated, running his hand around the white patch of his forehead.

Grace was dying to jump in there and pet the beautiful Morgan, get him trusting her, not just Isaac. But she knew full well that part of working as a team was not overstimulating the animal. She would have her time with Cincinnati soon enough. Until then, she watched almost greedily as Isaac stroked at his nose, the sides of his head, while whispering softly, peacefully, making even Grace feel calm.

"Your turn."

Despite the irritation Grace felt from just the existence of Isaac, she felt a giddy grin spread across her face as Isaac pushed open the gate, inviting her to come in beside him. "He's glorious," she whispered. "Aren't you, good boy?" she added when Cincinnati lowered his head to snuffle at the side of her face. Grace giggled, taking in the smell and the sounds, loving every second of the experience.

"I think he's ready for a lead," she said about twenty minutes later, after she was sure the horse was nice and relaxed.

Any training session—even with a new horse—could only be up to two hours. Much longer and the horse would lose interest, get tired, and want to rest or play. Grace was relieved Isaac felt the same way—she didn't want to clash with him about something so basic.

"I think he's ready to run," Isaac said, when the two hours was up.

"Ya think?" Grace said when Cincinnati jerked his head to the side, probably tired of the harness and lead. But they'd made good progress. They practiced putting on and taking off the tack, brushing him down, and simply getting him used to being around humans. Trusting them.

"Should we let him into the back pasture with the other horses?" Isaac asked, pulling at the collar of his shirt. It was getting warm in the stables.

"Maybe not yet," Grace replied. "I don't want him to lose focus on us, now that we finally have it."

Isaac didn't reply right away. Maybe he didn't

agree with her but didn't want to argue, either. Still, she wasn't about to end the morning in a dead heat.

"I, uh, I liked how you led him in by the chin that first time," she began. "I was impressed."

"*Jah?*"

"Oh, *jah*." As he walked past her, she made a point to glance up, batting her lashes flirtatiously like the way she'd seen Hannah do sometimes.

He paused and tilted his head. "Got something in your eye?" he asked.

"Uh—no," Grace said, jerking her chin away. "Oh…oh, *you*," she added, doing her best to familiarly shove at his shoulder.

"Don't lose your balance, there," he said. "Are you overtired? Need to sit?"

"Nay." Grace exhaled. "Never mind." Since the man still wasn't reacting the way she'd expected, and she loathed faking interest in him, she gave up her plan to flirt him into quitting.

For now.

"Before I go," she said, "I'll fill a cotton ball and put it in Cincinnati's stall for later. "It'll help."

"A cotton ball?" he asked. "For what?"

"The lavender oil."

He dipped his chin, staring at her through his brows. "Lavender?"

"Aye." She planted her hands on her hips, not appreciating the amused expression on his face. "Mixed with sweet almond and orange, it's very relaxing, calming."

Isaac removed his hat and ran a hand up the back of his hair. "Are you serious? You think a little flower is going make a difference in his behavior?"

"It's essential oil," she corrected him. "Folks have been using it medicinally for thousands of years. And yes, I think it will make a difference."

Grace had to press her lips together hard to stop herself from kicking Isaac King in the shins for looking at her like…like she was a dotty child, or maybe someone's great-grammie who'd seen better days.

"Is that *okay* with you?" she finally said, though she was not truly asking permission.

A long moment passed before Isaac lifted his hands. "Fine. Just don't get that stuff near me. And you're right about Cincinnati. He can run around the front ring until he's tired out. I'll be back this afternoon to check on him."

"You don't have to…" Grace cut herself off, not wanting to pick a fight. "See you then."

"Goodbye for now," Isaac said, pulling down the brim of his cowboy hat in a kind of gentlemanly way, making Grace want to scowl…or maybe smile. She wasn't quite sure.

* * *

For the rest of the day, Grace tended to her regular duties. She had five other horses that needed attention and training, one who was nearly ready to pull a buggy for the first time. She'd barely finished a young draft horse's lesson when Isaac returned.

"Why are you still out here?" he called. He'd changed into a clean blue shirt, maybe even taken a bath. Grace could only imagine how filthy she must've looked.

*Oh, well. My appearance doesn't matter to Isaac. He's married. Luckily. Otherwise, surely Papa would never allow us to work so closely together.* She smiled to herself. *And I wouldn't be able to walk by him and playfully push his shoulder like I did this morning.*

*Even though it didn't seem to even rattle him.*

"My twin is inside taking a nap," Grace said, going for a joke, wondering if someone like him would even get it, and then mildly surprised when he chuckled.

"Can I help you with this?" he asked, taking the lead of the tan draft horse.

"I'm all done with this girl. She's not stubborn, but she's not catching on." She blew out a breath. "About wore me out, all the tugging."

"Some horses are like that. I don't mind taking off the gear," he added.

Grace couldn't help eyeing him suspiciously. Why was he being so helpful? "Aye. *Danke*," she said. "Shall I bring out Sin? I corralled him earlier."

"*Jah*, that was my hope."

For a while, they stood inside the fence, watching Cincinnati run free. A few times, he actually slowed his gallop as he neared them, but never stopped. That would come soon enough. For now, they wanted him to feel calm and at home, trust them enough to learn.

"It's been a productive full first day," Grace said. "But I think it's good he'll have a rest tomorrow."

Isaac turned to her. "Tomorrow? Why?"

"Why…because it's Sunday. Preaching Sunday." The blank expression on his face confused her.

"You don't want to train because it's Sunday?"

"It's the Sabbath. It's the day of rest and for us to honor *Gott*."

"Right." Isaac removed his hat and placed it over his chest. "Right," he repeated. "Of course, sorry."

Grace was a bit puzzled. Was his congregation in Silver Springs that much different than Honey Brook? Maybe his village didn't have traditional Sunday services like hers did. How else were they different?

"Looking good," a new voice said, and Grace turned to see her father. "Just look at that gait."

"I know," Grace agreed, happy for the interruption. "I think he's a natural for dressage." She inwardly cringed when she heard Isaac clear his throat. "*We* think that," she tweaked, uncomfortable even thinking that they were on the same page. She needed to stay on her toes, remember her goal of being the finest horse trainer around.

"Could be," *Daed* said.

"We'll make him into a grand jumper," Isaac added. "Might take a little longer at the beginning, but good things come to those who wait."

"I have no doubt," her father said, his eyes narrowing as they followed Cincinnati around the ring. The sun was hitting the tops of the trees, and the empty feeling in Grace's stomach told her it must be near dinnertime.

"Why don't you come for supper?"

Horrified, Grace gawked at her father, who'd addressed Isaac.

"Won't be for over an hour or so," *Daed* added. "Give you time to go home and fetch, uh, Sadie."

"That's very kind of you," Isaac said. For some reason, he looked at Grace, as if he needed her permission first.

The invitation had been a complete shock to Grace. Didn't her father understand that Isaac King was trying to muscle in and take her job? And honestly, *Daed* should've asked her first to see if it was okay that he came to dinner. And he *really* should've checked with Sarah. Oh heavens.

"Umm… Of course," Grace said, doing her best to smile pleasantly, even though being with the man after hours was the last thing she wanted.

"Well, okay then." Isaac blinked a few times, then scratched his chin. But Grace couldn't fathom why he would seem confused at a simple dinner invitation for him and his wife.

"He's going that way—don't let him into the corner," Isaac said a few minutes later while they attempted to corral Cincinnati together for the first time.

"I know what I'm doing," Grace said, blowing the loose hair out of her face. When she glanced over at Isaac, it was infuriating that he was grinning at her. Was this some kind of test? Did he not understand how intrusive his mere presence was? Or did the smile mean he was finally giving in to her…her completely unsuccessful flirtations from earlier?

Finally, the horse was back in his stall, having taken them twice as long to do it than Grace could've done on her own. So much for teamwork.

Without a polite goodbye, Isaac jumped on his Arabian and headed home to fetch Sadie. Grace stared after him, feeling bewildered. First he grinned all charmingly at her, then he disappeared without a word?

"Aren't you going to change your dress?" Sarah asked as Grace washed her hands at the kitchen sink.

Grace looked down at herself. Yes, she was dirty, but not dirty enough to get anyone else dirty.

"Let me give you a hand," Amos said, helping Grace's mother from her spot on the sofa to her chair at the long dinner table. She always preferred to be close to the activities in the house, never wanting to miss a conversation if she could.

"*Danke*, son," *Maam* said, patting Amos's hand. "Gracie, go put on a clean dress. Make your family proud."

Grace turned off the water. "*Jah, Maam*," she said obediently, sending a quick sideways glance at Sarah, who was grinning smugly. While she was upstairs, Grace decided to give her hands a better scrub, up to her elbows, then wash her face well. The clean dress she decided on was mauve with short sleeves. The evenings were warm. She adjusted her *kapp* and slid on a clean apron.

Just as she was walking down the stairs, she heard the front door close and new voices in the house. Isaac stood at the foot of the stairs, looking up at her. He'd changed again into a snow-white shirt, the sleeves down to his wrists, black vest, and black hat.

"*Guder owed*," he said.

Grace nearly froze mid-step. Gracious, but he looked handsome. As handsome a man as she'd ever seen. *Good thing he's the enemy*, she thought as she continued down. *And of course, good thing he's got Sadie with him*—keeping Grace on her best behavior.

As soon as she got to the bottom of the stairs, a little girl came running up to her. She looked to be about six years old, had brown hair under her tiny black bonnet, the sweetest face, and a big smile displaying a missing front tooth.

"Hallo there," Grace said after the girl had practically run into her.

"Hi!" the little girl said. "Are you Grace? Daddy said he works with Grace."

Grace cleared her throat and looked at Isaac. "I am. What's your name?"

"Sadie!" she said brightly. "I'm Sadie."

Grace stared at the little girl for a second, trying to process what she'd said. *Oh! Isaac and Sadie have a daughter, and they named her…Sadie, too?*

Again, Grace glanced around the room, looking

for the new face of the real, grownup Sadie.

"Will you sit next to me?" little Sadie asked, reaching for Grace's hand.

"Sure," Grace replied. She shot a bewildered glance toward Isaac, who looked as confused as she felt.

"Say please, *dochder*," Isaac said.

As Grace's brain sluggishly began putting the pieces together, her head started to hurt, and she knew the front of her throat was turning pink and marbled with embarrassment.

"What's the matter with you, Grace?" Sarah said, causing her head to throb even worse. "We're ready to eat."

"Nothing, I…" She forced herself to lift half a smile, then was practically dragged by the hand by Isaac's *daughter*, Sadie, to the designated spot at the table.

"Daddy can sit over there," Sadie pointed to the empty chair across from them.

"Good plan," *Maam* said, smiling sweetly at the little girl, always the perfect hostess, when she was up to it.

"Let us pray," said *Daed*. They all bowed their heads for the food blessing, but Grace opened one eye, glancing first at the little girl beside her, then across the table at her…father.

Her heart leaped into her throat when she saw Isaac looking back at her.

# CHAPTER TWELVE

Isaac's impulse was to shut his eyes but, since Grace had caught him looking at her, it was just as well he kept staring right through the prayer. She opened her other eye, evidently unafraid to stare right back.

He shrugged one shoulder. She shrugged both of hers. Then the next moment she slammed her eyes shut.

"Amen," John Zook said.

"Who wants the first slice of meatloaf? I made it myself."

Right before Grace had come down the stairs, Isaac had been introduced to some of John's family. So he knew that the woman who'd just spoken was Sarah, John's son Amos's wife. Grace's sister-in-law. *That* Sarah.

Because of the "lemonade," Isaac couldn't help glancing at Grace again. Were they all about to get food poisoning? When their eyes met, a coy smile sat upon Grace's lips. She was clearly anticipating his worries.

"I do," Grace said, lifting her plate.

"You love my meatloaf," Sarah said, giving Grace a mighty large slice.

Grace held a fist over her mouth, but Isaac caught the stifled giggle behind it. She met his gaze again, and it looked like she was about to smile, but then the grin disappeared, her expression turning stony. She abruptly broke eye contact and stared down at her plate.

*What just happened?* Isaac wondered. *Is she*

*embarrassed about what she said to me about Sarah?
Or maybe... Does it have something to do with Sadie?*
He looked across the table at his daughter. Everyone
on that side of the table was fussing over her—filling
her milk cup, cutting her food.

He hadn't exactly felt overly welcomed by Grace
when John had invited him to dinner. In fact, before
then, she'd been combative with him practically every
time they disagreed about how to handle Cincinnati.

Isaac felt awkward enough being in the Zooks'
house in the first place. He'd only just settled into
Honey Brook, and he'd rather not drag Sadie around
from place to place—meeting people she may never
see again—more than he needed to. But he had to
admit, he'd felt a bit pressured to accept his boss's
invitation. So there they were.

Soon enough, the meatloaf plate made its way to
Isaac. He glanced at Grace to see if she was watching
for how big a slice he took. But her attention was
elsewhere. This deflated Isaac some. After all, the one
reason he'd been looking forward to dinner at all was
the hopes of getting to know his "apprentice" a little
better.

But apparently, she didn't want to talk to him.

Isaac took his first bite. It wasn't...bad. Maybe the
vegetables needed to be a little softer before being
added to the meat. Or maybe all the ingredients of
the dish could have been blended a little better. He
took a second bite, then a spoonful of mashed
potatoes, then a big drink of water. Regardless, he was
always grateful for a meal he didn't have to cook
himself.

"Stop that, Amos." Sarah slapped her husband's
hand when he'd reached across the table for a slice of
bread.

"Apologies," Amos said under his breath as he pulled back his arm, laying his hand in his lap.

"Can't even mind your manners when we have guests."

Besides the sound of Sadie talking to her food—which had become a new thing with her—silence filled the room, a very tense silence that, when he glanced around, he knew was felt by everyone.

Grace was staring down at her plate. Even with her chin lowered, he could tell she was blushing. But it wasn't her who should feel embarrassed. He wanted to say something. Not to Sarah—that wasn't his business—but to Grace; something to soothe her or preoccupy her. Maybe tell the joke about the Mennonite and the cow.

He chuckled inside at the memory of their first meeting out in the front pasture. Suddenly, all eyes in the room were on him. Maybe his chuckle hadn't been internal.

"Sorry," he said after a quick throat clear. "Tickle in my throat. Uh, Sarah, this sure is good." But Sarah only stared back. "Amos, what kind of work do you do?"

"I have a position down at Keim's sawmill."

"*Jah*?" Isaac added, then nodded for him to go on. "Sounds interesting. Sadie, careful not to spill." While Amos spoke about his job, Isaac kept an eye on Sadie, not wanting her to cause much trouble, though she was usually very well-behaved when they were at someone else's house. Goodness knew she hadn't picked up her good habits back home with his in-laws. Their evening meals could look like something out of a pigpen.

Isaac was about to lose his appetite. Not only was the food a bit questionable, but he felt guilty about what he'd just thought about his in-laws, and Grace was still ignoring him, and he worried that Sadie was too much to handle, and even with Amos talking and Sarah occupied with her supper, there was still an air of tension in the room.

He wondered if it were always there.

Every time he looked at Grace, it was as if she'd just been looking at him but then glanced away. The times he did catch her eye, that expression of confusion from when he'd first arrived—and maybe even frustration now—still colored her face.

It was going to be a difficult few months if he didn't find a way to get Grace to like him, let along work as a team. To trust each other.

"Another fire was set in town," John said.

"Moses told me," said Amos. "They're getting closer to houses."

"I heard about that," Isaac said, putting down his fork, needing to engage in any kind of conversation. "The Chupps were talking about it the other night." He paused to wipe his mouth with a cloth napkin. "They said it's a group of kids from a few towns over."

"Aye." John nodded. "That's what I suspect."

"Fires?" Grace said, looking at her father. "You told me they only spray-painted some sidewalks."

"It's been escalating," her father said, then he glanced at Eve, his *fraa*. "Nothing for us to worry about," he added, putting a hand on Eve's arm. "We're a safe distance. It's just boys being boys, I suppose."

"Someone ought to give them a good licking." No surprise, this had come from Sarah.

"They might just be bored," Amos said. "School's about to be out for the summer. Hopefully, they'll be put to work then, and not have time to mess around over here."

"I tell you, they need to be punished," Sarah said. "If I was their mother, I'd…" Surprisingly, her voice trailed off, leaving behind more tense silence. "Well, anyone want seconds?"

When no one spoke up, Isaac lifted his plate. "The mashed potatoes were delicious. I'd love another helping." It wasn't an actual lie because the potatoes were the most edible thing on his plate.

"Of course," Sarah said, smiling at him, then glaring down at her husband as she passed by him. Isaac wasn't sure if he'd made matters better or worse.

"*Danke*," he said after she'd given him two heaping servings. As he shoveled in his first bite, he noticed that Sadie and the two little Zook girls were away from the table. He pushed back his chair to stand.

"They're upstairs with a puzzle." Grace's voice sounded distant, and she'd barely even looked at him when she spoke.

"Okay." He looked at Eve, who—despite Sarah's overbearingness—was the matriarchal head of the house. "If it's okay with you."

"They're just fine," Eve said with a smile. As she reached out to take her glass of milk, she suddenly flinched as if in pain.

"Are you all right, *liebchen*?" John asked softly, leaning in to her side.

"Fine, fine, don't fuss." Eve was holding her right hand, rubbing the palm. "End-of-the-day aches."

*She's ill, or…injured*, Isaac considered when he realized he'd never seen her standing or walking on her own—someone was always helping. His thoughts wandered, wondered. He'd have to ask Grace about it.

At the thought, his gaze automatically turned to her, but she was watching her mother, a definite look of concern in her eyes, maybe even fear. Isaac was about to ask if he could help, then decided not to. Hadn't he already interjected when he shouldn't have?

Again, the room fell silent. He knew an Englisher idiom about the "elephant in the room," and wasn't sure if there were always a level of unspoken tension in the house, or if no one was talking because *he* was there.

He began to feel pressure on his chest, pure discomfort for simply existing.

Just then, Sadie came running down the stairs. "We finished the puzzle, Daddy!" she said. "It's a horse drinking water, and it says for ages eight and up." She grinned. "And we did it, even though I'm only six."

"*Wunderbar*, Sadie," he said, standing up.

"It's a brown horse," Sadie went on. "Is that the color of the horse you're training?"

"It is," Isaac said, sweeping her up in his arms. "How did you know that?"

"I don't know, I just *did*." She giggled but then pinched her eyes closed as she yawned. Isaac leaped at the excuse.

"Looks like someone is ready for bed. It's getting late for you after such an eventful few days."

"Not yet, *Daed*."

Isaac turned to Eve. "Do you mind if we call it a night? I should get this one home."

"Of course not," Eve said. "It was wonderful to meet both of you. Please come back soon."

"*Danke*. And thank you for our supper," he said to Sarah.

"You're more than welcome." Sarah smiled, but then crossed her arms and sent a sideways glance to Amos. "I'll be sure to make extra of my mashed potatoes next time you come."

Isaac swallowed, not knowing what to say. All he knew was he was more than anxious to get out of the house. "See you later?" he said, shifting his eyes to Grace. It looked like she'd finally let go of that breath she'd been holding. Perhaps she was just as anxious for him to be gone as he was.

"*Jah*," she said, standing up from the table. "*Guti nacht.*"

"*Nacht*," he said, then addressed John. "*Danke* again for the invitation." When they'd all said their goodbyes, Isaac turned to the front door and was out on the porch before he could take his next breath.

When the door was safely closed behind him, he took in a deep breath, then another. That had been one strange, mighty awkward situation. And what had been the matter with Grace this time? She'd hardly said two words after he'd arrived. Though maybe that was better than arguing with him about Cincinnati.

Although, he did kind of enjoy how fiery her blue eyes got when she was annoyed. Not that he would annoy her on purpose, but there was something about her that he still couldn't figure out. Like the puzzle Sadie had worked on, Isaac was more than tempted to work on Grace Zook.

"Can I get down?"

"Oh, *jah*!" Isaac had been walking so quickly away from the house that he'd almost forgotten where he was going. "Do you want to drive?" he said, setting his daughter down on the front seat of the buggy.

All the way home, Isaac ran the evening over and over through his mind, but came up with no idea of what he would say to Grace when he saw her next. Or if she would speak to him at all.

# CHAPTER THIRTEEN

Grace helped her little sisters get ready for bed, then came back downstairs, finding Sarah alone at the oversized farm sink, washing dishes by the light of a battery-powered lamp above her head. For a moment, she considered tiptoeing upstairs unnoticed, forgetting the book she'd come down to fetch.

But wasn't it enough that her sister-in-law had to fix three meals a day for seven people—nine tonight—and then clean up on her own? *It must be even more trying if you're not getting along with your spouse,* Grace thought. *Is there any way I can help them?*

Grace was not even close to being an expert in relationships, though. After all, she'd never been in one, had only a handful of dates to her credit, in fact.

What she was an expert in—handling horses—didn't apply to Sarah's situation.

Or did it?

*The first step in heeding is to connect with your horse, build trust, show them you're there for them. Communicate.*

"Want some help?" Grace asked, walking barefooted into the kitchen.

"I'd never deny you the *pleasure.*"

*Whoa there, girl. It's okay. I'm your friend...*

"Do you have to be sarcastic twenty-four hours a day?" Grace asked, as if figuratively reaching for control of Sarah's harness.

Sarah threw a glance her way that would usually send Grace back three paces and completely end the subject.

*When an ornery horse tries to get the upper hand, make sure you show no fear.*

So instead of giving Sarah her way, Grace shot back her own look, holding the beast in the eyes.

Sarah sighed. "It's not easy, you know."

"What isn't?" Grace began clearing plates from the table, pleased at the tiny victory of keeping her sister-in-law from changing subjects for once.

Sarah paused what she was doing and turned to Grace. For a moment, her expression looked soft, eager, as if she were about to open her heart to Grace.

*That's a good girl…*

"Nothing," she finally said.

*Offer the horse kind, soft words so she knows you're on her side.*

"*Daed* should've asked you first before he invited guests to dinner," Grace said.

"It's not that," Sarah said, looking down into the sink full of bubbles. "Heaven knows there's always enough food. Some members of this family don't eat enough—especially you."

Grace was on the thin side, but she'd always been the petite one in the family. Not that she should give Sarah that as an excuse as to why she'd rarely been an eager eater when it came to her sister-in-law's cooking.

"Your meatloaf was as good as ever," she said, taking the glass Sarah had just washed and drying it with a towel.

"*Danke*," Sarah said, then paused again and shook her head.

"Is it Amos?" Grace couldn't help asking, knowing she was dipping her toe into very hot water. But she loved her brother and felt so badly for him whenever she'd witnessed his wife treating him poorly. He deserved better.

They both did.

Watching their example might've been one of the reasons why Grace wasn't very keen on getting married herself. She'd never enjoyed housekeeping or holding everyone's babies, or most of the other things she knew women her age preferred. No, being with the horses was what she'd always loved. And if she could only get Isaac King out of the way, she was sure *Daed* would give her the training farm when he retired.

Sarah lifted her chin. "Is what Amos?"

Grace blinked, needing to remember what they'd been talking about. It was right then that she realized she should feel just as badly for Sarah as she did for Amos. "The reason you're so sad all the time," she said after whispering a silent prayer for guidance.

"I'm not sad all the time."

"Okay, annoyed, then." Grace leaned a hip against the counter, feeling brave. "And then you take it out on whoever else is in the room."

Sarah huffed and slammed down a fist. "I do *not*..." She took in a breath. Then she turned to look at Grace. Her expression was soft again, open. Was she about to speak freely or ask her help?

Before she knew it, though, that expression was gone.

"Amos needs to spend more time at home," Sarah finally said.

Grace was about to jump in with how her *bruder* had to work long hours at the sawmill, and that he had been for years, even before they'd gotten married, and how it was unfair for Sarah to demand he work less now.

But she didn't. The moment had truly passed.

Without much more talking, they finished washing the supper dishes, the pots and pans, and Grace was wiping down the last counter right as her wristwatch read ten p.m. But she couldn't get Sarah out of her mind.

Grace quietly moved by her parents' bedroom on her way to her own. When she noticed a light was on, she peeked her head in.

"Why are you still awake?" she asked her *maam*, who was seated in her big, comfortable armchair, a paperback on her lap.

"Wasn't ready for sleep yet." She closed the book. "Come sit with me for a minute." Grace glanced over at the bed to her sleeping father. "He's out." *Maam* smiled. "And it's just as well. I think I'll sleep right here. Feels better for my back sometimes."

Grace kneeled beside her. "Are you in pain tonight?"

"Only a little. I'm sorry your new friend had to see that."

"Who?" Grace asked, making sure the quilt around her mother's shoulders was in place.

"Isaac King."

"Oh." Grace blinked. "We're not friends. I mean, we're working together—*Daed* is making us work together."

"What?" *Maam* asked, a quizzical look on her face.

"Nothing." Grace shook her head around, trying to focus. "I doubt he noticed when you flinched." She pulled her eyebrows together. "I noticed, though. I fear your pain is getting worse."

For a moment, Grace couldn't speak another word. It didn't take an Englisher surgeon to see that her mother's condition was worsening. *She needs that operation*, Grace said to herself, noticing how *Maam* cringed when she tried to shift positions. *And the quickest way we can afford it is if we make a lot of money—now—with Cincinnati.*

Grace allowed herself to think about Isaac, how he'd been hired to lead the training of the important horse. Was the payment from the owner going to their company, and Isaac would receive only a tiny portion for his services?

Grace's stomach clenched, hating to admit that it seemed more likely that Isaac would get the majority. She suddenly realized she had no idea about the money, how it would be split, and if their portion would be enough for her mother's surgery.

A new determination to train better and faster than Isaac King filled her mind and soul.

"Want me to wake *Daed*?" she asked when *Maam* winced again.

"Of course not," her mother said. "And I didn't mean about my hand hurting during dinner. I meant I was sorry Isaac had to see Sarah and Amos like that."

"Oh." Grace paused, fussing with her mother's blanket. "It was…embarrassing. It's always embarrassing whether there is a witness or not." Grace put a hand over her mother's. "I usually just blow it off, but tonight I felt different. When we were alone, I actually asked Sarah about it. She said something about how it isn't easy."

"How what isn't easy?"

Grace shrugged, feeling deflated again. "She wouldn't say. For a split second, I hoped she might want to talk to me, but she shut me out like always. I thought it best not to pry any further."

"That is best," *Maam* said, squeezing her hand. "All we can do is pray for guidance and trust the Lord while trying to be the best examples of loving and forgiving, patient Christians that we can. It might rub off on Sarah. You never know." Smiling, she gave Grace's hand another squeeze. "I know she loves your *bruder*, but whatever she's going through now is making her miserable. It's up to Sarah and *Gott* to heal that."

"I guess so," Grace said. But then she couldn't help thinking that maybe it wasn't only *Gott* who could help Sarah, but perhaps Grace could, too. Maybe instead of allowing Sarah's attitude to get under her skin, she could be a better friend to her. And if Sarah's constant bad mood was due to marital issues, Grace could be someone Sarah could talk to. After all, they'd have a more peaceful home, and Amos would be happier.

"What are you thinking, dear one?" *Maam* asked; she must have read something in Grace's expression.

"Mm…nothing," Grace replied, even though she'd just decided that from now on, every time she was with Sarah, she would be her friend. Her best friend. No matter how painful.

After making sure *Maam* was as comfortable as possible, Grace retired to her bedroom. Jane, her youngest sister, had crept in from her room and crawled under Grace's covers. She didn't mind. With everything going on in her head, Grace could use the company.

*At least tomorrow is preaching Sunday*, she thought with relief as she slipped her nightgown over her head, moonlight shining into the room. *Maybe Isaac will ride back to Silver Springs to attend his own services.* She felt a knot in her stomach, still mortified by…well, everything.

Despite how she'd wrongfully assumed he was

married, Grace's behavior had been utterly inappropriate. She inwardly cringed at the thought of the things she had done, trying to make him behave just as improperly as she had. All the playful touching or letting her gaze settle on him for too long, shamelessly fluttering her eyelashes. She cringed again when she remembered how she even pretended to almost faint! All that innocent flirting was nothing less than a sin.

And then she'd met Sadie, his sweet little daughter. And she'd wished for the Lord to yank Grace up to heaven instead of having to deal with what she'd done.

*Ack!* She climbed under the covers and threw both arms over her face, feeling hot with mortification at her improper conduct. *Should I admit to* Maam *what I've done?* she wondered as she clenched her eyes shut. *Or the bishop? How big a sin is it?*

With these questions racing through her mind, it was a miracle Grace was able to fall asleep. Jane was already dressed for church when she woke up. "Will you wear your orange dress to match mine?" her little sister asked.

"What a splendid idea," Grace said after a long stretch. "Should we ask Sarah, too?" she added, not forgetting the promise she'd made to herself last night.

"She's already wearing her blue dress, the one she got married in."

"Ah," Grace said, standing up and stretching again, having momentarily forgotten the Amish custom of the wedding dress becoming the bride's future Sunday dress. She'd just been wanting to include Sarah in something simple.

"Get dressed," Jane said, excitedly pushing Grace toward the closet.

"I need to wash up and brush my teeth first." She put her hands on her hips and looked down at Jane. "Did you forget to do that?"

Her sister didn't reply right away. "I'll go do it now," she finally said, then disappeared down the hall.

Grace laughed cheerfully, grateful for the feeling of peace she had the moment she woke up. After kneeling for her morning prayer, she felt almost energetic. That sensation of weight off her shoulders stayed with her all through breakfast, while washing the dishes before Sarah had the chance, and as they started out walking to the Brennemans', where this week's Sunday service was taking place. It was only a few farms over, and walking was simpler than hitching up two buggies.

There was a large crowd already gathered; seeing the whole village together ready to hear *Gott*'s word made her heart feel even lighter, like she hadn't a care in the world.

"*Guder mariye*, Grace."

Grace nearly tripped over her own feet at the familiar voice, deep and manly. Before she could stop it, last night's embarrassment figuratively hit her between the eyes, an unstoppable heat creeping up her chest and throat, onto her cheeks for all to see.

"That's a pretty dress," said another voice, young and charming.

Grace turned to see Sadie…holding Isaac's hand.

# CHAPTER FOURTEEN

If Sadie hadn't pointed her out, then dragged him over to say hello, Isaac might not have recognized Grace. Her pale orange dress had full sleeves at the shoulders and was pulled in at her elbows, the color going well with the late spring tan on her face and arms. She wore a black bonnet over her black *kapp*, matching her pristine black apron. He'd never seen her without dirt on her clothing or face.

"*Wie geht's*," Grace said in formal High German—which was appropriate for church—after he greeted her. "I didn't know you'd be coming to…" She paused to press her lips together. "Never mind. Of course you're here."

"Of course." Isaac tilted his head, wondering why she was still behaving so strangely, barely making eye contact.

"*Grossmammi* made my dress," Sadie said, holding out the ends of her skirt. He'd have a little talk with her later about not drawing attention to herself. Though she was certainly the most beautiful child in Pennsylvania, even Isaac knew that modesty, humility, and piety were more important to the Lord than a physically attractive face.

At the thought, he looked at Grace again. All cleaned up like that, she was more attractive than he'd realized—well, maybe only since his nephew had practically forced him to ponder the question.

"I like it," Grace said, kneeling down to Sadie's level. "You look like a slice of lemon pie."

Sadie put her little hands over her mouth and

giggled. "Will you sit with us?"

Grace's blue eyes widened as she lifted her chin to look up at Isaac.

"Sadie," Isaac said, taking his daughter's hand. "You know the grownup men and women sit separately during the preaching. But you can sit on my lap. How about that?"

"Well…" Sadie reached out for Grace's hand, holding both hers and his now. He was glad his daughter felt comfortable around Grace. After all, he'd be working with her for a few months, and Sadie should get to know her.

"Is that what *Gott* wants?" Sadie asked.

Isaac couldn't help smiling, his heart filling with more love than was possible for his little girl. "That's exactly what *Gott* wants. He wants us to be obedient."

Sadie blinked as if thinking it through. "And you not sitting with Grace is obedient."

"It is," Grace answered. "But my sisters, Jane and Leah, will save you a seat at lunch afterward, if you want."

Sadie clapped her hands and leaned in to her father's side, suddenly shy.

"*Guder mariye*, Isaac," John Zook said, coming up behind them.

"*Mariye*" Isaac stuck out his hand to shake his boss's. He glanced over his shoulder, noticing that Eve was not with him. He still wished to find out what ailed her. Maybe he could help.

"Gracie," John said, glancing at his daughter then shifting his glance over to Isaac, perhaps noticing that they were standing rather close together. "Don't you have somewhere to be?"

"I'm waiting for Sarah. Coming, dear?" Grace smiled over her shoulder toward her sister-in-law, and it was such a big, cheesy grin that Isaac wondered it if were real.

He didn't have much chance to mull it over, because John cleared his throat, sending another glance his way. Isaac felt this look down to his toes. He hadn't meant to gaze at Grace so intently, and he certainly hadn't meant to grin while intently gazing. Not in front of her father, at least.

*No gazing, no lingering, nothing but business*, Isaac thought to himself as he dropped his chin, doing his best to convey to his boss that there would be no trouble.

After saying a quick hello to Amos and Sarah, Isaac made his way to one of the few dozen folding chairs set up in the grassy area beside the house. He looked forward to meeting the owners, wanting to ask them what kind of wood they used for their pigpen.

"Up you go," he said to Sadie, lifting her and planting her on his lap. "Comfortable? Because you know the preaching can be long sometimes."

"I'm okay, Daddy. I can see Grace over there. Look!" She pointed her chubby arm across to where the women sat separately from the men. "Hi Grace!"

It felt as if a few hundred eyes were aimed directly at him. He coughed under his breath and tipped his black felt hat at Grace, who looked as uncomfortable as he felt. "It's not polite to point," Isaac said in a whisper, pushing Sadie's arm down. "Time to be reverent."

Although he didn't search for him in the crowd, Isaac hoped John Zook hadn't witnessed the event. He respected his boss and enjoyed the few conversations they'd had. Isaac was not about to risk his job by being overly friendly with Grace.

The songs began, then the opening prayer by one

of the Elders. Even way over in Silver Springs, Isaac had heard good things about Bishop Turner, and was looking forward to his sermon.

By the end, Isaac wasn't disappointed. Even his daughter had been engaged when the bishop retold the story of Jonah and the Whale, reminding all to never shirk a calling from *Gott*, no matter how small.

"There's Eliza," Sadie said, wiggling off his lap. "Can I go play?"

"Keep your dress clean," he called as she ran away. Then he sighed, noting a group of men chatting in a circle. There'd been a time when that's exactly where he would've been at the end of the preaching. But now he had to be father *and* mother to his child.

"Can I help?" Isaac asked as the men began setting up the long tables for lunch, the women already inside helping the hostess with meal preparations. Grace was certainly with them, even though he half expected her to be outside with the menfolk. Though maybe his Silver Springs upbringing was making him think that way. The two communities did have plenty of subtle differences.

"I'd never turn down a hand," one of the men said. He was younger than most, looked just a bit older than Isaac, in fact. "Could ya help me carry this table over there? It's one of the heavier ones."

"Sure." Isaac felt good helping out, serving where he could, as his heart was full of all the good sermons he'd just heard. "What is this made out of?"

The man laughed. "Feels like concrete, doesn't it?"

"Heavy enough." Without much real effort, they set up the long table, then began pulling over folding chairs.

"You're Isaac King from Silver Springs, *jah*?" the man asked, readjusting his black hat.

"I am." Isaac nodded. "That's my daughter, Sadie, playing with John Zook's girls."

"Ah. I'm Lucas Brenneman. Happy to meet you." The two men shook hands. "This is my house—Esther's and mine—she's probably in the kitchen trying to delegate while watching the *kinnahs*. We have two." He stopped to smile. "Our newest came just two months ago."

"*Wunderbar*," Isaac said. "Such a blessing."

"He is. Already got me wrapped around his finger. Named him Ephraim after my father."

"Good, strong name."

"Aye." Lucas wiped his forehead with the back of his hand. "You're staying with the Chupps. Good family. Have you been out to their *daadi hous*? Met old Abram Chupp?"

"Not yet, though I've heard his name often enough."

Lucas bowed his head and chuckled. "He's quite a character. Seemed ancient when even I was a kid. When I came back, I was shocked he was still alive."

"Came back?" Isaac asked.

"*Jah*. Sorry, I'm used to everyone knowing. I was… away for a while."

"*Rumspringa?*"

"Well, it started out that way. I suppose it's no secret, but I left the church, lived on my own for almost ten years."

"You don't say," Isaac replied, interested. It wasn't too often a person came back to the faith and way of life after a long absence.

"I studied medicine to help my brother, who was ill." He paused and looked up at the sky. "He passed on before I could do any real good. After that, though, the urge to come home wouldn't leave me, so I came back, even worked at the medical clinic in town for a while."

"I'm sorry about your *bruder*," Isaac said. Then for some reason, he felt the desire to tell him about Martha—his greatest loss, in many ways.

"*Danke*," Lucas said. "I wasn't here long before I met Esther—well, remet her. We grew up together. I wanted to marry her almost instantly, but she wouldn't even consider it until I came back to the church, reconciled with the brethren and my family." That same smile returned. "My life's changed so much over the past two years. It's really incredible."

Isaac didn't know what to say, but it wasn't hard to be happy for Lucas Brenneman, nor was it difficult to like him straightaway and to be curious about his life away from the Amish world.

"I can see I've shocked you," Lucas said, putting a hand on Isaac's shoulder.

"Not at all," Isaac said. "Nothing I love better than a story of redemption. It's good for all of us."

"We'll have to get together sometime, then." Lucas grinned. "My wife says I'm the biggest talker in the village. She's Sarah's sister, you know?"

"Amos Zook's *fraa*?"

Lucas nodded.

"Ah." It was all Isaac could think of to say, not wanting to be rude.

Lucas burst out laughing, then glanced over his shoulders, lowering his voice. "She's very…different from Esther. Thank the good Lord."

Isaac blew out the breath he was holding. "So it's not just me?"

"Nay." Lucas laughed again. "She's my family now, so I love her as I must, but let's just say we don't visit over at the Zooks' all that often, not with the *kinnahs*.

It's a shame, actually. I should do better, be more forgiving."

"Nobody's perfect," Isaac said. "That's why we come to church, *jah*?"

"I knew I'd like you," Lucas said. "Esther will, too. We really must have you and your *dochder* over for supper."

"I'd like that," Isaac said. "Sadie loves *bobbeils*. Baby humans, baby chicks, baby chipmunks."

"Baby goats?" he asked. "We have a friend who raises pigmy goats as pets. It's Esther's favorite place to be. Your Sadie will love it."

"*Danke*, I'm sure she would."

"It's getting hot already." Lucas took off his hat and began fanning his face. "How has it been, working for John Zook?"

"Good, great," Isaac said, though he couldn't forget that glare his boss had shot him when he and Grace were standing together. "I really like him."

"Can't believe Grace agreed to having an outsider come in."

Isaac tried not to smile. It shouldn't have surprised him, though. In a village as small as Honey Brook, everybody knew everyone else's business. How else would Lucas Brenneman already know so much about him?

"I don't think she agreed to anything," Isaac admitted, his attention automatically turning toward the house, wondering where Grace was, wishing for a quick glance at her. "I was a big surprise to her—and not a welcome one. She's talented with horses, though, very talented. We work well together. At least…" He paused and tipped his hat back. "I suppose we will in time."

Lucas's eyebrows shot up. "She's working with

you? You're both training the one horse? Together?"

"*Jah*," Isaac said, not wondering in the least about why Lucas looked so surprised.

"John has no problem with it?" Lucas scratched the side of his short beard. "You two working together. You and his daughter alone. His single twenty-three-year-old daughter."

"Grace is twenty-three?" He wasn't sure why that information shocked him. He hadn't really considered her age. Despite her wisdom and experience with horses, he'd assumed she was younger. She was short and…thin…and…

When he did take a moment to think about it, obviously she was older. After all, hadn't Collin Chupp been asking to court her for years and years? And that warning look from John… Things were getting clearer.

"Unusual for two single people of marrying age to be alone together like that."

*Unmarried? Two single people?*

Isaac didn't know what to say. Impropriety had never once crossed his mind when he'd been alone with Grace. Perhaps because it had been all business, he hadn't thought of her as a single, available woman.

"I shouldn't have brought it up," Lucas said, probably because Isaac hadn't managed to speak one word. "As long as John Zook doesn't have a problem, no one else should. I certainly don't."

"*Danke*," Isaac said, still a bit rattled. He vowed then and there that his boss would have zero problems with him. Innocent flirtation was not worth losing this important job. "Should we help carry out the food?" he asked, enjoying Lucas's company but wanting to change the subject.

"*Jah.*" Lucas put a hand on Isaac's shoulder. "I

truly am sorry. It wasn't my business to pry."

Isaac smiled. "It's okay. To be perfectly honest, it hadn't crossed my mind—hadn't thought about her that way."

"That's surprising," Lucas said as they both paused their work to look at Grace coming out of the house. Her black bonnet off, strands of red-brown hair escaping from her *kapp*, slim waist, long neck, unexpectedly elegant in her movements, now that he noticed.

"Suppose it is," Isaac heard himself say as he watched her.

"Hallo, Grace Zook," Lucas called out when she neared the table they'd set up.

Grace stood in place and stared back at the two men. Isaac felt a strange pressure in his chest as they gazed at one another. Then Lucas waved his fingers at her, sending Grace back into the house.

The second Isaac had promised himself that Grace was off-limits was the same second he knew he was interested.

# CHAPTER FIFTEEN

Grace wanted to be up extra early on Monday morning, so she managed to bow out of most of the Sunday evening activities. She still couldn't look at Isaac without wanting to crawl into a hole and die, Sarah had been cranky as a mule, and Collin Chupp kept trying to initiate conversations when she'd been talking to Hannah and Mary.

"Sun's not even up."

As Grace pulled on her boot, she turned to see Sarah coming down the dark stairs. "I want to get out there before he… Uh, before the other animals wake."

"Ah," Sarah said, then covered a yawn. "I hope Amos brought in the milk from last night. I need it for the oatmeal and he always forgets."

*He doesn't* always *forget*, Grace wanted to say, but then remembered her goal of killing Sarah with kindness. "It's in the fridge," she said, then waited to see if Sarah would complain about it anyway.

"That's a miracle."

"You know," Grace said as she pulled on her second boot, "don't tell anyone, but I always loathed dealing with the cows. The bigger dairy farms have those electric-type milkers, but we've always had to do it by hand." She shivered. "Grosses me out."

"Same with me," Sarah said. "Such dirty work."

"I suppose it's quite a blessing, then, that Amos takes care of the milking, so we don't have to."

"*Jah*," Sarah said slowly, maybe not wanting to admit that her husband was good for anything.

"Compared to some," Grace added, "we really are spoiled. Think of the Old Order Amish near Lancaster. They're still using oil lamps and candles." Grace smiled as she turned on the battery-operated lamp, flooding the kitchen with light.

"Guess so," Sarah said, looking thoughtful. "Want coffee before you go out? I'll start brewing it right away."

Grace pressed her lips together, hiding a smile. Sarah had never offered her morning coffee before. "*Danke*, sister, but I need to get out there."

"Ew-key." Sarah's voice was singsong as she turned on the propane stove, the blue flame coming to life.

Grace allowed that repressed smile to spread across her face as she went out the side door, feeling pleased as punch that she was able to diffuse a bitter thought from Sarah's mind. Maybe she wouldn't be so hard on Amos this morning. Maybe today was going to be a precious gift from *Gott* for everyone.

"*Guder daag.* How are you this morning?" Grace said to Honey Pot, scratching him behind the ears. "We're going to pull a plow today. Are you ready for that, good boy?" She continued down the line, greeting each horse along the way.

Cincinnati was far back in his pen. When Grace stopped to reach her hands out to him, he backed up even farther. "Hey there, boy. It's okay, it's me, Grace. You know me, remember?" When the Morgan still wouldn't come out of the corner, Grace opened the gate and went in. The horse shook his big head and snorted.

"Oh, I know it's early and you were in the middle of a lovely dream about green pastures for miles, but we sometimes do our best work first thing in the morning when our minds are clear and fresh."

Grace kept speaking in a soft, calm voice as she neared the horse. He wasn't moving now, and Grace slowly reached up a hand, holding it under his nose. She knew it would take only a few seconds until he recognized her and wasn't so nervous.

*Trust is everything*, Grace thought as Cincinnati bowed his head, allowing her to pet him. *That goes for horses* and *people. Cincinnati needs to trust me, just like Sarah needs to trust me.* She paused and pushed out a breath. *And like Isaac King and I need to trust each other if the training is going to go smoothly, giving me at least a chance at some of the money. But how in the world will that happen if I don't even want him here?*

She spent the next twenty minutes contently brushing out the beautiful horse. He even let her slip on a harness.

"Such a brave boy," she cooed. "Should we go out to the front ring? Nice and easy? Should we? Oh, good boy." Though slowly at first, Cincinnati followed behind, right at her shoulder, as Grace walked past the other horses and toward the pasture.

"Maybe another few rounds of heeding practice, you'll be as serene and obedient as any of my horses." She led him straight to the gate and into the pasture. Normally, she might let him run free for a while, wake up his muscles after a long night's sleep. But Grace decided it might be best to walk him with a lead first to keep him comfortable with her.

"He's looking real good."

Hearing the voice made Grace jump and her breath catch. Irrationally irritated that he'd decided to show up, she turned to see Isaac leaning against a fence post, his tall Arabian tied up near the water.

How had she not noticed him riding in? And how long had he been watching her? She felt a tingling at the back of her neck, embarrassment returning.

"Ears are up and alert, too," Isaac added, walking toward them. "Not back in agitation like the other day."

"*Jah*," Grace replied, patting the side of Cincinnati's neck. She'd noticed that, too.

"He's progressing." Isaac stood on the other side of the horse, now, running a hand down the side of his face. The morning sun was behind him, silhouetting his face, body, hat.

"*Jah*," Grace repeated, then made herself look away from his striking profile.

"Mind if I take over for a while?"

"Uh, nay," Grace said, handing him the lead rope, still keeping her eyes turned away from him. "We, uh, walked the perimeter three times. He was distracted by a flock of ducks landing on the pond, but, uh, I got him focused again."

"Are you feeling okay?"

"Sure." She was forced to look at him now. "Wh-why?"

Isaac shrugged. "I don't know, you seemed out of sorts yesterday." He adjusted his hat. "The evening before, too, actually. Just wondered if something was wrong."

*You mean, something besides you riding up and trying to take away my future?*

Grace heard her own noisy breaths, felt her muscles tensing up again, making her both physically and mentally tired. She'd been frustrated at the mere thought of him for too long now. It had never been in her nature to hold grudges and be unkind on purpose. She didn't want to be that type of person, but how was she supposed to like Isaac King, let alone trust him enough to be her training partner?

She forced herself to look him in the eyes and hold a steady smile. "I'm fine." But then, remembering how overly familiar she'd behaved with him when she thought he was married made her embarrassed on a whole other level. A small part of her wondered if she should just be honest and apologize for her improper behavior the other day.

"Um, maybe we should walk him through the stables? Work on his concentration."

Isaac pursed his lips and pushed them to the side, thinking. "Sounds like a good plan." He didn't move, though, and his gaze held heavily on hers, making her palms tingle. He wasn't convinced that she was okay, and suddenly Grace would rather die naked in the middle of town than bring up their…situation.

When she couldn't find the words to speak, Isaac moved toward the stables, Cincinnati right at his shoulder.

Having to concentrate on work allowed Grace's spinning mind to relax. Cincinnati had trouble with only one horse, but when Isaac had them stand nose to nose, his aggression dissolved.

Despite herself, Grace couldn't help being impressed; she'd never used that tactic before. And she had to admit that his methods might've been different from hers, but he never treated the horse badly or stunted their progress.

The two hours of training flew by, and the horse was improving by the minute. It wouldn't be much longer before they could begin breaking him. How had that happened so quickly?

"How about another glass of that delicious lemonade?" After closing the stall gate, Grace looked up at Isaac, trying hard to fight back a snicker. And losing.

"There it is." Isaac tipped his hat to the side. "That's the first time I've seen you smile in two days."

Grace pressed her lips together, wanting to turn away from him again, to hide her oncoming blush, not quite ready to stop disliking him yet or to admit that she was still in shock that he wasn't married, and therefore mortified by what she'd done—or tried to do to him.

"Grace." When she tried to walk around him, to ignore his comment about her smile, Isaac stood in her way, blocking her path out of the stables. "I don't know what's going on, but something's happened." He crossed his arms at his chest. "Did I do something wrong?"

"Nay," she replied, honestly—the way her mother, the bishop, and *Gott* would expect—while looking down at the dirt.

"*Say* something offensive to you?"

She shook her head.

After a pause, he added, "Is it Sadie?"

"Nay!" Grace lifted her chin to look at him. "I mean, I thought that…" She had no idea how to continue without making a brand-new fool of herself.

"You thought what?"

*Oh heavens, just get if off your chest, Grace!*

"To be honest…" Heat was building under her hair again, and she was sure her face was as red as a freshly picked beet. She slammed her eyes shut and blew out a long breath. "I thought she was your wife," she said, keeping her eyes closed.

"You thought I was married to a six-year-old?"

"Nay." Grace almost laughed. "I thought…I mean, when Papa said you moved here…you *and Sadie*…I just assumed. He didn't mention you were — or *weren't*, I mean."

"Why should it matter if I'm not married?"

Grace finally opened her eyes, then had to blink a few times to prevent tears from falling. "Why?" she asked, amazed by his question — was it only women who thought about this kind of thing? She peeled her lips apart, ready to tell him a hundred reasons why it mattered that she'd thought he'd been married this whole time — married and off-limits to her, and not a single man with soft hazel eyes and strong hands who loved horses.

"Why?" she couldn't help repeating. But then all she could do was stare at the handsome, eligible man staring back at her — the man who stood in the way of her dreams.

# CHAPTER SIXTEEN

He didn't comprehend it at first—for he hadn't seen it directed at him in many years. But as a pink blush swept up the woman's face, Isaac would've had to be blind to not recognize the look.

Staring into Grace Zook's blue eyes, not blinking, he finally realized what was going on.

"Oh," was all he could utter.

Grace dipped her gaze to stare down at the ground. He was grateful, for the shock of what he'd just realized had stunned him into silence, too.

He'd wondered why the woman ran so hot and cold toward him. He wasn't naive; he knew she wasn't overjoyed about him being there to train Cincinnati—apparently, she'd assumed it was her job. But how was that Isaac's fault?

He also hadn't been naive about the moments she'd been, well, *friendly* with him. Maybe overly friendly, now that he thought about it. Her giggles, gazes, and spirited touching that had seemed so out of place. Not that he hadn't enjoyed the attention. Despite her odd behavior, Grace Zook was still as attractive and interesting as the first day he'd seen her. And all the time, she hadn't known he was single.

Isaac understood now why she was embarrassed.

"I get it." He removed his hat and ran his fingers through his hair, his head feeling hot and heavy—but not from being in the sun. "Grace, I..." Before he said what he'd been about to say, he remembered that warning look from John. His boss. "I suppose it hasn't been horrible working with you, though you know I was surprised that I had a partner."

"Not *horrible*?" she repeated, finally looking at him. "You're aware I was shocked when you showed up." She paused. It seemed as though she was about to add more, but then stopped.

"Aye." He nodded. "I understand that. So far, though, you haven't gotten in my way."

"Well, *you've* gotten in *mine*," she said. "Plenty of times."

"I'm sure I have." He made himself smile, needing to lighten the mood. "Despite the…the issues between us, do you think we can work together?"

He'd meant the question strictly for Grace, but after he'd spoken, he realized it was for him, as well. Could he work platonically, side by side, with a woman who had sky-blue eyes, could handle even the most aggressive horse, and yet was completely off-limits? Not even the tiniest flirtation would be allowed going forward.

"Of course!" Grace answered without missing a beat. "I have no issue whatsoever." She crossed her arms, looking like she had plenty of issues with it.

"Good," Isaac said, nodding. "Good. Well then. That's settled." Though he hadn't yet answered the question for himself.

"Done for the morning?" John Zook walked into the stable, a coil of rope slung over one shoulder. Almost impulsively, Isaac stepped backward, far away from Grace.

"*Jah*," Grace answered. Isaac noticed how she was wiping her palms across the front of her apron. "Meet back here later this afternoon?" she added, looking at Isaac. "Try putting on a blanket and saddle pad?"

"Okay," Isaac said, feeling an unexplainable guilt as he looked from Grace to John. "Perfect." When he didn't know what else to do, he turned on his heel. "I'll go check on Sadie," he said, which seemed like a reasonable excuse to leave the scene immediately.

As he mounted Scout, ready to ride away as quickly as he could, he still couldn't get "that look" from Grace out of his mind. Picturing it clearly. Picturing *her* clearly.

"We'll see you later then," John called out. John Zook. Grace's father. Grace's big, burly father. The man who'd hired him. His *boss*.

As he rode away, keeping Scout at a steady trot, Isaac felt a weight lift off his shoulders. *She's my boss's daughter.* He'd inwardly repeat the sentence until his brain truly understood.

He'd been hired for a job. An important job. *Very* important. He ordered his mind to remember just how important. If he was successful with Cincinnati, Travis Carlson would spread the news. New clients could change everything for him. For him and for Sadie.

"Reckless," he sneered under his breath. If he'd been just a little less proper and dutiful with his actions, he might've messed up his entire reason for being in Honey Brook. He promised the Lord and himself that he would never lose focus again.

• • •

Monday must've been one of the trading days in town, for there were many plain folks out on the streets. Some walking, some on rollerblades and scooters, but he was the only one on horseback. Not wanting to be conspicuous, he fastened Scout to a hitching rail, then ducked into the nearest store.

It was full of customers, both plain and Englishers.

A group of English women were huddled around a display at the end of an aisle. The sign read: Moses Miller's Esther's Organic Soap. And there was a phone number, email address, and even a website. Isaac wondered if this Esther was Lucas Brenneman's wife. Surely there were more than a few Esthers in Honey Brook.

Still, once the crowd cleared, he was curious to see what the big draw was. Unfortunately, all the soap was gone, though a sweet smell of lavender and wildflowers hung in the air. "Will you be restocking soon?" he asked the middle-aged woman straightening the shelf a few rows over. From her dress and head covering, he could tell she was Beachy, maybe even New Order like him.

"You can have a catalog emailed to you," she said, keeping her focus on the shelf in front of her. "The sign-up form's over…" When she moved to point in the direction of the front counter, she glanced at him. "Oh." She smiled and touched the side of her head. "Hallo."

"*Guder daag*," he said, politely. "When will you have more soap?"

"Soap?"

Isaac gestured at the empty shelf. "I'd like to send some to my sisters. And my daughter loves the smell of roses."

The woman raised her eyebrows. "Your…daughter?"

Isaac nodded. "Aye."

The woman blinked a few times, as if coming out of a trance. "Oh, um, yes, the soap. Well, depends on when Esther's in the mood to make it. She has two children now, one is brand-new, praise to the Lord."

Ah, so it *was* Lucas Brenneman's wife. How

interesting that she would be making soap and selling it in public. Things like that were rare, even in Silver Springs. Isaac's village was more modern in some ways, like courting traditions, reading from the Bible, and handling important work matters on the Sabbath. He'd learned that fact from Grace.

"I don't do email for personal use," Isaac replied, even while touching the small cell phone in his pocket. "But I believe I know who makes it."

The woman's face brightened. "You know Esther?"

"I know Lucas—met him yesterday, in fact."

"Well, when you do see Esther, tell her we're sold out again. I just can't keep enough on the shelf."

"Will do," Isaac said, though he had no idea if he would ever meet her. Or see Lucas anytime soon, for that matter.

He chose some rock candy dyed green as a surprise for Sadie, then left the store. He browsed past the bank, a small grocery market, and the medical clinic, reminding him again of Lucas Brenneman. Maybe he should pay them a visit this afternoon while he was free, see if they needed help cleaning up after hosting church services yesterday.

As he made the plan in his head, he noticed a group of teenaged boys surrounding Scout. They weren't Amish.

"The harness is so weird," one of them was saying, "don't you think?"

"Yeah," another added. "Like something out of the dark ages. Totally Sims Medieval."

"Yeah, or D and D."

"Can I help ya fellas?" Isaac said, stepping between his horse and the teen touching the harness.

"Uh, ha-ha, no," the kid chuckled. "Just checking

nks something's ailing her.
ed only first year med stu-
omething private. "Anyway,
and asked me to rush right
t on her arm."
about?"
ok his head. "A freckle. Maybe
dramatic like an age spot. The
" After another chuckle, Lucas
l be getting back home. I don't
ointments this afternoon, but I'm
se a hand with the *kinnahs*."
nto you."
do need to have you over for sup-
t saying that. I remember what it's
town. How about day after tomor-
othed down his beard. "I'll have to
er first."
d, not forgetting what it was like to be
ve a partner to check with. Though he
urprised by the additional feeling of
die will be thrilled."
inned. "Let's plan on it, then." He stuck
d for Isaac to shake. "See you soon."
s *gut*," Isaac said, and then the two men
ys.

he led Scout away from town, he thought,
out the differences between Honey Brook
er Springs, even though they were only thirty
way from each other. Their basic Amish
he was the same, but different Ordnungs,
ent traditions. One being that women here
ed to have more…freedom—if that was the
ct word. More responsibilities outside the home.
hen again, he hadn't yet been in Honey Brook

out your ride, dude."

"My ride?"

"Yeah, your totally prehistoric mode of transport." He reached out to touch Scout, but the clever horse backed away.

"Whoa, boy," Isaac said. "You guys from around here?"

"Couple towns away," the same kid replied. He looked to be about fourteen, shirt untucked, hair uncombed, and was obviously the group's spokesman. "We like to come on the first Monday of the month." He cocked a corner of his mouth. "Lots of interesting people watching." He chuckled, elbowing one of his buddies, making the rest of the group chuckle.

"Yeah—*interesting*," another boy chimed in. "Nice one, Kenny!"

"Shouldn't you be in school?" Isaac asked, mimicking his own father's stern tone.

The kids laughed. "Uh, sure, sure we are. See, we're in history class."

"No—sociology," another added. "Studying different cultures." This made the group laugh even harder, but an uncomfortable feeling was growing in Isaac's chest.

"I suppose you all know how to ride?" He patted Scout's neck.

"Why would we?" Kenny answered. He seemed to be their leader. "Ever heard of cars?"

Isaac shifted his weight. "You're old enough to drive, huh?"

The kid narrowed his eyes. "Not yet, but my cousin let me drive his truck once."

"Ah, now *that's* impressive," Isaac said. He knew it was impolite, maybe even immoral to tease the kids like that, but he couldn't help himself. They were being so prideful.

"Yeah, and my brother said he'd take me driving on old Wertztown Road, past Elwood."

Isaac happened to know exactly where they were talking about. He'd once helped with a new foal at a farm down Elwood Street. The place was between Honey Brook and Silver Springs, in fact.

"Well, I guess you're about to ride off into the sunset," Kenny said, smirking.

"Reckon I will," Isaac said, running his thumbs up his suspenders, playing along to keep the scene calm, even though their disrespect and need to be near his horse were really getting to him.

The boys started backing up toward the sidewalk. "I'm sure we'll be seeing you," Kenny said.

"Yeah," chimed in another. "Maybe even to-night—ow!"

"Shut up," Kenny hissed, after elbowing his friend in the stomach. Without another word, they ran up the street, glancing back at Isaac a few times. One of them dropped a candy bar wrapper, missing the garbage can by a mile.

That uneasy feeling pressed against Isaac's chest again. *Boys that age have no business hanging out here. They can only be up to no good.*

"Isaac, hello."

Almost as if emerging from his very thoughts, Lucas Brenneman appeared.

"Hi," Isaac said, but then turned his gaze back to the group of kids.

"Anything wrong?" Lucas asked, noticing his stare.

"You know those boys?" Isaac asked.

"Don't think so. Why?"

Isaac sighed. "Dunno, just had an encounter with them. Got a funny feeling."

long enough to recognize all of the differences between their two communities.

He thought about his mother, his sisters, even Martha, how they'd been perfectly content to stay home and take care of their families. *Or…were they actually content?* Did housekeeping carry a badge of righteousness in Silver Springs, and was it sinful to have any aspects beyond that?

Isaac knew what he'd had. *He'd* been content. Up to a point.

Suddenly, he stopped walking when he realized he'd absentmindedly passed by the Chupps' farm and was standing in the front pasture of the Zooks'. Grace was in the side field, working with the horse she'd been with the first time he'd seen her.

He felt a grin stretch across his face as he watched her stomp through the mud, trying to get the horse to pull a plow. The gelding was not having it. Isaac's impulse was to run out and help, but he knew full well she would resent him for it. To her, it was bad enough that he was "helping" her train Cincinnati.

*She's definitely a modern Amish woman*, he thought as she hiked up the bottom of her dress, showing muddy boots and knees, her apron smeared with dirt and who knew what else.

*The most non-traditional Amish woman I've ever known.*

Isaac's grin dropped and he began chewing on the inside of his cheek, still watching her, torn between intrigue and the need to look away and pray.

# CHAPTER SEVENTEEN

"You can always add flour, but you can't take it out."

Grace fidgeted but forced a smile. After all, it had been her idea to bake cookies with Sarah, have some quality sister-sister time. Grace conceded that she wasn't the best cook, but she did know how to use a measuring cup. And this afternoon really had nothing to do with cookies.

*Bonding with your horse is one of the best ways to gain their trust…*

"Good tip," she said, inwardly rolling her eyes. "I'll remember that."

Taking a short break from being outside during the heat of the day had been a necessity. She'd gotten a sunburn yesterday, and her muscles were sore from working in the field with Honey Pot. Her afternoon training session with Cincinnati had been the brightest spot of her day. And it hadn't been just because Isaac taught her a new way to approach with a saddle pad from the rear.

Instinctively, she moved to look out the window, trying to see the group outside. One of the barn cats had had a litter a few days ago, and that morning, she'd asked Isaac if he wanted to bring Sadie to see them. After their schooling, Grace's younger sisters had joined them in the barn.

"You can't help it, can you?" Sarah said.

"Help what?" Grace asked, spotting one of her sisters. She really shouldn't be holding the kittens yet.

"Am I boring you?"

Grace blinked. "*Jah*—I mean, nay. Sorry. Just

looking after the girls."

"Isn't Isaac with them?"

Grace felt herself smile as that very person walked into view. His hat was off, sleeves pushed up, straw stuck to his black wool pants. "Aye."

Sarah joined her at the window. For a moment, they watched in silence. "You'd never catch Amos out there like that."

"Why do you say that?"

"Because he's always away from home."

"Working, you mean? Earning money for the family."

Sarah grumbled and went back to the kitchen. "He could be here if he wanted." She picked up a pot in the sink and started scrubbing.

Grace was tempted to say that she was right… Maybe Amos would want to be home more often if his homelife wasn't so stressful. Her brother would hate to leave home if he had a kind wife who greeted him with appreciation and tenderness after a long day.

*Never forget that first step in heeding a horse. Connection. Building trust. Show her you're a team.*

"Let me do that," Grace said, stepping in to finish washing the pot. "Smells like the first batch of cookies is ready to come out of the oven."

"*Danke*," Sarah said, moving away from the sink.

Grace was about to say, "*Good girl,*" but refrained. "Mmm, those look delicious," she said. "You're going to have folks from all over following the scent to this kitchen."

Sarah chuckled lightly under her breath, making Grace smile to herself. "Want one while they're warm? I've got fresh milk, too."

"In a minute," Grace said. "I'll get all the dishes washed first."

"You don't have to."

Grace shrugged one shoulder. "I don't mind." *Nobody in her right mind wants to scrub pans while there is a cookie straight from the oven waiting for her. But building trust is more important right now.*

"*Danke* for your help," Sarah said while pulling the second batch from the oven. The kitchen really did smell amazing. "We should do this more often."

Grace smiled and looked down into the sink. "I'd like that, Sarah." She reached out to put a hand on Sarah's arm, but her sister-in-law flinched.

*Whoa, girl. Sorry, I understand. We're not there yet.*

"Amos used to love when I baked especially for him."

"I remember you coming over here in the evenings after you were engaged," Grace said. "What was that pastry with the cherries on top?"

*Let the horse come to you on her own. If she trusts you, it will feel natural.*

"Cheery Cherry Danishes." Sarah draped a kitchen towel over one shoulder. "*Maam* taught Esther and me how to make them…about a million years ago." She turned to gaze out the window. "He sure did love those. He'd burn his mouth every time, not waiting for them to cool even ten seconds."

Grace was almost shocked at how open Sarah suddenly was. *But sometimes that happens with horses. You may think there's no hope, and the next thing you know, they're eating out of your hand.*

Sarah went to smile at the memory, but then suddenly her expression changed. Her lips curled down at the sides, her eyes carrying a world of sadness. "Everything is different now."

"Sister?" Grace said, genuinely this time. She longed to reach out and touch her arm, offer some kind of comfort, but hadn't Sarah just recoiled?

"It'll never happen now. He won't come near me." Sarah took in a deep breath, and Grace clearly heard her chest rattling, her voice shaking. "I don't know what to do."

Grace's heart started beating fast. She thought no more about treating Sarah like an untrained horse, for she was looking at a woman in distress. But it was Sarah…and she didn't know how to handle her breed.

So she waited, her chest squeezing when she noticed tears trickling down her sister-in-law's cheeks.

"I want a baby," Sarah finally said in a quiet whimper, lifting her gaze, eyes wet. "I thought I was expecting three times, but the pain always came…"

Grace didn't hesitate this time; she rushed to Sarah and wrapped her into a hug, squeezing tighter when Sarah sobbed. For a while, they stood like that, neither speaking, but Grace was praying for guidance, for something to say that could offer comfort or understanding.

"I married a year before Esther," Sarah whispered, "and she's been blessed with two *bobbeils*. I think *Gott* has forgotten me."

"Heavens!" Grace said. "He hasn't, I'm sure of that. Jesus taught in Matthew to consider the lilies. Remember?"

"But the psalmist said that children are a gift, a reward from *Gott*."

Grace had to think fast. "True, but doesn't Proverbs say that a foolish child brings grief to his mother?" She pulled back to look Sarah in the eyes. "Think of all the grief you've been spared, sister."

Grace had meant it as a little joke to lighten the mood, and her heart stopped, waiting for Sarah's reaction. She exhaled in relief when Sarah's shoulders shook with a quiet laugh.

"I want children so very badly," Sarah said, taking in a deep breath, then leaning back against the counter. "But with the way things are, it's impossible now."

"Did a doctor tell you that? Have you seen Lucas?"

Sarah nodded. "He said there's nothing medically wrong with me, and that it's in *Gott*'s hands."

Grace wasn't about to argue with that.

"I know it's not a health issue—I feel that in my bones." Sarah paused to wipe her cheeks with a corner of her apron. "But it would be something of a miracle if I did get pregnant now."

"Why?"

Sarah looked away, but not before Grace noticed her eyes filling with tears again. "Amos won't come near me," she finally said. "We're never alone together anymore; we hardly speak."

This was the moment Grace had been waiting for. She loved her brother, wanted him to be happy, while she was also beginning to understand Sarah on a new level.

"Sister," Grace said softly, taking one of Sarah's hands. "Do you love your husband like Christ loves His church?"

"What do you mean?"

"I guess first of all, we can look to the Ten Commandments. *Gott* commanded that we must love one another. Everyone—with no exceptions. Even the Englishers who make fun of us, and our neighbor who sometimes takes peaches from our tree without asking." She paused. "Even a husband—if we have one—who works long, hard hours. *Gott* doesn't say we must love only those who we think deserve it. I would think he meant we should love those closest to us the most, forgive them the quickest, appreciate them for everything they do."

"You think I don't love Amos?"

Grace shrugged. "I don't know what's in your heart." Grace pressed her hands over her own heart. "All I witness is how you treat him, the way you speak." She took in a breath and held it before speaking again. "I know it's not my place, but I love you both, and change has to start with someone. If you choose to soften your heart—and your words— don't you think Amos would respond? If you love him better, don't you think he'll love you back the same way?"

Sarah didn't say anything for a while, and Grace feared she'd really stepped over the line this time. Would Sarah ever trust her again?

Just then, her two young sisters came running into the house, followed by Sadie. Grace waited a beat, but Isaac did not appear. She exhaled, grateful to not have to explain the current situation to an adult.

"Can we have some cookies?" Leah asked, jumping up and down.

"Wash your hands first," Grace said. "All of you." She smiled at Sadie and gave the top of her head a little rub. Besides her younger sisters, Grace wasn't around children all that much. "Um, how cute are those kitties?" she finally added.

"They're the cutest I've ever seen!" Sadie exclaimed. "But Daddy said I can't have one yet. Maybe as a special gift if we ever get our own house again."

Grace handed her a cookie with a napkin, which seemed like the natural thing to do. "You don't have your own house in Silver Springs?"

Sadie shook her head. "Not since Mommy went to

Heaven." She took a bite of the cookie. "We stayed in our house for a while, I think, but I was only three. We lived with *Mammi* before we came here, but…" The little girl lowered her chin.

"But what?"

"Well…" She dropped her voice to a whisper. "I heard Daddy praying once that he hoped *Gott* would help us leave there." She smiled. "I guess his prayer came true, because then we came here! Can I have one more, please?"

"Sure," Grace said, handing the child another cookie. A second later, all three girls ran out the door in a flutter of giggles.

Grace stood up and stretched, wondering what Sadie had meant about Isaac wanting a new place to live. Did he intend to settle in Honey Brook, or build a new house in Silver Springs when this job was over? Then again, she'd never been very good at translating a child's words into logical sentences.

"Did you…?" She'd turned to speak to Sarah but found herself alone in the kitchen.

# CHAPTER EIGHTEEN

Wind rushed through Isaac's hair as Scout climbed the hill. He wasn't sure how long they'd been away or how far they'd traveled. All Isaac knew was he'd had to get away.

It hadn't been on purpose that he'd overheard Grace talking to her sister-in-law. The little girls were still in the barn with the kittens and he'd been wanting to check on Cincinnati. As he'd passed by the house, the kitchen window had been open, and he'd caught what Sarah had said about having three miscarriages. Pain had shot through his brain as memories flooded back. He'd almost fled the scene right then, but then he'd heard Grace.

She'd spoken of love and forgiveness, having a change of heart and trusting *Gott*. Back then, he'd been plagued with wondering—hundreds of times—if it had been *Gott*'s will that Martha pass away when they'd just discovered she was carrying their second child.

"Whoa, boy," he said, allowing Scout to slow down, catch his breath.

Almost before the doubt and pain could return and grab on to his heart, Isaac looked to heaven and was instantly filled with peace. He knew it was the Holy Spirit, for he'd felt it before when he'd struggled with confusion over his unhappy marriage and then the loss of his wife, finally understanding what it truly meant to give everything over to the Lord.

Grace had spoken of treating others kindlier, and she'd borne witness of the commandment to love one another no matter what. Isaac climbed off his horse, needing to catch his own breath. He hadn't heard her speak that way before, so strong in her convictions. Her faith ran deep.

"She's more mature than I gave her credit for," he said to Scout, but the horse just neighed. "When we first met, I thought of her as a little sister, maybe. Though she constantly surprises me with her training experience, I didn't know the layers of her personality, that she's a grown woman with faith, and compassion, and patience for the most stubborn horse and the most troubled sister."

It was all too easy then to picture her face, the way she smiled at him and how she made him laugh. The jokes and the clever comments.

At twenty-three, how in the world was the woman not married?

Isaac swallowed. Why would a question like that pop into his mind? It wasn't any of his business—the reasons she was single or not. She was only his training partner…his boss's daughter. Hands off. Remember?

But the twinge of a new feeling in his heart didn't go away so easily this time. In fact, when he closed his eyes to see her face more clearly, his pulse sped up and heat pushed through his bloodstream.

"Okay, okay," he said aloud, squinting up at the sun. "So, you like her—that's no sin. She's very… likable. Which doesn't mean your thoughts have to go any further than that." He pushed out a deep breath. "Your feelings do not have to evolve, man. You have complete control over your actions. Grace Zook will never know a thing. More importantly, neither will her father."

With that firmly settled, he dismounted Scout to

walk for a while, but as he neared the outskirts of the first farm, he couldn't help mounting his retired racing horse and speeding toward the Zook farm.

. . .

"The girls are upstairs coloring!" Grace called out as she waved to him. "And there're cookies in the kitchen!" Thanks to his spying, Isaac already knew that, though he was rather surprised at her cheery countenance toward him. Maybe she was ready to make peace.

"*Danke*," he said. "Maybe later."

"A man turning down freshly baked chocolate chip cookies." She tilted her head. "You feeling okay?"

Isaac exhaled a laugh that sounded more nervous than happy.

*Get a grip, brother.*

"I'll take one in a few," he said, backing away. "Gotta brush down Scout first, maybe hose him off."

"Ew-key," Grace said with a shrug. "I'm about finished with the draft horse—owner's picking him up tomorrow. Want to work with Sin in a while?"

"Sure thing," Isaac said, noticing how her cheeks glowed with exercise. "I'll just, ouch—" He tripped over a garden tool and got tangled in Scout's reins. "I-I'll see you in a minute." He jerked himself free and could practically feel Grace's questioning stare boring into his back as he walked away.

So much for acting normal.

Isaac led Scout through the stables, bringing him to an empty stall.

"How's the breaking going?"

Hearing the voice, Isaac poked his head into the office, finding John wearing reading glasses and sitting behind a closed laptop computer. "Good. Could go faster, but I'd be afraid to rush it. He acts tough, but I think he's been more mistreated than we thought."

"Exactly what Gracie said."

"Oh?"

"She's concerned about the front end of his training." He chuckled and capped a pen. "Thinks he's a delicate soul."

Isaac echoed the chuckle. "She would say that."

John removed his glasses, standing. "How are you two getting along?"

"Grace and I? Oh, well, fine—we're just fine." He hooked his thumbs around his suspenders and slid them up and down. "Why? Did she say something?"

"Nay. But I know neither of you was expecting the other. To tell you the truth, I was plain afraid to tell Grace about you before you got here. She's a right little thing, but…whew. I wouldn't want to be one of those horses that gives her grief."

Isaac couldn't help laughing. "I know what you mean. She's an excellent trainer, more knowledgeable than I expected. In the few days I've been here, I admit, she's taught me a thing or two. I thought I was patient, but I've never seen anyone like Grace."

"She gets that from her mama," John said, then paused. Isaac wondered whether his boss was about to tell him what ailed Eve. "She prays with them— Grace does. With the horses."

"I know. At first, I didn't realize that's what she was doing, but each morning, she goes down the row, petting and whispering to every single one of those horses."

Isaac found this conversation pleasing, being able to talk about Grace with her father. The entire ride home on Scout, he'd done nothing but think about her, so it felt good to speak her name aloud, even if he wasn't saying what he was truly thinking.

"She's a delicate soul, too," John said. "She doesn't like to show it because she thinks her job is to be strong and hard like a man. I sometimes regret letting her train her first pony to pull a cart, but she has a gift, and her mother and I decided to encourage it." He blew out a long breath. "Some plain folks around here think it's odd, but we pay them little mind at this point. Though I do honestly worry about her future. She doesn't seem at all interested in settling down like she should."

Isaac didn't know what to say. Was this any of his business?

"You know Collin Chupp, *jah*?" John continued.

"*Jah*," Isaac replied. "We've crossed paths at the house a few times."

"He's a fine enough fellow. Maybe not the strongest or the brightest, but fine enough." John leaned back in his chair. "He's been interested in Grace since they were knee-high. I sure wish she'd agree to marry him."

This made Isaac stand at attention. "Grace and Collin?"

John shrugged. "Wouldn't be a bad match. Comes from a good family."

Though Isaac was suddenly speechless, he couldn't disagree. The Chupps were a very upstanding family, and he respected Samuel Chupp quite a lot. But...

"Shhh—" John put a finger over his lips and nodded toward the opening of the barn.

"Back field this time," Grace said as she breezed by the two men. "Same saddle pad, but I'm letting Honey Pot inside the gate, too. Would you grab the brushes?"

"Uh…okay," Isaac said. Then he turned to her father, who was still holding the gesture of silence.

"Best get to it," John finally said, tipping his hat. "She has the patience of Job but the focus of a charging bull. Don't get run over."

Isaac tried to control the mixture of thoughts and feelings now swirling inside his head. But when he looked over at Grace, she was tapping her foot on the ground, most impatiently.

# CHAPTER NINETEEN

Just as Grace came to terms with Isaac being an eligible widower, he was the one who started acting strangely. While in the back field working with Cincinnati, she kept catching him looking at her when he should've been paying attention to the *gaul*.

"First you don't want a cookie," she said, looping a piece of rope around her palm and elbow, "and now you can't get a harness over his nose." Moving swiftly, but not so much as to startle the horse, Grace easily slipped the thick leather straps into place, patting Cincinnati on the side afterward.

"I was trying to be gentle."

"There's a time for that and a time for improvement," Grace said, asserting herself, making sure that her opinions were known. She might be stuck with Isaac for the time being, but she wasn't about to let him fully take over. "He's an intelligent boy and he'll get bored with us if we're not careful."

"Do you see how his ears are back?" Isaac pointed.

"Yes," Grace answered, keeping her chin level. "He's alert."

"He's anxious. Look at his tail. He's not ready for you to be so familiar."

By the tone of his voice, Grace couldn't help but think he was speaking about them, as well. Of course, Grace agreed. They were training together, that was it. They didn't have to be friends.

"Let me show you how it's done."

Grace didn't wait to see what Isaac was about to

show her. "There's more than one way."

She could easily see that Isaac was clenching his teeth at her reply. "Since your way doesn't seem to be working, I'll show you how I do it, then."

Though Grace wanted to stomp her foot and tell him to back off, she did her best to swallow her pride and hand over the reins.

"He's fine on the longer lead, isn't pulling back anymore. Do you see what I'm doing?"

Grace blew out a breath, clenching her own teeth. "I see it."

"Now watch when I do this…"

What she saw made her speechless, and at times, nearly burst into tears of frustration. Frustration at her own lack of skills. What she witnessed Isaac doing was something she'd never seen in her life. She crossed her arms, trying to hold in the pain, but mostly trying to not feel dejected over her obvious lack of knowledge about this method of breaking a horse.

• • •

"It couldn't have been that bad."

"No?" Grace said to Mary as she paced back and forth across her sister's front porch later that morning. "I couldn't believe my own eyes. He got that ornery horse bowed into position, down on his front knee in complete submission, faster than I've ever seen."

"I don't know what any of that means," Mary said as she forced Grace into one of the rocking chairs, the mid-morning sun warming the air. "But it sounds impressive."

"It *was* impressive." Grace felt more frustration clawing at her. "I mean, I guess that's why he's called the Amish Cowboy, and why *Daed* hired him in the first place." She blew out a breath. "He must be into black magic or something."

"Grace," Mary said, her voice sharp. "That's not funny." She leaned down to kiss Rose on the top of her head. "Shouldn't even joke about it."

"I'm sorry, I didn't mean that about the magic." She began massaging the back of her own neck. "He's better than me. I guess I didn't want to admit it." She looked over at her sister. "No one's ever been better than me. Not even Papa."

"Pride, sister," Mary said, lifting her eyebrows.

Grace thought coming over to visit Mary would make her feel better, but so far, it hadn't. "Everything out of my mouth today is wrong. I don't know what's the matter with me. I left home to take a walk right after I fed the horses." She stared into the middle distance. "I can't face him."

"So that's why you came for this unexpected morning visit." Mary smiled. "You're hiding."

"Maybe. I just feel so…lacking. You don't know what that means to me. I needed this job to be perfect. *I* needed to be perfect. Or at least better than…"

"It's not healthy to compare yourself to others," Mary said after Grace decided not to finish her sentence. "We know that seeking praise from the world repels the Spirit. And you know what happens when we covet."

Her sister's words should've brought peace of mind, but they didn't. "I know," Grace said, looking over when Rose stirred. "I sometimes wonder why I was given the desire to work with horses, this gift to know how to train them."

"Do you want more tea?" Mary asked.

"Nay." Grace lifted her eyes and took in a deep

breath. "You and Simon were always a match, ever since you were children. You married young, so you don't know what it's like."

"Grace." Mary chuckled. "You're twenty-three. Even in our culture, that's hardly an old maid."

"But that's just it. In our culture, men want tradition. They want a wife who will cook and clean and have their babies."

"Are you speaking of *this* baby?" Mary said, gesturing down at Rose. "Because let me tell you, she is just as much mine as his."

"Okay," Grace conceded.

"And honestly, Hannah is getting to be one of the most skilled cooks around. She loves being in the kitchen. Her fried chicken last night was delicious. And the *kinnahs* clean up after supper."

"Okay, okay," Grace said. "So you don't cook or clean and half of Rose is yours." She paused to laugh at the absurd image. "What I meant was, I'm sitting here, looking at your precious baby, enjoying a peaceful, reflective morning, and all I want to do is pull on some trousers, climb onto a horse, and ride until my *kapp* flies off." She turned to her sister. "Will any man ever want that? Do I even want a man who wants that?"

Neither of them spoke for a moment, and Grace knew exactly what Mary was thinking.

*No self-respecting Amish man will.*

"I am wondering one other thing," Mary said.

*"Jah?"*

"Are you sure the only reason you're hiding from him is because you think he's a better trainer?"

Grace sat up straight. "Meaning?"

"I saw this Isaac King on Sunday." She rolled her eyes up to heaven. "You were holding back on us when you said he was handsome."

"You don't think he is?"

"Um, Grace, not that I notice any other man in that way besides my husband, but he's more than handsome. He looks like those posters we saw outside the mall in Harrisburg."

Grace's gaze drifted to the side, not remembering any posters but picturing Isaac. His strong jaw and nice arms and the smile that could sometimes tickle her heart. "Ahem." She cleared her throat. "Can I help you make the beds?" she asked after a minute.

"Done," Mary said, taking a careful sip of tea.

"Make lunch?"

"We're visiting the Yoders this afternoon."

Grace sighed. "What am I supposed to do, then?"

"Go home," Mary said. "Walk straight up to the horse, make him kneel in submission or whatnot, and don't worry a stitch about what anyone thinks. I love you, *Gott* loves you, and that's all you ever need to know."

Grace still wasn't ready to return to the farm, but her sister was right. Staying away because her pride was hurt, when she yearned for the smell of hay and the touch of smooth, silky mane, was not solving anything.

"Okay then." She leaned over to give her sister and Rose gentle kisses on the cheeks. "I can't covet my neighbor's training skills?"

Mary grinned. "No, you may not."

Grace smiled when an idea flashed into her mind. It was time she stopped thinking about herself but remember another "horse" in her life who needed her attention. "If you're free later this week, would you pay us a visit? I think Sarah would love to hold the baby."

# CHAPTER TWENTY

Instead of taking a ride or wandering around town, during the break between training sessions, Isaac stayed at the Zook farm, helping John with some of the other horses. That was what he told himself, but the real reason he was staying close was because Grace hadn't come out to work with Cincinnati that morning. The only word she'd left was that she had something more important to do.

It was true that Isaac didn't know her like the back of his hand, but from what he did know, there were few things more important to Grace Zook than being around her horses.

"*Danke*," John said, passing him the buggy harness he'd just used on the small painted pony. "He'll be ready to pull the girls' cart by end of the week." Isaac nodded, but his mind was elsewhere. "Not to worry." John put a hand on Isaac's shoulder. "She'll be back."

Isaac looked up, wondering if his thoughts could be seen on his face. "Who?"

"It's happened before—not often, mind you."

Isaac followed as John exited the stables and walked toward the house. "What's happened before?"

John scratched his beard. "Oh, she disappears like that out of the blue. She usually ends up at her sister's; usually comes back with bread or a pie, something she baked. Or she'll be at one of the aunts' cleaning their mud room or kitchen, sitting with one of the widowed mammies. Always something…I don't know…women's work, I guess is the best way to put it. Completely unrelated to working on the farm."

John leaned an elbow on the porch rail. "Her mother told me that she suspects she needs a break here and there."

"A break from what?" Isaac asked, curious, even though he half expected John was going to say that she needed a break from *him*.

"Gracie grew up playing in the dirt, but she's still a woman."

The words made Isaac hold his breath.

"I figure she needs a break from being outside with the men. There must be a part of her—maybe only a small part—that wishes for a homelife, even though she rarely shows it and never talks about settling down. With or without the Chupp boy." He paused to chuckle. "She always comes back to the horses. Can't stay away long."

Isaac flinched at hearing that name again. The more he thought about it, the more he was certain a strong-willed woman like Grace would never be happy with someone like Collin Chupp, who seemed dead set on having a submissive wife.

Isaac hoped what John said was true—that Grace would return home soon. His morning training session without her wasn't nearly as fun or productive. Even though they still butted heads at times, he found he missed bouncing ideas off his...partner.

"I best check on the chickens," John said. "Something's cut through the wire, or some*one*. Thanks again for your help today."

"Sure." Isaac nodded; his mind now wondering if Grace really did want to settle down someday, or if her life would always revolve around working outside with horses. And why on earth was that any of his business? Hadn't he already promised that he wouldn't think about her in that way? He mustn't if he wanted to keep this job.

It wasn't quite time yet, but Isaac decided to start the afternoon training session with Cincinnati a bit early. The horse had been fed and watered and had been resting for almost three hours, and Isaac would keep it easy, since Sin had worked very hard the day before. As he walked into the shadowy stables, he immediately noticed the Morgan wasn't in his stall.

His stomach dropped as a feeling of ice ran through his bloodstream. He checked the gate. The latch didn't look broken or like the animal had pushed his way out. No, someone had opened the gate. It was probably Grace, but Isaac had to be sure. He ran to check the side field but saw only the cows. The field behind the house was also empty, so he raced past the other field that led to the far back pasture with the tall grass.

That was when he heard the singing…

*"Gott is die Liebe, las mich erlosen, Gott is die Liebe, er liebt auch mich."*

*God is love*, Grace sang while stroking Cincinnati, her voice pulling him in. *God is love, He also loves me*.

Her beautiful, feminine voice practically called out to him, but what was more magnetic was that her hair was loose, no *kapp*, bonnet, or covering. Just long reddish-brown tresses falling down her back, over her shoulders. Isaac couldn't move. All he could do was stand in place, watch her hum and sing, gently running her fingers down the horse's mane—which, he'd hadn't noticed until now, matched the color of Grace's. Dark underneath, with red highlights in the sun.

Cincinnati nuzzled his nose into the crook of her neck. One side, then the other, as if kissing her on both cheeks.

Warmth spread through Isaac's chest as his heart

began to beat hard. It was the most beautiful sight he'd ever seen.

"Good boy," Grace said, her voice light as air. "Such a special boy." She moved one of her hands to the back of her neck, then pulled it away, tossing her hair just as a bit of wind picked up.

When that warmth in his chest moved down to his stomach, Isaac knew it was ill-mannered—at the very least—to keep watching Grace in her private moment.

"*Guder nummidaag*," he said as gently as possible, knowing he was about to startle her.

She whipped around, that long hair curtaining the sides of her face, blue eyes wide. "What are you doing here?"

"Looking for Sin," Isaac said as he took a step toward her.

"I took him out early," she said, the tall grass nearly up to her waist.

He couldn't help smiling. "I see that."

As he got closer, he easily saw that her cheeks and throat were pink. She was embarrassed. He should've been, too, but he couldn't seem to look away.

"Would you mind…?" She twirled one finger.

It took Isaac a moment to interpret the gesture. After chuckling under his breath, he obediently turned around. "I didn't see anything," he said. *Not your hair down, not your blushing cheeks.*

"There was nothing to see."

"That's what I meant."

"Then why didn't you say that?"

"I'm saying it now."

Despite the almost intimate setting of the situation, Isaac couldn't help teasing her, picking a friendly fight like he sometimes did while they were training.

He heard her sigh. "Okay, you can turn around."

When he did, her hair was pulled back and up, black heart-shaped prayer *kapp* in place. But it was no use; he'd never get the picture of her out of his mind. "What are you doing out here?" she repeated, her voice almost accusatory. But she couldn't fool him anymore—he saw she was trying not to smile.

"I told you, I was looking for Cincinnati." He put a hand over his chest. "About gave me a heart attack when he wasn't in his stall."

"Oh." Her cheeks were still a bit pink as he reached up to pet the horse. "I wanted some alone time with him. I should've left a note."

"I missed you this morning." The words were out of his mouth before he could stop them. "*We* did, I mean." He patted the horse, hoping to keep his own blush away. "Didn't we, boy?"

She looked at him, then lowered her head. "I, uh, was really impressed by what you did yesterday. I've never seen a horse respond like that so quickly." He heard her sigh. "I was shocked—humbled by my lack of knowledge."

So John had been right. "That's why you didn't show up this morning?"

She nodded but was still looking down.

"You're twenty-three, *jah*?"

She glanced up at him, blinked in confusion, then nodded. "Aye."

"Well, I'm twenty-seven—*four* years older than you, which means four more years of experience." He wasn't sure why he was trying to make her feel better, but he couldn't help it, even though her father—his boss—would definitely not approve of them being alone in the back meadow like this.

"Well, Papa is twenty years older than me, but I'm

still better than…" Her voice dropped off as she pressed her lips together. "I'm having trouble with humility these days."

"It's hard to be humble when you're so gifted," he said. She blinked again, but her eyes were brighter. "Comparison can make you miserable; believe me, I know. Plus, there's something in the Bible against it."

"That's what my sister said." She looked at him for a moment, then bit her lip. "Would you tell me how you did that yesterday?"

"No," Isaac said. Before Grace's frown could set, he added, "But I'll show you. Do you have a shorter lead with you?"

"*Jah.*" Grace displayed a bag she must've carried all the way from the barn. "His harness, too."

Together, they got the horse properly situated, gave him a few extra rubs, then Isaac took hold of the lead. "Come here," he said. "Stand right beside me behind his back legs, like this, bending at the hips."

When he glanced back at her, she seemed frozen in place. Was it because crouching directly behind a horse like Sin could be dangerous? Or was she afraid to stand so close to *him*?

"What's wrong?" he asked. "Don't you trust me?"

"No."

Her reply had come so quickly, so automatically, that Isaac almost flinched. He stood up straight, feeling his brows pull together, a frown curving his lips. *Maybe she really is afraid of me. Did I cross a line? Or is it me in general she doesn't trust?*

He dropped his chin to stare down at the ground, wondering what to do or say that would help her feel comfortable. *Trust*, he thought. *That has to be the basis of our partnership, or this whole thing could be a miserable failure for both of us.*

"Well," he said. "Will you trust me to show you how to do this right now?"

Before she answered, she bit her lip. "Aye," she finally replied.

Isaac offered her a smile, just a little one, hoping to put her more at ease. "What is most important is Sin has to know who's in charge," he said. "I'm in charge now—I'm the boss, the leader. When you're holding the lead, you're the boss. Here."

Grace took the rope, sent a glance toward Isaac, then stared straight into Cincinnati's eyes. Of course, she already knew how to gain and keep a horse's attention—he wasn't teaching her anything new, but it was the setup to breaking that he always found so key.

"Pull him this way, now," Isaac said. "Down at an angle, he'll lift his foot on his own."

"He's...*not*," Grace said, panting with effort. Isaac knew it took practice, and he didn't expect it to work for her the first time. Still, after she'd disappeared on him that morning, he didn't want her to feel discouraged again.

"Angle the rope like this," he said, coming up behind her. "Pull gently." He reached out and took ahold of the rope, wrapping his hand around hers. It was the only way he could demonstrate exactly how to do it.

Or at least, that was what he told himself as he pressed his body to the back of her, both of them grasping the rope, tugging in unison.

Ever so slowly, Cincinnati succumbed, obeying perfectly, bending down onto his knees, then rolling onto his side.

"Well done," Isaac said, his voice almost a whisper. "You did great."

"Are you talking to me or the horse?"

Because of his position standing right at her back, he couldn't see her face. But then he felt her shoulders shake as she quietly laughed.

"Both," Isaac said, making himself move back, for he was noticing the unique, flowery scent of her skin too much. "It's a team effort. Here, let's get him back up."

A moment later, Cincinnati was standing on all fours, his long tail swishing.

"*Danke*," Grace said. "That was pretty incredible."

"That was you trusting me." When he took a beat to let that sink in, Grace looked at him, her pretty blue eyes locking onto his, almost hesitantly at first. "Trust is important between any two beings," he added before he allowed himself to analyze the look in her eyes. "Do you agree?"

He waited, and Grace finally nodded. "Yes, I do definitely agree."

"I couldn't have done it without you." Isaac had no idea why he said such a thing. It wasn't really the truth, and the tone as it had come out of his mouth sounded almost…flirtatious.

Grace was looking at him, chin tilting up, eyes as blue as the sky above, making Isaac's mouth go dry. Then she looked down at her hand—*their* hands, for Isaac's was still wrapped around hers. He knew he should let go immediately, but something made him pause, to memorize the feeling of her soft skin touching his.

But a moment was all he took.

"Well done," he said again, dropping her hand, then pushing that same hand through his hair, bobbing his head up and down. "That was great."

Grace lowered her gaze but then laughed lightly.

"It really was. And you were right. Sin had to trust me, but first I…I had to trust you."

He waited until he knew his voice would be steady. "I'm glad you did—*do*." He stepped back and raked his fingers through his hair once more.

"About your training skills, I meant," she added quickly as she turned her attention to Sin. She lifted her hand that he'd been holding and pressed it against her cheek for just one second. Then she shook her head and reached for the lead. "Let's do it again. But on my own, this time."

Isaac made the motion of a bow, then stepped aside, way back, giving both of them plenty of space. Heaven knew Isaac needed it.

• • •

"That was really delicious," Isaac said as he handed his empty dinner plate to Dorothy Chupp. "Those green beans tasted just like my mother's."

"*Danke*," Dorothy said. "It's the lard. Makes everything taste better."

Isaac nodded, then wiped his mouth with a napkin. Sadie had already finished supper and was upstairs playing with the new doll he'd bought her at the mercantile in town, the two Chupp girls tagging along. Isaac knew he was probably spoiling Sadie, but her short life had been uprooted so many times, he never wanted her to feel like she was doing without because of that.

When this job was over and his business was bringing in more money, he would build them a house of their own. He'd make sure Sadie would grow up in a loving, peaceful, obedient home.

"Well," Samuel Chupp said, laying his palms flat

on the table. "I'm heading over to the bishop's in a while."

"On a Friday?" Dorothy asked.

Samuel sniffed and rubbed his beard. "Been some trouble out near Ben Stolzenfus's."

"Another fire," said Collin, helping himself to a second plateful of roasted chicken. "Heard talk of it at the iron shop. Only lasted a minute."

"Fire's not to be taken lightly, son," Samuel said. "Even the smallest flames. Say the wind picks up or there's no water close by." He shook his head. "Could be real devastating."

Collin shrugged one shoulder. Isaac hoped the gesture was made in understanding and not passivity. But it made him once again think that Collin wasn't the right man for Grace.

"Think I might stop by the Zooks' on the way," Samuel added. "See if John and Amos want to come."

This made Collin sit up. "The Zooks'? I'll come too, Pa."

"You're interested in attending the meeting?" Samuel asked his son, his head tipped to one side.

"Meeting? Uh, no, I was just thinking of paying a visit to Grace. I was out at their place earlier, dropping off some molasses from *Maam*." He leaned back in his chair. "Asked her for a date, even."

Suddenly, Collin Chupp had Isaac's complete attention.

"A date?" Dorothy said. "And what did she say this time?"

*You took the words right out of my mouth*, Isaac thought, though he wouldn't be so bold as to ask the question himself. But after that moment in the field today with Grace, being so close to her, holding her hand, even, Isaac knew Collin shouldn't be anywhere near her.

"It'll happen," Collin answered, the corners of his mouth turning up. "I have no doubt."

"So she said no," Dorothy replied.

Collin's crestfallen expression made Isaac want to laugh out loud. Yet he was surprised by how relieved he also felt at Collin's answer.

"She said she's real busy." He pursed his lips. "Training some new horse." He looked at Isaac, who was trying not to smile. "Hey, thought that's what they hired *you* for."

"I…" Isaac lifted both hands, not sure what to say. "We're working as a team. A partnership."

"Well…" Collin narrowed his eyes. "I don't reckon my girl should be partners with anyone."

"Collin." Samuel stood up from the table. "Is Grace Zook your girl?"

"She will be someday," Collin said. "Soon as she gives up all that horse training. A girl like her should be in the house. Ain't that right, Pa?"

"That's John and Eve Zook's business," Samuel said. "Not mine. And definitely not yours. Now, don't you have some feeding to do?"

"Yes, *Daed*," Collin said. But right before leaving the room, he sent Isaac a look that was probably meant to scare him, but all it made him want to do was laugh.

"That boy," Samuel said, sitting back in his chair. "Don't know what I'm gonna do with him. Can't even seem to find steady work."

"What does he do now?" Isaac asked, sensing permission to pry.

"Helps out at the farm mostly. Works part-time at the feed store and makes deliveries for the market on his scooter. Can't support a family on that."

Isaac thought for a moment, then said, "What about logging? Still a lot of trees to fell, especially around Silver Springs. Got a big logging group of plain folks out there."

"Really?" Samuel rubbed his beard. "Silver Springs, huh? Might be good for the boy to get away from home. Try life on his own."

"Might be the best thing for him," Isaac agreed. "I might be able to put you in contact with the hiring agent."

"*Jah?*"

Isaac nodded, feeling good because he was helping out his host, but also completely guilty for practically running Collin Chupp out of town. Away from Grace.

# CHAPTER TWENTY-ONE

Grace pressed her lips to the back of her hand, the one Isaac had been holding—well, *sort of* holding. She had a small scratch there, and she'd nearly convinced herself that that was why she kept running her thumb over it.

No matter what she tried, however, she couldn't get the "incident" out of her mind, even as she attempted to fall asleep in the darkness of her room. It had been terribly thrilling to get Cincinnati to obey her so easily, but the shock of being touched like that by a man left her head spinning. She wasn't sure if she liked it or not.

Strangely enough, however, it had been a pleasure working with him this morning. Grace always thought she was the most patient trainer around, but Isaac King had her beat. When first Cincinnati would not let Isaac near him with a harness in his hand, Isaac had stood three feet away from the horse, just holding it and staring into Sin's eyes, not making a sound. Amazingly, it was Cincinnati who'd made the first move by walking over to Isaac, softly butting his nose against Isaac's head.

Initially, Grace hadn't been sure if she'd be able to work with a partner, but sometimes it was as if Isaac was reading her mind—they worked together almost…better than alone.

She turned over onto her side, remembering the moment he'd seen her with her hair down. She knew she was never to not have it covered with a *kapp*, but out there in the back pasture, where she thought she'd been alone, she hadn't seen the harm in it.

She felt herself smiling, tucking her chin, picturing that enthralled look in his eyes, wondering if a man would ever look at her like that again—like she was a woman and not just a horse trainer in a grimy dress.

Then again, would she welcome it?

• • •

The next morning, Grace practically jumped out of bed, eager to get her morning chores out of the way so she could head straight to Cincinnati. Rounding the corner into the stable, she stopped short, panting to catch her breath.

"You're up early," she said, feeling almost accusatory as she placed her hands on her hips. But then she remembered the trust. She wanted Sarah to trust her. She wanted Sin to trust her. And Isaac had even said the words: "Do you trust me?"

Grace hadn't then, but she did now.

"Couldn't stay asleep," Isaac said. "And I wanted to see if I could get here before you for a change." He ran his hand under Cincinnati's chin, then turned to Grace and smiled. "All it took was sleeping in my clothes, then breaking the speed of light."

Grace wasn't sure what that last part meant, but for some reason, seeing him in the early morning light put a smile on her face. "Maybe we can squeeze in three training sessions today," she suggested. "If we don't work him too hard. He's proven to be pretty durable."

"I was thinking the same thing." He looked down and brushed at the front of his blue shirt. "Maybe we can go out to the back pasture again."

The way he looked at her, his hazel eyes big and

inviting, made her stomach do another of those funny back flips. She was about to agree, but then thought better of it… As if an invisible angel were sitting on her shoulder.

"M-maybe not," she said instead, staring at him with a level, steady gaze. "Three of the Millers' horses are loose in the front, rehab after they were spooked a few days ago. I think it would behoove Sin to be around more horses." She shrugged one shoulder. "Just an idea."

"A very good one," Isaac said. "One I should've thought of." He bowed his head. "Thank you, partner."

Grace couldn't help laughing, grateful that there was less awkwardness between them now. She knew that was best for Sin, and she also needed to work more at forgiving…both her father for hiring him and Isaac himself, for simply being there.

They brushed Cincinnati for a while, small talking in between making plans for their afternoon training sessions. Right as she got to the gate of the front pasture, Isaac and the horse behind her, her father came running out of the house.

"Call Lucas Brenneman!" he shouted, practically throwing his cell phone at Grace. "Hurry!"

"What's wrong?" she yelled back, seeing the alarm on her father's face.

"Your mother fell," *Daed* said. "I need to get her to a doctor or hospital. I don't know what—"

"Where is she?" Isaac said.

"On the floor by the couch. She's not opening her eyes. I don't know…"

"Come with me to check on her," Isaac said, taking ahold of her father's arm. "Call Lucas, quickly," he added, glancing at Grace.

"I've never called someone on a phone before," she said, holding it up like it had appeared out of nowhere, feeling panicked and useless.

"Is his number in your favorites?" Isaac asked *Daed*.

"First one."

"Just hit the down arrow once," Isaac said as he began pulling *Daed* toward the house. "Then hit the big green button."

Grace looked down at the phone in a daze, already feeling lost.

"The down arrow," Isaac repeated as he rushed into the house. "Trust me, Grace. You can do it."

Grace swallowed and nodded. She found the arrow, which moved something on the face of the phone that she couldn't read, then she hit the green button in the middle, the one shaped like the big phone her grandfather used to have in his barn.

"John?" someone said.

"Lucas!" Grace shouted at the phone. "Lucas, it's Grace Zook. Something happened to my *maam*!"

Right as she ended the call, *Daed* came running out of the house. "Is he coming?"

"Nay," Grace called. "He said to get her to the medical clinic in town as fast as possible but to be very careful. He'll meet us there."

As if he'd been prepared for the instructions, Isaac came onto the front porch, holding *Maam* in his arms. Her eyes were closed, head bobbing.

"*Maam*!" Grace called out, feeling hot tears in her throat. "What happened?"

"It's okay," Isaac said. "Her heart feels strong and her hands and feet are warm. Help your father with the buggy."

*Daed* was already pulling the horses around,

hitching them to his largest buggy.

"Open the back door," Isaac said. Grace obeyed instantly. "Get inside. I'm going to lay her down flat. Can her head rest on your dress?"

"Aye." There was plenty of room in the back of the buggy, so Grace climbed in, helping Isaac lay *Maam* down as gently as she could.

"John," Isaac called out. "I need you back here to keep her steady. I'll drive."

Without a word, her father was in the back, doing what he could to keep his wife from rolling around. The buggy jerked at first, but then it was a steady ride. The whole way to town, Grace prayed and prayed, begging *Gott* to spare her sweet mother, to keep her alive.

Grace's heart sped faster when the horses slowed. She saw the medical clinic ahead, Lucas and two other men standing on the curb. Before the buggy came to a complete stop, the back door flew open and an English man wearing a white coat jumped inside.

"Is she breathing?"

"*Jah*," *Daed* said. "I listened to it the entire way here."

"Good," the man said. He knelt by *Maam*'s head, leaned down, and put his ear to her mouth, then he laid fingers on the side of her neck. "Steady pulse—that's good. Luke, Greg, let's get her inside for X-rays." He turned to Grace. "It's okay, you can let go."

Grace looked down to see she was grasping onto the sleeve of her *maam*'s dress. But instead of letting so, Grace tightened her grip like iron.

"What's your name?" the man asked, calmness in his voice.

"It's Grace."

Grace wasn't the one who had spoken. She gulped in a breath when she saw Isaac standing outside the open doors of the buggy.

"Grace," the man said. "I'm Kevin. I've got your mom now. Trust me."

Trust was never the first thing Grace felt when it came to Englishers she didn't know. But she knew Lucas, and she trusted him now. In fact, just seeing him made her not as frightened somehow. After they pulled out her mother on a long, flat bed, Grace and her father followed the doctors inside until they disappeared behind a pair of white double doors. Lucas led them to the waiting room.

"We'll run tests," he said, touching her father's arm. "And we'll give her fluids. I didn't notice any bumps on her head, but we'll scan for that, and to see if there's new damage to the vertebra. I'll come back with news as soon as possible."

"*Danke*," *Daed* said, his bottom lip trembling.

Grace ran to his side and wrapped her arms around him. "What happened? Were you in the room?"

"Aye." He wiped his nose with a hanky. "She was reaching for a book—I told her I'd get it, but she can be so stubborn. Next thing I know, she yelled for me from the floor, hands behind her back, pushing in right…right where it happened."

Grace shut her eyes. It had been two years since the accident, and her mother was still in daily pain. This time the pain had knocked her unconscious.

"She needs that surgery," she said.

"I know."

"Can't you borrow the money for it?"

Her father dropped his chin. "It's very expensive, Grace, and the church can offer only so much."

Grace bit down on her lip, tasting blood. "Would we have enough if I was training the Morgan on my own?" When her father didn't answer, Grace felt the heat of a roaring fire under her hair. "We would, wouldn't we? *Daed*…" She stood up, taking a few steps away. "*Maam* could be getting better right now if all the money was ours. Why are you paying someone else to do a job I can? I want to take over the family business when you retire. Don't you know that?"

Grace realized she was being disrespectful and completely irrational, but she was scared and angry, and she truly didn't understand her father's decisions lately.

"Why are you wasting our money?" she said, her voice hitching, heart beating fast in her chest. "Why?"

"Gracie, I…" Her father's eyes brimmed with tears, but Grace's panic and confusion were overpowering her empathy.

She opened her mouth to say one more thing, but then closed it, knowing the new words would hurt her father's feelings even worse. Instead, she ground her back teeth and ran toward the exit, barely registering that Isaac had been standing there the whole time.

# CHAPTER TWENTY-TWO

Isaac stared as the doors of the medical clinic closed behind Grace. He wasn't sure what to think; everything had happened so fast. When he heard John slump into a waiting room chair, he forgot about his own problems and rushed over to his boss.

"Can I get a glass of water over here?" Isaac called to the woman at the reception desk.

"Sure," she said, pushing back from her desk. "Bottled or tap?"

"Doesn't matter—bottled," Isaac said, annoyed at the question. "It's going to be all right," he said to John. "Eve is in good hands."

"*Jah*," John said, but Isaac saw worry in his eyes. "She's getting worse, I fear. The last doctor we saw said she should be on complete bedrest, but that wife of mine…" His voice shook. "She can be as pigheaded as anyone I know—*Gott* love her."

"Hopefully, you'll get some answers after the doctors do their tests," Isaac said, handing John the bottle of water. "These Englishers aren't like us. They have decades of education. They'll know how to help."

"We already know what she needs. I just can't give it to her."

"Grace—" Isaac cleared his throat. "Grace said something about surgery."

John bobbed his head up and down. "The two doctors we saw in Hershey both said the same thing. But it will cost more money than I've ever had at one time."

Isaac opened his mouth, ready to give another suggestion. But he had none. "Do you want me to fetch Amos?" he asked. "Send word to the sawmill?"

"Not yet," John said, wiping his eyes with the heel of his hand. "Not until I know what happened." He leaned over to look at the double doors that Eve had gone through. "I think if it was real serious, Lucas would've told me by now. He knows we want the whole family here if…"

When John's voice faded out, a cold shudder ran up and down Isaac's back. Surely this wasn't life-threatening. Though…Isaac was well aware he didn't have all the facts. Had Eve Zook been in an accident, or was this a chronic illness she'd been battling for years?

The two men sat in silence for a while, both given fresh cups of coffee as the time ticked on. Other people and patients came and went. No one stared at them. No one cared. When they weren't closed in prayer, John's eyes were fixed on those double doors.

Isaac crossed his arms tightly, trying to squelch the nervous feeling in his stomach. For he knew what it was like to stand on one side of a door when your spouse was on the other side.

"I don't know what I'd do without her," John said, staring down at his hat. "I've loved her since we were children. My family's everything to me." His voice hitched as he exhaled. "That's why I don't want Gracie to…" The words quivered. "It scares me to death every day—the thought of it."

Isaac leaned in closer. "Grace is okay. She left for a while, but she's not in danger."

After shaking his head a few times, John lifted his gaze to Isaac's. Pain and fear sat behind his blue eyes. "She's a horse trainer," he said after a deep inhale.

"And she wants to keep doing it, you heard her. Wants the farm when I retire—keep the training company going. She's capable, that's plain to anyone."

"*Jah*," Isaac said when John didn't go on. Of course, he knew Grace was a very skilled trainer, and if he knew her at all, he'd guess she'd want to keep it up as long as possible…until she settled down.

Suddenly, Isaac couldn't help thinking of Collin Chupp. Was the young man just waiting in the wings until Grace decided to stop training full-time? And would John really encourage the match? Isaac felt himself shaking his head, clenching his jaw.

Isaac glanced at John when the man chuckled under his breath. "I wish someone good like *you* wanted to buy the company. It would ease my mind just fine." He paused and swallowed as a fresh patch of tears filled his eyes.

Though this moment was about John's situation, Isaac couldn't help feeling honored that his boss thought so highly of him. The respect was certainly mutual.

"It was an accident that done it." John continued.

"Accident?"

"My Evie," he said. "Out of the clear blue sky. She was removing the harness like she's done a hundred times—always careful, knew what she was doing, and that horse kicked her with both back legs, sent her five feet away. I thought he'd killed her on the spot."

"Eve?" Isaac asked, a horrific picture forming in his mind. "Her injury was from a horse kick?"

John nodded, wiping at his eyes. "Don't you see? They can be dangerous enough, and my…my precious daughter is out there every day, deliberately putting herself in peril." He paused to pinch the bridge of his nose. "Please don't ever tell her this, but that's why I hired you. I hoped Cincinnati would be her last horse, that she'll see how good you are and just...I don't know...get on with her life."

The whole picture was becoming clearer. Problem was, Isaac had been observing Grace since the day he'd arrived; she was an excellent trainer, never took unnecessary risks, respected the animals like Mother Nature herself.

In the back of his head, Isaac had wondered a few times why exactly John had hired him when he didn't need to. So far, Grace was just as good as he was.

Now he knew. And it did not sit well.

He needed this job. He needed to provide a better life for Sadie. Was it any of his business *why* he'd been hired? At the same time, however, he'd hate for Grace to think *he* didn't trust her.

"Would you go after her?"

Isaac glanced at John, not sure who he meant, so he gestured to the white double doors and lifted his eyebrows.

"Gracie," John said. "Would you bring her back?"

"Of course," Isaac said, happy to be of service, ready to be put to work. He was out the front door of the medical clinic in two seconds, though he had no idea where she might've gone or how long ago it had been since she'd left. He squinted up and down the streets, scanning the mix of plain and English folks on the sidewalks.

"Grace!" he called out, spotting the back of a woman's head who looked like she could be Grace. His muscles were flexed, ready to fly down the street after her.

"Is she okay?"

He jumped at the soft voice, his muscles burning for relief.

"Is she?" Grace was standing outside of the medical clinic, leaning against a cement pillar right by the door, looking small. Isaac must've raced out so quickly that he didn't notice her.

"Hey," he said, a bit rattled, glancing at her, then at the woman down the street who was definitely not Grace Zook.

"Will *Maam* be okay?"

Isaac exhaled, strangely winded. "We don't know anything yet."

Grace nodded and moved a hand up to her throat. Her face was white as a bedsheet drying on the line, and her eyes were red, cheeks wet. Despite everything he now knew, or maybe *because* of it, Isaac couldn't stop himself from moving closer.

"I've never seen her like that," she said, her voice almost too quiet to hear over the street noise. "It looked like she was asleep, but she wouldn't wake up. I thought she was…" She covered her face with both hands. Isaac could easily hear her sobs. "I'm so scared," she cried. "I don't know what to do. I can't stop shaking."

"Come with me," Isaac said in a low voice, gently taking her by the arm and leading her a few feet away into the doorway of an empty storefront. "Just stand here," he said, moving her so her back was against the door.

Grace nodded, her hands still covering her face.

Isaac sent one glace over his shoulder, making sure they had at least some privacy. Then he leaned in, putting his hands on the wall behind her, her head between them so the two of them were in their own little huddle.

"Dear Heavenly Father…" he said, his voice hushed in reverence. He prayed for Eve's body, for calmness to come to John's mind, for the doctors to know what to do, and then Isaac prayed for Grace. "Please bring peace to her heart. Help her know she is stronger than she thinks, and that she brings joy and happiness to everyone in her life."

He hadn't meant for his prayer to make her cry harder; he'd hoped it would ease her pain some. But when he said "amen," Grace burst into heart-wrenching sobs.

"I'm sorry," Isaac said, his heart breaking for her. "I thought I could help—"

"Nay, *I'm* sorry," Grace said, rushing forward, wrapping her arms all the way around him. "I'm so sorry, Isaac."

Isaac nearly stumbled back, surprised by the sudden embrace and the sheer inappropriate nature of it. After Grace had barely been willing to stand beside him the other day, her hug about shocked him to death. "It's…okay," he said, though he had no idea why she should be apologizing to him for saying a prayer.

"No, it's not," she said, her cheek pressed against his chest. "I can't believe what I said in there."

Confused, Isaac was about to ask what she meant. But when she burst into another wave of fresh sobs, he had no choice but to wrap his arms around her and hold her tight. Otherwise, he was afraid she'd break into a million pieces.

So he selfishly allowed himself to feel Grace inside his embrace, listen to her breathing—fast with sobs, then slow when crying tired her out. She was shorter than he was, but her head fit perfectly right under his chin. She sniffed and blew out a deep breath. Isaac knew that at any second she would pull away and it would all be over.

*Her skin smells like lavender*, he mused, quickly adding to the memory. He was surprised because the other day, she'd smelled more of hay and freshly cut grass.

"*Danke*," she finally said. And just like he thought, she dropped her arms. She was looking down at her hands now, slowly rubbing them together.

"You're welcome," Isaac said, missing her warmth. On the heels of that, he remembered what John had said about wishing Collin could get Grace to settle down. He also recalled that John hadn't hired Isaac because he was the best trainer around, but in hopes he would help get Grace to quit. Isaac felt his stomach roll when his thoughts added that John had specifically asked him not to divulge any of that to his daughter.

If he did, would his job be on the line?

*And could it be even more on the line if John sees us together like this?*

He quickly stepped back. "I still don't know why you were apologizing to me, though."

"I know you heard what I said to my father," she clarified, running a hand across her forehead. "I shouldn't have lost my temper like that. I was scared." She took in a shaky breath. "I *am* scared."

"Do you want to go back in? John was asking for you."

Grace swallowed, as if not wanting to move just yet, but held her chin level. "I need to apologize to him, too." Isaac could tell she was about to start crying again. "He must be so worried."

"Let's go inside."

Grace nodded, and Isaac held the door open for her to enter the medical clinic. "*Daed*?" she said, standing a few feet away from him, like she was afraid he might really be angry.

"Come here, Gracie," John said, standing up and opening his arms to his daughter.

Grace ran straight to him.

Isaac knew it would be this way, for there was nothing his own daughter could say or do that would keep him from welcoming her to his open arms. He stood a ways off for a while, not wanting to intrude. He heard them whispering to each other, Grace sniffling, then hugging her father around his neck.

"I'm sorry, again." Grace was looking at Isaac now. "Please forgive me."

"Don't worry about it," Isaac said, walking toward them. "Everything was…heightened."

"You're a good man," John said. His eyes were still wet, but he put out his hand. Isaac shook it, squeezing it a little firmer this time. John Zook wasn't just his boss. Isaac was beginning to respect the man as highly as his bishop back home, even though the man held his future in his hands.

They sat down again, still waiting for Lucas to give them an update. Now that things were calmer, Isaac couldn't help but recall Grace's words from earlier. He'd known since day one that she hadn't wanted him there, that he had somehow taken "her" job.

But Isaac couldn't have imagined how dire the Zooks' situation was. Was his salary when the job was done actually taking money that could be used for a surgery to save Eve's life? Or at least improve the quality of her life?

Guilt washed over him…a guilt that might not have been from his conscious doing, but he felt it just as strongly. Then he thought of Sadie and remembered his own reason for being in Honey Brook. Which problem was more important? His heart knew it was neither right nor fair to compare the two situations. And hadn't he preached the same thing to Grace earlier?

He didn't have time to dwell on the matter, for Lucas appeared, followed by the doctor who'd been in the back of the buggy.

"John," Lucas said, "this is Kevin—Doctor Kevin McBride. Kevin, this is John Zook."

"It's nice to meet you, John," the doctor said, putting a hand on John's arm.

"Pleasure, pleasure," John said. "M-my wife?"

"She's resting. I gave her a mild painkiller. She said it was okay, but should I have checked with you first?"

"Nay, nay, it's fine." John blinked, his eyes rimmed with tears. "Can I see her?"

"In a minute," Kevin said. "She woke up almost as soon as we finished the X-rays."

"Hard not to with all that yelling," Lucas said. "Was that you, Grace?"

Grace nodded, then kept her chin lowered. "I'm sorry if I disturbed anyone. I…I have no excuse."

"Please, please," Kevin said to her, probably noticing that she was two seconds away from crying. "There's nothing major to worry about at this point." He looked at John. "The compressed vertebra from the accident—you said it was from a horse kick two years ago?"

Isaac held his breath.

"Aye," John answered.

Kevin nodded. "It hasn't caused any additional damage that I can see, though X-rays show only so much. I can tell, however, that there's a great amount of inflammation. Due to swelling, one of her discs has moved, pushing the two vertebrae farther apart. That is causing your wife a lot of pain." He paused and glanced at Lucas. Lucas nodded, as if the two men had already consulted. "What she really needs, John, is a CT Scan and an MRI."

"Fine, fine," John said. "Do whatever you have to."

"Thing is," Lucas said, "we don't have that equipment here. She'll have to go to the Medical Center in Hershey. It has all the machines and specialists she needs." Lucas leaned in closer. "And I've taught seminars there…back before I rejoined the church. They know a lot more about us plain folks than they used to. Eve will be treated with the greatest respect and care."

"Hershey." John made a fist and ran it over his mouth.

Isaac waited nervously for his answer—not knowing what John Zook would say. Though Isaac knew what his answer would've been. Suddenly, it wasn't Martha with an injury that he was picturing but Grace. He tried shaking his head to get that thought out of his mind.

"*Jah*," John finally said. "We can do that."

Isaac exhaled in relief. "Want me to pull the buggy around?" he asked, needing to be busy, helpful.

"Aye," John replied. "We can take her right now."

"John," Lucas said. "Hershey is fifty miles away. She needs to go in a car."

"Oh." John frowned momentarily, but then said, "Yes, of course. Will you take her?" he asked, grabbing Lucas's arm.

"I don't have a driver's license anymore, but…"

"I'll take her," Kevin said. "I've got an SUV with a big back seat. She won't be able to lie down completely, but at least it will be a fast trip."

"John will be able to go, too, *jah*?" Isaac asked,

jumping in. He would demand it if the man said no.

"Yes," Kevin said. "As soon as Eve's ready, I'm going to give her a shot of steroids. It will help with the pain and inflammation, since the drive will still be a bit bumpy. She might need to spend a few days in the hospital. Why don't you go home and pack a bag?" he said to John. "I think we'll be ready to go in about an hour."

"*Danke*," John said. Then, after saying his good-byes, the doctor walked away.

"Is that all?" Isaac asked, looking at Lucas. "Anything else we need to know?"

"I don't think so. Kevin already reserved the CT and MRI for testing as soon as she arrives. We'll know more in a few hours."

"We should get you home, then," Isaac said, knowing how anxious John must've been, not wanting to waste a minute. "Should I drive?"

"Aye," John said, looking older somehow, worn out. "Gracie?"

"I'm here," she said, sliding up to her father.

"I'm going to be gone for a while."

"I know, *Daed*."

"It would worry me less if I knew you were taking care of things at home—at the farm, I mean."

"Don't worry, *Daed*," she said, putting an arm around him as they walked outside into the afternoon sunshine. "We'll take care of everything. Won't we?"

Isaac was surprised to see that the question was aimed at him.

"Isaac and I will keep things going just as normal as can be." Grace tried to laugh. "Why, the farm will probably run smoother than it ever has...without you around."

John chuckled. "I'm sure it will. *Danke*," he said,

reaching for Isaac's hand, squeezing it so hard, causing a lump to form in Isaac's throat. "Having you here is such a blessing. *Gott* must be looking out for us."

Isaac wasn't sure what to say, because it wasn't *Gott* that had brought him to the Zook farm. It had been John, and though his reasons for that might've been off the mark, Isaac was ever so grateful that he was right where he was.

"*Danke*," Grace whispered to Isaac as she climbed onto the buggy next to him. "I was just saying that so *Daed* wouldn't fret."

"I'll do anything you need," he said, telling the absolute truth.

# CHAPTER TWENTY-THREE

Grace felt tired all the way to her bones. Everything was a rush, helping *Daed* pack his bag, gathering items she knew her mother would want with her in the hospital, saying goodbye to both of her parents as they settled into Dr. McBride's big vehicle.

"Feel better soon," Grace said, touching her mother's arm, trying to keep her voice from shaking. "Take care of her," she added, looking at her father. "Bring her home safe."

"It's going to be okay, my girl," *Maam* said, but her voice sounded weak, not convincing at all to Grace's ears.

Grace forced a smile and stepped back as the SUV pulled away from the house. Her heart was still beating hard and fast in her chest as it disappeared out of sight, leaving only a cloud of dust.

"When will she be home?" little Jane asked, tugging on Grace's skirt.

Grace picked her up. "You're getting so heavy," she said, swinging around her youngest sister. "You'll be tall as me before I know it."

"But when?" Jane repeated, looking into Grace's eyes.

"Soon," said a voice.

Grace turned to see Isaac and immediately felt grateful.

In the most respectful and helpful way, he'd taken control from practically the very beginning, almost reading her mind about their needs…just as he sometimes did when they were working with Sin.

Isaac had jumped into action the second *Daed* had run out of the house. Grace felt a shiver up her spine at the memory. And she'd never forget the scene when Isaac had come out of the house a few minutes later, holding her unconscious mother in his arms. He'd loaded them all in the buggy, then taken them safely to the medical clinic, explaining everything to Lucas when they'd arrived. All she and her father had had to do was sit in the back, keeping *Maam* as still as possible.

Isaac had taken care of the rest.

And he'd sat with her father in the waiting room after Grace had been so foolish and cruel and stormed out. She still hadn't forgiven herself for that and knew it would take a long conversation with *Gott* before she did.

"Soon?" Jane said, scrambling out of Grace's arms, looking up at Isaac now. "How soon?"

"Well…" He knelt down to her, crooking his finger so her sister Leah would join them, too. "You know those brand new kittens in the barn?"

"Uh-huh," Jane said.

"In about three days, they'll be ready to come out onto the front lawn for you to play with. That's about the same time we expect word from your papa telling us when they'll be home from the hospital."

"Three days?" Leah asked, looking at Isaac first and then at Grace. "That's not so long."

"And we can play with the kittens then, too, *jah*?" Jane said, clasping her finger under her chin.

"*Jah*," Grace said, nodding excitedly, hoping to cast all worry from her younger sisters' minds. Once the girls had run off, she turned to Isaac. "*Danke*," she said inside an exhale.

"I know what it's like," Isaac began, "having to

explain something very difficult to a child. There's little else that's worse."

When Grace looked at him he was squinting, and his jaw muscles were working. Of course, she'd wondered about it…why Isaac wasn't married anymore. He didn't seem like a man who would ever get divorced.

Then she recalled what Sadie had said about her mama going to Heaven.

When reality solidly settled on Grace, she looked at Isaac as he stared off into the middle distance, caught up in his own moment of pain. Grace felt the pressure of new tears in her eyes. How had he gotten through it? And how had he explained it to Sadie?

"Would you stay for supper?" Grace asked without thinking.

It took a moment for him to answer, so long that Grace wondered if he'd heard.

"Sure," he finally replied, sliding his hands into his back pockets. "That would be real nice."

"Won't be for a while," Grace added, relieved at his acceptance. "I'll go inside and help Sarah, but would you mind checking on Cincinnati?"

She relaxed when he turned to her with a smile. "Good idea. Mind if I come inside to wash up first?"

Grace smiled back at him, the expression feeling natural. "Of course."

Grace must've had a radar to detect it, because the second they stepped foot inside the house, she felt tension roll over her like a burst of wind, making her smile instantly drop.

"I won't allow you to talk to me that way. It's gone on too long."

Grace froze in place when she realized it was Amos speaking harshly to Sarah, and not the other way around. The couple was standing in the kitchen, not noticing they had an audience. Or not caring.

"It's not *Gott*'s will, nor is it mine," her brother continued.

"Fine," Sarah said, slamming down a small pot. "I'll take to my closet and pray for forgiveness all night. Is that what you want, husband?"

Amos shook his head. "All I want is for you to respect me. I'm tired of coming home and getting unkindness from you every night. And now this thing with my mother—" He stopped speaking and put a fist over his mouth. "I need your support more than ever. I need you, this family needs you."

Grace held her breath, eyes moving to Sarah.

None of her training methods were coming to mind. It was like watching two wild stallions in the heat of battle.

Sarah was wearing a deep frown, eyes narrowed. "I can't remember the last time you *needed* me, Amos." She tossed a dish towel over her shoulder. "You seem to get along just fine without me."

"I don't want—" Amos cut off, probably hearing the floorboards creak. "Oh. Grace," he said, his voice clipped. "Isaac." He nodded politely. "Evening."

"Evening," Isaac said, then cleared his throat.

It was so quiet, Grace could hear her pulse inside her ears. There was so much tension in the air, she almost couldn't move.

"I'm leaving to do the milking," Amos said, not looking at or addressing anyone. "Don't expect me back anytime soon." He put on his hat and, a second later, was out the door.

Grace glanced at Isaac, who looked like he was holding his breath.

"Did you enjoy that?" Sarah turned her back to them then started up the water faucet. A moment later, she shut it off. "You see?" she said, pointing at the front door. "Even when I think I'm trying to do better, I…" She shook her head and hissed a breath out through her teeth. "You all can have supper without me for a change." Sarah untied her apron then went up the stairs without another word.

"I…um, think I should go." Isaac had his hat off and was running his fingers through his hair.

"I don't blame you," Grace replied, feeling tears of embarrassment and frustration burning in her eyes. "I'm sorry you had to see—"

"It's okay," he said, his hand up, palm out. "I'll check on all the horses, so don't worry about that. See you in the morning? I'll get here early."

Grace exhaled, her shoulders slumping the moment Isaac was gone. She was grateful for his tact but was absolutely mortified that he had to witness her family at their worst today. First *Maam* getting hurt and then witnessing front row to Sarah and Amos fighting like stallions brawling for territory.

*What must he think of us?* Grace asked herself as she moved to the stove, seeing what kind of supper Sarah had started.

*What must he think of* me?

She took in a deep breath and held it. She'd felt close to him just a few hours ago. He'd been so incredibly sweet to pray with her like that. No one had ever offered her such a kindness before.

*And then I hugged him— Ach! I couldn't help it!*

Grace shook her head, her shoulders heavy again with burden.

*And then he couldn't get out of here fast enough*, her thoughts added. Not that she'd expect him to stay after that, she just… She just liked it better when he was around.

After giving the boiling sweet potatoes a stir and checking the slices of ham in the oven, Grace sat down at one of the kitchen chairs, put her hands over her face, and allowed her final tears of the day to escape.

# CHAPTER TWENTY-FOUR

Isaac felt terrible for ducking out on Grace, but he could tell she was embarrassed and wouldn't want to talk about it with him. Family issues were private — even more so in Amish communities.

After entering the stables, he went down the line, talking to and petting each *gaul*, but he knew he was no substitute for Grace. She had a special way with animals, there was no doubt about it. Isaac could only wish for such a gift.

"Hallo, good boy," he said, spending an extra few minutes with Cincinnati. "We were going to train you three times today," he continued, scratching the horse behind his ears. "Imagine that, buddy, being with Grace three times in one day." He felt his mouth form into a crooked smile as he dipped his chin. "I think I would've liked that, too." He paused when the horse shook his head. "I hope so, fella. I really do hope everything works out."

Isaac fed the horses, watered and brushed them, hopefully as thoroughly as Grace would. By the time he'd finished, the sun was finally about to set after a very long day. On his way to Scout, he passed by the house. Lights were on in the kitchen but nothing on the second level. Isaac hoped that meant that Sarah was downstairs having supper with the family, maybe even making amends.

For all he knew, however, she could be self-isolating in her room, no one in the house daring to disturb her.

He felt for Grace. She was a kind person, wore her

heart on her sleeve, he suddenly realized. It must've been often depressing to live in a home where you could cut the stress in the air with a knife.

She didn't deserve that. No one did—not even Sarah.

The days were growing longer, more daylight, and as he rode through town, Isaac passed by a few small groups of teenagers who he recognized from church, some on roller skates and some in small courting buggies. He couldn't help smiling, remembering those days.

"Feels like a million years ago," he said to Scout. "A different lifetime, in fact." Yet again, his thoughts wandered back in time.

He should've gotten to know Martha better. Spent more time with her alone, more time with her family. It wasn't until after they were married that he knew what they were really like.

Isaac felt a fist grab his gut. He needed to get Sadie away from them. He needed the money from this job to get him started on their new life as quickly as possible.

That fist in his gut grew larger, gripped tighter when he remembered what he'd heard Grace say earlier that day…that her family needed the money, too, for Eve's operation. Then his thoughts bounced to what John had told him about why he didn't want Grace to be a trainer anymore—how terrified he was that what had happened to Eve could someday happen to Grace. So much so that he'd hoped by hiring Isaac, she'd quit training altogether.

More heaviness sat on his shoulders when he remembered he was not to tell Grace any of that. Isaac knew without a doubt that John loved his daughter, and that his decisions weren't meant to punish her or make her unhappy, but that, as her father, he was doing what he thought was best to protect her.

Isaac felt awful—caught in the middle. There was no good answer, and he had no one to talk to about it. His brain was spinning too fast.

"Evening."

The voice came from out of nowhere, causing Isaac to jump in his saddle.

"Sorry." Lucas waved from his front unlit porch. "Didn't mean to startle you. A voice in the darkness…"

Isaac relaxed. He hadn't realized his detour had wound him all the way to the Brennemans' place. "Never know what's lurking in the bushes in a town like this," he joked, climbing off his horse.

"You looked in deep thought," Lucas said.

"I was." Isaac ran a hand through his hair, scratching the back of his skull.

"Worried about Eve? I heard from Kevin an hour ago. They're still running tests, but Eve is comfortable, and John hasn't left her side." He smiled and shook his head. "The devotion those two have toward each other, it's certainly enviable." He tilted his head. "Not that I envy."

Isaac couldn't help exhaling a snicker. "Never." He sighed and looked up at the sky, the first stars appearing. "It wasn't Eve I was thinking about, but thank you for the update. Does the family know?"

"I called John's phone—Grace still has it. They know."

"Good. That's good."

"So something else is on your mind?"

Isaac wasn't sure what to say. There was a lot sitting on his mind and heart right then, actually, but was he allowed to talk about it? He'd feel like he was prying.

When his answer didn't come quickly enough, Lucas said, "Why don't you come inside for a while? Esther put the *kinnahs* down and I think she's just about to pull a cinnamon cake out of the oven. Please don't make me eat it by myself."

Isaac still didn't reply, unsure of everything.

"Come," Lucas said, reaching out his hand. "Let's be good friends."

Finally Isaac exhaled, a weight lifting off his shoulders. "I'd like that."

Their home was small but comfortable, candles mixed with battery-powered lights giving a homey glow to the room, as did the pile of quilts draped over the living room furniture.

"Have you met Esther?" Lucas asked.

Isaac recognized his wife from church, but they hadn't yet spoken. "Not officially," Isaac said. "Please forgive my intrusion at this hour."

"I had to practically drag him in," Lucas said, coming up behind his wife and giving her a kiss on the cheek.

To Isaac, the gesture looked so sweet, so natural, that he didn't even think about glancing away to give them privacy.

"It's nice to finally meet you in person," Esther said. "Luke told me about what happened with Eve today. Shocking." She put a hand over her heart. "Though something like this was bound to happen sooner or later. She really needs that surgery." She turned to Lucas. "Are you sure the doctors in Hershey won't consider cutting the cost some?" She crossed her arms. "I thought they were eager to work with plain folks."

"I'll keep asking," Lucas said. "But so far it's a no-go. The hospital has a new administrator; things have changed there."

"Well, it's just awful," Esther said. "Don't you think?" She looked at Isaac.

Isaac didn't know what to say. He felt like he had a target on his forehead no matter what he said. *It's his fault*, the target was saying. He's *the reason Eve can't get the surgery*.

"Awful," he said, genuinely agreeing with Esther. Everything about the situation was awful.

"Have a seat," Lucas said to Isaac, gesturing to a chair at the long kitchen table.

"Sure I'm not disturbing you?"

Esther fell into the chair across from Isaac. "My husband was about to serve me dessert," she said, gazing over at Lucas. "He knows it was a long day for me, too."

"Sit," Lucas said.

Isaac decided to give in and relax. After all, hadn't he just been wishing for someone to talk to? Maybe not about what was really on his mind, but with Grace unavailable, he needed another friend.

His thoughts paused for a moment, realizing that he and Grace really were friends now—at least Isaac thought so.

"*Danke*," he said, finally sitting down.

"I heard you have a daughter," Esther said. "Would you pour me some tea?" she asked Lucas. "Tea for you?" she asked Isaac.

"Please," Isaac said. "And yes, my daughter Sadie is six years old."

"Is she in school?"

"Goes to the schoolhouse with the Chupp girls. Her English is coming along. Must have good teachers here."

Esther grinned and looked at Lucas. "See?"

Lucas spread his arms, held breath in his cheeks then blew it out. "What did I say?"

Esther rested an elbow on the table and leaned toward Isaac. "My mother is one of the teachers there. This is her first year. *Someone*—" she shot her husband a look—"thought she might be too old."

"I never said that." Lucas set a plate and fork before Esther and then Isaac. The cinnamon cake smelled scrumptious. "What I said was she was used to homeschooling her own *kinnahs* and might not be able to keep up with an entire classroom."

"Anyway," Esther said, "*Maam* teaches English. I'm glad Sadie is learning well."

"Thank your mother for me," Isaac said. "Sadie can be a handful."

"What six-year-old isn't?" Esther said, pouring the tea. "How is it working at the Zooks? Sarah's my sister, you know."

Feeling a sudden heat behind his ears, Isaac swallowed then took a bite of cake. "This is delicious." He took another bite—totally stalling. "I like John Zook a lot, very good man," he said, his mouth half full. "Eve is a sweetheart, Amos seems like a hardworking fella, though I haven't spent much time with him, and the two little girls are so good to Sadie. She loves playing with them."

"Notice how he dodged the second part?" Lucas said, lacing his fingers under his chin.

Isaac stared down at his plate for a moment. "Wh-which part?"

Lucas burst out laughing.

"I know, I know," Esther said, fanning a hand in the air toward her husband. "Sarah can be a little much. Try sharing a bedroom with her. I think I paid the highest price when we were children."

"She takes care of the house very well," Isaac insisted, racking his brain for another compliment that sounded genuine. "And she's an excellent cook."

Esther snorted. "No she's not. She's a terrible cook." She sat up straight, covering her mouth with both hands. "Sorry, that was horrible of me to say. My sister is talented in *other* ways—let's leave it at that."

"So…" Lucas finally took a seat. "You mentioned John and Eve, Amos and the girls." He paused and took a bite. "But you failed to say anything about Grace."

"Oh." Isaac went to take another bite of cake, but he'd already used that stalling tactic once. "Grace is…" His brain that had been void of words was suddenly full of them. "Grace is…a very talented horse trainer."

"And?" Esther said.

Isaac began playing with his fork.

*And…she has the sweetest smile and warm hands, a* Gott-*loving humble heart, and she has about the most beautiful hair I've ever seen.*

"And she's a pleasure to work with. Taught me a few tricks of the trade I didn't know."

"You like…*working* with her?" Esther said, eyes narrowed.

*"Jah."* Isaac nodded, afraid to confess more.

"Well, it's a wonder to me she isn't married," Lucas said. "Baffling why no one's snatched her up."

"Snatched," Esther said, shaking her head. "Make her sound like a chicken's egg waiting to be gathered. She's my sister Evie's age—or maybe a bit older," she said to Isaac. "Her group is always playing volleyball or tag, staying late after Sunday services for games and singing. Grace was never like that."

"She has her horses," Lucas said.

Esther sighed. "I suppose."

"When did she start training?" Isaac asked. It seemed like a safe subject.

"I don't know, exactly," Esther said. "But every time *Maam* and I went for a visit, Grace was outside either riding one or behind one teaching it to pull a plow."

"She's got energy," Isaac said, unable to hold back a smile. "She's up before the crack of dawn, taking care of all those horses. John doesn't seem to train much anymore—at least not when I'm there. It's all her."

He felt another fist in his gut when he thought about how John's hiring him hadn't really been necessary. Just because her father was worried that she might get injured didn't mean she couldn't successfully train Sin all by herself.

"What was she like before her mother got hurt?" Isaac asked, wondering if more information would stop him from feeling guilty. "Seems John is by Eve's side a good part of every day. Not that I blame him. I just wonder if Grace used to have more time to herself." He paused and stared at the wall across from him. "And what about Collin Chupp? She claims she's never gone on a date with him, but he practically swears they're getting married someday—though I can't picture Grace with a man like that. Nay, she needs someone more sure of himself, a man who can keep up with her, but also give her space when she needs it. She's got this strange self-doubt thing." He shook his head. "I still don't understand where that comes from."

He laughed under his breath, picturing her the

other day with her hair down. Then almost feeling what it was like to hold her in his arms.

"Huh." Esther leaned forward, elbows on the table, holding her cup in two hands. "You seem mighty interested in Grace."

Isaac felt his face get hot; the back of his neck was suddenly sweating, too.

When he opened his mouth, hoping some kind of rebuttal would fall out, Esther winked at him, then merely looked off to the side, taking another sip from her cup.

# CHAPTER TWENTY-FIVE

"Here's your oatmeal. Is that enough?"

"*Too* much," little Jane complained.

Grace dabbed at her forehead with a dish towel. "Well, eat as much as you can; you don't want to be late for school. You too, Leah. Don't forget your lunch boxes."

"Can't I just stay home today?" Jane frowned down at her breakfast. "Maybe I'm sick like Aunt Sarah."

"Your aunt's not sick," Grace said as she wiped off the counter. "She's just…tired. Hopefully, she'll be downstairs by the time you get home from school." She glanced toward the stairs, wishing her sister-in-law would appear like magic.

But she hadn't seen Sarah or Amos in person since their argument. Though Amos had left dirty dishes in the sink that Grace discovered in the morning, and Sarah had left a pile of washing on the bathroom floor.

*If I can just get the girls washed, dressed, fed, and off to school*, Grace thought as she tightened her apron, *then I'll consider this morning a success.*

After Isaac had left last night, Grace had sat sulkily at the table, wishing things were different. But that had lasted only a few minutes. Never one to mope, she'd gone to work finishing supper, getting the *kinnahs* to bed, then tidying the kitchen.

It had been too long since she'd been in charge of the housekeeping. A part of her almost missed it, but then when she'd taken the leftover scraps of food out to the pigs and heard Isaac in with the horses, Grace's heart longed to be there more than anywhere.

"*Mach's gut!*" Grace said, kissing her little sisters on the tops of their sweet little bonnets before they took off running to meet their friends. "Happy learning!"

"*Guder mariye,*" Isaac said, stepping up onto the porch.

"Hi," Grace said. It surprised her how happy she was to see him, but she also still felt a bit shamed by her family's behavior last night and couldn't quite look him in the eyes.

"Horses are fed. I worked with the one at the end."

"Pete?"

"*Jah.* I knew you wanted to get him behind a buggy by today. He was skittish at first, but after a while, he seemed to like it. Calmed right down once at a trot. Sin's already been out in the back pasture with a few of the other horses." Isaac smiled. "He seems to have taken a fancy to Honey Pot. I had to break the bad news that they're both geldings."

Grace blinked in amazement. "You did all that this morning?"

"I told you last night that I would get here early." He leaned against the railing. "'Course I didn't sing to each of them like you do. Or pray with them and recite scriptures." He grinned. "I'm sure they're all missing their daily devotionals with you."

Grace wasn't sure if he was teasing her or being genuine, but either way, she couldn't help giggling. "It's not my fault that I love them so much."

"They love you, too." He took off his hat. "You can't imagine all the frowns I got when they saw *I* was the one giving them their morning oats."

Grace laughed again, her load already feeling lighter. "Have you had breakfast? There's oatmeal inside. Fruit and yogurt. Fresh baked raisin bread."

Isaac lifted his eyebrows. "Did *you* or Sarah make the bread dough?"

"Well, Sarah did a few days ago—but I baked it this morning!" Grace said, enjoying their easy banter.

Isaac laughed, his hazel eyes squinting. "*Danke*, but I've already eaten. Besides, is it safe to go in there?"

Grace followed his gaze to the front door, shame about last night returning. "I'm so sorry you had to see that," she said, lowering her eyes, feeling her cheeks getting hot. "I'm completely mortified."

"Why?" She heard Isaac moving closer to her. "It wasn't your fault. Nothing you did."

"I know," she said. "But it was still painful to know someone else witnessed it. And then you left so fast—"

"I only did that because I could see how embarrassed you were. I didn't want to add to it."

Grace looked up to see Isaac's kind eyes watching her, his brows bent in compassion. "Won't you at least come in for coffee?" she asked, not wanting him to leave just yet. "I see we got a bit of rain last night; you must be cold."

"I'm not," Isaac said, "but I'd still love to have coffee with you." Without waiting for her, he walked into the house, slipping off his boots at the door.

Grace pulled down her favorite blue pottery mug and filled it with coffee. "Here's the cream," she said, handing it to him. "And sugar's on the counter, though I prefer brown sugar in mine."

"Really?" Isaac asked, holding the mug in his hands.

"Only if it's homemade, though. Not that stuff from the store. The molasses has to be fresh." She pushed a small white porcelain bowl toward him. "Try it."

He took a scoop with a spoon and was about to add it to his coffee when he suddenly froze. "You're not tricking me like with the lemonade?"

Grace's chest vibrated, holding back a laugh. "I promise—watch." She added a heaping spoonful of brown sugar, stirred it around, then took a long drink. She closed her eyes, the comforting liquid filling her mouth then going down her throat, warming her entire body.

"Judging by your expression," Isaac said, adding some to his own coffee, "this I have to try." He took a drink, then his expression turned puzzled, like he didn't know quite what to think. "It's good," he finally said. "Tastes like…like…"

"Christmastime?"

His eyes went wide. "Exactly." He took another long sip. "Mmm. That's very good."

Grace couldn't help smiling, enjoying a moment of normalcy, two people having coffee, the house quiet, chores done. And it didn't feel strange in the least that it was with Isaac—the very person who'd been a thorn in her side from the first week she knew him.

*How things have changed so quickly…evolved*, she thought as she took another sip. *I no longer feel resentful toward him. He's turned out to be an excellent training partner and…and even a good friend.* She was so peaceful in the thought that she absolutely refused to remind herself of all the negative things about him being in her life in the first place.

Perhaps *Gott* was softening her heart. And wasn't that more important than anything?

"I heard from your father," Isaac said.

"When?" Grace asked, setting down her mug.

"Earlier this morning. He has my phone number."

"Are they coming home?" Her heart skipped a beat in hope.

"Nay." Isaac shook his head. "He thinks not for a few more days. But he did ask me to take care of some things for the farm. He needs supplies. Gave me a list of items from around town, a few to get way out past Nickel Mines, but I know somewhere I can get everything in one place, and for a much better price."

"Isaac." Grace chuckled inside her throat, a little taken aback. "You don't have to do all that. Papa hired you for one job, not to hold the whole place together while he's gone."

She watched as the corners of his mouth turned down into a frown. "It must sound a mite strange to you, but this place is beginning to feel like home to me—maybe not living at the Chupps, but working here on this farm. And your father has become more than just my boss. If a friend of mine—or anyone, for that matter—asks for help and I can give it…" He held his hands out to his sides.

It did sound strange to Grace. But on the other hand, she was beginning to see that kindness and sacrifice were part of Isaac's nature. He served when he could and helped wherever it was needed.

"That's very kind of you. I don't know what to say."

"Say you'll let me."

"Of course. *Danke*." She exhaled a little laugh. "So you were saying you know a place where you can get everything at once? Where?"

"Have you ever heard of a mud sale?"

"*Jah*," Grace said slowly, trying to think. "It's a... big auction, mostly Amish and Mennonites. I've never been."

"Englishers attend, too. We buy, sell, and trade with them just as naturally. And it's more than just an auction. Every kind of country vendor is there. Farming equipment, buggies, food, sweets, quilts, books, hats, and boots. Sometimes in the afternoons after the bidding, folks hold friendly three-legged races or other contests. It's always an exciting day."

"Sounds really fun," Grace said, almost picturing the place. "But I thought they're held only once a year and earlier in the spring."

"There are a few throughout the year, some bigger than others. This is one of the biggest. It's held twice a year."

"And it's tomorrow? How far away?"

"Reading," Isaac said. "Three hour buggy ride each direction."

"All that way? You think it's worth it?"

"Definitely. Especially if you've never been." He paused and lifted his eyebrows, smiling at her.

"Oh, *I* can't go with you," she said firmly, though in her heart she suddenly yearned to. "I can't be away from home for that long, not all day, what with how things are right now. Who'd cook and watch after Jane and Leah?"

"*I* would."

They both whipped around to see Sarah standing halfway down the stairs, still in her nightgown and dressing robe, hair covered with a scarf.

"Oh, uh, morning," Grace said, trying to sound cheerful.

"Morning," Sarah said, her voice tired and grumpy, but at least she was out of bed. "It's fine with me if you're gone tomorrow. Won't matter much to my routine."

"So you're…" Grace lifted her eyebrows. "Up?"

"Of course I am. See?" She motioned at the fact that she was standing. "Up."

Grace blinked a few times, not allowing herself to smile yet.

"Mud sales are also fundraisers for the county's volunteer fire departments," Isaac said, tapping his chin. "I'm pretty sure there are a few men in Honey Brook who are involved in that."

"*Jah*." Grace blinked again. "Samuel Chupp and Jeremiah Brenneman. And Lucas. I'm sure there're more."

"Just go then," Sarah said, pouring herself a cup of coffee. "I know you're dying to."

"Well…" Grace felt a smile spread across her face at the prospect of a new adventure.

"I'll be here at five in the morning," Isaac said, interpreting her expression as affirmation. "We'll take care of the horses, set them up for the day, then be on our way by six. Home by eleven?" He glanced at Sarah as if asking permission.

"Heavens, I'll be dead asleep by then." Sarah took her mug and headed toward the stairs. "Just don't make a ruckus when you get back."

"I'll take that as a yes," Isaac said, looking at Grace eagerly.

Grace couldn't hold back her smile this time. "Yes!"

# CHAPTER TWENTY-SIX

Isaac was pretty sure he knew the way. Still, he tucked the map to Reading into the pocket of his black vest. It was still dark and calm as he drove the buggy toward the Zook farm. He couldn't help grinning as he recalled the look in Grace's eyes, how excited she'd been about going to the mud sale. He would enjoy her company, for sure, but that hadn't been why he'd invited her.

She deserved a day away, a chance to relax and have fun. She was a hard worker—he admired that about her—and a good sister and daughter. But the last few days, weeks even, Isaac knew had been extra stressful for her. What bothered him worse was discovering that a lot of it had to do with money.

Amish were never rich, never seemed to have enough money for extras. Humility and self-reliance was the culture. Isaac loved this about the community, but he knew money issues could make even the humblest Christian feel helpless, hopeless, and unworthy. Grace Zook should never feel that way. Especially because of something that was in no way her fault.

"We'll just have to show her a great day," Isaac said, moving the reins. Samuel Chupp had been generous enough to lend him two of his horses for the trip. Six hours might've been too much even for Scout.

When he got to the farm, there were no lights on in the house, though he noticed a soft glow coming from the stables.

"I'm ready," Grace said as soon as he entered, touching her forehead to Cincinnati's. She was in a light purple dress, black apron, black pullover sweater, and slim black athletic shoes. She looked as clean and fresh as she had on preaching Sunday.

"How long have you been up?" Isaac asked, offering Cincinnati his own scratches and tender pats.

"I didn't want to be late," was all Grace gave as an answer. "I could barely sleep last night."

Isaac grinned. "Excited, *jah*?"

Grace's face brightened. "Oh, *jah*. Am I dressed okay?"

It wasn't customary in their culture to aim attention on what someone was wearing...clothing and everything one owned was to show modesty, obedience, and devotion to *Gott*.

Still, Isaac couldn't help admiring how Grace looked. Her excited smile and eager bright blue eyes only enhanced her appearance. And for a moment, he couldn't believe he was going to be spending the whole day with her.

"Fine." Isaac cleared his throat, for his answer was nowhere sufficient. "Fine. You'll fit right in. No one will know it's your first time at a mud sale."

Grace clasped her fingers together as if in prayer, but then let out a little squeal of delight and turned in a circle, acting as thrilled as Sadie might if she saw a white bunny in a field.

"I'm ready," she said. "Can we go now?" Isaac glanced down the line of horses. "I told you," Grace added, "everything's done. I might not have spent as much time with Honey Pot as I usually do, but he'll be fine. Amos is letting them into the field after he finishes milking."

"You really did cover everything."

Grace only smiled then walked to the porch and grabbed a backpack. "Supplies," she said as she climbed aboard the awaiting buggy.

*I'm definitely going to show her a good time today*, Isaac thought as he climbed in, sitting next to her. It wasn't a big buggy to hold a family, so their shoulders couldn't help touching. Grace sent him a little glance, then set her gaze forward. The woman was ready to go, all right.

Neither of them spoke until they were almost out of town. Isaac didn't know what was on Grace's mind — maybe too excited or nervous to talk — but Isaac couldn't help catching that same lavender scent he'd noticed the other day.

*Maybe she uses a special soap*, he mused. *Perhaps one of the kinds Esther Brenneman makes.* The idea made him think of his visit with them the other night. How considerate Lucas had been to invite him in, even at that late hour. They'd been having such a pleasant conversation, then Isaac didn't know what happened. Suddenly, he'd asked twenty questions about Grace.

*"You seem very interested in her,"* Esther had said, flat out. He'd felt the blood drain from his face and couldn't seem to find anywhere to look. Probably sensing Isaac's discomfort at such a blatant statement, Lucas had jumped in about a new type of hay he'd just ordered from Car-Mar-Farm. After that, it seemed that Esther couldn't keep from snickering about something every time their eyes had met.

"I think you missed a turn."

Grace's voice snapped Isaac awake from his thoughts. Yep, he'd most certainly missed a turn. "Shortcut," he said, lifting a crooked smile.

The sun was rising, and with it came the sounds of

other buggies and working farms, even a few cars driving safely past them.

"What is Sadie doing today?" Grace asked as she tucked her hands inside the sleeves of her sweater. Isaac was wearing a heavy black coat over his vest and white shirt, but hadn't realized being out so early this morning might be cold.

"I think there's a blanket in the back," he said.

"There is." Grace nodded. "Under the bench seat. I've been in this buggy a few times."

"With Collin Chupp?" he blurted without thinking, feeling a tightness in his chest that he didn't like at all.

"Maybe," Grace said, her blue eyes turned to him. "Or maybe with his mother. And I was asking about Sadie. It's a Saturday, so no school. What does she do when you're not home?"

"Actually," Isaac said after a few deep breaths, "Esther Brenneman is taking her for the day. Apparently, they have friends who raise pigmy goats as pets."

"Oh my goodness!" Grace gasped. "In Honey Brook?"

"Few miles north of town," he replied. Then, noticing how she'd turned to face him, excitement in her expression, he added, "Maybe you and I can go with them next time."

"I'd love that," she said. A moment later, she laughed under her breath. "I'm not all that natural with children, but your daughter's adorable, by the way."

Isaac smiled and bowed his head. "*Danke*. She hasn't had the easiest life thus far. I pray her future is much better."

Grace didn't reply, didn't speak at all. And when

Isaac glanced her way, he saw that she was frowning, chewing on a fingernail.

"Are you okay?" he asked.

"*Jah*." She nodded. "She said something to me the first time she was over playing with my sisters."

"Sadie did?"

"Something about how she hopes you two will have a house of your own again, and I guess she must've overheard you talking about the people you were living with in Silver Springs. She said you didn't want to stay there."

As he listened, Isaac's throat grew tight, and he pulled at the collar of his shirt. "I should've been more careful about that," he said quietly, after a long pause. "She doesn't need to know anything about… that." He heard himself exhale loudly, mostly in frustration at himself.

Grace didn't say anything but drew something out of her backpack. "Hot coffee with brown sugar," she said, passing him a thermos. Her gaze on him was so sympathetic, as if sensing he needed extra kindness.

"*Danke*," he said, taking it, though instead of going for a drink, he put it on his lap. "After my wife passed away," he began slowly, while staring at the tips of the horses' ears, "I had to sell our house. The bank would've repossessed it in time because I couldn't work as much—couldn't be away from home. Sadie was only a baby." He kept his gaze straight ahead. "Most of my siblings live in Silver Springs, but they all have very busy lives, large families. I didn't want to impose on them." He pressed his lips together. "I didn't have much choice other than for Sadie and me to move in with Martha's folks."

"That was your wife's name?" Grace asked, her voice gentle. "Martha?"

"Aye. We married young." He paused to chuckle. "Young even by Amish standards. We grew up in the same village, but I didn't know her family very well, though they seemed like normal folks." He paused again. "I was naive. I didn't understand yet that appearances can be deceiving."

When his breathing became noticeably heavy and he didn't continue speaking, Grace asked, "Would you like me to drive for a while?"

Isaac focused on the road, realizing they'd already traveled quite far, and he hadn't been paying attention. The street sign ahead showed that they weren't lost, at least. But still, he couldn't get carried away by his thoughts like that again, dwell on a subject so hard on his heart.

But then he looked at Grace—the woman who somehow in just a few weeks had become a good friend to him, someone he knew he could talk to.

"I was working long hours back then, sometimes training ten horses at the same time. Business was getting better as my reputation became more widespread, but Sadie still needed looking after. I couldn't be both mother and father to her then. There just wasn't time."

"I understand," Grace said. "I'd think her *gross-daadi* and *mammi* were taking care of her?"

"My in-laws," Isaac said after taking a beat, "they aren't the people I thought they were. I want Sadie to be raised in a true Christian home, full of kindness and love, forgiveness and obedience. Just because a family may appear to be all those things doesn't mean that sometimes they're not." He took off his hat and massaged the back of his neck. "The words I heard Sadie repeating—my innocent daughter." He shook his head, anger brewing in his heart again.

Suddenly, he felt pressure on his arm. When he looked down, Grace's hand was there, wrapping around it just above his elbow. The simple touch was so calming to him, so welcome, that he felt no shame in continuing.

"We can't go back to that house," Isaac added. "I won't allow it. A few months ago, I decided that I'd do whatever it takes to earn enough to move her out of that environment for good. Some Mennonite friends of mine helped me build a website, get a phone, and learn how to email. That brought in more business, but not enough." He sighed. "I needed to figure out how to reach the next level, find a higher level of clientele."

Lost in his thoughts again, Isaac balled his hands into fists and squeezed; otherwise, he might be tempted to let out a yell at the top of his lungs.

"And that's why you came to Honey Brook." Grace's voice was soft, but there was a ring of understanding behind it, distracting him enough to feel calm again. "To train Cincinnati. To use that income to buy a house and also get the Englisher customers, like Travis Carlson said."

"Grace." Isaac didn't know what to say. She was exactly right, although now his motivations and expectations were suddenly muddled.

She exhaled softly. "I understand. We both really need that money. Me for *Maam*'s surgery, and you to make a better life for Sadie. It's a problem."

He nodded, guilt giving him a slight headache, but he was also relieved that she finally knew where he was coming from. Though that didn't solve anything.

"Can we still be friends?" she asked.

The question made Isaac chuckle. When he didn't answer, Grace gave his arm a little squeeze.

"I really hope we can," she added.

It wasn't until right then—at the first thought that something like this might cause them to not be friends—that Isaac realized how important Grace's friendship was to him. He felt comfortable sharing with her…even something as personal as the situation with Sadie.

But socializing with her, chitchatting during their many training sessions together, had also become vital to his happiness. He loved being around her, teaching her. Learning from her.

Feeling her hand on his arm.

"You offered to drive earlier," he said, needing to clear his head. Thinking about Grace Zook in that way wasn't going to solve anything, either. "Do you mind?"

Grace lowered her chin and looked at him through her eyelashes. "Please," she scoffed lightly. "Didn't I tell you once that I probably drive a buggy better than you?"

Isaac laughed, then slowed the buggy to a stop. Normally, if they were going to switch seats, one of them would climb out of the buggy while the other would slide over. Instead, Isaac simply leaned back and placed his hands on Grace's waist, pulling her to stand then across his lap as he slid over.

"Mercy," she whispered after taking in a sharp breath.

"Did I shock you?"

A hand was at her throat, shoulders rising and falling with her quick breaths, keeping her eyes away from him. Isaac reckoned she would be just fine.

"I'm sure you know that the Ordnungs in Honey Brook and Silver Springs vary a bit, *jah*? Did you know the courting allowances are quite different, too?" he asked conversationally, teasingly, as he handed her the reins.

"N-no," Grace said, still staring straight ahead.

"We're allowed to touch, hold hands, even before the first date if there's a known intention between the couple. And when you're dating, me touching you like I just did…" He paused, waiting for her reaction, not disappointed when she sent him a lightning-fast glance. "Well, that'd be perfectly acceptable."

"We're not…dating," Grace said, finally turning to face him. Her cheeks were pink, as Isaac knew they would be.

"True." He tapped his chin with an index finger, teasing her again. "Nor has it ever once crossed my mind."

# CHAPTER TWENTY-SEVEN

"You're a very wicked man, Isaac King," Grace said after snorting a laugh, swatting him on the arm in a playful way, like back when she'd thought he was married. Once she realized he was teasing her, she managed to pull herself together. Though it might've been difficult getting the memory out of her mind of him holding her around the waist like that, his hands strong and confident as they'd switched seats.

"Don't know what you're referring to," Isaac said, moving the front of his hat down over his eyes. "Less than a mile now," he added, pointing to a makeshift street sign, advertising the West Reading Auction and Mud Sale.

Seeing the sign, Grace's heart began beating faster, excitement flowing through her body. "How fast do these horses go?" she said, flicking the reins, noticing the number of buggies suddenly on the road with them.

*Are they* all *on the way to the big event?*

Isaac tapped the face of his watch. "It's barely eight thirty," he said. "Don't worry, they won't dare start without us."

Grace couldn't help giggling as she carefully guided their buggy behind the one in front of them, the procession of trucks, buggies, and carriages forming an organized line. The marginal wait to enter the huge grassy field—the temporary parking lot—was almost more than she could take. She filled the time by asking Isaac every question she could think of about what to expect… Where should they go first? Eat first? See first?

"Over there," Isaac said once her questions ran out. "We'll water the horses then let them loose in the pasture with the others."

As soon as she parked the buggy, Isaac taking care of the horses, Grace felt almost overwhelmed by her surroundings. She'd attended a wedding once for people from two different villages. It had seemed everyone from both communities was there. But that was nothing compared to the number of people at the mud sale.

And it wasn't just the crowds, but so many different cultures all in one place. Mixed among the many Englisher trucks and trailers, she saw plenty of gray Amish carriages, more than a few market wagons—indicating that bishops or preachers were there—rows of black buggies driven by the Mennonites, and even a spattering of spring wagons, which were traditionally driven by youth in the county.

"Ya doing okay?" Isaac asked, coming up from behind.

"Why?" Grace asked, wondering if she was standing out.

"That smile on your face." He pointed at her mouth. "I wasn't sure if it was because you're happy, or if two hummingbirds were holding up the corners of your lips."

Grace threw her hands over her grinning mouth. "Happy," she said.

As they neared the entrance, Grace counted four large stages, two livestock rings, plows and other farming equipment lined up in rows, and at least half a dozen brightly colored tents set up right in the middle.

"Heavens," she said under her breath, trying to take it all in. A group of children ran by, none of them over ten years old, some in solid colored dresses, others in calico. Grace couldn't help wondering if they were all from one family, or even from the same Anabaptist sect.

Maybe strangers were already making new friends at the mud sale. Her heart warmed at the idea.

"Anything catching your eye?" Isaac asked, unbuttoning his heavy black coat, as the air was finally warming.

Grace could only shake her head. "I'm speechless," she finally said, turning in a small circle.

"Well, I'm feeling pretty hungry after that long drive. How about food?"

"Aye. Can we go there?" Straight ahead, she saw a sign selling Pennsylvania Dutch chicken corn soup. "That sounds delicious."

"Judging by the long line," Isaac said, "It must be."

"Do you mind?"

He smiled and shook his head. "It's where I was going to suggest we head first. Chicken corn soup is a staple at these auctions. Why don't you stand in line? I'll meet you there in a few minutes."

"Alone?" Grace said, suddenly feeling like an ant in a world of giants.

"Grace Zook," Isaac said, crossing his arms. "I've never known you to be afraid of anything."

"I'm not…afraid," she said, trying to shoo away the nervous butterflies in her stomach. Without another word, she marched right over to the soup line and took her place at the end.

She watched Isaac laugh, wave a goodbye, then disappear into the crowd.

Grace took in a deep breath, begging herself to have courage. She'd faced down more than a few aggressive four-legged animals in her life, and Isaac was right: she'd never backed away.

*This is a new experience for me*, she silently told herself. *A new place. That's all.*

"Hey."

Grace turned around to see two English women in line behind her. Youngish—maybe slightly younger than herself. They were both dressed in pants, tall rubber boots, and sweaters that zipped up the front. The dark-haired woman's boots were bright pink.

"*Guder daag*," she replied out of politeness, unconsciously touching the front of her plain black sweater.

"Have you ever had this soup before?" the other one asked. She had short blonde hair that fell to different lengths on either side of her face.

"Nay." Grace shook her head. She was about to turn around, signifying an end to their conversation, but wasn't this her day to try new and exciting things? "But I hear it's very good," she added, trying to speak clear English.

"*Gut*," the blonde said with a smile. "I like how you say that. Your accent is super beautiful."

Grace couldn't help smiling, for it was *they* who had the accents. "*Danke*—thank you," she said.

"I've never been to one of these," the dark-haired girl said as she rubbed her hands together.

"Neither have I," Grace said. "It's a bit…ah… astonishing, to be honest."

The blonde elbowed her friend. "See, Lola, I'm not the only one who's freaking out." She paused and swiveled her head around, eyes wide. "I'm afraid I'll get lost."

"We're from DC," the other one said, as the line began to move. Lola—that was her name. "We're here on vacation. Well—not really vacation. I'm rushing

Sigma Delta Tau at Temple this fall. They usually don't take upperclassmen, but I really wanna get in. My mom and Aunt Ashlee were both Sig Delts, so I'm practically a legacy."

"I told you, that doesn't matter," the blonde said to her friend. "Bethany Ann and Tyler's girlfriend are both on the admission board." She tucked some hair behind one ear. "It's grades and extracurricular. You shouldn't have quit cheer last year."

"Geez, Hollis, don't you think I know?"

The girls were talking so fast that Grace almost couldn't keep up. Temple, she knew, was a college in Philadelphia. They must've been talking about classes they were taking.

"Anyway," Hollis continued, addressing Grace. "It's not a vacation. My cousin's from Philly and they own land out here, so we decided to take a road trip."

"*Jah*. Fun," Grace offered when she'd stopped talking. "We road trip, too. 'Course it takes a lot longer for us."

There was a heavy pause, and Grace hoped she wasn't going to have to explain her little joke.

"Ohmigosh! That's hilarious!" Lola grabbed onto her friend's arm and they both dissolved in laughter.

"Yeah, because you don't drive cars!" Hollis added, laughing so hard that tears were clinging to her long, dark eyelashes. "You're so *clever*—that means like smart-funny. How long did it take you to get here today?"

"Almost three hours," Grace said, nearing the counter to order their food. "I don't know how many miles, but I'm sure it would take less than half the time in a car."

"So, you came in one of those horse-drawn buggies?" Hollis gestured toward the parking lot.

"Aye." Grace nodded. "I even drove half the time."

"Whoooooa…" The girls said in unison, gazing at Grace with matching expressions of amazement. Grace was tempted to add that she'd been a horse trainer for most of her life but didn't want to brag.

"That is so dang cool," Lola said.

"Yeah," her friend added. "*Majorly* impressed, here. I love your top. Is it homemade?"

Grace smiled and ran her hands down the sleeves of her sweater, feeling its softness. "My *mammi* knit it for my mother when she was my age. *Mammi*—that means grandma."

"Oh, awesome."

"I like your boots," Grace said to Lola, returning the compliment.

"*Danke*," she said with a little smile, then grabbed Grace's arm. "Is it okay if I say that?"

Grace laughed. "Of course!"

"Hiya." Isaac was suddenly beside her, sliding in to take his place right at her side, causing Grace to take in a breath of surprise. "Here. I knew the line would take a while, so I thought we could split this in the meantime." He handed her a sticky bun wrapped in a napkin. It was still warm. "Got extra napkins in my pocket."

"*Danke*," Grace said, her heart warming at his thoughtfulness.

"Ohmigosh… That is soooo sweeeet." Hollis was gazing at them, her hands pressed over her heart. "Did you see that, Lola?"

"Yes. And I totally just died a little." She leaned over to speak quietly to her friend. "He's a total hottie."

"Um, hello, yeah, like I didn't notice that small fact."

Isaac looked at Grace, confused amusement in his eyes. "You've been making friends," he said, leaning down to her, speaking Pennsylvania Dutch. He was so close that Grace felt his warm breath against her face.

"How long have you been together?" Lola asked.

"Do you have kids? I bet they're adorable."

It took a moment for Grace to register what they were talking about. She lifted her eyes to Isaac, who was looking down at her, eyebrows bent.

Simultaneously, they stepped away from each other.

"Friends," Grace said to them, pointing back and forth at herself and Isaac. "Just friends."

"Noooo." Lola said with a big frown, her shoulders slumping.

"Truly?" Hollis added. "That breaks my heart. Are either of you with anyone else?"

"Married, you mean?" Grace asked. "Nay. Single."

"Ah!" Lola perked up. "Well then. It might totally happen." She narrowed her eyes and nodded sagely. "I have a feeling about you two. Oh! You're next in line!"

"It was nice visiting with you," Grace said, smiling at both of them. "It made the time go by."

"I was afraid you wouldn't want to talk to us," Hollis said. "Gunner's brother said Amish people don't mingle with anyone else. But then we got in line behind you and you looked so friendly, and…" She lifted her shoulders. "We decided to try."

Grace felt a bigger smile spreading across her face. "I'm so glad you did. I hope you have a wonderful day." She turned to Isaac, who'd already ordered two cups of soup.

"Want crackers?" he asked.

"Sure," Grace said, feeling sunny beams from

heaven shining down.

She felt good inside and gratified she'd decided to engage with the English ladies. Being with mostly plain folk made her sometimes shy around other types of people. But they'd been very respectful to her, interested, and so amusing.

"Bye," Hollis said, waving her fingers as they walked away.

*They thought we were a couple*, Grace couldn't help remembering as they strolled to a picnic table. Was the assumption impertinent? Or had they seen something in how they behaved together?

"You have a crumb right there." Isaac reached out and touched the corner of her mouth with his pinkie finger.

At the touch, Grace felt a wave of heat gush through her chest, sending tingles down her arms and hands, leaving a strange sort of giddiness in her head. It was the same kind of feeling she'd had when he'd shown her his breaking style, and then again when he'd held her around the waist when they'd switched seats in the buggy.

When Grace realized she'd never felt that way before, the tiniest voice in the back of her mind wondered if that might be how it felt when you were falling for someone.

# CHAPTER TWENTY-EIGHT

Isaac knew bringing Grace here had been an inspired idea. He just hadn't realized how much fun *he* would have, too. If they weren't listening to one of the many auction callers, or snacking on a funnel cake, they were laughing or pointing out funny things to each other. Grace had taken to the mud sale like a fish to water.

Every so often, he worried that John wouldn't approve of Isaac inviting his daughter to spend the day with him. But he managed to block that out of his head every time he saw Grace smile.

"What do you think of that one?"

"Uh-uh." Grace tilted her head. "See the sway in his back? I wouldn't bid more than fifty."

They were standing front row at the fence, arms resting on the top rung, watching the horses up for auction being paraded in and out of the ring. It was almost one p.m., and the chilly start to the day had turned quite warm. Isaac had already taken off his coat and left it in their buggy, leaving him in his best white shirt and black vest.

Grace had removed her black sweater and tied it around her waist. It wasn't common for an Amish woman to openly display her figure in public or in private, but she'd told Isaac how special the sweater was to her and she didn't want to risk it being stolen.

Isaac knew her decision wasn't out of vanity. Though he'd been fighting an inward battle with himself to stop noticing the curves of her body. It made him remember how he'd touched her in the buggy when they'd switched seats. Despite what he knew was right, it made him want to touch her like that again.

"Pretty," Grace said when a rusty-brown American saddlebred mare trotted into the ring. Her mane was dark brown and she had a white splotch on her forehead.

"Remind you of someone?" Isaac asked.

Grace smiled and dipped her chin. "I miss him. Is that silly?" She was wearing dark sunglasses that she'd purchased at a stand, so Isaac couldn't read her eyes. But he was pretty sure they'd be rimmed with sentimental tears.

"He's a good boy, our Cincinnati," he said. "I miss him, too. We'll get to those three training sessions tomorrow."

When she turned to examine the mare, Isaac kept his eyes on her profile. From personal experience, he already knew her skin was soft and warm and sometimes smelled of lavender. He could sketch her smile blindfolded, and the blueness of her eyes could be matched only by the heavenly sky—a work of art painted by *Gott*.

"I heard that. Are you bored?" she asked, suddenly turning to him.

Isaac flinched, realizing he'd just…sighed.

Sighed while looking at her. While thinking about what a special woman she was. How he couldn't get her out of his mind lately no matter what the distraction.

"Nay, uh…" He ran a fist under his chin, realizing the danger he'd put himself in. "Just admiring the… the *gaul*. It's going to get top bid."

"How can you tell?" Grace rested her chin on her hands. "I can barely understand him. Is that English or Dutch? Sounds like gibberish to me."

She was obviously referring to the auctioneer. He was an Amish man with some kind of microphone attached to his head. His voice was speedy singsong, the typical rushed rhythm of an experienced auctioneer.

"You have to let your brain go kind of soft," he said. "You'll pick up the cadence after a while."

"*Jah*," Grace said. "And if I were asleep, I'd probably understand him even better."

Isaac laughed, always enjoying her little jokes.

"*Sold!*" The auctioneer banged a gavel on his table and the crowd around them erupted in cheers. An older Amish man near the front lifted his arms over his head as if he'd won a grand prize.

"How much did she sell for?" Grace asked.

"Uhhh." Isaac struggled to remember the last bid he'd registered. But the auctioneer had already moved on to the next horse, his singsong rhythm over the speakers making it impossible for Isaac to think.

"I missed it, too," he admitted. "Must be out of practice. Want to walk around?"

Grace's face brightened and she gripped the strap of her bag. "I should pick up a little something special for the girls—oh! and I saw a booth back there that sells essential oils."

Isaac grinned and shook his head. "Are you truly into that stuff?"

He'd meant it as a joke. Because really, wasn't the woman more intelligent than to waste her money on a magic potion?

"Hey, do not make fun of me." She pointed at him, as if reading his mind. "And aren't you supposed to be getting supplies for my *daed*?"

"I've been doing that along the way," he said. "You've just been distracted."

"Ahh." She lifted her chin. "Almost too much to take in. What's that?"

Isaac looked to where she was pointing, but Grace was already walking in that direction. "Goat yoga," she said, reading the sign outside a small tent. "What do you suppose that is?"

"Why don't you take a look?" He knew what yoga was, or had heard of it, at least. Englishers had all kinds of complicated ways to exercise. With plain folks, they naturally spent their time outside, working or playing, and walking most everywhere they went.

Grace gasped. "It's kids!" She whirled around to him. "Look, they're climbing on that woman's back!"

Inside the tent were about a dozen colorful mats on the ground. The people lying on them or kneeling on them were frozen in all sorts of strange body poses. Grace was right…most of them were engaging with one or more of the goats running around.

Isaac wasn't sure exactly what he was watching, but all of the people inside—mostly Englisher women—were giggling and laughing in delight.

"Should I try?" Grace said. She hadn't turned to him and probably wasn't actually asking his permission. She didn't need it, anyway.

"May I?" she asked in English to the person in charge. It cost her five dollars for fifteen minutes, but Grace didn't hesitate about handing over the money. She tore off her sunglasses, kicked off her shoes, and practically ran to one of the open mats, lowering onto her hands and knees. A tiny white goat immediately trotted over, bleating in her face.

"Aren't you coming?" she asked Isaac, laughing as her new friend leaped up, landing right in the middle of her back.

"There aren't any men," he said to her in Dutch.

"Oh, gracious, too embarrassing for you?" She waved him away, the goat still balancing in place.

With fifteen minutes on his hands, Isaac could round up the rest of the items on John's list. Or he could stand there and ogle inappropriately at Grace.

Mirroring the English woman on the mat next to her, she'd stood up straight, balancing on one foot while the other leg was bent, the bottom of that foot pressing into the inside of her standing leg. She was also holding the little white goat in her arms.

He had no idea how she wasn't falling over.

From the position of her body and her purple dress, Isaac could see quite a bit of her leg, almost up to her knee. He shut his eyes and turned around, not needing that image branded on his brain.

"I'll be back when you're done," he said to Grace, sending the quickest glance at her.

"Fine, fine." She barely gave him a goodbye wave before she slowly squatted down onto the mat, the nimble goat climbing to stand on the tops of her shoulders.

Isaac needed fresh air. He needed to clear his eyes and brain and try to focus on something besides Grace. "The new plow hitch," he said to himself, remembering the tasks he still had to accomplish that day. He squared his shoulders and marched toward the farming equipment.

After shaking out his hands and offering a few silent prayers, he worked quickly at making the rest of the purchases. Everything was boxed and in the back of the buggy by the time the fifteen minutes were up.

He found Grace outside the goat yoga tent, chatting with another Amish woman. Her cheeks were pink from exercise and her eyes glowed. "This is Louisa," Grace said when Isaac joined them. "She's from Honey Brook, too."

"Ah. Pleasure," Isaac said. "Good to meet you."

"Isaac King." Louisa crossed her arms and nodded. "Grace was just telling me about you."

"Is Levy here?" Grace asked, practically cutting off her friend's last word.

"*Jah*," Louisa said. "He's over at the center ring with his brothers and cousins. Apparently, there's some kind of race for the men about to happen. Obstacle course, I think it's called." She rolled her eyes but smiled. "That husband of mine will do anything to one-up his brothers."

"Obstacle course?" Isaac asked, looking over the crowd in the direction of the center ring. "Huh."

"You want to race, too?" Grace said. "What is it with men and the need to play around in the dirt?"

Louisa laughed as she adjusted her *kapp*. "I don't know, but they've all got it."

Isaac wasn't about to deny it. He'd run plenty of obstacle courses in his day, mostly at mud sales just like this one. He'd won first place a few times, but his pride was never even bruised when he didn't. It was about the challenge and the fun, seeing if he could do better than last time.

"Mercy me, Isaac King, the look in your eyes," Grace said. "I supposed we better get over there and sign you up."

"You don't mind?"

She shook her head. "It'll be fun to watch."

By the time they arrived at the center ring, there was quite a crowd, both plain and English folks. The racers—a pretty even mix of plain and English men— were already getting lined up. Isaac paid the entry fee then took off his hat and black vest, handing those to Grace to hold.

"Good luck," she said with a big smile, but then she shrugged. "Though I'm not sure I'm supposed to say that. Have fun, at least."

Isaac returned her smile, adrenaline already pumping through his blood. *"Danke."* He gave her one last look, rubbed his hands together, then strolled over to take his place along the inside of the fence.

"Howdy," the man next to him said. He wore torn jeans and a shirt that Isaac recognized as supporting a sports team.

"Hi," Isaac replied.

Neither of them spoke again. Isaac was concentrating on the layout of the obstacles, the path of the race. First, they would be climbing over huge tractor tires, then jumping over logs. Next was a wooden wall they'd probably have to scale. The other side of the wall might have a rope, and he'd swing down. A balance beam about three feet off the ground was after that, then what looked to be a set of wooden ladders to climb.

Before he could see the rest of the course, a voice came out of the loudspeakers.

"Runners, take your mark!"

Isaac's muscles flexed, blood rushing, heart racing. The crowd cheered.

"Go!"

His boots dug into the ground, giving him a fast start. The hurdles were easy, and Isaac had a good rhythm going as he leaped over the tires, logs, and ropes that he hadn't noticed before. He could hear grunts from the men behind him, so he slowed his speed slightly, letting them get closer.

He was first over the wall, but when he landed, he didn't move out of the way fast enough before someone landed right on top of him. They both fell to the ground, Isaac's face in the soft dirt.

"Sorry," said a panting voice. "Are ya okay?"

"Fine," Isaac said, rolling up to his knees, dusting dirt out of his eyes. "Don't let me stop you," he said to the other man, encouragingly. "You could still win."

The guy scrambled to his feet and headed off toward the balance beams.

After having to dodge yet another flying body jumping off the wall, Isaac knew he would never beat his best time. It didn't bother him that he wouldn't win, though he was determined to finish the race strong. He climbed the ladder with ease, accidentally swallowing only a little bit of dirt. What he hadn't been able to see before was the final obstacle.

Up ahead, the ground took a gradual decline, then a sharp incline. In the middle were three large puddles of water, probably created with shovels and a water hose provided by the volunteer fire company. Isaac quickly gauged that the one to the far left must've been the shallowest of the three because the few racers ahead of him were choosing to trudge through that one.

Just as he was about to take that path, he noticed Grace standing at the fence by the finish line. Even from that distance, he noticed that her face was pale, and she was clutching the front of her apron. The worried look in her blue eyes while she watched him was unmistakable.

Had she witnessed him take that crash at the wall? And the next one? Had she also noticed that he was suddenly limping? *Just a little twinge of pain*. He was so close to finishing, though, and really, there was nothing he could do to take away her fear.

Or was there?

In the split second he had before reaching the

puddles, Isaac noticed that not a single racer had gone through the one on the far right. As he got closer, he realized why.

Before his body could even respond, the decision was made. He managed to send Grace a lightning fast glance before he leaped into the air, hitting the water in what the Englishers called a belly flop.

# CHAPTER TWENTY-NINE

Grace couldn't breathe. As she scrambled over the fence, a part of her brain heard the crowd burst into some kind of roar—laughing, howling, she couldn't distinguish.

"Isaac!" she called as she ran toward where he'd landed facedown in the water, still unable to catch her breath. As she got to him, he rose onto his knees.

She stared, frozen.

He looked at her, the front of his body covered in mud. "Did I win?"

Grace gaped down at him, her heart racing. "Are you…hurt?"

"From *that*?" He made a face and waved a hand. "It was plenty deep enough, not to mention the layer of mud on the bottom. Nice, soft landing."

"You did that on purpose?"

"I saw you watching." He ran a hand over his face, then pushed his wet hair back off his forehead. "Thought it'd be funny."

"Funny?"

He shrugged. *"Jah."*

Grace could only stare at him, no words coming to mind. He didn't seem to be injured at all, just… soaked. His big smile, probably meant to assure her that he was okay, helped her heart to slow down from its racing panic.

He stood up, shaking out his arms. "Wait." He pointed at her. "You *didn't* think it was funny?"

"Isaac." She stepped forward and shoved at his chest. He stumbled back, chuckling heartily, wiping his eyes. "Isaac King," she added, crossing her arms, "you have an impressionable six-year-old daughter."

"*She* would have thought it was funny."

Grace shook her head, unable to stop the belly laugh from escaping. "What are we gonna do?" She gestured wildly at his clothes. "You're completely drenched."

"I noticed."

"And all to get me to laugh?"

"It worked, didn't it?" After a shrug, Isaac turned his back to her, took hold of the front of his shirt, and started fanning it out, probably trying to flick the big chunks of mud off without hitting her in the face.

When he turned back around, Grace found herself fixated.

His white shirt, wet through but now void of mud, was stuck to Isaac's chest, the thin material molded to the shape of his muscles, his long torso, open a bit at the throat, showing more bare skin than she'd ever seen on a man.

*Ooooh*… She felt herself sway a little, lightheaded, thoroughly dazzled.

She knew she swallowed. She tried to blink, but honestly, she was simply unable to remove her very unladylike, and most un-Amish-like gape from him.

"You okay?"

"Aye," she replied, still swaying.

"You're not blinking."

Somehow, Grace was able to pull herself out of the daze and take in a sharp breath. When she could breathe normally again, she felt her heart racing, heat at the back of her neck, down her spine. She looked up into his eyes, then quickly away from him altogether.

"And an extra ten points," said a voice from the

loud speakers, "to the gentleman who took a swan dive into the mud." Suddenly, they were surrounded by people, some cheering, offering Isaac congratulations in both Dutch and English, others slapping him on the back.

Then Isaac was being physically moved away by the crowd; Grace was left behind. She stood up on her toes. "Isaac? What's going on?"

"Jackson's always cheating," a man standing next to her said. "Judges saw what he did at the wall and disqualified him straight-up. They said your fella was far enough ahead of most of the other runners and declared him the winner."

"What?" Grace rose higher on her toes, trying to get Isaac to see her. "Isaac won?" Right then, he managed to look over his shoulder and send her a smile and a big old shrug of bewilderment. Grace couldn't help laughing again.

Something like that could happen only to Isaac King.

Grace watched as he was brought all the way up to the judges' table. They tried to give him some kind of gold statue, but Isaac waved it away good-naturedly.

"*Danke*," he said into the microphone, then gave one small, modest wave to the crowd. As he was en route to her, Isaac was sieged again, this time by a swarm of Amish men. They were all wearing matching slick black coats with two bright yellow reflective stripes encircling the arms.

Reading Volunteer Fire Company read a logo on the back of their jackets. All were laughing, and Isaac didn't look to be in the least bit of danger. She watched as they hustled him to what she'd thought was just a normal house on the edge of the property. As she looked closer, the same logo was on a sign on the front of the house.

She ran after him, curious to see what would happen next.

"Whoa there." She was stopped by one of those Amish men outside a tall door with a high arch, where Isaac had disappeared. "No females allowed unless your spouse is inside. You're not married to Isaac, are you?"

Grace huffed out a breath and planted her hands on her hips. "No, but… What's going on in there?"

"We're letting him shower," he explained. "We've got dry clothes for him, too. He'll be out in a minute." He dropped his chin and laughed. "Wasn't surprising to see him pull a stunt like that, ain't so?"

Grace was suddenly at attention. "You know Isaac?" she asked, pointing at the house.

"We grew up together, our farms not half a mile apart."

"You're kidding!"

"I'm an Isaac, too," the man said. "Isaac Hochstetler."

"Grace, nice to meet you."

"I moved my family up here two years ago," the other Isaac said, "but I knew it was him the second he came out of that mud hole, spitting water."

Grace couldn't help laughing, replaying that moment in her head. "He's wild."

"Always has been. Great to see the guy again. We really missed him."

"After you moved here?" she asked.

"Nay. After he got married. We didn't see him out as much after that."

"Oh," Grace said, recalling what they'd talked about in the buggy on the way to the mud sale that morning. He'd mentioned that he should've gotten to know Martha better before they married, and how badly he now wanted to get Sadie away from his in-laws.

"He's a good man—the best horse trainer I've ever seen," the other Isaac added. "He can break a stallion from scratch in less than four weeks. Not that he'd ever brag about that, or anything for that matter. His humility is most likely one of the reasons he struggled building a business."

"Struggled?" Grace couldn't help asking.

"Well, maybe that's not the right word." He stroked his short beard and glanced toward the house. "Not my place to talk about."

"We're friends," Grace said after a moment. "And you're right, he's a very good man, and a very humble, wonderful father."

"You've met Sadie?"

Grace couldn't help smiling. "Aye. She's lovely, good manners, just like her father."

The other Isaac turned to her, his eyes suddenly focused on her face. *"Jah?"* He tilted his head. "How did you say you know each other?"

"Umm." Grace's throat got tight and her stomach pinched. "He, uh, he's training a horse at my father's farm in Honey Brook."

"He's in Honey Brook now?"

*"Jah."*

"And that's where you live, too? You're both in Honey Brook?"

"J-just temporarily," she quickly added. "I mean, he's there for the job, just until the job is over."

"Ah. I see."

Grace was satisfied that she'd diffused whatever the other Isaac may have been presuming about their relationship. After all, there was nothing going on between them. They were friends, partners.

So then why did her heart suddenly feel heavy, as well as her shoulders?

And why hadn't she mentioned she was training the horse, too? Why had she made such a point that he was in Honey Brook only until Cincinnati was done training? And why had she tried so hard to downplay their friendship, how much he meant to her?

It seemed that for the first time, Grace was grasping that fact herself.

The other Isaac asked her what else they'd seen and done at the mud sale. They chatted for another few minutes, but Grace was stuck pondering over the day that Isaac would eventually return to Silver Springs, her shoulders feeling even heavier.

Soon enough, Isaac—*her* Isaac—came outside. He was wearing black pants and a blue shirt that didn't fit him quite right, a bit tight around the upper arms and chest. Grace blinked and looked away, whispering a prayer for strength to think of him in respectful and pious ways from now on.

"How did I know you two would eventually meet?" Isaac said, pushing up the sleeves of his borrowed shirt.

"*Gott* moves in mysterious ways," the other Isaac said. "*Bruder.*" Then the two men hugged, slapping each other on their backs.

The friends chatted, addressing Grace whenever there was the need for further explanation about a story or private joke between them. A few other Amish men joined them, all friends from Isaac's past. He introduced her around, and only a few of them looked at her questioningly as the other Isaac had earlier, wondering why they'd come to the mud sale together.

Grace couldn't help wondering the same thing. If her father had been at home instead of at the hospital, would she have been allowed to go?

Since there was nothing either of them could do about that now, Grace stood back and watched Isaac interact with his friends. She could easily see how much they liked, respected, and probably missed him. More than a few asked after Sadie and offered condolences about Martha—which Grace found strange. Had his friends from Silver Springs really not seen him in two years?

"I promised Grace we'd stop by the crafts tent before they close," Isaac said. "Wonderful to see everyone. Please give my regards to Bishop Lambright and his family."

More hugs were exchanged, and Grace's cheeks were starting to ache from all the smiling. She'd had such an eventful day, and she owed it all to Isaac.

"What's that for?" he asked her as they stood in line to get one last funnel cake.

"What's what?"

"You're looking at me funny," Isaac said.

Grace pushed out her bottom lip and shrugged innocently, even though her eyes had been glued on him for a very long moment. "It was fun watching you with your friends."

Isaac chuckled and rubbed the back of his neck. "They're good people," he said. "Some I've known my whole life."

Grace dropped her gaze to the ground and shifted her feet. "I supposed you're pretty anxious, then, to get back to Silver Springs, *jah*?"

Isaac didn't reply, and when she lifted her chin, he was looking at her, a dent forming between his brows.

"I…" he began then stopped, rubbing his neck again.

His hazel eyes were soft as they settled on her, but there was a curious intensity behind them, almost as if he were seeing her for the first time, or in a different way. She felt a fluttering in her stomach and a tingling on her lips that was becoming common whenever he looked at her. She tried swallowing to wash it away, but the feelings grew only stronger.

"I hadn't thought about that," he finally said, running a fist across his forehead. "I've been focused so much on…on the horse—Cincinnati."

His answer surprised her. "Cincinnati?"

"*Jah*. Uh, do you want strawberries or syrup on top?" he added as they moved down the funnel cake line.

Grace knew she was about as inexperienced as a toddler when it came to relations between men and women, but she also knew something had just changed, because from the way he'd been looking at her, she'd never believe that Isaac King was thinking about a horse.

"Strawberries," she said, and for the life of her, she couldn't keep from smiling, gazing up at him like she was seeing him for the first time, too.

As thoughts filled her head, memories of his laugh, his touch, the way she felt when he looked at her, she knew her breaths were coming fast, making her shoulders go up and down. All in response to a sensation that was brand new, and oh, so welcome.

# CHAPTER THIRTY

Isaac wanted to start back before it got too late in the afternoon. The roads would be busy with various modes of transportation, so after they finished their funnel cakes, and made sure all of their purchases of the day were secure in back, they climbed aboard the buggy and began the long trip back to Honey Brook.

A little sunburned and a bit worn out, he settled into his seat, enjoying the beautiful scenery. After the third time he heard Grace softly chuckle to herself, he turned her way. Her eyes were closed but a little smile sat on her lips, chin tipped up toward the arching sun. Her upper body shook as, again, she laughed to herself.

"What's so funny?" he finally asked when he knew he'd enjoyed watching her for too long.

"Mmm." Her eyes remained closed, but her smile grew. "I was just thinking about today."

"You had a good time?"

Her eyes popped open. "The best. I can't believe I've never been—" She cut herself off and turned to him. "Thank you for bringing me, Isaac. I'll never forget this day as long as I live."

Isaac had hoped to show her a good time at the mud sale, so he mentally gave himself a humble nod of congratulations, and a simple prayer thanking *Gott* for inspiring him.

"Remember all those tomato plants in the gardening tent?" she said. "There must've been a hundred this morning."

"Most were gone by the time we left," he said.

"But it was sad to see all the okra that was left. I suppose folks who like that have already planted their own crop."

"Maybe." Her eyes fluttered closed again. "Lunch was so good. My pork sandwich was delicious."

"You didn't share one bite with me," Isaac said.

She turned to him again. "Because you ordered three hot dogs just for yourself."

He snickered under his breath. "They were small."

Grace chuckled along with him. "I'll never forget it." She put a hand over her mouth as her laugh increased. "You coming up from the mud like that."

"And what about you standing there on one leg holding a goat?"

"It was to help my circulation."

"So was the mud." Isaac pressed his lips together, but it wasn't long before they both broke into a fit of happy belly laughs so irreverent that the buggy started to shake.

"Gracious," Grace said, wiping the bottoms of her eyelids. "What a day."

"Did I tell you about my first mud sale?" Isaac asked. When Grace shook her head, he went on. "I was around ten, and my father brought the whole family. Two of my sisters hadn't been born yet, but it was still a pretty full carriage. It rained the day before, so the ground was soft, puddles everywhere. Even though my mother reminded me more than once, I forgot to bring my rubber boots. By noon, I'd lost my shoes in the mud somewhere. Had to spend the rest of the day barefoot. Not like that wasn't how I spent most of my time at that age, anyway."

"You and mud." Grace clicked her tongue. "Some boys never grow up all the way."

He chuckled. "My brothers joshed me about it for

years. I'd find muddy boots under my bed or behind a chair. Once my sister molded my mashed potatoes into the shape of a boot."

Grace was an engrossed audience, prompting him to tell her about the time Daniel got sick from eating a whole crate of apples, and when Lucy slept in the barn for a week, and *Daed* helping him train his first pony.

"Your family sounds fun," Grace said, handing him a granola bar from her backpack. "I can't wait to meet—" She cut herself off by taking a bite of her own granola bar and glancing away.

"I like your family, too," Isaac said. "I don't know them all very well yet, but what I know, I like." He chuckled to himself. "Though I might never look at a glass of lemonade the same again."

He'd meant it as a joke, but when Grace didn't laugh, he looked over at her. His stomach dropped when he saw she was silently crying.

"Grace?" He put his hand behind her seat. "Are you okay? Did I say something wrong?"

"Nay," she said, though she didn't stop weeping. "I'm…I'm fine."

She obviously wasn't fine because the tears kept coming. And, since Isaac couldn't just sit there, he pulled the buggy over onto the wide shoulder.

"Grace," he said, rotating in his seat so they were face-to-face. Seeing her like that, eyes clenched tight, mouth slightly open, letting out a quiet, agonized sob, broke his heart right down the middle.

"Please," he said. "Do you not feel well? Are you hurt?"

"I wanted to help, I *tried* to help," she said, finally speaking. "Maybe I tried too late, or tried wrong, or it wasn't my place to try at all—even *Maam* said so."

She was speaking rapidly as she covered one eye with the heel of her hand. "I thought I'd actually gotten through to her once, but I was wrong." She lowered her hand and looked at him. "You saw her the other night. Both of them." Another heartbreaking sob shook her shoulders.

"Amos and Sarah?"

Grace pressed her lips together and nodded, fresh tears trickling down her cheeks. "You talked about getting away from the negative atmosphere of your in-laws' house. Mine is no better, is it?"

"Grace…"

"There's always tension, no matter how cheerful the rest of us are, no matter how hard I pray for peace. I keep thinking that if I'm more righteous, *Gott* will help me with Sarah and Amos, bless me to know what to say. But sometimes I'm not sure if I'm doing anything that *Gott* intends for me. Like, I love working with horses, but even *I* know it's not *traditional.*"

She was talking faster now, jumping subjects, as if she wasn't thinking about what she was saying.

"Maybe I've already messed up."

"Messed up what?" he asked when she paused to take a breath.

"My life. Maybe training isn't *Gott*'s plan for me anymore—I've never prayed very hard about it. I know it isn't a woman's place in our culture, but I suppose I assumed the rules didn't apply to me because it's all I've ever wanted. How can *Gott* bless me if I'm not obedient? Should I be praying for Him to bless me to want what I'm supposed to want? I'm supposed to get married and have babies, right?" She barely got the words out before she started sobbing again, as if simply saying them was breaking her own heart.

If the conversation hadn't turned so serious, he might've laughed. She was being irrational now, for—despite what her father thought—Isaac didn't know anyone who was more in sync and talented when it came to those animals, more familiar with how they behaved and their needs than Grace Zook. Her willingness to care for each individual horse was beyond even his expertise.

A talent like that had to have come straight from Heaven like a laser beam pointed directly at her.

"Maybe Bishop Turner is right," she continued, her words coming faster. "And Hannah and Mary." She sniffed. "They say I shouldn't spend so much time with horses. I could always just get it over with and marry Collin Chupp. He's—"

*"No!"* Isaac hadn't meant to cut her off, but he couldn't listen to one more word. His voice was so strong and firm that Grace flinched in her seat. "You cannot do that, Grace."

She stared at him, her blue eyes wide, breathing shallow and fast as if she'd been the one in the mud race.

His heart was speeding, too, but his mind was crystal clear. He'd known it was coming on for days, maybe longer, though he'd tried everything to ignore his feelings.

He knew she would never stop working with horses—it was her lifeblood—but the thought that she would even entertain the idea of marrying Collin...

"No," he said, softer. "You can't marry that man." He swallowed as he gazed into her eyes. "Or any other man."

"Why?" Her voice was shaky, almost a whisper, yet her gaze hadn't moved from his.

Despite the tricky conversation he would have to have with John Zook, and the countless potential ramifications to his future, Isaac knew if he didn't admit it now, he might never.

"Grace," he said, then paused to remove his hat. "If you marry that Chupp fellow, you won't be able to go on a date with me."

"Are…are you asking me for a date?" She was blinking now, maybe attempting to wrap her brain around the question, or maybe…maybe hesitating while she thought of a way to turn him down gently.

Suddenly, a rock of doubt sat in Isaac's stomach. He'd said it all wrong—wrong time, wrong place. Who does something like this on the side of the road, for heaven's sake?

Still, the words had come out, he'd said them, and now he had to be man enough to mean them.

"Yes, I am," he said, then sat back and waited for the blow.

Her eyes fixed on him again, and before his heart could take another excruciating beat, her pretty pink lips turned up into a smile.

Without her needing to say a word, warm, comforting relief washed through his body. He knew he was smiling, too, for he felt almost giddy. She pressed her lips together and lowered her chin. He did the same, though he leaned in so his forehead touched hers.

Isaac wasn't sure how long they remained in that position, which was why he was startled when he heard a horn honking. He could tell by the way it sounded that a car was coming toward them, and probably going much faster than the posted speed.

The honking was getting closer, but there was nothing Isaac could do to move the buggy farther off the road if it was in the way; he didn't have time. Luckily, it honked once more, then drove past them. It was for sure going way too fast, because the sheer wake of it passing gave the buggy a mighty shake, metal clinking against metal.

He'd been braced for it, but Grace let out an earsplitting scream. The next thing Isaac knew, she'd leaped forward, throwing herself into his arms.

# CHAPTER THIRTY-ONE

Grace didn't want to move an inch. She didn't want to breathe or blink or do anything to remove herself from this moment. Isaac King wanted to take her on a date. Isaac—the man whose presence had so unexpectedly brightened her life—was interested in her.

She pressed her nose into his shirt, still warm from the heat of the day. It didn't smell like him, exactly, and Grace wondered if the volunteer fire company used an electric clothes dryer.

"Are you okay?" His soft words came drifting down to her ears.

She didn't reply right away, didn't want to break the spell.

"Grace?"

She felt his warm palms press to her back.

"Mmm-hmm," she breathed out. "I'm better than okay."

His body shook from a silent laugh. "I think you need to sit up, then."

But she didn't want to. It was all too wonderful. She would be content to feel his arms around her for hours and hours. But then the picture of him in that wet shirt popped into her mind, causing a burst of heat to stir at a place deep in her core.

She quickly pulled away and sat back, though unable to look up at him just yet.

"You've become very special to me," Isaac said. "I hope you feel the same."

Before answering, she pressed her smiling lips

together. "*Jah*," she said simply, knowing her cheeks were turning pink. "But I am wondering about something."

"What?" He shifted in his seat, moving an inch closer to her. "You can ask me anything."

"Well…" She finally looked up at him. "You said the courting rules are different where you come from."

"*Jah.*" He nodded slowly. "And?"

She swallowed. "And you said something about how kissing is allowed."

"Uh-huh," he said, sounding suspicious. "Before the official engagement."

"You mean like even now?"

"Mmm… More like after date number five."

"*Five*?" she couldn't help shrieking.

"Five," he confirmed with a nod.

"Five," she muttered, chewing on a fingernail. "I don't know if I can wait that long."

Grace couldn't believe she'd been so bold. Never in her life had she pondered what physical things happened on a date or during courtships. There'd never been anyone she was interested in doing any of that with, so why even wonder?

And then Isaac had ridden into her life.

As they gazed at each other, Grace's muscles felt weak as noodles, and her throat dried up, butterflies in her stomach, as his hazel eyes on her grew intense. She braced herself for something she knew she wasn't ready for but desired just the same.

"Grace," Isaac said, a corner of his mouth turning up. "Your father would kill me."

She couldn't help breathing out a soft laugh. "I don't care."

"Yes you do. I think you're feeling things for the

first time." He paused to exhale. "I am, too, if I'm being honest. We need to be careful. I've been married before, so I know how easy…" When he cut himself off, he glanced away.

Grace wasn't sure what he'd been about to say, but he seemed embarrassed by it.

"It's going to be tricky, since we work together," he continued a moment later. "I honestly don't know how it will work. And I wasn't kidding about your father. I know he respects me as a trainer and he trusts me to be alone with you." He ran a hand through his hair. "But I don't know how he's going to take this. My job could be in jeopardy."

Grace hadn't thought about that. Would *Daed* actually punish Isaac? Would he allow them to spend hours together alone while training Cincinnati and then permit them to go on a date alone?

Just as a sinking feeling of disappointment was about to replace her happiness, Isaac reached for her hand.

"I do think this is okay." He intertwined their fingers. "Do you?"

"Aye." She grinned in relief, moving their hands to rest on her knee. For a moment, she stared forward, trying to memorize his touch, while also trying to feel calm and natural, holding his hand like that for the first time.

After only a few moments of shy awkwardness, it felt as natural as praying.

"Your skin is soft," Isaac said, running a thumb over the top of her hand. Grace trembled.

"Yours is rough," she said, opening his palm, tracing the tip of her index finger over a callus. "But I like it." She looked up at him, then looked away. "So, what do we do now?" When he squeezed her hand, she wondered if he might put an arm around her shoulders next.

"Now?" Isaac said after blowing out a deep breath. "Now, we go back to Honey Brook."

Grace felt her bottom lip push out. "So soon?"

He chuckled. "Grace, it's getting dark already. I don't like being on the road at night." He reached out and touched her chin. "Not with such precious cargo."

Grace grinned and knew she was blushing, but she didn't care. "I suppose you're right. I don't want Sarah to worry."

Isaac freed one of his hands so he could pick up the reins. "She said she'd be long asleep by the time we got back."

"She did say that," Grace admitted, "but I think she'll stay awake." She looked up at the setting sun, orange and yellow and stripes of blue. "I think she's got a kinder heart than we all realize."

Isaac smiled at her. "You have the biggest heart I know."

Grace couldn't help squeezing his hand. In fact, she didn't let it go during the rest of their trip home, the milky-blue sky lit up by a full moon to guide him. As they were about a quarter mile from town, they started discussing what to do with Cincinnati the next day. Grace agreed that he was ready to hold a rider now and probably would be keen to start jumping in another few days.

A strange feeling came over Grace when she suddenly realized that they were not only in sync about Sin, but also about their feelings for each other. Well, maybe not strange, but almost comforting, like two pieces of a puzzle finally fit together.

With tomorrow's plan settled, Grace leaned in to his shoulder and let her eyes drift to the horizon. But then she blinked and sat up. "What is that?"

"I don't know," Isaac said, letting go of her hand so he could take ahold of both reins, needing to concentrate. Because of the brilliance of the moon, the bright orange splotch in the distance backed by black clouds was perfectly clear. Hauntingly clear.

"It's a fire!" Grace exclaimed, clutching his arm.

The horses were already racing at full speed.

"I know," Isaac said, pushing them to run at a flat-out gallop.

Frantically, Grace tried to gauge their location as they neared town, Isaac driving straight toward that horrifying ball of orange. Dread filled her pounding heart. "It's the Brennemans'!" she cried.

"Lucas?"

"His brother Jeremiah." She turned to him, a shudder running down her spine. "Isaac, they have eight children."

Isaac whipped the horses, demanding they speed up. They were getting closer now; Grace could feel heat from the fire, smoke in the air. Seemed everyone in town was awake and gathered in the Brennemans' front pasture. Two fire engines were there, and Grace saw both Amish and Mennonites rushing toward the flames carrying hoses, wearing helmets. Other men from the village were filling buckets with water.

"It's the barn, not the house," Isaac said. This gave Grace some momentary comfort, but then Isaac's wide eyes shot to her. "Sadie's spending the night here." He glanced toward the house, dread in his expression.

"Go," Grace said, in sync with his thoughts yet again, taking the reins, slowing the horses just enough for Isaac to jump out and sprint toward the crowd gathered at the house.

As quickly as she could, she tied up the horses then raced to the house, noticing her brother Amos was among the ones helping put out the fire. She didn't stop to talk but kept running until she reached the house. She saw Elizabeth Brenneman holding a baby in her arms, Esther, and a group of women surrounding her and her children. But she didn't see Sadie.

"Sadie!" she shouted, panic making her heart race, her vision blurry. She spun in a circle, looking everywhere, the smoke making the chaos worse. Grace was first to admit that she had little know-how when it came to *kinnahs*, but she trembled at the thought of what could happen in a dangerous situation like this. Finally, she spotted them. Isaac was kneeling, holding Sadie in his arms. Without thinking, Grace ran to them.

"Is she all right?" she asked, going down onto her knees.

"Aye," Isaac said, picking up his shivering daughter. She was in only a thin sleeping gown, and the night air was cold despite the fire. Isaac walked them away from the house to an empty bench. "Do you see an extra blanket?" he asked Grace.

Grace glanced around, noticing a small pile someone must have brought out. "I found one!" Without missing a beat, she went for the blanket before it was gone. Returning, she handed it to Isaac. He gently draped it around Sadie, who was now whimpering.

Isaac held her tight in his arms, but Grace noticed his dread-filled expression moving to the fire and the men trying desperately to put it out. Lucas was there, and Amos and Jeremiah, and the Chupps. Even Bishop Tanner.

Isaac looked at Sadie. Then he looked at Grace.

"Isaac," Grace said, without pausing to think. "I've got her. I'll take care of her. Go." She wasn't exactly sure what to do for Sadie besides keep her away from danger, but just like Isaac, she knew she had to help. "Here." She pulled out her white handkerchief. "Tie this to cover your nose and mouth."

"*Danke*," he said. He didn't move for a moment, but then kissed Sadie on the forehead and whispered something into her ear. "Are you sure?"

Grace had practically zero experience with children who weren't in her immediate family. And quite frankly, they scared her a little. But right now, she did not even hesitate. "*Go!*" she said as sharply as possible without startling Sadie, taking the frightened child into her arms.

He gave her a long look that spoke of gratitude and courage before running toward the closest fire truck. Grace's heart thumped hard as she watched him disappear into the smoke and chaos.

"I've got you," she said when Sadie started to fuss. "Just…just, um, close your eyes and think of…all those kittens in the barn, okay. Isn't that nice?"

Sadie sniffed then lifted her head, looking Grace in the eyes. *I hope she can't see the anxiety on my face. Don't children sense fear?*

"Can I think of the goats instead?" Sadie asked, a sweet pout on her lips. "I got to meet them today at Miss Vivian's." She blinked her big eyes. "And I dressed one up like a puppy."

Grace hugged her little bundle, trying to make herself feel calmer. "Of course you can think about the goats. Whatever makes you happy." While Sadie told her more about her day, dozing off now and then, Grace tried to spot Isaac in the group.

Thanks to the volunteer fire department and the

brave men of Honey Brook, the flames were starting
to diminish. But the damage was done. Even Grace
knew the barn would be a total loss. She could only
hope and pray that all the animals had escaped free
from harm and be grateful that the house seemed
untouched.

"Do they know what caused it?" Grace asked as
Hannah came to her side, looking sleepy and worried.
Grace knew the feeling.

"At first, someone thought it was an electrical fire.
Jeremiah keeps a generator in there," Hannah replied.
"But then I guess they thought one of the cows
kicked an electrical socket."

"It was arson."

Grace almost jumped when she saw Isaac. He was
wearing a pair of heavy black gloves and her once-
white handkerchief—now black with soot—was tied
around his nose and mouth. His clothes were wet
from water and sweat, and even though it was half
covered, Grace could see that his face was red from
exhaustion.

"Arson?" She echoed, alarm bells going off in her
head. "How do you know?"

Isaac bent in half, resting his hands on his knees as
if catching his breath.

"You need water," Grace said. "Hannah, can you
find him a drink?"

"I'm fine," Isaac said. "There was a witness, though
he didn't speak up right away." She watched as Isaac
turned to look over his shoulder at a group of older
men surrounding one of the teenagers from the
village. "We think we know who's responsible," he
added. "We're getting a group together to go after
them."

"Tonight?" Grace said, confused. "Isaac, it's one in

the morning. How will you track down anyone?"

"Lucas thinks he knows where they live. And I definitely know what they look like. We have to do it now."

"Isaac?" someone shouted from the crowd.

"I'm coming," he called back. "I have to help if I can," he said to Grace. "Would you please keep her?" He touched a hand to the back of Sadie's head, who was fast asleep. "I couldn't leave her now unless I knew she was safe with you."

Grace felt pressure against her chest. First, from alarm that she would be in charge of Sadie for even longer. She forced that feeling away, but it was quickly replaced by fear of Isaac going off on some kind of manhunt in the middle of the night. Half a moment later, that was replaced by tenderness that he trusted her with his child.

"Go," she said, feeling tears press behind her eyelids. "Don't worry."

"I won't now," he said, going down on one knee so they were eye to eye. "I don't know what I'd do without you."

"Please be safe. *Go!*"

Isaac swallowed; then it looked as though he was blinking back tears, too. "*Danke*," he said, his voice cracking. A moment later, he was gone, leaving Grace to stare off into the last of the red and orange flames, clutching Sadie with all her might.

# CHAPTER THIRTY-TWO

"They think it's the same boys who did all the vandalizing," Hannah said. "And shot off fireworks."

"I guess that wouldn't surprise me," Grace replied, heartsick that anyone could be so full of hate that they'd purposefully cause major property damage. Not to mention the potential of lives being lost.

Though it was still dark outside, the cleanup efforts had begun. Curls of black smoke rose from the pile of ashes that had once been Jeremiah Brenneman's barn. Most of the women had gone home, though a few—like her best friend, Hannah— had stayed to help where they could, making sure the men were provided with plenty of water and dry clothing.

Grace couldn't offer much help with Sadie asleep in her arms. And she wasn't about to let her go, not after she'd promised Isaac that she would be safe. She should've gone home, but she couldn't seem to make herself move from the scene, hoping Isaac would reappear at any moment.

"You look like a mother," Hannah said, plopping down beside Grace.

Grace straightened her shoulders. "Ya think so?"

"Oh, *jah*."

"Well, you should see how hard my heart is beating. I feel like a complete fraud—I have no idea what I'm doing. Do…do you want to hold her?"

"You're doing grand." Hannah leaned over to get a closer look at Sadie. "She's adorable."

"I'm sure she was terrified to death, being dragged from bed and not knowing where her daddy was." At the thought, Grace hugged Sadie a little bit tighter.

"I saw you and Isaac arrive here at the same time," Hannah said, rubbing black ashes off her arms. "Did you get word together and come over?"

"Your dress is ruined," Grace said, instead of answering the question. "The fabric is singed. Hannah, how close did you get to the fire?"

Her friend shrugged. "A mite close. Our farm backs up to theirs, you know."

"Were you outside when it happened? Wasn't it after dark?"

*"Jah."* Hannah sniffed and turned her head, looking the other way.

"Were you alone?" When Hannah wouldn't look at her, Grace sent a soft elbow into her ribs. "Who were you with all alone after dark?"

"No one." She shrugged a shoulder. "Just Peter Shetler."

"Peter?" Grace hoped her shriek wouldn't wake Sadie. "P-Peter Shetler. I thought you said—"

"I know, I know," Hannah said. "But he really is a sweet man. He came over yesterday to help me pick green beans for lunch for Sunday services. *Maam* asked him to stay for supper and, I don't know. I'd meant to walk him out to the gate, but the hours passed." She began playing with a corner of her dress. "You know how that can happen."

Grace did. The hours she'd spent with Isaac yesterday seemed to fly by. But that wasn't the topic at hand.

"Did he ask you on a date?" Even with only gas lamps and flashlights, Grace could easily see her friend was smiling. "Hannah, I'm so happy for you.

Peter is solid. He has a good job at the buggy-making company, and he's always early to help set up the tables and chairs for church. Amos considers him a good friend."

"I think he has a kind heart," Hannah said. "Always have."

Grace couldn't help being excited for her friend. Maybe Peter would want to marry Hannah. Maybe yesterday was the last time Hannah would ever be alone. Grace looked down at Sadie, not allowing herself to think of a future like that with Isaac. That all seemed miles away as she stared at the last place she'd seen him before he'd left with the group in search of the arsonists.

"Don't think I didn't see what you did there," Hannah said. "You didn't answer *my* question."

Grace adjusted the blanket around Sadie like she'd seen other mothers do. "Which question?"

"Now you know that Peter and I arrived at the fire at the same time because we were together. Were you and Isaac together?" She touched Grace's arm. "You don't have to worry. I'm not one to judge." She stopped to smile. "Obviously."

"He took me to a mud sale up in Reading," Grace said, deciding to trust her friend with *some* of the information. "It wasn't a date or anything like that. *Daed*'s still at the hospital with *Maam*, and he asked Isaac to buy some things for the farm." She bit her lip, not sure how to phrase the next part. "He, uh, he asked me to go with him—he must've thought he'd need help."

"Reading's nearly three hours away."

"*Jah*," Grace said. She could see by the look on Hannah's face that her friend was calculating how long it had taken them to drive back from Reading, knowing that the mud sale would've ended no later than three. "Don't ask," Grace said. "Because there's nothing to tell."

"Sure," Hannah said. "Just like I have nothing to tell, either."

The two women stared at each other for a moment, neither willing to spill their guts. From the pleasant distraction, Grace had nearly forgotten why she was sitting outside in the middle of the night.

"Look!" someone shouted. "I think that's Sol Hooley!"

Grace took in a sharp breath and sat up. Sol had been part of the group that had ridden off on horseback with Isaac. Suddenly a dozen people were surrounding Sol, shouting questions as he climbed off his horse. Grace looked behind him, but no one else appeared. Was he alone? She couldn't hear what he was saying, if something had gone wrong, causing her stomach to roil with nausea.

Not more than five minutes later, Sol was off again.

"What's going on?" Grace asked as the group dispersed. "What happened?"

"They're still looking, Sol says," Bishop Turner's wife replied. "Apparently one of the group that set out is injured. I told Joseph it was too dangerous at night, but he didn't listen."

"Injured?" Panic flooded Grace's chest, her heart beating hard and fast. "Who was it? Does he know? Did he say?"

"Didn't say," she replied. "Lucas is with them— he's practically a doctor."

This brought a temporary calmness to Grace's heart, but it didn't last long. "Are they coming back soon?"

"Doesn't sound like it. They could be gone for hours."

Grace nodded, then stood up, keeping Sadie close to her body. She stared into the darkness, smoke making her cough. She couldn't help worrying about the safety of every man out there, yet her heart kept returning to Isaac.

*If anything happens to him…*

Her heart pounded again, and her head began to ache, the pressure of tears in her eyes.

"Please be safe," she whispered into the night sky. "Please come back."

"Daddy?"

"Shhhh," Grace said as Sadie began to stir. "It's me, Grace."

"Where's my daddy?"

"It's okay, Sadie. There was a fire last night, remember? Your daddy…is helping."

"I wanna go home," Sadie said, though her eyes were closed.

Grace pondered that for a moment, not sure what was best for the child. "I…I think that's a very good idea." It would be better to get Sadie out of the night air, but also, Grace was becoming more and more worried the longer she stayed out there, surrounded by smoke and ashes, gazing into the dark.

After making sure Sadie was bundled up, she carried her to the Chupps' buggy, the one she and Isaac had used that day…or yesterday. The horses were tired, but it wasn't a long way home. By the time they reached the front pasture, Sadie was stirring again. As carefully and quietly as she could, Grace hitched the horses and buggy then took Sadie inside.

The family room was dark, but there was evidence that Sarah had been up late. Mugs half filled with hot cocoa and her sister-in-law's favorite cookies were left out on the counter.

For the tiniest of seconds, Grace placed Sadie onto the sofa, needing a quick trip to the bathroom before the night got too long. When she returned to the living room, Sadie was sitting in the dark, both her hands up, palms out, whispering something singsong.

"Sadie," Grace said in a quiet voice. "What are you doing, sweetie?"

"Playing," Sadie said. "With Lilly."

Grace tipped her head to the side. "Who's Lilly?" *And where?*

Sadie glanced up at her then down at the empty sofa cushion beside her. "She's my friend. Actually…" the child said after a little sigh. "She's my pretend sister 'cause I want a baby sister so bad. I keep hoping Daddy will bring me one."

Grace nearly lost her breath as her mind skipped ahead to a not-so-far-off future.

*If I go on a date with Isaac, I'll probably want to go on another, and another. What if we get serious? What if…* She paused as the happy flutter in her stomach from the idea of being courted by Isaac was replaced by a knot of insecurity deep in her gut. *What if I want to marry him? Will he expect me to give Sadie a baby sister?*

"Where's Daddy?" Sadie said, blinking up at Grace as if she'd just realized she wasn't at home.

"He'll be here soon," Grace said as she sat on the couch beside her. "Shhhh. Don't worry, sweetheart." When the little girl didn't settle, Grace didn't know what else to do. She stared up at the ceiling, tears threatening to fill her eyes. "Shall we…shall we say a prayer for him?"

Luckily, this seemed to comfort Sadie, for she adjusted herself on Grace's lap so she could fold her arms reverently. "Dear *Gott*…"

Sadie began the sweet, simple prayer, but when her voice began to fade out with sleep, Grace took over, asking the good Lord to please protect "Daddy" and all the other men out that night. To please bring them home safely. Privately, Grace continued the prayer, reminding *Gott* how much she cared for Isaac, how he'd become more than just a good friend, how special he was to her heart.

Then she prayed for herself... For strength and guidance and to feel at peace in a world that was spinning out of control.

Her heavenly pleading went on for so long that Grace didn't remember saying amen. Eventually, her chin lowered, resting on the top of Sadie's head.

Two guardian angels fast asleep.

# CHAPTER THIRTY-THREE

It was just after dawn. Isaac stopped by the stables to check on the horses first. Despite not sleeping for over twenty-four hours, seeing that Cincinnati looked strong and alert lifted his spirits.

He removed his hat and boots before entering the house, hoping he wouldn't disturb anyone at such an early hour—everyone had been up late.

The moment he stepped inside, he saw them.

And his heart skipped.

Grace was reclined on the sofa, propped up by a single pillow. Sadie was stretched out on top of her, tummy down, her chubby arms limp around Grace's neck, while Grace's arms were holding his daughter securely in place.

After a moment, it was difficult for Isaac to look, for his heart was so full, so enamored by the scene. He never dreamed he could care for someone as quickly and naturally as he'd come to care for Grace.

He quietly sat in the armchair opposite the couch, stretching out his weary legs, propping his chin in one hand so he didn't have to move a muscle to watch them. So many thoughts were running through his head. Things he wanted to tell her, show her, do with her...when the time was right.

They hadn't even been on a date yet, and they wouldn't until he figured out how to speak to John about it. The sudden nervousness about that conversation caused his stomach to clench. Could his feelings for Grace really jeopardize his future?

Maybe he should have kissed her when he'd had

the chance. With the way he anticipated the next few weeks would go, it might be quite a long time before they could have that first date.

Isaac's focus was diverted when he saw a shadow coming down the stairs. "Shhh…" He gestured at the sleeping pair on the couch, then placed an index finger over his mouth.

Sarah froze in place, then she seemed to understand as she crept silently into the kitchen. She held up the coffeepot and raised her eyebrows at him.

Isaac shook his head but mouthed, "*Danke.*"

Sarah went about her early-morning routine while Isaac happily remained right where he was. Amos was next to appear in the kitchen. He said a few words to Sarah that Isaac couldn't hear, then went out the door.

Amos had been with him and the other men as they'd gone after the arsonists, but he'd returned to town with the first group a few hours ago. Isaac had been glad of that. He didn't want Grace to have her brother to worry about, too.

"Isaac?"

"Hey." He quickly got to his feet and moved to the couch, kneeling down. "Keep sleeping, if you want."

Grace blinked her beautiful blue eyes then breathed in a sharp inhale. "Are you okay?" She tried to sit up. "What happened?"

"Shhh," Isaac whispered. "I'm fine. Everything's okay." When Sadie began to stir, Isaac took the opportunity to pick her up, her warm little body slumping against him. "There, there, sweet angel. Thank you for taking care of her."

"Of course," Grace said. "I should've taken her to the Chupps' so she could sleep in her own bed, but…"

"No, no," Isaac said. "Here with you is where I pictured her the whole time." He slid onto the couch next to her, smiling down at Sadie. He was sure Grace had taken good care of his precious daughter.

The thought gave him pause. When he'd asked her for a date, he hadn't yet considered the whole picture. What if they went on a second date? Ten dates? What if things progressed and he wanted to marry her? How would Grace feel about being an instant mother to his child?

Another stab of nervousness made him wonder if following his heart was the right thing to do.

"I'm glad you're home safe." Grace put a hand to her chest. "I was so worried, I…" As her voice faded away, she moved her other hand to cover her mouth. "I didn't know if you…"

"Hey, hey." Isaac moved to her quickly. "I'm sorry I made you worry. I won't do that again."

Grace dipped her chin. "Promise?"

Those early concerns and wonders didn't seem to be so important now. Not while they were together.

As he sat with Grace, Sadie in his arms, he felt peaceful and safe for the first time in years.

"Glory be—why don't you just take her upstairs to the bedroom?" Sarah said.

Isaac frowned at the lewd suggestion, breaking his gaze on Grace to see Sarah watching them as they sat close and snug to each other.

"*Sadie*, I mean," Sarah added. "Take *Sadie* to the bedroom. Lord have mercy."

The heat of embarrassment rushed into his cheeks at where his thoughts had gone. "That's a…a good idea," he said. "Do you mind?"

Grace cleared her throat, sending a hasty, surreptitious glance toward Sarah. "Up the stairs," she whispered to him, "last door to the right."

Isaac stood up and headed toward the stairs, not

bothering to look in Sarah's direction but feeling her eyes boring into him the whole way. Once at the top of the stairs, he breathed out an exhale. He needed to be more careful. Still, he couldn't help chuckling inside at how they must've appeared to Sarah.

Not wanting to invade Grace's privacy by examining her room, he quickly pulled back the covers and placed Sadie on the bed, tucking the soft quilts up to her chin. He gave his daughter a quick kiss on the forehead before creeping out of the room.

He should've made more noise while coming down the stairs, for when he reached the bottom, he found Grace and Sarah huddled close together in the kitchen. Looked to Isaac as if Sarah was giving Grace an earful.

"It's *fine*, it's *nothing*," Grace was saying in a speedy whisper.

"What if Jane saw you? Or Leah?" Sarah whispered back. "She's getting old enough to wonder. She asks questions."

Grace put her hands on her hips. "There's nothing to tell."

"Mm-hmm." Sarah shook her head, and pulled out a big saucepan. "*Guder mariye*, Isaac King. Since we're all up, why don't you stay for breakfast?"

He looked at Grace first, gauging her reaction. She nodded, pulling back a smile that made his heart melt. "*Danke*," Isaac said. "Can I help?"

"What you can help with," Sarah said, "is to sit down right there"—she pointed to a chair at the kitchen table—"and tell us what happened last night." She dumped dried oats into the pot, more violently than was necessary. "Amos won't speak more than two words about it."

"I'd like to hear about it, too," said Grace.

Isaac massaged the back of his neck, knowing he'd have to tell them about it sooner or later. "Like I told you last night, Grace, Lucas knew who'd set the fire — or he thought he knew. There were two witnesses to confirm it."

"One of them was Hannah," Grace said to Sarah. "She was hanging out with Peter Shetler alone after dark."

"Ain't so?" Sarah said, her mouth holding the "*O*."

"It'll be all over town by morning." Grace glanced to the window. "Oh." She smiled and shrugged. "I guess it is morning." She held a mug of coffee up to her mouth, unsuccessfully hiding a grin. "Poor Hannah."

"Are you finished?" Isaac said, his voice mock-stern, though rather enjoying the temporary truce between Sarah and…well, everyone.

"*Jah* — sorry," Grace said, lowering her mug and straightening her shoulders. "Continue."

"They were English; two of them had been to see Lucas at the medical center a year back. He remembered them because of their bad language, and also because they were there to be treated for burns on their hands." He addressed Sarah. "They'd been caught setting a neighbor's doghouse on fire."

"Mercy me," Sarah said.

"Were their parents with them back then?" Grace asked.

"*Jah*," Isaac replied. "Lucas said he remembered their names, and he knew their address because it rhymed with a place he used to live."

"That was lucky," Grace said.

"Honestly, it was a hunch at best," Isaac said. "But Lucas wanted to go after them. Jeremiah, too — I don't blame him. Before I knew it, there were twenty men ready to form a search party." He looked at Sarah again. "Your husband led one of the groups. He took them down by the river."

"My Amos knows the trails along those riverbanks like the back of his hand," Sarah said.

"Did you find them?"

Isaac was glad Grace wanted to jump to the end of the story, for there were details she didn't need to know about. What they'd done was dangerous and foolish, and someone could've been badly hurt.

"The hunch paid off, and it was exactly who we guessed," Isaac said. "They were hiding in the woods outside Weaver's Feed Mill." He paused to run a hand down his face. "They'd lit another fire."

"Good gracious!" Grace cried, cupping her hands over both cheeks. "Did you put it out in time?"

"Aye. It did little damage. There were four teens, ten of us men. They fessed up to what they'd done right quick, though they blamed one another, didn't stop pointing fingers until we dropped the last one off at home." He paused to shake his head. "Their parents were furious and very apologetic to Jeremiah."

"What happens now?" Grace asked.

"I'm not exactly sure. Lucas and Jeremiah were the ones talking with all the parents. Jeremiah didn't have fire insurance on the barn, so—"

"So, *he* has to pay to rebuild it?" Grace cut in, banging a fist on the table. "That's not fair. That's not fair at all."

"Grace," Sarah hushed. "People are trying to sleep in this house."

"Sorry," Grace said, forcing herself to breathe out. But Isaac could still see the fury in her expression. "Why are the Brennemans responsible for something they didn't do?"

"You didn't let me finish," Isaac said, putting a hand on Grace's arm, hoping to calm her down. He didn't care if Sarah approved or not. "The Jacksons—they're the family with the two brothers—they offered to pay for the rebuild if Jeremiah didn't press charges."

"You mean tell the police on them?"

Isaac nodded. Then waited.

"But…" Grace bit her thumbnail. "But plain folks wouldn't go to the English police anyway."

Isaac pulled back a corner of his mouth. "Apparently, the Jacksons don't know that."

Grace's gaze moved to the side, then up. "You mean…" She covered her smile with a hand. "Is that even…moral?"

"I suppose that's for *Gott* to decide," Isaac said. "Though Bishop Turner was standing right there with Jeremiah the whole time."

Hearing Grace's giggle made Isaac's spirits soar.

"Well, I guess we're to take the Lord's tender mercies no matter how they come to us." Grace walked over to Sarah, offering to help with the oatmeal.

Isaac leaned an elbow on the table, resting his chin in his palm, allowing his eyes to follow Grace around the room. He wondered if she knew he was watching, because she never stopped smiling while a little pink blush stained her cheeks, a twinkle in her blue eyes. After the third time Sarah cleared her throat, Isaac knew he'd outworn his welcome.

"I should go home," he said. "Back to the Chupps', I mean. Clean up and change clothes for the day. Do you mind if Sadie stays here until she wakes up?"

"'Course not," Grace said. "I'll walk you out."

Isaac couldn't help feeling Sarah's disapproving stare following them until he walked out onto the porch.

"I'm so glad you're safe," Grace said, pulling the door closed behind her. The yellow light of the early morning sun gathered around her like she was the sun itself. "I couldn't stop worrying. Word came back that someone was injured. I was frantic."

"Oh." Isaac rubbed his chin. "Uh, *jah*. That was me."

*"You?"* Grace stared at him, then her eyes ran down his body. "Are you hurt? What happened?"

Isaac shouldn't have brought it up. It had been embarrassing enough in front of the other men. "I, uh, c-came off a horse."

"While it was running? Isaac, you could've been trampled to death out there in the dark."

"Not while it was running." He sniffed and rubbed his nose. "You know that handkerchief you gave me earlier?"

*"Jah?"* Grace nodded, eyes fixed on him.

"I put it in my pocket before we left. Anyway, we were stopping to water the horses, so I slowed the gelding way down, practically walking."

"And?"

"I wanted to touch the handkerchief, like it would bring me good luck or something." He paused to chuckle, feeling a bit silly. "I was looking down at it, not paying attention to where I was going. Long story short, a tree branch came out of nowhere and hit me in the face."

Grace was holding back pretty well, but after a few seconds, she burst into giggles.

"I know, I know," Isaac said, unable to suppress his own laugh. "So much for my 'Amish Cowboy' reputation. I'm grateful only half of the group witnessed it."

"Oh." Grace wiped the corners of her eyes. "This is a very forgiving community. I'm sure everyone's forgotten about it."

They stood on the porch in silence. Isaac knew he needed to be on his way but didn't want to say goodbye. "Well," he finally said, "I have a lot to do today."

"I'll see you later, then?" Grace said. "We're going to saddle and ride Cincinnati today, remember?"

"I hate to miss that, but something important's come up that I can't shirk." He looked down and ran a hand through his hair. "I fear I won't be available to train as much as we planned this week. Maybe even the week after."

"Why?"

"The Jacksons are paying for the materials for the barn to be rebuilt, but not the actual rebuild. There's a lot to prepare for, clean up, plan, and draft. Jeremiah has his farm to take care of, re-corralling the loose livestock. Lucas has a busy job, too. The cleanup alone is going to be a community endeavor, not to mention the rebuild." He paused, hoping and praying he'd made the right decision. "I volunteered to lead the project."

"You? But, Isaac, you don't even live…" Her voice trailed off as she stared at him. Then something seemed to occur to her, and she lifted a little smile.

"I know," he said, smiling back. "Feels like home, though."

# CHAPTER THIRTY-FOUR

It was strange, working with Cincinnati alone. With the other horses, Grace had always been accustomed to being the sole trainer, but Sin felt different.

"Good boy," she said, leaning forward to rub along Sin's shoulder. Just as she'd suspected, he'd taken to the blanket and soft saddle pad without a single issue. The heavier leather saddle with stirrups and the thicker belt around his belly took a bit more time, but by noon, Grace was riding him around the perimeter of the front ring with complete ease.

Still, with every accomplishment the grand horse made, Grace wished Isaac were there to commemorate it. They were a team. It didn't feel the same without sharing those moments with her partner.

Or maybe she simply missed his presence altogether.

She clicked her tongue and angled the reins. Cincinnati obeyed the prompt and made the turn perfectly. She smiled to herself, daydreaming about what Isaac would have said.

She'd seen him a few hours ago, just checking in before going out to the site of last night's fire. Cleanup and rebuilding projects were huge undertakings, ending with a barn raising.

Grace wasn't surprised in the least by Isaac's desire to help the village, a community of which he was only a temporary member. Didn't she see that so often in his personality now?

*Maybe this means he wants to stay?* Grace asked herself as she climbed off the horse. *Maybe he's thinking of a future in Honey Brook.*

But Grace knew it was dangerous to let her thoughts drift there. It wasn't fair to either of them, and it could all end in disappointment.

*Sometimes it's better to not give your heart away,* she'd told herself a million times. But then she pictured Isaac's eyes and smile, his sometimes scruffy hair, and the way just hearing his voice brought a thrill to her entire being.

Wasn't it foolish to have jumped to conclusions? They'd never once talked about marriage. It wasn't Isaac's fault that Grace had allowed her worries about the future to get the best of her the night before.

*For all I know, Isaac wants a traditional wife to keep house and have children, be his helpmeet like Mother Eve was to Father Adam. If so, should either of us be wasting our time with even one date?*

As Grace let that thought settle, it didn't feel quite right. After all, wasn't Silver Springs New Order? She didn't know all the differences between their two Ordnungs yet, but so far she'd surmised that Isaac's home was more progressive in rules like technology use and worship services...not to mention their courting restrictions were much more lax.

At the same time, Grace also understood that didn't necessarily mean the same for rules about wives staying home or other Amish traditions.

But what if it did?

*Maybe he wants to pair himself with a more independent woman. Someone who matches his talents and intellect.*

Yes, that sat much better in Grace's mind. She could always ask Isaac about it, flat-out. But how embarrassing would that conversation be? Instead, she decided to follow his lead—after all, he'd been an amazing teacher so far.

Grace felt herself smiling as she brushed Cincinnati, feeling the warmth of the noonday sun on her face, also feeling warmth spread through her soul. After releasing the horse into the back pasture, she headed to the house. She'd slept only a few hours last night and was beginning to feel the weariness of tired muscles.

When she entered the house, Sarah was in the kitchen, mixing something in a bowl, gazing out the window over the sink. Amos was seated at the table, looking down into his plate of chicken casserole. To Grace, it appeared that neither was acknowledging that the other was in the same room.

It made her heart ache to see her brother and sister-in-law unhappy. She didn't know what else to do—or if anything she might do would make a difference.

"Hallo," she said, walking to the sink to wash her hands.

"Want lunch?" Sarah asked without looking at her.

"*Danke*, yes, please." She walked over to Amos, gesturing at his food. "This looks delicious. I'd love some if there's any left."

Sarah uncovered a casserole dish that was sitting on the counter. "Bring me your plate."

Grace quickly obeyed, wanting to show her gratitude. "Yum." She put her nose over the steaming dish and inhaled. "Did you make this last night?"

"*Jah.*" Sarah handed her the plate. Her face looked drained of energy, eyes red and weary.

"*Danke.*" Grace sat across from her brother and took a heaping forkful. "Sarah," she said with her mouth full, "this is so good. Mmm…did you add celery?"

"Aye." Sarah finally turned to her. "It's nice to hear some appreciation once in a while." She looked at Amos, but he didn't even twitch.

"I really appreciate this—and you," Grace quickly added. "You know cooking isn't my favorite. I appreciate every time I don't have to make a meal."

"You're welcome, Grace," Sarah said, still looking across the room at her husband.

When Amos didn't offer a single word, Grace's heart sank. Were they so angry at each other that not even one kind sentiment could be shared between them?

Grace ate slowly, wanting to ask Amos to share his story about last night but fearing saying anything might cause a fight between them.

"Sadie woke up at about eight," Sarah said, pouring batter into a round cake pan. "She's upstairs with Jane."

"Oh!" Grace said, alarmed that she'd almost forgotten Isaac's daughter had spent the night. "I'll go get her. She needs a bath and change of clothes."

"Don't worry," Sarah said. "I took care of it."

"You gave her a bath?" Grace asked.

Sarah opened the oven. "Janie and Leah too. I put them all in the big tub together, let them play in the water for a while with some paper boats I folded. They were having fun."

Grace couldn't help being shocked.

"She's a little smaller than Jane," Sarah continued, "but she's wearing one of her old dresses. I double-wrapped the apron ties."

"You…" Grace knew the tone of her voice sounded much too surprised. "You did all that?"

"Why, 'course!" Sarah said. "She's a guest in our home. Or did you think I don't know how to take care of *kinnahs*?"

"Nay," Grace said, lowering her fork. "I just—" She cut herself off before she said something she shouldn't. "*Danke*, sister. That was really wonderful of you."

Sarah merely shrugged and continued her routine.

Grace slid her gaze over to Amos, startled to see that his eyes were fixed on his wife, looking first confused and then...pleasantly surprised?

"More chicken?" Sarah asked, addressing Amos.

"Uh, please," he replied, holding up his plate. "*Danke*, Sarah."

Something changed in the air—maybe only slightly, but Grace felt it as she looked back and forth at Sarah and Amos. She didn't want to move, fearing she'd break the mood, but she also thought it best that she get out of that room as soon as possible, in case they wanted to talk to each other.

"More milk?" Sarah asked her husband.

That was the last thing Grace heard before she snuck out of the house. While standing on the porch, she closed her eyes, offering a sincere prayer of thanksgiving, then asking *Gott* to please continue to bless her brother and sister-in-law, to help them forgive each other, to remember the wedding vows they'd made, and how they'd once been crazy in love with each other.

"Grace?"

Recognizing the voice, warmth immediately filled her chest, happy little flutters in her tummy. "Hi," she said, opening her eyes.

"How is your day so far?" Isaac asked, walking to the porch.

"Shhh," Grace hushed, padding down the stairs and taking Isaac at the elbow, leading him away from the house. "I think they're talking."

Isaac hunched his shoulders, as if trying to shrink his body. "Who?" he whispered.

"Shhh—Sarah and Amos."

"Ahh." He nodded a few times. "And that's good?"

Grace glanced over her shoulder at the house. "I don't know." She held her shoulders up in a shrug. "Maybe."

"Grace." Isaac spoke the single word, lifting a big smile.

"What?"

"I just…" He chuckled softly, shaking his head. "I sure do like you."

"Oh." Grace knew she was blushing, but she'd stopped feeling self-conscious in front of Isaac long ago. "I like you, too." Playing it safe, she removed her hand that was still clutching his arm. "And if I didn't tell you yesterday, what you're doing is making me like you more and more."

"What am I doing?" he asked, leaning his face toward hers, making Grace's lips tingle.

"The b-barn," she managed to sputter. "Rebuilding."

"Nah," he whispered. "Folks in Honey Brook have been so kind to Sadie and me. I reckon she has more friends here than she did back home."

Grace tried to not make that daydreaming leap about Isaac staying in Honey Brook. One step at a time.

"Sadie's inside playing with Jane," Grace said. "Do you want to say hello?"

"I thought the house was off-limits."

"Well…"

Isaac smiled. "I'm sure she's fine, and I wouldn't want to interrupt…um, anything. I do have time before I'm meeting with the cleanup volunteers. How's Sin?"

Grace grinned, and she couldn't talk fast enough, reporting everything to Isaac about how well that morning's training had gone, as they strolled toward the stables.

"Amazing job," Isaac said, after easily mounting Cincinnati, the horse finally behaving like the champion thoroughbred he was. What Grace thought was amazing was how elegant and poised Isaac looked atop the horse.

"How did you do it so fast?" he added, leading Cincinnati to make a right-hand turn.

Grace shrugged. "Something my father taught me. 'Training with the Spirit,' he used to call it. Do you know he prefers to hear 'I'll Do a Golden Deed'?"

"Your father?"

"Nay—*Sin*." Grace giggled. "He's calm as a summer's day after I sing the second chorus. I think it puts him in the mood to be taught." She reached out and gave the horse a tender pat. "Always does for me."

"Grace."

"Aye?"

He didn't continue right away, but simply kept those intense hazel eyes fixed on her, causing her heart to skip a beat. "Don't make me say what I'm thinking right now."

"That bad?" she grinned. "Or that good?"

"Very good." He chuckled and adjusted his hat. "Mind if I ride him a while?"

"He'll love it."

While Isaac took all the spare time he had to work with Cincinnati, Grace led Daisy, one of the new mares, into the pasture. They weren't working together, but at least she could watch him, wave as he rode by. But it wasn't long before time was up, and Isaac had to leave. He insisted on removing the saddle and tack and then brushing out Cincinnati before returning him to the back pasture.

"I'll come for Sadie later this afternoon, if that's okay," he said.

"She's fine here," Grace replied. "As long as she wants."

There was nothing more to say, as they both had work to do on their own. Still, Grace wasn't going to be the first to say "*mach's gut*" this time.

"Well then." Isaac began backing up, while Grace's heart took a leap into her throat, missing him already. "I'll see you soon." He took a few steps away before turning back. "'I'll Do a Golden Deed,' you said? All the verses?"

Grace smiled and nodded. "Works every time."

She heard Isaac chuckle, then he waved before mounting Scout and leaving the farm. She could've sworn she heard him humming the old Protestant hymn as he rode away.

"Don't look at me like that," Grace said when Daisy shook her head, black mane spreading down her back. "I wasn't *really* thinking about…" She bit down on her bottom lip. "He's just so handsome—anyone would think so." She tilted her head, gazing into the distance. "And generous and caring, and so thoughtful. Humble, too. Okay, okay." She gave the mare a stroke down the nose. "My complete focus is on you now."

Grace got Daisy to pull a light wagon, though when she reared at the sight of a larger cart, Grace knew the mare's training was done for the day. She walked down the row, spending time with each horse, though her mind wasn't completely on them this time, but wondering what might be happening at the Brenneman farm.

It was time she peeked in on Sadie and Jane to see what the little girls had been up to all day. The second Grace stepped into the house, she froze in place.

The kitchen was empty, but Grace found Sarah and Amos beside each other on the couch. No lights on. Not a sound. Sarah was sitting up, while Amos was tipped toward her, eyes closed, his head leaning against her chest. Sarah cradled it gently, while his arms were low around her waist.

"Shhh." Sarah held a finger to her lips. "He's exhausted after last night."

Grace nodded, still not sure what she'd walked into, though she knew instantly it was a private moment where she didn't belong.

"Good news," Sarah continued, her voice barely a whisper. "Your father called. Eve's condition has improved. Coming home soon."

Not wanting to make a sound, Grace clasped her fingers together and held them under her chin. "*Danke*," she mouthed, her heart flooding with gratitude.

Sarah nodded an inch, then tipped her chin to look down at her husband, running a hand through his hair.

Grace left them, tiptoeing up the stairs. When she reached the top, she lowered onto her knees, giving proper thanks to her Heavenly Father with everything in her heart.

# CHAPTER THIRTY-FIVE

"Add the water slowly. Right into the center. There ya go."

"I do know how to mix concrete, Isaac," Lucas said, leaning on his shovel, looking at Isaac with narrowed eyes.

Isaac chuckled. "I'm kidding you, brother."

"I *was* away for ten years," Lucas admitted, wiping his brow. "But it's all coming back to me."

"Once you participate in your first barn raising," Isaac said, "it's in your blood forever. That's what my father used to say. I can't tell you how many I've done."

"We couldn't have a better crew chief than you," said Lucas, pushing a wheelbarrow full of freshly mixed concrete to where the foundation was being poured. "So far, this is one of the smoothest barn raisings I've attended. You're a fine leader."

Isaac looked down at the notes on his clipboard. "I'll try not to let that go to my head."

The actual barn raising was tomorrow, but the concrete foundation block had to be laid at least a day before, giving it time to set. More than fifty men had shown up to work that morning, which wasn't a surprise. Barn raisings involved every person in the community: men, boys, women, and children. Everyone had their part.

"Isaac!"

For the past ten days, his reaction had become the same every time he heard her calling his name. First it hit him in the chest, a soft, inviting punch, which settled as a warm, slow shiver meandering down his limbs.

"Have some water." Grace was holding up a glass, enticing him to take a break.

She'd been bringing snacks and cold drinks to the workers all morning. Even before they poured the foundation, she'd been there the days when the crew had been removing the ashes, seared wood, and other debris of the original barn. That late evening when the shipment of reclaimed lumber had finally shown up from the mill, Grace was there, offering hot coffee and warm shoofly pie by the slice. One day, at high noon, she'd arrived at the Brennemans' riding Cincinnati.

Isaac had heard a few gasps and whispered observations, but mostly, seemed folks didn't give her behavior a second look, as if seeing a beautiful woman on horseback was commonplace. Perhaps it was…where Grace Zook lived.

She never seemed to tire but was strong and helpful, thoughtful, showing service and a maturity he hadn't seen in her before then.

"*Danke*," he said, taking the cold glass gratefully.

She wore a blue dress, the black apron tied at her waist instead of through her arms. She smiled at everyone, cheerful in her duties.

"What?" she asked when he felt his own smile broaden.

"I'm happy to see you," Isaac stated simply, "so I'm smiling at you."

She dipped her chin, a feminine, bashful blush on her cheeks. "Well, stop. Someone might see you."

Isaac felt a pinch in his stomach. He still hadn't asked John for permission to take Grace on a date, though it had been on his mind practically every darn second. It wasn't as though they were purposefully sneaking around, he just hadn't found the right time for a serious discussion with her father. In the week and a half since his boss had returned from the hospital in Hershey, the two men had grown even closer—which was a natural result of working side by side. Isaac respected him even more now, so naturally, he felt horribly guilty that he'd been flirting with John's daughter behind his back for so long.

Isaac couldn't stop worrying what would happen if John disapproved of their dating. Could he fire him, and Isaac would lose the money from the job, also impeding his plans for the future with Sadie?

"I better go, then," Isaac said. "Maybe I'll see you later?"

"You *have* to see me later," Grace said. "Cincinnati has two more weeks of training. You can't expect me to keep up the pace without you."

He exhaled a laugh out his nose—a temporary reprieve from the guilt. "I meant after the day's training." He took a step closer. "I meant a proper date after the sun goes down. I meant taking you on a ride in an open buggy, you allowing me to hold your hand. Maybe you'd loop your arm through mine if we take a moonlit stroll."

"I think that could be arranged," Grace said, her voice dropping to a whisper. "When?"

"Soon." Isaac looked around, wishing he could leave his post right then and sweep her away. "I, well, I still have to speak to your father."

"Papa likes you a good much," Grace said cheerily.

"He likes me because I'm a hard worker and a decent man." He paused to shake his head, feeling that guilt again. "At least, he *thinks* I'm decent. He doesn't know what we've…done."

Just like his, Grace's smile took a dip. "Not like we've sinned or anything. We've just…we've done things a bit out of order from what's traditional."

"That's one way of putting it."

"Really though, since when have I done anything traditional?" Her smile was back, and when she laughed, it was impossible for Isaac not to feel at peace.

If someone hadn't called his name, he was quite sure he would've remained exactly where he was.

"I'll be right there!" he called over his shoulder, not ready yet to take his eyes off her.

"You better get going," she said. "You're in charge, you know."

"*Jah.*"

"See you tomorrow?"

"You're leaving?"

Grace ran her hands down the front of her apron. "I have other responsibilities." She paused. "I think Sin misses seeing us together, though."

"I'll make it up to you," Isaac promised. "I know I've been leaving a great deal of the training to you."

"What you're doing now is more important." She lowered her chin and said something he couldn't make out.

"What was that?" He turned his ear to her.

"I said I'm very proud of you. In the most modest way, of course."

He laughed. "*Danke*, Grace Zook." There wasn't much more to say, and Isaac did need to get back to laying the foundation. Grace was first to walk away that time, waving as she handed another man a cold drink.

But instead of returning to his chores, Isaac had no choice but to watch her, while feeling a legitimate weakness in his knees, a lightness in his head, a flutter in his heart, all leading to a realization that he was on a path he'd only dreamed of.

• • •

The next day's festivities began early. Family carriages started arriving at the Brenneman's right as Isaac got there at seven. He and Jeremiah greeted everyone, directing where the buggies, carriages, and wagons should park.

"Morning." Isaac waved to the Chupps. "Right over there," he motioned.

"I *know*," Collin Chupp grumbled. He was driving the family buggy and gave Isaac a glare that he felt all the way to the back of his eyeballs.

"What was that about?" Jeremiah asked, obviously noticing the glare.

Isaac shrugged. "No idea."

But he did know. At least he suspected. How could anyone observe him and Grace together and not presume something besides friendship might be going on between them?

*If Collin noticed, John might have, too.*

When was the right time to swallow his concern and talk to Grace's father properly? With only a few weeks of training left, it felt as though time was running out.

"*Guder mariye,*" he repeated over and over before it was time to go to work.

Just as he was about to leave the rest of the greetings to Jeremiah, the Zook family arrived. He felt his heart begin to beat hard in his chest in anticipation of seeing her. And nervousness about seeing his boss.

He knew Eve wouldn't be coming—she being one of the few members of the congregation who was excused. He tipped his hat to John, who was driving, and waved at the two little girls, who practically jumped out of the back of the buggy and ran toward a group of *kinnahs*. Sadie was already there.

"Morning," Amos said as he climbed out, holding a hammer in one hand and a saw in the other. "Put me to work."

"How are you at sawing floor joists?" Isaac asked, shading his eyes from the sun.

Amos was already peeling off his black jacket. "Just point me to where I'm needed."

"Be careful, husband."

The voice was female, but not Grace's. Isaac was astonished when he saw Sarah lean out the front of the buggy and stretch a hand to Amos.

"Aye, I will," Amos replied, reaching up to take his wife's hand in a way Isaac had never imagined was possible between these two from his own observations and from what Grace had told him.

Just then, Grace poked her head out. Isaac gawked at her, knowing his mouth was still hanging open in disbelief. Grace looked over at the couple, smiled, and shrugged one shoulder.

*I'll get the whole story later,* he said to himself. *By the way Grace is grinning, I'm sure it's a good one.*

Grace climbed out of the back of the buggy, clad in a peach-colored dress, appearing as clean and fine as ever.

"Can I help you with that? Here, let me carry—"

"You certainly will not," Grace said, turning a shoulder to him, guarding the two large bags of potatoes she was holding in her arms. "You know very well what my job is today and what yours is." She lowered her voice. "And you're not to treat me differently."

Isaac stepped back, grinned, and crossed his arms. "Oh aye. I'd *never* do that." He tapped his chin and motioned with his head. "House is that way, but I'm sure you knew that."

"*Danke*," she said, holding eye contact with him longer than was necessary. Or discreet.

"*Danke!*" Sarah cheerfully echoed as she practically bounced out of the buggy and headed toward the farmhouse, lugging a stack of Dutch ovens.

When he looked at Grace again, she only gave him that same mysterious shrug.

"I'll see you at lunchtime," she said.

He took off his hat. "*Danke*, Grace, for all you do for me."

"Oh stop it," she whispered under her breath. "You're making me blush."

Isaac didn't say another word. He didn't have to. He just gazed at her, feeling happy and warm as they stood together under the morning sunshine.

"*Ahem.*"

Isaac jumped back when John came up beside them. "M-morning, John. How are you?"

"Mornin'." He stood between them, big and tall, chest out, methodically slapping the head of a hammer into his palm. "Got a job for an old man like me?"

Isaac swallowed, wishing he'd already had the looming conversation with his boss. He was anxious about his future, but he was nearly just as anxious at the notion of not being allowed to court Grace. Sometimes it felt like he was torn down the middle.

"The *old* men are most likely with the teenagers pulling out nails from the refurbished beams," Isaac said to him. "Experienced men like yourself are handling the bigger projects, like posting the main frame."

"Well, then, I suppose I best be going that way." John sent a glace to his daughter first—who seemed to be frozen in an abnormal position—then he looked at Isaac…who was beginning to feel too hot under the collar. A moment later, the corners of John's eyes crinkled. Was he…smiling at them? "You kids have fun today, *jah*? But be safe."

The moment John walked away, Isaac felt a heavy tension loosen in his shoulder muscles, and he allowed himself to feel optimistic that his talk with John would be a success. "You too!" he called, following the need to shake out his stiff arms and hands.

"You're lucky he respects you," Grace said with a wink, then turned to the house.

Since it wouldn't be Christian to leer at her so obviously as she strolled away, Isaac went back to his own job, happy for the distraction and to be of service. Since barn raisings in Amish country were as common as a winter cold, everyone seemed to know where to go and what to do. It was a perfect group of men working like a well-oiled machine.

Isaac found himself nailing down rafters next to Amos, for which he was grateful. They hadn't spent much time together, and to Isaac's shame, he'd formed an unfair opinion of the man.

After all, Isaac himself understood that no one really knows what's going on in someone else's marriage.

"Got any longer nails?" Amos asked him as they worked side by side.

*"Jah."* Isaac passed him a handful. "I can send for more."

"I'm good for now," Amos replied. "This is going to make a fine barn. Word is that Jerry wanted to expand his herd. I think he'll get to after this."

"I guess that's one good thing about what happened."

"Aye. Here—let me hold that in place for you."

Isaac hadn't expected to have any kind of deep and meaningful conversation with Amos as they'd been clinging to the rafters like frogs to a lily pad, but he was grateful to have some kind of relationship with him.

Noon came, along with the lunchtime bell. Isaac had been smelling the delicious food cooking for the past hour. His parched mouth and growling belly told him it was time to stop. At one of the long tables, he was wedged between Lucas and Samuel Chupp, across from Bishop Turner and his sons, ensnared through the entire meal by answering questions about Silver Springs.

Folks were curious about him, which he understood, but he'd hoped he would be able to spend some of his break with Grace. The few times he saw her, Collin Chupp was either talking to her or following behind her.

Isaac might've felt jealous or envious that someone else was occupying her attention, but he knew where Grace's heart was.

It might've taken until sundown to finish the barn, but the folks of Honey Brook were hard workers, never taking unplanned breaks, always asking what else they could do. Isaac was amazed when families began loading up their carriages and buggies with the tools they'd brought and the pots and pans used for cooking.

Almost out of nothing, a sturdy barn now stood

where there once was only ashes.

"Fine day's work," John said, placing a hand on Isaac's shoulder.

"Mighty fine," Isaac agreed. "But you know it had little to do with me," he quickly added, not wanting to come across as proud or self-serving.

"Oh, nay," John said. "I *do* know that." He looked at Isaac, dead serious, then he broke out in a gleeful chortle. "Lighten up, son. I believe you managed to impress everyone around here." He glanced over his shoulder. "Some more than others, I reckon."

Isaac noticed Grace coming their way. The front of her dress and apron were spotted with splashes of food and hard work, but her eyes were smiling as she looked at him.

"John Zook, I'd like to have a talk with you…" Isaac began, squaring his shoulders. "About that very subject." The words had flowed out so naturally that he felt almost no nervousness.

"Oh?" John said, placing his large body between Isaac and his eyeshot of Grace. "What sort of talk?"

"I think you know, sir."

Isaac didn't go on, but let the words hang in the air. Settle in John's mind. He couldn't get a read on his boss's expression at all, but he did notice he was pinching his lips in and out, and his forward-leaning posture was definitely on guard.

"I'm a very busy man, but I reckon I can make time for you this evening—but late when everyone's retired for the night." He paused to blow out a long breath, "If it's that important."

"It is, sir. And tonight's fine," Isaac said. "Ten o'clock?"

John didn't actually grumble before walking away, but Isaac was grateful they had a good relationship before now. Isaac was no coward, but John Zook could be an intimidating fellow, despite the kindness he'd always shown since the day Isaac was hired.

"Hi," Grace said as she approached, sounding drained but cheerful.

"Hi," Isaac replied, probably sounding the same to her.

Who knew how long they might've remained there if not for the first raindrops falling to the ground.

"Say goodnight, Grace," John said. "Don't want to get stuck in the mud."

At the word "mud," Grace's eyes went wide, looking at Isaac like they had a special secret—which they did.

"*Guti nacht*," Isaac said.

"*Nacht.*" Grace grabbed onto the railing of the buggy, but then stopped. "See you in the morning?"

"I'll meet you there." He nodded at John, who only stared back.

As they drove away, Isaac was pretty sure he wouldn't be able to think straight until he laid it all on the line before Grace's father.

• • •

Isaac was a grown man. He had a six-year-old daughter and had come through more trials than people twice his age. So why did he feel about twelve years old when he knocked on the front door?

Only a few seconds passed before John opened it, holding it wide, speechlessly inviting Isaac inside. Besides a small, battery-operated table lamp by the couch, the rest of the downstairs was dark. Everyone else in the house, asleep.

"Evening," Isaac said as he removed his hat. "I

really appreciate you giving me the time."

"Yes, yes," John replied. "Have a seat." Isaac quickly obeyed, but John remained standing. "Uh, you want something from the kitchen? There's no coffee, though."

"I'm fine."

John grumbled something under his breath then glanced away, slowly rubbing his palms together, a gesture Isaac recognized as a stalling tactic of his own. Seemed his boss wasn't exactly sure where to start, either.

Finally, though, John took a seat in the armchair across from him. A picture suddenly appeared in Isaac's head…that early morning he'd come there to find Grace asleep on the couch, his daughter safe in her arms. The nerves making his hands shake practically dissolved.

"I think you know why I'm here," Isaac began.

John ran a hand down his beard. "Could be."

Isaac sat up straight and leaned forward. "After nearly two months, I've grown very fond of your… family—I respect *you* a great deal. I'll always be grateful for the opportunity you've given—"

"Oh, mercy, son." John cut in. "Are you in love with my daughter?"

"I…" Isaac had never felt so tongue-tied in his life.

"What? Too soon?" John sat back and crossed his arms, an almost amused expression on his face. "You said it's been nearly two months. Why, I saw Eve across the room at her cousin's wedding and told everyone in earshot I was gonna marry her."

*Marry?* He'd come there to ask John if he could take Grace on a date. Of course, he knew more dates would follow—he was dead certain about that. And then they'd be officially courting…which usually meant they had strong intentions to…

Did any of that scare Isaac? No. Was he not already looking forward to every step in that process with Grace Zook? Yes.

So? Did he love her?

"Since you're not willing to admit that yet, how about I rephrase it?" John cocked his head to the side. "Are you here to ask if you can court Gracie?"

Isaac exhaled, grateful John had let him off the hook. *"Jah."*

"I'm your boss, you know. I could fire you on the spot."

A shudder zipped up Isaac's spine, but after examining John's expression, he lifted a confident smile. "I don't think you'll do that."

"Aye." John leaned forward, resting his elbows on his knees. "I don't think I will, either." He laced his fingers in and out. "I do have some concerns, though. You're in Honey Brook temporarily. If Grace is already attached to you, won't dating make an inevitable separation worse?"

Isaac was about to reply, but John kept going.

"You've been married before, you have a child— now I'm not saying those are negatives, I'm just wondering how they fit into your plans for my daughter."

Isaac nodded, taking note, but didn't speak, sensing John still wasn't finished.

"Grace can be hardheaded. She gets that from me, and she's got her heart set on something I'm still not sure I can fully support—you know that."

John paused and looked down at his hands, giving Isaac a chance to recall the conversation he and John had had all those weeks ago at the medical clinic. He'd confided in Isaac that he was worried about

Grace continuing with horse training. He hadn't said it flat-out then, but Isaac suspected John would be perfectly at ease if his daughter gave up her passion and settled down. He'd be retiring soon, and he'd either shut down Zook's Horse Training Farm, sell it off, or pass it on to a member of the family.

Isaac suspected Grace hoped to keep the business—despite the rarity of women owning companies.

"You've thought all of this through, I assume," John said, lifting his eyes to Isaac's. "And more so, I reckon."

Because of Isaac's overall confidence, he sometimes wondered if people supposed he always had everything figured out. In this case, it couldn't be further from the truth.

"Those same questions have been keeping me up at night. But I truly care about your daughter, and she cares for me." Isaac wondered if he should elaborate, but then thought it better to keep it basic. "We've grown very close; we trust each other. When the time comes, I'm sure we can figure it out."

"I have little doubt," John said, nodding. "But there's the money, too. I hired you to do a job and plan on paying you exactly what you're worth—though the final decision will be on Travis."

"Oh?" Isaac asked, his mindset suddenly shifting. "I wasn't aware Travis would be involved."

"He wasn't at first. We've spoken a few times…he wanted updates on Sin. He's mighty impressed—so impressed that he intends to endow quite a bit of money to the lead trainer. Publicity, too. He's got all sorts of ideas about cross promotion at the shows and competitions. Sounds high level—career-changing, I'd expect." He paused to blow out a breath. "I hired you, but I always knew Grace would be a part of it.

Though I didn't know then how big a part she'd become. It's…different now. There's more at stake. I hope you understand that."

Isaac could almost feel the waves of concern rolling off his boss. He felt them, too. He and Grace were a partnership now—if solely for this one project. And if Travis was willing to endorse only one of them…

John was right. There was a lot more at stake. But what could be done?

After another long moment of thought, Isaac ran a hand through his hair. "I do understand. And frankly, I don't think I'd have it any other way. Your daughter's changed my life." When he looked at John, he felt even more at ease when he saw that he was smiling. "It puts her and me at a greater impasse," Isaac continued. "But we've been at one from the beginning."

"Well, you're a good man, Isaac King. And I think I'm a better person from knowing you. I know my sweet Gracie will be safe on a date with you."

"Thank you," Isaac said, not having expected such praise when he'd first entered the house. He enjoyed talking with John—always had. But when his boss rose to his feet, Isaac knew their conversation was over.

"Travel safely," John said, opening the door. As Isaac was about to leave, John reached for his arm. "It's about time you asked to talk to me about her." He grinned. "I was wondering what took you so long."

# CHAPTER THIRTY-SIX

It seemed the fates were against Grace taking that long-anticipated buggy ride with Isaac. When she'd said goodbye to him after the barn raising, feeling those little wet drops from heaven, it didn't stopped raining for three days.

Grace was grateful they had a big barn and an oversized stable with plenty of room to entertain the horses during the rainy days. Every morning, afternoon, and evening, she made sure to walk each one up and down the aisle, practicing liberty with those who'd yet to master it.

Her two little sisters, accompanied by Sadie, helped give Cincinnati, Honey Pot, and Lord Byron horsey makeovers. Leah was a whiz with the clippers, while Jane and Sadie took turns practicing their mane-braiding skills.

"It's about time we give these stalls a good deep clean," Grace said. The mere suggestion of working rather than playing scared the little girls away, leaving only Grace and Isaac in the stables.

"Did you know that would happen?" Isaac asked, using a pitchfork to haul out the old sawdust from Cincinnati's stall.

"I didn't think it would be so easy," Grace admitted, getting a broom so she could sweep off the bare mats. "Should've thought of it three days ago."

Isaac laughed. "And I figured it was only horses you have power over."

"I feel sorry for Sarah. She's the one who'll have to deal with all the muddy little boots and dirty dresses after they're done splashing in the puddles outside."

Isaac was quiet for a moment, concentrating on his work. Grace couldn't help taking the opportunity to observe—from afar. His shirtsleeves were pushed up above his elbows, showing tanned skin, dark arm hair, and big muscles. Once she felt her mouth go dry, she quickly looked away.

"I, uh, was thinking of trying a new hay for the fall," she said, going back to her sweeping. "I read about a nice grass-alfalfa mix, but it comes all the way from Cortez, Colorado."

Isaac looked up, leaning on the pitchfork. "Decker Hay Farm?"

Grace blinked in surprise. "I think that's the name. How in heavens did you guess?"

"They've got a great reputation, though I've never used them before. A bit extravagant for plain folks."

"That's true. But I might suggest it to Travis Carlson when he comes for Cincinnati." She held her breath, waiting to see Isaac's reaction.

It was a subject neither of them had spoken of in quite a while: the day their training the intelligent Morgan would be over. Grace didn't want to bring it up, but wouldn't they have to talk about it sometime?

Seemed Isaac didn't want to discuss the real issue, either. "That's a good idea," he said, going back to work, clearing out the old straw and sawdust even faster. "You should tell him."

Grace waited to see if he would say anything more, but he seemed fixated on his task.

"*Jah*, I will, then." Her heart felt mopey as she went about cleaning the stalls, moving the horses in and out, making sure to spend quality time with each of them. Their conversation was pleasant like it always was, but Grace had come to expect more.

Had something changed Isaac's mind? Or was he, too, feeling down at the thought of ending their partnership?

"I don't know what's going to happen."

Grace looked toward where Isaac was, three stalls over. "About what?"

"About Travis." He jammed his rake into a bale of hay. "The money he's going to pay for training Sin." He removed his straw hat and tossed it onto a chair. "Honestly, I don't like even thinking about it, but I can't help it now." He paused and gave her a long look.

Grace felt her shoulders relaxing some. At least they were finally talking about it.

"I know you're hoping to be able to afford the operation for your mother," he said. "I want that for her, too. And *you* know I need the money and connections to make a better life for Sadie." He raked both hands through his hair, looking mind-weary. "Believe me, I've been over it a hundred times."

"So have I," Grace said, wanting to take a step toward him, maybe reach out for his hand. *Maam* needed the surgery so badly now, and they'd have to scrape together every penny for that. But it made Grace want to burst into tears when she thought of Isaac having to move back in with his in-laws.

"I just wish…" he began, but paused to blow out a breath.

"Wish what?"

He looked down, running a hand over his forehead. "I have a little money saved. I wish I could pay for Eve's surgery myself and then—"

"Isaac King!" Grace cut in. She was about to reprimand him for even thinking of using his hard-earned money for anything besides his own future.

But then the sheer kindness of his words touched her so tenderly, all she could say was, "You're the most generous man I've ever known." After a moment of thought, she added, "In the end, though, it's not up to us. Not really. My father will decide on the money. He's seen how we've been training together. I'm sure it will be fair."

Isaac gave her the same long look as before, his mouth halfway open, but then he shook his head and glanced away.

"Isaac," she said. "We've known this from the start."

"*Jah*," he said, picking up the rake again. "But there's something you don't know. Travis and John have spoken recently about a change in the compensation deal, then John talked to me."

"*Daed* talked to Travis?" After Isaac nodded, she went on. "And…and my father spoke to you about it privately, without me?"

After a quiet moment, Isaac nodded, a strange look in his eyes.

Grace tried very hard to keep her initial reaction from feeling left out, or even betrayed. But really, shouldn't she be an equal member of the partnership? She looked at Isaac, ready to pepper him with a million questions. But she stopped, realizing repentance shone in his hazel eyes, not any kind of manipulation.

She took in a deep breath for preparation, then blew it out slowly. "Okay. What did Travis say?"

Grace stood right where she was as Isaac told her about the opportunities the "lead trainer" was going to receive from Travis. The advertising and promotion. The money…that both of them desperately needed. *Daed* had been more than hinting that he'd be retiring soon—he'd even mentioned wanting to spend more time with *Maam* in the near future. This could be Grace's only chance to make the kind of training farm she'd always dreamed of.

"What did you tell my father?" she asked when he'd finished.

"I told him I wouldn't have it any other way."

"You mean, you *want* to be in competition with me?"

One corner of his mouth pulled back. "I told him it's a complication, but if I'd never been brought here…" He paused and dipped his chin. "I never would've met you."

As he looked up at her, a pleasant little flutter settled in Grace's stomach. Her breaths were heavier and slower, her own lips curling into a smile.

After weeks of trying so hard to get along and respect each other, they were at odds again now— each out to win a single prize. But it was different this time. Grace had feelings for Isaac, very strong ones. And she'd be out of her mind if she didn't recognize how much Isaac cared for her.

Should their mutual attraction make this easier? Or harder?

"I have an idea," Isaac said, raking up a pile of used straw. "How about you let me do all the training the next few days. You handled so much of it while I was working on the barn raising." He shrugged. "Sound fair? You know, to sort of even up our time?"

For another uncomfortable second, the suspicious side of Grace was on high alert. Was Isaac trying to "even up" their training sessions so *he* would be in a better position to get Travis's endorsement?

Even considering that felt wrong to Grace, and a shiver of shame ran up the back of her neck. Isaac would never do something like that—to her or anyone. She'd never met a man with more integrity.

After a few quiet moments between them, Isaac walked over to her. "We'll figure it out," he said, then reached out and ran a finger over Grace's forearm. The touch sent a tingle all through her body, reminding her how much she liked and respected this tall, strong, good man before her. Trusted him with everything.

"Stay for supper?" she asked, unable to stop from smiling, forgetting the huge obstacle in their way.

"I shouldn't," he said. "I've been letting Sadie stay up late all week. She won't want to wake for school tomorrow if I don't get her back on a schedule."

"I understand," Grace said. And somehow that made her like him even more.

"Tomorrow, then?" he asked, rolling down his sleeves.

Grace nodded. "Tomorrow."

• • •

The loud bang shot Grace nearly out of her bed. Another flash of light, then an even louder crash. When had the storm rolled in? Last night, it drizzled, but not even the *Farmer's Almanac* had mentioned a thunderstorm.

She sat up in bed, listening, trying to gauge when the next flash of lightning would strike. It hit hard and close. In the silence afterward, she heard a sound from outside that sent her flying out of bed. She grabbed her dressing gown, throwing it on over her long nightdress as she ran down the stairs.

Her bare feet were muddy by the time she got to the stables. She grabbed the battery-powered lantern that *Daed* always kept in his office and turned it on. A few of the horses were making a fuss, but most of the whinnying was coming from Cincinnati. For all Grace knew, this was his first experience with torrential weather.

"Hey there, boy," she said as she carefully approached him. Lightning struck, followed by a loud clap of thunder. "Whoa," Grace said, keeping her distance. "It's okay, boy. I've got you." But the large, powerful Morgan wouldn't calm down, wouldn't let Grace within three feet of him.

It took another ten minutes or so, but finally, Grace was able to step inside Sin's stall, though she kept her back pressed to the gate, not getting too close. Then she suddenly remembered something her father had taught her years ago during a similar thunderstorm.

"I'll be right back," she said, making sure the horse was looking her straight in the eyes. "It's okay." Then she ran to the office, opened the bottom drawer of *Daed*'s desk, and pulled out a little box. "There it is," she said, removing a small brown bottle then running back to the stall.

"Hey boy. Good, good boy," Grace cooed as she slowly slid inside the stall. She opened the little bottle and sprinkled a few drops of the liquid on the palms of her hands. Carefully, so as not to startle the horse, she extended her hands in Sin's direction, palms forming a cup.

Grace exhaled slowly as the curious horse took a few steps toward her. "You like that, huh?" she whispered when Cincinnati allowed her to hold her hands up to his nose. "Smells nice, doesn't it? I like it, too. So calming, eh?"

Not too long later, she was stroking his neck with

one hand while keeping the other hand at his nose. Sin nuzzled her head, calming down, much to Grace's relief. But then suddenly, he lifted his head and backed into a corner of the stall. A split second later, Grace heard what Sin must've heard: footsteps running toward the stables.

"Isaac!" she exclaimed.

"I got here as fast as I could," he said, out of breath, hazel eyes looking frantic in the dim light. "Is he okay?"

Grace didn't think twice about how he'd appeared from out of nowhere in the middle of the night, completely soaked from the rain still pounding down outside. "I've been here for a while," she said, relieved that he was there. "He's calm for the moment, but the thunder makes him frantic."

"Should we secure him? Tie him up so he won't hurt himself?" Isaac opened the gate and stepped inside just as carefully as Grace had.

"I was wondering the same thing," Grace said. "But then I remembered the first time we saw him. How he'd been tied up in the back of that trailer."

"And he broke loose," Isaac finished for her. "You're right. That would probably stress him out even more."

"And bad memories," she added, turning back to the horse. "Shhh, good boy," she said, extending her hands again.

"Is that lavender?"

"Essential oil. It calmed him down a minute ago." She paused to roll her eyes. "I know, I know. You think it's nonsense."

Isaac opened his mouth, but then closed it. "Can I smell?" he said after a moment.

Grace pushed out her bottom lip in surprise.

"Really?"

He held out his open hand, so Grace passed him the bottle tentatively. She didn't think he would make fun of her like when she'd first told him about using the oil, but he could be just as strongly opinionated as she could.

Isaac sprinkled some into his palms, just as Grace had. "Hmm," he said, after taking a little sniff. "It's… nice." He smiled and pressed his nose into his hand. "Smells like a meadow." He chuckled softly. "Makes my eyelids feel droopy." He glanced at Sin. "I guess I can see how it might feel calming. Will you try it on him again while I watch?"

"Okay," Grace whispered. Much like before, she slowly approached the Morgan, arms outstretched, palms cupped. It happened quicker this time, as if Sin knew he had nothing to fear.

"Amazing," Isaac said in a low voice. "Look at that."

Grace couldn't help lifting a tiny smile of victory. Not that it was a competition, but she appreciated that Isaac saw merit in another of her techniques. When it came to training, it seemed as though there wasn't much they didn't agree on anymore.

"It's not me," she said as Sin nuzzled his nose into her palms, then nuzzled her neck, under Grace's hair. "It's the smell. He loves it." She couldn't help giggling at the sweet horse's sudden affection.

A moment later, Isaac joined her, and together they stroked Sin's neck, four hands working in unison. When the next clap of thunder struck, the horse barely seemed to notice.

"I think the storm's passing," Isaac said, giving Sin a scratch behind his ears.

Grace exhaled. "About time," she said. When she

heard Isaac laugh softly, she looked at him, clearly, for maybe the first time since he'd arrived. It had been nearly an hour since he'd shown up, but his hair, clothes, and skin were still damp.

"Drenched again, I see," she said with a doting smile.

Even by the dim lantern light, she saw him smile back. "You were expecting me to run a mile and a half through the rain and not be?"

"Run?" Grace was taken aback. "On foot? All the way from the Chupps'?"

He nodded. "When the thunder woke me, I knew Sin would be anxious. And I wasn't about to take another horse out into this mess." He pointed his chin outside.

"You didn't think I would take care of him?"

"I *knew* you would. But I didn't think — I just came."

When Isaac kept his eyes locked on hers, Grace couldn't help wondering if maybe it wasn't just Sin he'd wanted to check. When he still didn't look away, Grace took a step back. "You must be freezing. Let me find you a towel."

"I'll get it," he said. "I know where they are."

Grace nodded, then turned her attention back to Cincinnati, running a hand down his broad face, though she couldn't help looking over her shoulder to see Isaac walking toward the tack shelves. When he returned, he was carrying a towel in one hand and a big quilt in the other.

"Here," he said, handing her the quilt. He took the towel and began drying his face and behind his neck.

"*Danke*," Grace said reflexively. "But aren't you cold?" She attempted to hand the quilt back to him.

"Nay," he said while drying his hands and

forearms. "It's for you. I figure you weren't about to go back inside but wanted to stay with the horses."

Grace's chest felt warm, comforted by how well he knew her. "You're right," she admitted.

"I also figured you'd want to be comfortable." He pointed at the quilt. "And, since you're not leaving anytime soon, neither am I."

Grace had never felt like this before. Yes, her parents had always taken good care of her, but it was different coming from Isaac. She'd wanted to take care of him when he'd gotten hurt at the mud sale, and now here he was, taking care of her just the same.

Isaac arranged the quilt on the floor, giving Cincinnati plenty of room to walk around if he wanted. "Sit," Isaac said. Grace obeyed. But then Isaac disappeared, returning a moment later with another blanket. "Here," he said. "You got wet too, you know. And whatever that thing is doesn't look very, um, thick."

Grace suddenly remembered she'd come straight from bed, at least having the foresight to have grabbed her dressing gown on the way outside, but not dressed properly at all.

"Oh!" She reached for the blanket, immediately wrapping it around her body, covering robe and nightgown.

Isaac laughed softly. "Please don't be embarrassed. I hardly noticed." He sent her a look with a crooked grin that made her tingle.

"Sit," she said a moment later, gesturing to a spot on the opposite side of the quilt.

"Long day," he said after lowering to the ground. Grace noticed then that Isaac wasn't dressed all that properly, either. He was still in his sleeping shirt, which was looser and thinner and more open at the throat than his regular shirts. He must've caught her staring because a second later, he adjusted the towel to cover his chest.

Grace felt heat rise to her cheeks when she looked away. The physical desires swimming through her mind and body were coming more often, even when she tried to—halfheartedly—pray them away.

"Very long day," she agreed. "I realize rain is a blessing from *Gott*, but honestly, I've had enough blessings this week."

"It's been fun for the *kinnahs*," he said. "Sadie loves the rain. Even if it's only sprinkling, she'll find a puddle and stomp away until she's soaked to the skin." He dipped his head and smiled. "I was just like that as a boy."

Grace leaned back, balancing on her hands. "Tell me more about when you were a child."

While the flame of the lamp flickered gently and the rain continued outside, Isaac shared delightful stories about a childhood filled with boyhood adventures, lessons from goodly parents, and a security and happiness that could come only from a home full of love.

"Anna sounds like so much fun," Grace said after he'd shared about the time his youngest sister tried to train her twin goats to fetch like dogs. "I'd like to meet her someday."

"I'm sure you will, Grace," he said.

Another wave of warmth and tingles filled her chest. Similar waves had been washing over her ever since they'd sat down together in the dimly lit stable, the sounds of the rain and the random horse whinny filling the night.

"She was the last of us to marry," he continued. "She got engaged quite young, but her husband is a good man. Very upstanding. I was relieved because it happened right before Martha…"

"Before she passed away?" Grace finished for him.

"Aye. It was one less worry for me. Otherwise, she might've come to live with me at Martha's parents' home." He paused and bowed his head. "I would've hated to expose her to that."

Grace couldn't help it. She needed to touch him, to let him know she cared. So she reached out and took his hand.

"I'm sorry," Isaac said. "I don't mean to speak so harshly. They have positive qualities, too."

Grace couldn't help but exhale a light laugh. "You see the good in everyone."

"I try." He gave her hand a squeeze, and they shared a happy, meaningful look that made Grace feel like she was glowing. "Can I tell you something?"

"You can tell me anything, Isaac. Don't you know that?"

"I do," he said. "It's just… I can't believe how much my life has changed since…since I moved here."

*"Jah?"*

"I'm hopeful about the future for the first time in, well, I don't know how long it's been. I would never disrespect the memory of Sadie's mother, but we weren't very happy at the end. All I could do was try to be the best man and best father that I could."

"Isaac." She squeezed his hand. "I've seen you with Sadie. You're wonderful with her. She adores you." She moved closer and took his hand in both of hers. "You're the best man I know."

"You don't know how much that means to me. I never thought I'd…"

When his voice faded out and he dropped his chin, she pulled at his hand, nudging him to finish.

"I never thought I would meet someone like you," he finally said. "Being around you lifts me, makes me happy." He looked up. "I'm a better man because of you."

No one had ever said anything like that to Grace. She was so happy, she thought she just might fly up to heaven. For weeks, they'd been tiptoeing around their feelings for each other, but now Grace really knew.

"I've been thinking," Isaac continued. "I'm pretty sure we should go ahead and count the mud sale as our first date—non-officially."

"Why?" Grace asked.

"Wait." Isaac held up a finger. "You'll see my logic in a minute."

Grace smiled as his hazel eyes became animated, his face so handsome. So very kind.

"The evening ride home after the mud sale should definitely count as date number two."

"Okay," Grace agreed, though she didn't see what he was up to yet. "What about when you came home after the fire?" she asked. "We spent quite a bit of time together then. Is that date three?"

"I knew you were smart." Isaac grinned. "Date three, huh? Well, then…" Without removing his hand from inside her grip, he moved so he was sitting right at her side. "I think this is allowed."

Grace felt another wonderful rush as Isaac put an arm around her, gently pulling her close. "*Jah*?" she managed to say, though her breaths were shallow and short.

"The first day of the rainstorm," Isaac continued, "when we reorganized all the tack." Tenderly, Isaac shifted closer, moving his mouth right to her ear. "Pretty sure that was number four," he whispered, his warm breath tickling the side of her neck, sending delicious shivers all over her body.

Grace closed her eyes. "Wh-what about date five?"

"Do you think we've had one?" Isaac asked, his voice soft like a breeze.

*"Jah."* She let the word drift out of her mouth, unable to stop it. A moment later, she felt his hand on her cheek, his thumb stroking across her skin. Grace almost couldn't breathe. "Tonight," she whispered.

"Ah." He moved her hand that was holding his to press against his chest. Then a moment later, it moved to her other cheek. "Grace," he whispered, cupping her face, tilting it toward his. "Are you sure?"

It took everything in her, but Grace filled her lungs, then lifted her chin so she could show him she was sure; so she could look him in his hazel eyes and tell him everything else.

Before she could fill her lungs again, she felt herself slowly being pulled forward. The soft touch of his lips on hers felt as welcome and natural as anything. Then instantly, it felt as though her heart was on fire, her pulse galloping like a runaway horse. Instinctively, she leaned in to him, allowing herself to submit, to enjoy every touch and breath and explosion inside her body.

Her life would never be the same again.

# CHAPTER THIRTY-SEVEN

It hadn't been Isaac's plan to kiss Grace tonight, but somewhere inside he knew all the time they'd spent together would eventually come to a head. His feelings for her had been building stronger and stronger until she was all he could think about.

Thinking led to acting, and every bone in his body was calling to her as she sat on that quilt in the dimly lit horse stall, reminding him of all they'd been through and all the ways he'd been falling for her.

Just like her father had suspected.

A clap of sudden lightning startled him, and for a split second, he wondered if it was a sign from *Gott* to pull back. But then he felt Grace grasp the front of his shirt, their lips still connected, and Isaac knew it wasn't time yet to pull away.

Her skin was soft and smooth between his hands as he held her cheeks. He'd do anything to brand this memory onto his brain forever. But time could not last forever.

The sweetness of hearing Grace gasp for breath made his already pounding heart race even faster, as if he was the old Cincinnati, broken loose and running at top speed. Fearing he would want to kiss her again, right then, Isaac touched his forehead to hers. For a moment, they just breathed together, Grace still clutching the front of his shirt in her hands.

"Wow."

Her whisper made him chuckle softly.

"Yeah?" He whispered back.

"Oh *jah*."

They snickered at each other as the rain continued to pour, large drops hitting the barn roof.

"I didn't know…" Grace began in a whisper.

"Know what?" Isaac asked, his forehead still pressed to hers so he couldn't see her eyes.

She took a beat, then sighed. Isaac felt her breath like a warm wave on his face. "I didn't know it would feel like that," she said. "I didn't know *I* could feel like that." Finally she pulled back and lifted her chin. Her blue eyes were beautiful. "Like this."

"Can I tell you something?"

She smiled. "Of course."

Isaac first took a pause. He wasn't sure he should admit this, though he'd been thinking about it ever since the kiss had begun. "I didn't know I could feel like this, either. Grace, I never have." He reached down and took her hand. "Not with anyone." He lifted her hand and kissed her palm. "Not ever."

He hoped she understood what he meant. He'd been in love before—at least he'd thought so. He'd courted a woman, proposed, married, had a daughter. Yet, he'd never felt so happy, so alive and strong as he did right this second…sitting in a barn with Grace Zook in the middle of a rainstorm.

Grace gazed into his eyes, sparking all those physical yearnings to come alive again. He knew he shouldn't kiss her a second time. He wasn't that strong.

"I should go home."

"No!" Grace practically yelled the word. Then she dropped her chin and laughed quietly. "Please don't go yet."

Isaac took in a deep breath. "It's hard for me to sit here with you," he admitted. "I want to keep kissing you. I want to take you in my arms, Grace, and hold you close to me. You know I can't, though."

"I know," she said, nodding. Then she looked him in the eyes. "Maybe after another five dates?"

He couldn't help laughing. "I think it would be more appropriate then."

After her own quiet laugh, Grace reached up and took his face between her hands, staring him in the eyes. Isaac couldn't move, could barely breathe as she looked at him with an intensity he didn't realize she had.

"You're the best man I've ever known, Isaac King," she whispered. Then she leaned forward, kissing him on one cheek.

Isaac clenched his fists together, forcing himself not to touch her, not to give in to the physical desires to love this woman properly, fully.

And just before he might've yielded, Grace sat back. "I think it stopped raining."

Isaac wondered how she could tell, for all he could hear inside his head was his pounding heart, his own fast, labored breathing.

"The sun will be up before long," she continued, letting go of his face. "We'll be seeing each other again soon enough."

"That's true," he replied, though he still wasn't ready to move. Even though he'd been the one to stop the path they'd been on, in his heart, he didn't want to be separated from her for even an hour.

A moment later, she was on her feet, turning her attention to Cincinnati. Isaac was grateful for the space, for the fresh air to breathe that didn't fill his senses with all things Grace. For a second, he dipped his chin, offering one quick prayer of thanks that they hadn't gotten carried away and done anything regretful.

Finally he found the strength to rise to his feet, though his thigh muscles felt shaky, his head lighter than air. "Are you going back to bed?" he asked, joining her as she attended to the horse.

"I'm going inside," she said. "But I doubt I'll sleep a wink."

The flirtatious look she flashed made him grateful again for *Gott* blessing him so thoroughly. "Same," he admitted. "I'd hate for Sadie to wake up and find me gone."

"Go," Grace said. "Three training sessions today, okay?"

"Whatever you say."

It was a silly way to think, but after they'd said their extended goodbye, Isaac felt as though he was walking on clouds all the way back to the Chupps'. Had his feet ever touched the earth? Or had angels been his escorts?

• • •

The rest of that day was a blur, for in between morning training sessions, Isaac—quite nonchalantly—had asked Grace Zook for their first official date. After she'd accepted, Isaac knew he hadn't stopped grinning until he'd finished his day's work.

The roads were still muddy, and not many buggies were out as Isaac made his way to the Zooks' just as the sun had set, but this time, there was nothing that would keep him from beginning their courtship.

"I hesitate to ask where we're going," Grace said as she sat beside him in the open carriage. She wore a dark blue dress and black cape fastened at the throat, and her eyes and cheeks practically glowed, pink lips smiling.

"Afraid I'm planning a mud fight?" Isaac found it hard to keep his eyes on her and on the road.

"I wouldn't put it past you." She laughed. Then she cleared her throat. "I would ask you about your day along the way but, since I was with you practically every minute, there isn't much to catch up on."

"Sadie's very excited," he offered.

"You told her?"

"Yup." Isaac felt his own smile broaden.

"Does she understand?"

"Probably not. Since we work together, she knows us spending time together in the evening is different. The two oldest Chupp girls talk about dating and courtships as often as they can. Sadie may understand more than she realizes, but I doubt she understands the actual significance."

"Oh?" Grace straightened her posture and blinked several times, as if playing coy. "And what is the significance?"

"That I've been observing you, Grace Zook, for weeks now. And I've become very interested in getting to know you better." He paused. "If this were a more traditional situation, I would've sat across from you during singing time. I would've asked you one or two questions while we ate cookies and drank punch. And when I'd worked up the courage, I would've asked if I could drive you home—"

"I would've said yes," Grace said, cutting in. "To everything."

Isaac reached out and took her hand, sliding it into the crook of his elbow, relaxing into a smile when Grace took his arm. "We would have dessert with your folks on our first date," he continued. "Maybe meet up with another couple for supper on our second date."

"I guess not much about us has been traditional."

Isaac couldn't help glancing at her, relishing the way she'd said "us."

"And I don't mind that in the least," she added.

Isaac didn't reply, but dropped into deep thought for a moment. He'd done everything right the first time around, he'd prayed and followed his heart and been obedient down to the letter. He'd never, ever consider himself lucky that Martha had passed away. No matter how he'd felt about her at the end, he would never be happy that Sadie was left without her mother.

Still, because of all that, he was here with Grace now in the crisp night air. Anytime he wanted, he knew he could hold her hand, put an arm around her. Maybe he'd give her a tiny, chaste kiss. None of that would've been possible if their situation had started out traditionally.

"I think I know where you're taking me," Grace said. As she studied him through her eyelashes, she squeezed his arm.

"Is that so?"

"Mm-hmm."

Honestly, Isaac hadn't planned any kind of elaborate date, he was just looking forward to being alone with her, with them both away from the stables and dressed up, and especially with his intentions now known to her father.

It wasn't too much farther, and she'd see exactly where they were going. He'd walked by Annie's Sweet Shop and Creamery a dozen times but had never gone in, though the smell of homemade waffle cones wafting out of their open doorway was always tempting. He could almost taste the fresh strawberry ice cream now.

"Aren't you turning here?"

"Hmm?" Isaac asked. When he looked where Grace was pointing, he noticed that it wasn't on the way toward anywhere. It was just a dim and silent road that led to what seemed to be an even dimmer pasture.

"Grace Zook…" Isaac playfully squinted down at her. "Are you trying to get me alone?"

She tilted her head. "We're always alone."

"Are you trying to get me away from your father's property, in the dark, under a full moon?"

When she smiled and slowly blinked, her blue eyes seemed to be reflecting that very moon. "Maybe."

Suddenly, the last thing Isaac craved was ice cream.

# CHAPTER THIRTY-EIGHT

"Did you know I thought you were a boy when I first saw you?"

"That day in the pasture?"

Isaac laughed and took her hand. "That very day."

Grace loved how her hand fit inside his so naturally, as if it were always meant to be there. The other evening, when he'd been holding her hand, he'd said how soft her skin was. She'd nearly laughed, for she'd been working with ropes and leads and reins for most of her life. The palms of her hands were almost as rough as her father's.

At the time, though, she'd loved how he'd run a finger inside her palm, making her believe her skin was just as smooth as any other woman's — any traditional Amish woman's who worked with bread dough and oven mitts and babies instead of horses and all their rough tack.

Isaac King certainly had a way with words, and if Grace wasn't careful, she'd melt away under his sweet accolades.

"That was the first time I noticed your dimple, too."

Grace couldn't help smiling self-consciously, dipping her chin, blushing, because she knew her dimple was on full display.

"Not fair. I can't see it now — too dark," he said, lowering his voice to a whisper. "But wasn't that your plan all along?"

Grace felt another blush coming on. Although she hadn't been the one to plan their first date, she had assumed Isaac wanted nothing more than to be alone with her, for that was her wish, too. Though she'd never been there before now, the dead-end street between the pharmacy and the bookstore was a well-known spot for couples who wanted privacy.

But when Isaac had driven right past it, Grace had to say something. It hadn't dawned on her that Isaac wouldn't have known about the courting spot, since he hadn't grown up in Honey Brook. Grace felt a thrill in her stomach when Isaac had led the carriage in a circle, heading back to that dead-end street.

Standing under the moonlight with him, she wondered if she'd be nervous. But Grace had never been so happy.

"That's when I noticed that hat of yours," she said. He wasn't wearing the cowboy-hat-shaped straw hat now, but a black brimmed one that was for more formal occasions.

In fact, now that she thought about it, she hadn't seen that other hat in a while.

"You don't wear it anymore," she pointed out. "Why?"

Isaac touched his black hat then stared forward for a moment. "Someone gave it to me."

When he didn't go on, Grace wondered if it had been a gift from Martha. Though exchanging presents wasn't customary under the Ordnung, maybe it was okay in Silver Springs. After all, she was learning how different their communities really were. At the thought, Grace couldn't help rubbing her lips together, remembering that kiss in the barn. In Honey Brook, it was customary to save the first kiss for after the couple was engaged.

Grace looked at his profile under the moonlight. His strong jaw, broad forehead, intense eyes. She'd easily conformed to *his* rules under the Ordnung rather than hers when it came to dating.

"It was around the same time that folks started calling me Amish Cowboy," Isaac continued. "It was an innocent nickname that the church leaders didn't have a problem with. Anyway, one of my first customers saw it in a shop and gave it to me…maybe as a joke, I don't know. But enough people heard about it and it became this thing. Before I knew it, I'd been wearing it for years."

"What changed?" Grace asked.

"I came here." He turned to look at her. "Everything changed when I came here."

Knowing she was about to be kissed, Grace's heart started beating hard as a wonderful ball of heat formed in her stomach. In preparation, she sucked in a quick breath and closed her eyes.

"It's not right."

She loved hearing his voice when it dropped to a whisper like that, but after a moment, Grace didn't know what his words had to do with kissing. Finally, she opened her eyes. Isaac was looking the other way.

"What's not right?" she asked, trying to slow her breaths.

"Wearing that hat," he replied. "The rules of what is proper attire are more casual in Silver Springs, but they sure aren't here. My excuse at first was that I was an outsider, just visiting Honey Brook, so why bother changing my customs?"

"I see how that makes sense," Grace agreed.

"But like I said, things changed. I don't feel like an outsider anymore. I feel like I belong here just as much as I did back home. That hat—though still special to me—doesn't belong here. No matter where I go, I want to be obedient, I want *Gott* to know I will always do what is right."

"Isaac…" Grace said, looking into his eyes.

*"Jah?"*

She laughed softly under her breath. "Nothing. I don't know." She wanted to tell him everything she was feeling. How'd she'd grown to admire him—his good, righteous example. How she knew she'd never find a more obedient man in all of Lancaster County—not a kinder man, either. And how she knew he was raising a daughter who would follow in his footsteps.

"You miss the hat that much?" Isaac asked, touching her shoulder, then running his hand down her arm.

Instantaneously, heat returned to Grace's body, with a need and a longing she couldn't explain or control. She lifted her chin, hoping he'd kiss her this time.

"Anyway," he said, dropping his hand that was holding her arm, "as long as I'm in Honey Brook, I won't wear that hat."

"Such a stickler," Grace said after blowing out a long breath.

"I'm happy to say I'm guilty of that." He shrugged but smiled. "I'm feeling guilty about some other things, too, Grace."

"Like what?"

"Like what happened in the barn."

She knew her cheeks and throat were flushing, but she didn't care. "I don't feel guilty about that—and I'm from Honey Brook. Why should you?"

In a moment of bravery, she stepped up and put her arms around him, just like she would if it were Amos or her father or anyone else she'd hugged a thousand times in her life.

But hugging Isaac King felt nothing like anyone else.

His shirt smelled clean but with a hint of being around horses. She loved that smell, for it was a perfect definition of Isaac. His chest was solid as she rested her cheek against it. When she felt his arms go around her, she closed her eyes as swirls and flashes of lightning lit up her insides.

"Grace." The word was barely a whisper, and when he'd said it, his arms around her tightened.

She exhaled contentedly, never feeling so natural than when they were together like this. She felt sure of herself and of the future. She felt strong and soft at the same time, wanting him to hold her like that until the sun came up.

His hands moved to her shoulders, one stroking her cheek now, so gently. Grace's limbs felt weak, knowing what was about to happen. Screaming for it to happen.

"Open your eyes."

Grace was confused but obeyed. Isaac was staring down at her, his eyebrows bent. "I think we should go."

"Where?" Grace asked, puzzled. "Why?"

Isaac took both of her hands in his. "Because…" He exhaled and looked down at the ground. "Because things might get out of control."

"I know what I'm doing," Grace insisted. When he still wouldn't meet her gaze, she squeezed his hands. "I really do."

Finally, Isaac lifted his chin. The worried expression on his face was gone, and his smile was back. Seeing it made Grace breathe easy again. "I'm sure you think you do," he said.

It was Grace's turn to bend her eyebrows,

requesting further explanation.

"Look," he continued, "this is happening really fast for you—for us." He held up their entangled hands. "We need to take it slower, more customary. It's the right thing to do."

"I thought we were bucking tradition."

He chuckled under his breath. "You know I'd never really do that. Our customs might not be the same, but I am traditional at heart. I love our church and way of life. Always have." Despite his speech, he lifted their hands, kissing the back of hers then pressing it against his cheek.

"Mm-hmm," Grace hummed, not sure if she believed him 100 percent, but she did know she trusted him. Yes, when it came to courtship, he was the one with experience, not her, and Grace would never, ever want to be in a position where she had to choose between obedience and sin.

"Where to?" she asked as they strolled back to the carriage. Something about how it was parked under a bright streetlamp made Grace feel serene, obedient. Maybe she had been about to take things too far. Maybe a relationship like theirs was meant to always be in the light.

"Ice cream," Isaac said.

"Annie's?" Grace asked with a big smile.

"You read my mind."

As he was about to help her into the carriage, Grace said, "We can walk from here. Give Scout more of a rest."

"Sounds good." Isaac grinned then scooped up her hand.

Together, they crossed the street then began walking up the sidewalk. Most of the shops were closed, but the few that were open were brightly lit. A handful of couples and families—both English and plain—strolled along the streets, happy to be outside after all the rain.

There was a line to get into Annie's to order their ice cream, but Grace didn't mind. As they stood side by side, they fell into a comfortable conversation. Grace was amazed by how she could say anything to him. When he suggested a new training method for Cincinnati, Grace had a different idea in mind and had no problem sharing it with him.

"I think that might be even better," he said without an ounce of pride. "I know he's been raring to jump."

"*Jah*," Grace said, smiling. "And the ground should be dry enough tomorrow. His training has been structured so far; I think a day of free jumping will really get him ready."

"Do you have bounce rails?"

Grace nodded as they moved closer to the front of the line. "You've got a really nice, rising trot with him; I think you should do it first."

"I was about to say the same thing to you."

"No, no. Your balance is much better."

When Isaac lifted a hand, probably to deny it, Grace started laughing. "We're not getting anywhere with this."

They moved up a few more places in line. "How about whoever is in the stables earliest tomorrow morning gets to pick."

She grinned, knowing there was no way Isaac would win. "Good idea."

When Isaac began speaking to the person in line ahead of them, Grace let her eyes flutter closed as she sighed. She'd never worked so well with anybody, not even *Daed*. In the past few weeks, there'd been moments when it felt as though Isaac knew her thoughts before she did. Cincinnati had come to them as a wild, unruly animal. But because of their teamwork, the *gaul* was on his way to being a champion.

In Grace's mind, it had been almost organic for that teamwork to transfer into feelings of trust and admiration, and then into a blooming relationship that grew stronger day by day.

"Well, look who's here."

Grace opened her eyes to see three young men standing next to them in line. The one who'd just addressed them looked familiar, though Grace couldn't place him. It was strange, however, because when he locked eyes with her, Grace's stomach automatically tightened.

"Wade, hello," Isaac said. "How are you?"

Ack. It was Travis Cooper's son—the young man who'd been with him when he'd dropped off Cincinnati. No wonder her stomach had taken a roll when she'd seen him. She hadn't liked the way he'd leered at her then, nor did she like it now.

"Epically great," Wade answered. "These are those guys who took Sin," he said to his friends, displaying that same grin Grace remembered. "I told y'all about them, 'member?" He paused for reaction, and after shooting an elbow into the boy next to him, they all started to snicker. "What's your name again?"

"Isaac." His voice was steady. Polite. They still had to remain in good standing with Wade's family, after all. "And this is Grace Zook. Cincinnati is at her training farm."

Wade's gaze slid to Grace again. "Ah, yes. Grace. I sure do remember you. Say, you don't mind if we just get in line with you, like we're all together?"

Grace couldn't help noting how long the queue was behind them. Wasn't it cheating to allow Wade and his friends to cut the line like that? She wanted to speak up, but Wade's aggression made her so anxious that she could only look down at her hands.

"Cool, thanks! Ha ha, this is much better, isn't it?" Wade said, slipping in to stand right beside her before anyone gave him permission.

She shot Isaac a look, hoping he could read the unease in her eyes.

"I don't want to be rude to them," Isaac whispered to her in Pennsylvania Dutch.

"They're the ones being rude," Grace whispered back. "But he is Travis's son. I suppose we shouldn't stir anything up."

"That's what I'm thinking, too. The line is moving; it won't be much longer."

Grace sent him a private little eye roll, hoping he was right.

"Jeez, y'all are being real impolite talking that gibberish language right in front of us." Wade moved an inch toward Grace. "You're not talking about me, are ya, sweetheart?"

"Grace, why don't you go inside and check the flavors," Isaac said in English, stepping between them. "They have different specials every day." He leaned down to her. "I'll try to get rid of them while you're gone," he added, again speaking Dutch. "So, Wade, what grade are you in? Are you graduating soon?"

Grace was grateful she was able to slip away, at least momentarily. She felt all kinds of awkwardness with the group of boys. Thank heaven for Isaac's politeness and quick thinking. She'd witnessed him with Englishers on other occasions; he always seemed to find things in common with them and never failed to share opinions and somehow even form a quick bond. It was another of his natural talents.

She took her time noting that tonight's special flavors of ice cream were coconut, double stuffed Oreo, and peanut brittle. Hoping to have given Isaac enough time to get Wade's group to go to the back of the line, she meandered up the sidewalk, relieved to notice that the boys were gone. No, wait, the two friends were gone, but Wade was still there.

Not wanting to look silly by turning around again, Grace stood out of sight, pretending to read the signs on the side of the building, though close enough to hear their conversation—Wade's voice certainly carried.

"You're seriously not worried that she'll mess it up?" Wade was saying.

"Grace is very skilled."

"For a *woman*. Ha ha."

Grace didn't hear Isaac's reply or if he'd given one.

"All I'm saying is that even *my* mom stays home and cooks and cleans." Wade cocked his head to the side. "I thought your religion or whatever was, like, real strict about that."

"It is," Isaac replied, sounding like he was still straining to remain polite. "We've got rules and traditions like any other group, and there're definitely specific roles men and women play, but that's also the reason why our families and communities work so well. We each have our stations."

"Yeah, but you just said that Grace is basically as good as you are at training. How is she allowed to work with horses?"

Grace couldn't help smiling, knowing Isaac had been defending her. She'd think of a special way to thank him for that later.

"Grace is different," Isaac said. "She's got very special gifts."

"But still." Wade scratched his head and shifted his stance. "You're out on a date, right?"

"Yes," Isaac said. "Our first date." Grace couldn't help glancing at him, thrilled he admitted it so freely.

"So wouldn't it be better for you if she was, like, regular Amish? Aren't they supposed to be at home learning to churn butter and have babies and take care of their husbands? I mean, I don't know—I'm just asking."

"That...that is the tradition in the communities around here."

Grace felt her eyebrows pull together, wondering why Isaac hadn't added that *she* was an exception to the rules and he supported that she didn't want to be traditional. When those words didn't come, she knew she was frowning.

"What I really don't get," Wade continued, his voice dropping, "is that her father doesn't mind. If men like you expect to marry someone who stays home, isn't John freaking out that she'll never get married? I mean, he'd be a sucky father if he wasn't at least concerned. Surely he's talked to you about it—man-to-man."

Grace's spine stiffened. How dare the boy ask such personal questions? It would be different if Wade were legitimately interested in learning about their culture, but this wasn't curiosity, it was just plain disrespectful...to Isaac and to her family.

They were getting closer to the front of the line, and Grace suspected Isaac was simply making gracious conversation until Wade went away. He was great at chitchat.

"Her father is a good man. And he is...very concerned."

Grace's heart froze in place at Isaac's words. When

she took a quick peek at him, his face looked a little pale, and he was rubbing a fist across his forehead.

"He, uh, he talked to me about it one night," Isaac continued. "Because of personal circumstances with their family, he's hesitant about…well, in the future, he doesn't want her working at the training farm."

"And you think he's right?" Wade asked.

She watched as Isaac, looking uncomfortable, shrugged one shoulder. "I suppose, as his employee, I have to agree with John's decision."

It felt like someone just spiked a volleyball right at Grace's stomach, taking the wind out of her. The words she was pretending to read on the side of the building went blurry as she stared at the back of Isaac's black hat, feeling lightheaded.

"Seriously? Ha!" Wade's loud voice was like another volleyball spike, aimed at the side of her face. "So, he's like trying to get her to quit or something? Oh, man, that's classic!"

"Shh." Isaac hissed. "Lower your voice—I didn't mean…" His words faded out the second Grace forced herself to step into view. If he'd looked a little pale before, now Isaac's face was as white as winter snow. "Grace." His eyes held wide.

Grace had no words. She didn't know what to say or do. Almost as if on autopilot, she backed away from him and from the line outside the ice cream parlor. Off the curb and into the street.

"Better control your girl," she heard Wade say right before she turned around, marching away as fast as she could.

"Grace. Wait!"

She knew Isaac was following, and she wasn't sure where she was going. Just away.

"Grace. Hold on." He finally caught up to her

when she'd reached the other side of the street.

"What?" she said, swinging around after he'd taken her by the elbow.

Doubtless seeing the hurt and betrayal in her expression, Isaac dropped her elbow and took a step back. "What's wrong?"

Grace almost laughed. Was he kidding? "Headache," she said, truthfully, for it felt like her entire brain was about to explode. "I want to go home. Now." Noticing where they were, she began pacing toward where they'd left the buggy.

"Sure." Isaac stepped quicker so he was walking at her side, causing Grace to pick up speed. "Grace." He took her by the elbow again, forcing her to slow down. "Wait a second."

She stopped in place and spun to face him. "Did you really talk to my father about that?" She knew she didn't have to explain what "that" meant. And did she really have to ask the question in the first place? For she already knew Isaac and *Daed* had discussed Travis's new compensation plan in a conversation that purposely hadn't included her. What made her think they didn't talk behind her back all the time?

And just the other day, hadn't she felt the tiniest unease that Isaac was trying to "even things up" with training Sin? Was he trying to control the situation so *he'd* get the endorsements?

"*Jah*," Isaac admitted, looking her straight in the eyes as if he had nothing to hide.

Grace exhaled a scoff. "That's just perfect." She inwardly cringed at her sarcastic tone, but not enough to apologize. "And you felt the need to share that with Wade Carlson, of all people."

"That was a mistake," he said, looking over his shoulder, his ears turning red. "I'm sorry."

"You're sorry that I heard it or sorry you and my father have been keeping secrets from me?" She placed her hands on her hips, frustrated at the tears beginning to fill her eyes. "I thought we were a team."

"We are. Come on—just listen."

She scoffed again and began walking at an even faster pace. "Just take me home." Without waiting for his help, she climbed into the buggy, noticing with alarm how she was forced to touch shoulders with him when he got in next. She wanted to be small, alone. Far away.

Isaac took the reins, flicking them until the horses began to move. "I'm really sorry," he said. "Can we talk about it?"

Grace couldn't look at him. She felt sick to her stomach, bile rising into her throat every time they went over the tiniest bump in the road. Her mind reeled, confused to the point of nausea at what she knew. She felt something might have been off, and now she was ill to her very core that she'd been right all along.

"Please talk to me."

A part of her desperately wanted to hear what he had to say, wondering if he could clear the air.

But how was she supposed to trust anything he said now?

# CHAPTER THIRTY-NINE

Isaac felt terrible. He knew he'd really messed up by talking to Wade about such personal matters. Unknowingly, he'd betrayed Grace, and she had every reason to be disappointed with him. By now, he knew her pretty well and knew she wouldn't want to speak to him until she was calmer. They had that trait in common.

So Isaac kept a tight hold on the reins and silently followed the road home.

He'd make it up to her. When she was ready, he'd tell her everything he and John had talked about. She was right to feel betrayed. Isaac had had no business keeping that conversation from her, or any of the others he'd had with John concerning her. He'd even felt a little guilty that night, so the next day, he'd told her about Travis's new plan. He knew now that he should've shared with her the rest of what John had said…about how her father was sick to death with worry that Grace would be hurt like his wife had.

Being a father himself, Isaac couldn't help empathizing with John. Isaac would do anything to protect his own daughter. But it wasn't his place to tell Grace. After all, John hadn't given him permission to share.

"Can I ask you something?"

Isaac turned to Grace, grateful she was at least speaking to him. "Sure."

"Was Martha a homemaker? She stayed home to take care of Sadie?"

"*Jah.* Why?"

But Grace didn't reply. When he looked at her, the heels of her hands were over her eyes.

It broke his heart to see how upset she was, but Isaac wasn't sure what else he could do at that point. She said she had a headache, so he was doing everything he could to get her home quickly and safely. "Grace, sweetheart, just sit tight. Everything's going to be okay."

"Don't." The word was practically a whisper. Isaac might not have even heard it had it not been accompanied by Grace moving away from him.

"Careful—you'll fall out of the buggy," he said, adding a laugh to his voice, hoping to lighten the mood. "Didn't you promise to teach Sadie how to sing to the ponies? She's counting on you."

Suddenly, Grace went still as a board as he heard her suck in a breath. When she looked at him, Isaac flinched. Her face was as pale as Cincinnati's spot, but her cheeks and around her blue eyes were redder than a strawberry.

At first he thought she might be having an allergic reaction, until he noticed her eyes and cheeks were wet from tears.

"Grace, honey, are you crying?" He reached out to hold her hand, like he'd done a dozen times in the last few days—his attentions had always seemed welcomed by her. But Grace recoiled, staring wide-eyed at his hand like it was a snake.

"I hope…" she began, her voice weak, "I hope she has a good mother someday."

Isaac felt his brows furrow. "Who?"

She sniffed and rubbed her face with the corner of her cape. "Because I'm sure you'll marry someone who will raise her properly. Stop the buggy, I want to get out."

Pain pressed against Isaac's chest, his pulse fast with confusion. What was going on? This couldn't be just about talking to John behind her back.

"I mean it," she said, looking at him with a stern expression. "Stop or I'll jump out right here."

When he didn't slow down, she grabbed for the reins.

Isaac didn't wait to call her bluff. He'd never seen her more serious. "Whoa," he said, gently pulling at the reins. "Whoa there, boy."

Before they'd come to a stop, Grace was climbing off the buggy, much faster than Isaac could have imagined. "Good night—I mean, good*bye*," she called over her shoulder as she began running.

Isaac sprang off the buggy and followed. "Grace! Stop! I told you how sorry I am about what I said to Wade. I should've told you first."

"You don't get it, do you?" She didn't stop, but ran straight past the Chupps' house, heading down the hill toward her farm. For an instant, he thought about letting her go until she'd cooled off.

But no, he couldn't. Something was terribly wrong—something he couldn't figure out. He was not going to leave until he knew she was okay.

"Wait, please. I don't understand. Why won't you talk to me?" The night air burned his lungs, while hurt and bewilderment filled his head. "Grace, wh-what about Cincinnati?" It was the only thing he could think of that might get her to stop running away.

When she halted in place and turned back, Isaac stopped, too. He hoped she'd be reasonable and talk to him calmly, let him know why she was so upset, and how he could help.

"Is that all I am to you?"

"What?" He was tired of repeating himself over

and over, but she wasn't making sense.

Under the moonlight, she turned her face away from him, then lowered her chin. "Of course I'll finish Sin's training." When she finally lifted her head to face him, Isaac's heart nearly shattered seeing the fresh tears streaming down her cheeks. "But that's the only time I want to see you, Isaac. No more *chats*, no more *dates*. Do you understand?"

"*No*," he said boldly, though trying to remain calm. "No, I don't understand any of this." He reached out a hand to her, wanting desperately for her to come to him. He could explain everything better, if she'd only give him the chance. "Please, will you really not talk to me?"

She shook her head and crossed her arms. "Nothing more to talk about."

But he knew her voice. He knew her tones. She was scared and hurting like she'd been at the medical center that day, and when she'd told him about Sarah and Amos. Her heart was coming apart. But this time, it was breaking over him.

He couldn't deny it—he'd made a huge mistake, many mistakes, and from the look in her eyes, he knew the trust she'd finally given him was now gone.

"Is there nothing I can do?" he asked, his open hand still outstretched to her.

She shook her head. It was the kind of gesture that felt final.

Lowering his hand, he nodded and took a step back, as if allowing her to go.

She did go. But she didn't go alone.

After quickly securing the buggy, Isaac followed her, keeping in the shadows, making sure she got home safe and sound. He loved her too much to do otherwise.

• • •

As he checked on Sadie, kissing her good night, Isaac thought back through every conversation, every word they'd had on their date. He'd really messed up; there were no two ways about it. He'd destroyed their relationship in a matter of seconds. Not knowing what else to do, Isaac knelt by the bed and prayed, asking *Gott* to touch his heart, to give him discernment about what to do next.

He didn't sleep that night, but tossed and turned and worried—not so much about his own broken heart but about his sweet, lovely Grace. The pain she must be going through. Even though he wasn't able to sleep, Isaac prayed that *she* would be able to. That her mind and heart would be at peace enough to talk to him the next morning. He hoped this so much that when he got up to go to work, he was actually cheerful, certain it would happen.

"Morning," he said as he approached the opening of the stables.

She stood before Sin's stall, not singing a hymn or whispering a scripture passage, or even petting the horse.

"He's been brushed," she said, keeping her gaze away from his. "The poles and jumps are laid out in the front pasture. We'll walk him over those first."

Isaac had been holding his breath, but then released it at the word "we'll." It gave him hope.

"You can take the first training session," she continued. "No reason anymore for us both to be out there." She wiped her palms across her apron. "I'll take him this afternoon—"

"Grace," he said, knowing he was cutting her off,

but this couldn't wait. "Don't you think we should…" He paused and shrugged. "Shouldn't we talk about last night?"

Finally she met his gaze. Her face wasn't as pale, but the whites of her eyes were red, as if she hadn't slept a wink last night, either, and his heart sank. "Do you remember what I asked you?"

Isaac almost laughed. "You asked a lot of questions last night."

She sighed. "Do you remember that I said I would train Sin with you, but that was it?"

His eyes burned and his head throbbed, his hopes dissolving. "I do remember that."

"Then please respect my wishes."

Isaac pressed his hands over his throbbing heart. "But, Grace, I'm sorry—you don't know how sorry I am for saying what I did. You have every right to not trust me right now, and I have no excuse." He stopped to run a hand over his face. "You can ask me anything. Can't we forget last night?"

She shook her head. "You still don't get it."

He *didn't* get it. But still, as he looked at her, he wanted to tell her everything in his heart, all the tender, loving things he felt for her.

Grace dropped her gaze and was staring at the ground. "Don't make this worse."

*Worse? How could this get worse?*

It was like he'd lived a whole day but couldn't remember what happened. Somewhere in that forgotten day, he'd hurt Grace Zook irreversibly. How and why he would've done that still wasn't clear.

All he could do was stand and stare at her as she further explained how the training sessions should go that day and the rest of the week. Very seldom did it require them to be together.

"Fine," he said, feeling too beaten down to fight anymore. She was done with him—their partnership and whatever else they might've had was over.

She moved Cincinnati into the pasture, getting ready to start her part of the training. Isaac knew he was supposed to leave her there alone, but he couldn't. He stood outside the fence as she saddled the horse, then began dragging the trotting poles into place. One looked a little too far away from the others, but Isaac didn't say a thing.

He also didn't say a thing when Sin trotted over the poles perfectly, again and again. Nor when Grace got him going at a faster trot, posting him right down the middle of the poles. It was like they'd both suspected: Cincinnati was a born jumper.

He wanted to whoop and congratulate her, but he didn't. Not that Isaac relished being purposefully ignored for a full hour; he just couldn't get himself to walk away.

"Hallo!"

Isaac had to squint into the sun at the approaching figure coming from the road. He didn't recognize the person at first, but when he got near enough that Isaac could hear his greetings to Grace, he realized it was Collin Chupp.

Isaac's eyes automatically narrowed.

Grace sent Isaac a quick glance, then turned her full attention to Collin. He was there to bring a jar of his mother's chicken soup to Eve—that much Isaac heard perfectly. Though why was a grown man delivering food when he should've been working? And why hadn't Samuel Chupp reached out to Isaac's friends in Silver Springs about the job for Collin out there?

They continued chatting. And although Grace

wasn't behaving toward Collin like she'd behaved with Isaac, happy and open and uninhibited, Isaac still didn't like it. He didn't like them standing together by Sin. He didn't like how often she smiled at the boy.

"Do you know about the Lambrights' get-together after the singing next preaching Sunday?" Collin asked her.

"Hadn't heard about it," Grace said. "Why?"

Collin shuffled his feet, while a ball of hot fire lit inside Isaac's chest.

"Was just wondering if you'd like to go with me. I'll pick you up in my open carriage and everything."

Isaac felt his teeth grinding, ready to *escort* Collin Chupp all the way back home, by the scruff of his neck if necessary.

Then he saw Grace. Her lips were pressed together and her chin was tucked, the wind blowing strands of loose hair around her face. Ever so slightly, she shifted so her body was facing Isaac.

He already knew from the Chupp family and from Grace herself that she'd never gone on a date with Collin, no matter how many times he'd asked her.

"Okay," Grace said. Her eyes glanced toward Isaac, then quickly away, but so strong was their connection that, for a moment, Isaac thought she was speaking to him. "*Jah*," she added, looking at Collin next, "that sounds like a nice distraction from…from work."

Isaac felt a rage under his skin like he'd never known before, and he was two seconds from doing more than *escorting* Collin Chupp away.

They probably settled on a time and place, and maybe chatted about the weather, but Isaac heard nothing more. Blood whooshed inside his ears, his pumping heart making his body weak and drained as he nearly pulled a fence post out of the ground with his bare hands.

Hadn't he been the happiest of men less than a day ago? Hadn't he been making mental plans for weeks about his future—*their* future? And now he had to stand there and witness Grace accepting a date from another man.

He heard them saying goodbye to each other, even saw when Grace looked over at him again, then quickly glanced away. Was she trying to hurt him? Had the whole scene been for his benefit to show that Grace was moving on?

He didn't know anything anymore. Even *Gott* had gone silent as he stood at the fence, feeling like the biggest fool in Lancaster County.

# CHAPTER FORTY

Grace didn't think she'd be able to get out of bed this morning, let alone do anything productive like put on clothes or train horses…or work with the man who had broken her heart. She pulled the covers up over her head and willed herself not to cry again.

Even though it had been only three days, hadn't she cried enough?

It broke her heart anew when she remembered how shocked Isaac had looked the other night. How he'd chased her down the dark road when she'd jumped out of the buggy, needing to be away from him by any means.

Yes, he'd seemed shocked—and confused and distressed—but Grace had heard the things he'd said to Wade. It was better that she face reality now than weeks or months down the road, after she'd fallen in love with him even more.

Slowly, she got out of bed and went through her morning routine, halfheartedly, because half of her heart was gone. Neither Sarah nor Amos nor *Daed* said much to her when she went downstairs for breakfast.

When she'd come home after their date, much earlier than expected, the questions had begun. Luckily, *Maam* must've seen something in her eyes, because she'd told Grace to go right upstairs to bed. A while later, *Maam* had come into her room. She'd sat on the bed and let Grace sob into her lap, whimpering about how she'd had to end her relationship with Isaac.

Even now, while Grace attempted to choke down her oatmeal, she felt pressure building in her eyes and in her chest, making it hard to breathe as she replayed the horrible memories.

"My sister Esther's little Bella is still down with a cold," Sarah said as she started a new pot of coffee. "I've been meaning to pay a call but haven't had the time." She put one hand on her forehead and one on her stomach. "I haven't felt myself in a few days. Maybe there's something going around."

"Why don't you take it easy today?" Amos asked her, touching her arm.

"Wish I could," Sarah replied to him. "But my list is longer than a donkey's tail—just as ornery, too." Together, she and Amos laughed at the little joke.

Somewhere inside Grace's heart, she was happy her brother and sister-in-law were getting along, but all Grace could do was stare blankly at the table in front of her.

"I do wish I could sit with Esther today," Sarah continued, "just to make sure she isn't feeling overwhelmed with an ill child and a *bobbeil* on her hip. Hmm, what to do...what to do... More coffee, Grace?"

Suddenly, Grace lifted her head. "*I* can visit Esther."

"Oh?" Sarah's voice was high and lilted. "Why, do you think you have time?"

Grace had to think about it. She certainly deserved a day off, and hadn't Isaac wanted to "even up" their training time? The thought made her stomach drop. But not having to see him made her shoulders feel lighter, yet her heart was still heavy.

"I'll leave a note in the stables for...Isaac." Saying his name aloud and hearing how her voice trembled, made her head throb.

"Or I could talk to him," *Daed* offered.

Grace looked at him. "Would you?"

"Sure." He smiled. "Just leave it to me. I'll take care of the other horses today, too, if you'd like. Are their training notes up to date?"

"You don't have to do all that, Papa," Grace said. "It's quite a lot."

*Daed* chuckled. "Well now, my mind may be halfway retired, but my body still knows what to do with a *gaul*."

Grace felt tears in her eyes and a huge lump in her throat, but she refused to cry. She'd also refused to talk to her father about anything she'd overhead Isaac telling Wade. It was somehow okay to be angry with Isaac, but she was too much her mother's daughter to disrespect her father.

"*Danke, Daed*," was all she could get out.

She stayed in the kitchen longer than usual, waiting to hear the sound of Scout's hoofs approaching. Even if she didn't already recognize his gait, Grace would've known it was Isaac anyway, for he was the only man in Honey Brook who traveled by horseback.

*Here they come*, she thought, feeling the hoof vibrations like the beats of her heart. *He'll go past the house, let Scout into the back pasture, then he'll head straight to the stables.*

*Daed* was already outside waiting for him. Grace sat as still as a jackrabbit, but she heard only muffled mumbles.

*Is Isaac disappointed at my absence? Upset? Sad? Relieved?*

Thanks to her decision, it was none of her business now.

When *Daed* came back inside to fetch his hat,

Grace didn't dare look at him, though she felt his heavy gaze on her. She knew Sin would be working with the trotting poles in the front pasture. And yes, it might've made her the biggest coward, but when she left the house to go visit Esther, Grace took the long way by cutting through the back pasture, ensuring that she would not run into Isaac.

At last she was free. She took in a big breath, letting the fresh morning air fill her lungs. Other ailments could be helped by breathing good, clean air. Perhaps a broken heart could be, too.

• • •

"Grace, goodness, this is a surprise," said Esther Brenneman after opening her front door.

"Sarah said Bella's still under the weather and your hands are full."

"Sarah said that?" Esther replied, tilting her head.

Grace nodded. "She thought you might want my help today."

"Oh." Esther smiled and opened the door wider. "Please come in, then. I'm always happy to have company."

When Grace entered the house, the baby was down on the thick family room rug. "He's crawling already?"

"Aye," Esther said after a big sigh. "And he's got the energy of his father. None of us can keep up with him."

"What a…joy." Grace felt her chest cave in as she spoke the words. She had little idea how it felt to be a mother. She'd spent time with Sadie, and had become almost as comfortable taking care of her as she did with her own younger sisters. Was that the same as feeling like a real mother?

"He is a joy," Esther replied, luckily interrupting Grace's thoughts, for a new lump sat in her throat at the thought of not teaching Sadie to work with her first pony, or how to sing "Come Thou Fount" or all the other things Grace suddenly realized she would never do.

"Have you eaten yet?" Esther continued. "We're a little off schedule this morning. Bella was up early wanting breakfast, and I've already put her down for her first nap."

"She's eating, then?" Grace asked. "That's good."

"*Jah*," Esther said after a pause, but then bit her lip. "I, uh, I think she's on the mend—but I'm still so happy you came over. I love my family, but it's nice to see a different face every once in a while. Tea?"

After chatting in Esther's comfortable family room for a while, they moved into a back room off the kitchen. Grace knew Esther made soap to sell at Yoder's store, but she'd never been witness to its creation. There were so many detailed steps in the process, yet Esther barely seemed to consult the recipe tacked on the wall.

Grace volunteered to hold the *bobbeil* while Esther worked, wondering at how natural she looked.

"What do you think of this one?" Esther asked, passing Grace a small bottle of oil.

"Smells wonderful."

"*Jah?*" She smiled modestly. "I invented the blend myself a few months ago. The daffodils were in bloom, and I wondered what their essence would smell like." She held the bottle up to her nose and took a sniff. "It's strong, but I never use very much. It goes so well with the geranium." She closed the oil bottle. "Luke even likes a drop or two in his morning coffee. I get up early to make it special for him."

This instantly made Grace think of Isaac, and how they'd stood in her kitchen drinking coffee with brown sugar, then the brown sugar coffee she'd made for their trip to the mud sale. Before Grace could stop them, memories came flooding back...

The last time she'd seen him.

The agony in her heart hit so fast that she had to slam her eyes shut.

"I don't know how you do it," she said a moment later.

"Do what?"

She opened her eyes after willing away what she hoped were the last of her tears. "How do you... I don't know... How do you do both?"

"Both?"

Grace nodded after taking in a deep breath. "You take care of Lucas and the children and your home. But you also do this." She gestured at the stack of soap molds waiting to be filled. "It's like you have two jobs—two lives. How do you do both?"

Esther watched her for a moment, then pushed the soap molds back, wiping her hands on her apron. "Easy answer," she said. "I don't."

"But you do. I've been watching you for two hours."

Esther rubbed her lips together, then pulled up a chair to sit across from Grace. "I can see how it might seem like it. Do I prioritize and organize and sacrifice? *Jah.* But so does Luke. He has a job and is a hands-on father and husband. Otherwise, I couldn't do most of what fills my day. We're a team in every sense of the word."

Despite her efforts, Grace was blinking back tears, knowing they would spill over any second.

*I thought* we *were a team, too.*

"I'm not seeing Isaac King anymore," she sniveled, needing to get it out.

"Oh? Were you seeing him?" Esther asked. When Grace lifted her teary eyes to look at her, Esther's faux-inquisitive expression vanished. "I'm sorry. Of course, I knew you were interested in each other—even though we're not supposed to notice things like that until after the engagement is announced."

*Engagement?* Grace couldn't help it now. She threw her hands over her eyes and let the tears flow.

"I think I love him," she said, her heart beating faster and faster until she felt faint. "But he's not the person I thought he was. I've…I've lost faith in him."

"Oh Grace," Esther said, putting a hand on Grace's arm. "Do you mind me asking what happened? If you want to talk about it."

"Sure," Grace said, wiping her other cheek. "I know it was early in our relationship, but I thought we were a good fit," she began. "I mean, once we admitted our feelings, it all just happened. It was effortless." She took in a shaky breath. "We spent so much time together training Cincinnati that I assumed he wanted…" She had to stop and press both hands over her heart, needing to catch her breath.

"What did you assume?" Esther asked, kindness in her voice.

"I thought he didn't mind that I'd rather work outside than…" She let her voice trail off as she gestured to the baby in Esther's arms. "We never talked about marriage, but why did he waste his time with someone like me if he wants a traditional wife and a proper mother for Sadie?"

"He told you that's what he wanted?"

Weeping anew, she rubbed her eyes with her fists,

so as not to evoke the pain of recalling what his exact words had been. "I can't begrudge him for wanting that. *I'm* the odd one—the problem. Not even my father trusts me." When her heart felt heavier than a bucket of oats, she added, "Do you mind if we don't talk about it anymore? Makes me..." She couldn't even finish with the word "sad."

Esther reached out and squeezed her hand. "Whatever you want."

While Esther went back to her soap, Grace did her best to play with the baby—which wasn't so hard. She even fixed lunch while Esther finished up. Bella was awake now, and besides a slightly runny nose, she didn't seem ill in the least.

"Roast beef sandwich?" she said when Esther came into the kitchen.

"Wow." Esther grinned. "It looks delicious. Is this from the leftovers?"

"*Jah*," Grace said. "I hope you didn't have any other plans for the meat."

"Only to reheat it over the stove then eat it the same way as last night." Esther took a bite. "Delicious. Did you make this relish sauce out of that one last pickle?"

Grace chuckled under her breath, happy to be of help. "My mother taught me the recipe when I was just a girl."

"How is your mother these days?" Esther asked as she sat at the table with her sandwich. "Is she feeling better?"

"Some, I think," Grace said, wiping down the counter. "She still needs an operation, though."

"*Jah*." Esther nodded. "Luke has a meeting at the hospital in Hershey at the end of the week. He's going to discuss her case with them again."

"That's very kind of him," Grace said, even though she knew there was little hope. If her family didn't have the money, there would be no surgery, and *Maam* would get worse and worse.

Just then, the door swung open and Lucas Brenneman came inside. "Grace Zook," he said with a big smile. "What a nice surprise."

"Are you home for lunch?" Esther asked.

"If there's food," he said, "I'll eat."

"Grace made roast beef sandwiches," Esther said. "Here, have the rest of mine."

"There's enough for me to make one more," Grace offered, rising to her feet.

Lucas smiled. "Mighty grateful, then." He sat in the chair next to his wife, whispering something in her ear that made Esther giggle, then swat his shoulder. "I was out at your place earlier today," he added. "Checking on your mother."

"Oh?" Grace stopped what she was doing and looked at him. "Did my father call you? Is something wrong?"

"No, no," Lucas said. "It was a routine visit. She's doing fine. Maybe a bit sorer than usual, but that's to be expected."

Grace swallowed hard. It was killing her to know her mother was suffering and there was something she could do about it. Though truth be told, there was *nothing* she could do about it.

There was the possibility—she couldn't help thinking—that her family might actually soon have enough money for *Maam*'s surgery and then some. But before Grace got her hopes up, her excitement sagged, remembering that Isaac had been hired for the job of training Sin—and wouldn't that be all Travis Carlson would need to know when he saw how beautifully his horse was trained?

Her thoughts drifted further, remembering that rainy day in the barn, when Isaac had been so sweet as to confess that he'd wished he could offer his own money—little as it was—to pay for the operation. Simply recalling the kindhearted, magnanimous gesture touched Grace in a place she had assumed was dead.

"Your father tells me he's thinking of selling some land," Lucas said, forcing Grace back to the here and now. "Says he has a deal in the works."

"He did?" she said, feeling blindsided but trying not to show it. She shouldn't be surprised, though. Seemed Papa really didn't trust her to take over the farm.

"He's retiring soon, *jah*?" Lucas asked. "That's probably what he's planning for."

"Probably," Grace said slowly, though in actuality, she had no idea what was going on. Not only could Isaac be leaving as soon as next week, but now *Daed* was selling off their training land? Grace would be lost without her horses.

She couldn't take it. It seemed her whole life, all the plans she'd ever made were disappearing before her eyes. She knew she couldn't hide out in Esther's kitchen all day, so eventually, she waved everyone goodbye and headed home.

It was the time of day between the early afternoon training session and the later afternoon session, so she was fairly confident Isaac wouldn't be at the farm. As she walked past the empty front pasture, she noticed the jumps were arranged in the "gymnastic grid," meaning Cincinnati was progressing even faster than she'd expected. They could be setting up the riding course as early as the day after tomorrow at this pace.

And before the end of next week, good old Sin would be jumping like a champ.

But no, "they" wouldn't be doing anything like that. At least not together as the team they once were.

Suddenly, Grace froze in place, noticing a person standing by the front porch. From the pounding in her chest, she knew it was Isaac. Even if she crept away on tiptoe, he would see her.

"Oh," she said. "Hi."

Isaac turned around. The happy expression that used to greet her was gone, replaced by ashen skin and bags under his eyes like he hadn't slept in days.

"Hallo," he replied, wiping his hands on the backs of his black pants. "How are you?"

"Fine," Grace said, though her throat was closing up on her. "You?"

"Truthfully, Grace, I'm not doing all that well."

"Is something the matter with Sadie?"

"Sadie's fine, she's good." He looked down at the ground. "That's not why I'm not doing well."

Grace immediately wondered if there was a problem with Scout or Sin or any of the other horses in the back fields. "What's wrong, then?"

It took a moment, but finally, Isaac lifted his chin and looked at her. His hazel eyes were rimmed with red, no longer bright and intense like before. "I miss you."

The figurative kick from a wild mustang hit Grace squarely in the stomach.

"That's as honest as I know how to be," he added. "I miss being with you and talking to you. Every second of every day, I miss you. Everything about you."

"Don't," she whispered under her breath.

"I miss working with you." He glanced toward the

front pasture. "Did you know Sin is doing cross-rail jumping like it's nothing? He picked it up right away. I was so excited, but it meant nothing because you weren't there to share it with me."

"He'll be gone at the end of next week," she said, knowing how cold and detached she sounded. But if she couldn't protect herself, she would run into his arms, hug him tight, tell him she'd be any kind of woman he wanted her to be.

But that would be a lie, too. Grace would never be like the other women in Honey Brook. She knew that for sure now, and it should be just as clear to Isaac.

"You're still mad at me for keeping secrets, and I don't blame you," he said. "But can't you forgive me?"

Grace had to think for a moment, because she wanted to be honest. "I forgive you for that, Isaac," she said. "You and Papa had your reasons for not including me — he probably needed an impartial friend to talk to, and the future of our training farm doesn't really involve you, anyway." She paused to steady herself. "It's more than that, though. You and I...we're fooling ourselves to think any kind of long-term relationship would work. So yes, I forgive you, but I can't forget the rest."

He gaped at her, looking like blood had drained from his face. She knew this because she felt the same.

Isaac was pale, and he barely met her eye, but after a throat clear, he asked, "Is there anything else?"

"*Danke* for taking care of the training today."

He continued to stare, as if hoping to read something different on her face. Grace was ready to crumble, to take it all back...if only he could tell her just the right words.

"You're welcome," he finally said, dropping his gaze to look at the ground. "Seems there's nothing more to say, then. I left you a letter in the office." He pointed at the stables. "Don't worry, I didn't write anything that will embarrass you, just notes about Sin. We need to be on the same page if we're not going to be working together."

Grace leveled her chin, stoically, numbly, even though her legs were trembling. "Okay."

After the simple reply, Isaac started backing away, his hands in his pockets. "Want me to do today's last training, too?"

"Please." Grace swallowed. *"Danke."*

Without another word, he left on foot. Grace didn't have time to wonder where he was going and why he'd leave without Scout, because she had to reach out for the porch railing as she crumpled onto the steps.

"I miss you, too," she sobbed under her breath as she cried one more time over the man she loved, the man she still wanted more than anything. "Please come back."

"Gracie?"

It felt like her heart had stopped altogether. Had he actually heard? Had Isaac returned at her silent request?

She lifted her chin to see her father standing on the porch, his hand still holding the doorknob. Tears and audible sobs of sheer disappointment shook her body.

"Oh Gracie." He came down the stairs and sat beside her. She leaned in to his shoulder and blubbered. "Now, now, daughter. It's not as bad as all that. There'll be other horses."

Grace pulled back. "You think I'm crying over Cincinnati?"

*Daed* shrugged. "Aren't you?"

"Well, *jah*," she admitted. "That hardheaded horse changed my life." She sucked in a breath. "I'll never be the same because of…him."

*Daed* put an arm around her. "There will be more, many, many more."

Grace looked him in the eyes. "Not if you retire."

Her father chuckled and gave her shoulders a squeeze. "Well, not as many, that's true."

Grace had no idea why her father seemed amused when everything around her was falling apart. "You talked to Lucas today." She wiped at her eyes. "You're selling some land?"

"Some," *Daed* confirmed, scratching his long beard. "Seems like the right thing to do, and certainly the right time. Don't need so much for just myself anymore. I thought you'd agree."

Grace was utterly speechless. All she could do was shake her head, gently enough to not cause any additional pain. If she moved too much, she might vomit.

"Honestly, Papa," Grace forced herself to say, gathering what strength she had left. "Why don't you want me to take over the business? I've asked you before, but you've never truly answered." She sniffed. "Don't you think I can do it?"

"Gracie." *Daed* took her hand. "Of course I know you can. Why, you're the best trainer around; got a fine head for business, too. Everyone knows that."

Grace couldn't help exhaling, more confused than ever. "I know this sounds selfish, but why aren't you giving it to me, then?"

*Daed* turned away from her, staring straight ahead. Grace watched his profile…watched as he blinked, rubbed a hand over his mouth, his chin suddenly trembling. "I've never been able to get the picture out of my head," he began. "It happened in the blink of an eye. Your mother nearly died that day." He paused to wipe at his nose. "I don't know what I'd do if anything like that happened to you. It would kill me."

Grace fell speechless as she stared at him, understanding finally at least part of her father's struggles. When a single tear ran down *Daed's* cheek, the thought of his intense worry over her for all this time made Grace's heart nearly stop, an inhale freezing inside her lungs.

*Daed* squeezed her hand with both of his as more tears came. Grace had never seen him cry over anything besides her mother.

"Papa," she said, trying to be strong while noting the tremor in her voice, remembering perfectly the day of *Maam's* accident. "I understand—it can be dangerous if you don't know what you're doing. I never wanted to make you worry so much."

He lifted a teary smile, a familiar twinkle in his eye. "That's my job."

She tried to swallow but felt pain at the back of her throat, not knowing how to calm his fears.

"I'm very careful," she offered after a moment.

He sniffed again. "So was she."

Grace didn't know what else to say. It wasn't as if she could promise him she'd never get injured by a horse—that was something no one but *Gott* knew.

"It means so much to me," she added, wanting her father to know her whole heart. "It's all I've ever wanted—I know you don't approve because it's not traditional, but I've been wearing Amos's trousers under my dresses ever since I was six years old."

*Daed* exhaled a little chuckle and gave Grace's hand another squeeze. "Aye, and I've loved you all the more for it, *dochder*. But can I help it if your old papa is set in his ways?"

"Nay, I guess you can't," she said.

He didn't want her to get hurt, and apparently he also didn't trust her to run the farm. Seemed there was nothing more to say.

Her father was starting to sell off the farm piece by piece, and there was nothing Grace could do to stop it. She loved her father with all her heart, and though she might never understand his decision, she had to respect it.

"Isaac's taking care of Sin this afternoon," she said, knowing the only person she had left to lean on was *Gott*. "I'll see you later."

# CHAPTER FORTY-ONE

Isaac had never been so attached to a place, a person, and an animal as he was to Honey Brook, Grace, and good old Cincinnati. He hadn't realized just how strong the bond was until the day before Travis Carlson was due to return in his big truck.

The last week had become a blur with getting Sin ready to go back home and begin his jumping career, preparing Sadie for yet another big change, and from trying to steal glimpses of Grace whenever he could.

He always felt her presence, especially when it was his turn with the *gaul* after Grace had been training him. Sin was always just a little more focused then, a little calmer, a little more ready for the next part of his life.

Isaac had had a plan for the next part of his life, too. But now, if it didn't include at least Grace and Honey Brook, he didn't know what was left.

"*Guder mariye*," he said to Grace as he entered the stables. It was the first time they'd been alone since that moment on the porch...when he'd poured out his heart to her one last time, and she still said no.

Would he ever forgive himself?

"Hi," Grace replied. She was standing inside the stall, her forehead pressed to Cincinnati's. He saw she had tears in her eyes as she whispered something he couldn't hear to the magnificent horse. If Isaac knew her at all, it would be scriptures or a sweet prayer of parting or she might've been singing one of her favorite hymns.

He stood silent, giving her all the time she needed,

for she'd become just as attached to Sin as he had. He wished he could comfort her, but those days were gone.

Their solitude was disturbed when John began chatting with Travis Carlson on the phone in his office. Isaac wasn't trying to eavesdrop on the conversation, but John's voice was loud and clear when he said, "So your decision is already made, then?"

Grace pulled away from the horse and looked toward the office. Isaac watched her, holding his breath.

"I see," John continued. "Well, I suppose that seems fair. All right, then, I'll see you tomorrow afternoon."

Even though Isaac had spent well over a month in John's presence, he couldn't even begin to interpret his tone. To which of them had Travis decided to give his endorsement?

Before his thoughts could start down one road or the other, Isaac heard Grace take a sharp but quiet inhale. "I guess it's done, then," she said, rubbing absently at her arms. She opened her mouth as if about to say more, but closed it again and turned back to Sin. "I'm going to miss you so much—miss *him*, I mean."

"Are you okay?" Isaac asked her in a soft voice.

"No," Grace said, looking over at him. "I'm not okay with any of this."

"Yes." Isaac exhaled. "It's hard to say goodbye to something—or some*one*—you've grown to love."

Grace stared at him for a long moment, her beautiful blue eyes filling with tears. "He...he was such a mess when he came to us," she said, stroking Sin's neck with both hands. "That first day."

"That dented trailer," Isaac added. "And when I

thought he was going to run you over in the pasture…" Something came alive in his heart when he heard Grace's light giggle.

But then, as if she'd been caught talking in church, Grace sealed her lips shut and looked away.

"It all started with kindness," Isaac couldn't help adding, wanting so much to simply walk over and stand beside her.

"Communication, too," Grace said.

"And trust." Isaac let the words hang in the air for a few seconds. "Trust and honest communication are the most important things in any relationship," he finally continued, hoping she'd catch the double meaning in his words…hoping against hope she'd talk to him about what was really going on between them.

But she didn't—not even to agree or disagree.

"You know what we should do when Travis comes tomorrow?" Isaac said, not wanting to waste any of their remaining time together in awkward silence.

"What?" Grace asked as she wrapped her arms around her torso.

He took one step toward her. "We need to show Travis what an amazing horse he's got. I think you should ride Sin out."

Grace gawked at him, blinking. "You mean, me ride him out of here, just like that? Isn't that a little boastful?"

Isaac shrugged and offered a smile. "Well, it's Sin who's done all the work, *jah*? Horses can't have pride."

Grace's eyes went wide as she glanced at Cincinnati then back at Isaac.

"What do you say?" Isaac asked. "Trust me one more time?"

She stared at him in silence, and Isaac so wished

he could read what was going on inside her mind. He wished he could go back in time and fix everything, all the mistakes he'd made that caused Grace to lose faith in him. To stop loving him.

"I'll have to think about it," she finally said. Isaac knew he couldn't convince her to do anything—and Lord, he loved that about her. So he simply let the subject drop.

"What are you going to do after tomorrow?" she asked, the question surprising Isaac. Or was he more surprised that she was choosing to further converse with him at all? "After Travis makes the decision, I mean."

"Head to Silver Springs."

"What?" Grace's hands dropped to her sides. "Back there?"

"We're staying with my brother—a few days at most, I hope." He was pleased she was interested in his future enough to inquire, but did it really matter to her?

"And then what?" she asked.

"I'm not exactly sure yet, Grace." He lowered his eyes and kicked at a rock, his heart feeling heavy and sluggish. "Boarding in Honey Brook costs money, and I don't…" He let the rest trail off, knowing he didn't need to explain the situation further. "I have one or two plans in mind, though—I always do."

She nodded while tugging at the front of her apron. "Why don't you take Sin out today," she said. "Keep him as long as you want." She dropped her chin, breaking eye contact. "Take him now, out to the far back pasture where there's privacy. I'm sure you'd like to say goodbye on your own."

Isaac didn't want to be on his own; he wanted to be with her. But, since she was practically shoving him out the barn doors, what else could he do but agree?

"*Danke*," he said.

After another quiet moment, Grace broke the silence. "Well, uh, I suppose I'll leave you to it." She began backing away slowly. Right before she turned around, Isaac saw her clamp a hand over her mouth, though not soon enough to block a heartbreaking sob as she ran out of the stables.

As his gaze helplessly followed her, Isaac's chest felt hollow, empty, even while fighting back the urge to go after her. But he'd tried that and failed. Grace had made her feelings perfectly clear. She didn't want him.

For the next few hours, Isaac rode Cincinnati all around the Zooks' property, even out to the further-most corner of the very back acre. He didn't give Sin a normal training session because, knowing this may be the last time he'd be alone with the grand *gaul*, he wanted the final memories to be special.

By the time he returned to the stables, he was breathing hard, his hairline damp with perspiration, and he'd even lost his hat somewhere along the way. Sin was ready for a rest, too, and as Isaac led him to his stall, he was relieved to feel the first presence of peace return to his soul—despite the sadness he felt about a future he could no longer count on.

After watering and brushing, Isaac took one last moment alone with Sin. He stroked his face and ears and down his long, graceful neck. "You've been such a good boy," he whispered, feeling a lump in his throat. "Thank you for bringing me to this wonderful place with all these *gut, gut* people." He touched his forehead to Sin's in the way Grace always did. "Don't forget to lift that back leg high on the first jump like Grace said. And get ready to be a star."

Before he got any more choked up, Isaac walked down the long row of horses, saying goodbye to each of them, and then smiling to himself at how much he'd learned the past few weeks—about training horses and about himself.

Lessons he wouldn't have learned anywhere else.

# CHAPTER FORTY-TWO

Grace gazed out the window of the SUV as Dr. McBride drove them onto the winding road leading to the farm.

It had been three days since she'd left home. *Maam* had been anxious after her surgery, and Dr. McBride had seen no reason why she and *Daed* couldn't stay a few more days. Just that morning, *Maam* was moved to a rehab center where she would get her legs, stomach, and back muscles working strong again. Lucas had given her a phone, and *Maam* had already called them twice since Grace had left.

*Daed* had also reached out to Travis Carlson, changing their plan for Cincinnati to be picked up later today. Grace couldn't help smiling—though it was a melancholy smile—knowing that Isaac had been able to spend a few more days with Sin.

"Just five more minutes," *Daed* said, grinning from the seat beside her, looking about ten years younger. "That hospital's real nice, but I can't wait to sleep in my own bed."

"Same," Grace agreed, feeling a tweak in her back.

She didn't say a word to either of her parents, or to Lucas, but she'd been thinking about Isaac the whole time she'd been in Hershey. Wondering what the future held—for both of them. She knew how badly he and Sadie needed to start a new life apart from his in-laws in Silver Springs. Even though they couldn't be together like they'd been before, she couldn't bear the thought of Isaac not getting exactly what he wanted, what he'd worked so hard for.

But hadn't she worked hard, too?

"I wonder what Isaac will do if he doesn't get the endorsement from Travis," Grace said, staring out the window, not really wanting to discuss the money but longing to speak of anything concerning Isaac. "Will he stay in Honey Brook, do you think?"

When *Daed* didn't reply, Grace glanced over to find him looking down at his cell phone, his two index fingers tapping at the numbers. She'd seen it before—her father was texting.

"Could be," *Daed* said, but she could tell he wasn't giving her his full attention.

"He has some money, I know that," she continued, not caring if she was talking to herself now. "He's been saving for a few years. Hopefully, it's enough for them to—"

"I know for a fact," *Daed* said, putting his phone on the seat beside him, "that money has been spent."

"On what?" Grace sat up straight. "And how do you know?"

Before her father could even open his mouth to reply, his phone rang. "It's your mama," *Daed* said, quickly putting it to his ear. "How are you, dearest? *Gut, gut. Jah*, I know, only a few more days, eh? Ha-ha."

Despite not getting an answer, Grace couldn't help pulling back a little smile, so thankful her mother would be returning to them soon, and on the road to a healthier life.

"Aye, I know, *liebling*," *Daed* continued. "What an unexpected blessing—nay, *miracle* that money was. A surprise, oh, surely, for how else could we've ever paid for your surgery?"

Grace glanced at her father, who was beaming as he spoke to *Maam*. What surprise was he talking about? A miracle? Grace thought for a moment, realizing that—in all the excitement—she'd barely even wondered how *Daed* had finally come up with the cash for the surgery. Maybe he'd made some deal with Dr. McBride, or Lucas.

So then, what had *Daed* meant when he'd said he knew for a fact that the money Isaac had been saving was spent? How in the world would he be privy to that? Unless…

Her hands flew to her throat when she brought to mind that rainy day not so long ago, when Isaac had said he'd wished he could pay for the surgery himself.

*Had* he? Could he really have done such a massively generous thing? Given up *his* money for *her* family?

Grace almost couldn't believe it.

Then again, did she expect anything less than miracles from Isaac King?

Suddenly her skin began to shiver, and she had trouble catching her breath.

"*Daed*!" she nearly shouted, grabbing his elbow.

"I know, I know," her father replied. "He's early."

"Early?" Grace's mind spun. "Isaac?"

"Nay." He leaned forward to stare out the front windshield. "Travis Carlson."

Grace's stomach dropped when she realized they were pulling into their long gravel driveway; Travis's truck and silver trailer were parked beside the front pasture. But Isaac…Isaac was nowhere to be seen.

*Good gracious! Travis is early, and Isaac doesn't know!*

"Call him," she said, turning frantically to her father.

"Just did," *Daed* replied, holding up his cell. "Straight to voicemail."

Grace bit down on her lip as the car slowed to idle in front of their house.

"*Danke*, for everything," *Daed* was saying to Dr. McBride. "Words cannot express how much…"

Grace dashed out of the car, ran up the porch steps, and threw open the front door. "Isaac? Is Isaac here?"

Sarah and Amos jumped apart from each other. Grace would have to think about it later, but she could've sworn she'd caught them in an embrace behind the icebox.

"Isaac?" Sarah echoed, smoothing down her apron, rubbing a thumb along her bottom lip. "Haven't seen him in two days."

"Two days?" Grace put her hands on top of her head, pushing in her *kapp*, trying to think.

"Grace!" her father called not five seconds later. "Would you bring out Cincinnati? It's time."

Grace's heart pounded as she glanced about the room, hoping Isaac would somehow appear out of nowhere. She couldn't possibly do this without him, not with what she now knew.

"Gracie?"

Taking in a deep breath, trying to steady her wobbly knees, she called back, "Coming!" As she entered the stables, eyeing the tops of Sin's ears, she knew the time was far spent for any last goodbyes. At the hospital, she'd privately wept over knowing she would miss her last training session with Cincinnati, but how grateful she'd been to know Isaac would be there to do it.

So where was he now?

Grace felt frantic. And lost. Lost without her partner.

"Good boy," she said to Sin as she approached his

stall. "You've been such a good boy, but it's time for you to go home now. *Jah*, I know, but it'll be okay." She pressed her forehead to his, taking in one big inhale, hoping to never forget how the events surrounding the tenacious, marvelous horse had altered her life forever.

"Hey, boy," she said after a thought suddenly popped into her head. "Are you up for a bit of showing off?" She gave his neck a pat, eyeing the soft saddle on the tack wall. "Because your friend Isaac gave me a wonderful idea the other day."

She worked quickly but safely, sitting tall and proud—proud of her beloved Cincinnati—as the two of them trotted out of the stables and into the bright sunshine. She was confident that the *gaul*'s knees were high, head up, chin tucked, prettier than any show horse.

Not making any sort of eye contact with her father, Grace led Sin forward, backward, and side to side. Then, just as Isaac had probably envisioned, she galloped him into the front pasture where all of the jumping equipment was still in place.

"I can't believe it," she heard Travis say after Sin took the jumps perfectly, not missing one beat. "Is that really old Sin?"

"He likes to show off!" Grace called out, unable to stop from grinning.

"I'll say!"

After running the course four times, Grace slid off the horse, gave him some long strokes down the neck, then led him over to Travis and her father, whispering soft praises to Sin along the way.

"I can't tell y'all how impressed I am," Travis said. "It's like I can't believe my own eyes. What an entrance!"

"It all started with kindness," Grace said, a bit out of breath, coming to stand beside her father. "And trust."

"I'll certainly do my part at spreading the word about this training farm," Travis said, shaking John's hand vigorously. "Now, let's get to the lead trainer endorsements." He paused and looked around. "Where's Isaac?"

"He's, uh, he's not—" *Daed* began, but Grace cut him off.

"Isaac had urgent family business but wishes he were here." She took in a deep breath, sent one glance to her father, then stepped up to Travis. "Before you say anything more, I must insist that you give the endorsements, the publicity, the money…give it all to Isaac."

"Grace," she heard her father whisper, but it didn't stop her.

"I brought some of my own expertise to the table, and we were a true partnership, but Isaac was the leader, and he deserves everything." She put up a hand when Travis tried to speak. "I don't want to know what your earlier decision was, because it doesn't matter. Isaac earned it."

She finally stopped, needing to still her racing heart, let her words process. When she glanced at *Daed*, his mouth was open. Grace knew she'd shocked him more than anyone, but she'd decided—maybe almost the very second she'd realized what Isaac had done for her and her family—that she'd do whatever it took to keep him and Sadie in Honey Brook. It tore at her heart to think she would never be with Isaac in the way she'd hoped, but still, it was more important that he was happy and raising his daughter in a stable home with a real future.

"Gracie," *Daed* began, speaking in Dutch, "you

should've talked to me first—"

Her father was cut off when Travis started laughing. "This is the strangest day I've had in a while," he said after taking off his ball cap, slapping it against the side of his leg.

*Daed* let out an exasperated sigh Grace knew was meant for her. "How so?"

"Isaac King had me on the phone late last night," Travis said, pulling a small piece of paper from his shirt pocket and holding it out to Grace. "He made me promise—no, practically *swear* on the Bible that I would give the endorsement to you, Grace Zook. Insisted I put it in writing, in fact. See?"

When Grace was too stunned to move, her father reached for the folded piece of paper. "This isn't legal."

Travis chuckled again. "No, but I'd never renege on a promise like this. And not to someone like Isaac." He slid on a pair of sunglasses that had been hanging around his neck. "Seems I've been dealing with some mighty generous folks here." He smiled at Grace. "Too generous to take credit where credit is due. Nice, though, for a change."

Grace's mind was whirling. She couldn't believe what was going on. Why on earth would Isaac insist she was the lead trainer? Didn't he know he was throwing away his future? Tears began to burn her eyes when she thought of the sacrifice he was making, an even greater one than she'd first assumed.

Suddenly, she had so much love in her heart, she felt almost giddy.

"Suppose we should get our Cincinnati ready to travel," Travis said.

"Aye," her father replied. "I've got all his tack here."

"He likes sour apples," Grace said, trying her best to engage in the matters at hand.

"Thank you," Travis said. "For everything. I mean it."

Grace could only go through the motions as they loaded the now obedient horse into the trailer. So much different than the first time, she couldn't help recalling, then almost laughing at the way Isaac had looked that day when Sin had nearly kicked off the back of the trailer.

"You and I have some business to conduct, young lady," Travis said once Sin was safe and sound. "And you, sir."

The next hour was a whirlwind as Grace and *Daed* sat in the office with Travis, going over the details of the new collaboration.

Their first new horse would be arriving in three days. Two mares the day after. And Grace would be attending a rodeo at the end of the month to inspect the potential booth that would be used for advertising Zook's Horse Training Farm all around the state. If neither of them wanted to man it, they were free to hire and train someone else. Grace couldn't help thinking that she'd love if they hired a young Englisher woman who adored horses as much as she did.

Her mind was still in a haze when she and *Daed* waved goodbye to Travis. The second the truck and trailer were out of sight, she felt another gush of warmth toward Isaac wash over her, followed by a sadness of what might have been. Despite everything, she knew she'd never meet a better man.

"Looks like it's already started."

Hearing her father speak, Grace opened her eyes. She was surprised to see the number of buggies and carriages parked by the house, the side field filled with grazing horses she didn't recognize, but who most likely belonged to those buggies.

"What's going on?" she asked. "We were only inside for an hour. What's started?"

Daed was smiling. "Told you I sold some land."

Grace's mouth fell open, her mind whirling in confusion for not the first time today. "But you don't need to now. We won the endorsement."

"I made this deal before today," *Daed* said, rubbing his hands together as he gazed toward a group of men. "Don't forget, when your mama comes home, she's gonna need me around the clock the first few months." He paused to grin. "My favorite job— nothing I'd rather do."

"I don't understand," Grace said, alarmed by the growing number of people gathered by the lane that led to the back pasture. "Why are all these folks here? It looks like they're getting ready for a barn raising."

"Well, Gracie…" *Daed* took off his hat and scratched his head, motioning for them to sit on the porch. "A lot's been happening lately; forced me to do some real hard thinking."

"Okay." After they sat, she patted her father's arm, offering comfort. "Is there anything I can do to help?"

Her *daed* pulled back a crooked grin. "Come to think of it…" He touched his index finger to the tip of Grace's nose. "You can take over the family business—and the sooner the better."

Grace blinked slowly, unsure of what she'd just heard. "Take over?"

"The training, all of it. I'm retired." He threw his hands in the air. "I don't wanna have to be involved in all that promotion and whatnot. I'm too old and set in my ways. Travis needs someone more energetic and forward-thinking than me to run things." He put an arm around her shoulders. "I should've admitted this a long time ago, Gracie. You're the right person for the job, you always have been—no matter what dangers are associated with it. I guess I didn't want to admit it." He lowered his eyes. "Will you forgive your father for being such an old fool?"

Grace didn't have to think twice, but flung her arms around her father, both of them shaking with sobs of joy. "There's nothing to forgive," she said when she could finally speak again. She felt a swelling in her heart like a pot on the stove ready to boil over. "I can't believe it. Are you sure? Even after what happened with *Maam*?"

"Never been surer of anything," he answered.

"But…" She sat back and wiped the tear trickling down her cheek. "You told Isaac it isn't proper that I keep training. It's not traditional for a woman—"

"Old fool." *Daed* pointed at his own chest. "Say, why was Isaac telling you about our private conversation?"

Feeling shameful, Grace looked down at the ground. "He didn't tell me that part," she admitted, a wave of guilt washing over her as she ran that fateful night through her head one more time. "I overheard him telling someone else." She pressed a hand to her forehead, pondering how to express her next thought. "But…after everything that's happened today, I'm not so sure he meant anything by repeating it, I mean, I can't imagine he agrees with that philosophy."

"It might've been a mistake, then, huh?" *Daed* said. "One he feels real bad about." He leaned forward and lowered his voice. "And don't we all make mistakes?"

If she could now entertain the notion that Isaac

might not actually share the beliefs Wade had basically forced him to say that night, maybe she'd gotten even more wrong.

Just as Grace was ready to jump to her feet and ride Honey Pot all the way to Silver Springs, *Daed* pulled back to look her right in the eyes.

"I'm very proud of you, my Gracie." He cupped her face and ran his thumbs over her cheeks. "And if we're telling the truth, I've been having quite a few personal discussions with Isaac lately." He kissed her forehead. "Seems a smart girl like you would want to sit down with him for a proper talk."

"Hallo, Grace."

Recognizing the deep, manly voice, Grace looked up to see Isaac on the bottom step of the porch. Hadn't he been staying with his brother in Silver Springs? And if not, why had he missed the meeting with Travis?

While her confused subconscious ran in circles, her body instantly reacted to his presence: her tummy filling with nervous butterflies, an uncontrollable desire to take his hand, slide into his embrace. He was so handsome that it made her heart ache.

She'd expected being away from him for all those days would've helped her get over him, but the second their eyes met, she knew, despite everything, that her feelings had grown only stronger.

Was he still interested in her, though? Could she have really gotten everything so wrong that night, and every day since?

"Hi," she replied, trying to hold herself together. "I'm surprised to see you here."

"Oh?" Isaac said. "I've been taking care of the horses. Barnaby and Tater Tot are ready to be saddled. Big Smokey still won't settle in at night without your lullabies. Not to mention Honey Pot."

"You?" She couldn't help pointing to him.

"Didn't you tell her?" Isaac asked *Daed*.

*Daed* scratched his beard and stood. "I guess not. So much on my mind these days."

Grace exhaled in bemusement. "And what's happening to the back pasture? Why are so many men from the village here? Is there a church meeting?"

She looked at her *daed* first, then at Isaac, who was holding air in his cheeks, his arms out to his sides.

"I asked Isaac to help with the horses," *Daed* finally explained.

"And I gathered the men from the village."

"Okay." Grace said, though still baffled, even more so...seeing Isaac when she'd thought he'd already left town.

"I'm going to get washed up," *Daed* said. He gave Isaac a shake of the shoulder before disappearing inside the house.

"You seem confused," Isaac said to her, removing his hat.

"I am." Grace couldn't help chuckling sarcastically. "It's one thing after another today. First, I must ask. Did you...?" She paused when her chest suddenly went tight. "Isaac, did you give your savings to the hospital for *Maam*'s surgery?"

He stared at her, his brows furrowing. "I... I wish I could have," he said, dropping his chin. "I'm sorry. You don't know how much I wanted to help your family, Grace—"

"Please don't apologize for that. I'm so relieved. I really am." She felt choked up, her voice starting to shake, but she needed him to know she was sincere. "I was sick with worry about you and Sadie going back to Silver Springs."

"That's all worked out now," he said. "I mean, I *hope* it is." He flipped his hat in his hands. "Wonderful, though, that the hospital did the surgery for free. Pro bono, they call it. There's usually so much red tape." He paused to chuckle. "Lucas said it was a miracle."

"A miracle?" Grace echoed, recalling what her father had said on the phone to *Maam*. He'd used that exact word. *Miracle.*

"So that's what happened." She rose to her feet and put a hand to the side of her face as if her head really was reeling. "I assumed…"

"I've been assuming a lot, too," Isaac said after her voice faded out. "Wrongly assuming, I should say. It feels better now that I'm trying to set things straight."

Grace closed her eyes, knowing the flutter in her stomach would not go away until he set a few more things straight for her.

"Isaac," she said after taking in a deep breath. "You're New Order. How do you feel about women working outside the home?"

His brows shot up, then he pointed a finger at her. "You mean, like *you* owning and running your own horse training company?"

At the sudden introduction of the subject, Grace felt flushed, and her whole body began to tremble. "Why?" she said, more hot tears creeping up her throat. "Why did you tell Travis to give the endorsement to me?"

The calm expression that had been on Isaac's face suddenly dissolved. "I don't know what you're…" He paused and ran a hand along the side of his head. "He wasn't supposed to tell you about that."

"Well, he kind of had to."

"Why?

"Because." She couldn't help shaking her head. "Because *I* insisted he give it to *you*. Apparently, you got to him first, though." Her shoulders slumped as she pressed her palms together in the manner of prayer. "You deserve it," she whispered.

"No," he whispered back. "*You* do." He placed his hands over hers, holding them together.

For a moment, neither of them moved. Grace felt her pulse in her ears, blood rushing up to her cheeks, as she breathed in the scent of sunshine and hard work that always surrounded Isaac like a second skin.

She was unable to meet his gaze, even though she knew his eyes were pinned on her. "*Danke*," she managed to exhale in the tiniest of whispers. Isaac didn't speak, but she felt the gentlest pressure of his hands squeezing hers.

"Well, it's done now," he said as he stepped back, turned around, and walked down the porch steps. "And I believe all is right."

But all wasn't right. Not yet. "You didn't answer my question," she said, following him down the stairs.

"What question was that?" he asked. He seemed a little frustrated as he pushed his fingers up the back of his head. And when he finally turned around to her, his face was flushing, jaw muscles flexed under his skin.

"About how you're New Order," she said a bit tentatively, for she was nervous at how unsettled he now seemed. "It's none of my business, but how do you feel about women working outside the home?"

He stopped pacing, fixed his eyes on her, and then it was like all his tense muscles finally relaxed. "What makes you think my answer is none of your business?"

"I…" She hardly knew what to say to that. "*Daed*'s

retiring, giving the training farm to me. You don't think that's…improper?"

He pulled back a familiar smile, the one that always put Grace at ease, and not so long ago, the same smile that had sent a screaming desire through her body to kiss him. But she couldn't think that until all was really settled between them.

"So?" she asked, widening her eyes.

"Well…" Isaac fingered his chin, thoughtfully. "Some folks around here might have a problem with it, but I never would."

Grace's heart gave an optimistic leap, but before she had the chance to reply, a mule-driven cart came close to running them over. They had to jump out of the way as it continued toward the trail leading to the back pasture where other carts and men were gathered.

"We're ready to start." Bishop Turner suddenly appeared, coming up to Isaac with a hammer in his hand. "Any other instructions?"

"Keep it as standard as any other in Honey Brook," Isaac said.

"What's going on?" Grace asked as she noticed men were unloading long planks of wood onto the ground.

"Oh, afternoon, Grace," the bishop said. "We're all very excited about this. See you both later."

Grace stared at him as he walked away to join the others, her jaw going slack. *Daed* had given her the business, but he owned all the land, even the back pasture that looked like it was about to be turned into a building site.

"From your expression," Isaac said, catching up to her after she'd began following the bishop, "I get the feeling you're still a little confused."

"A little?" Grace replied, walking faster. "What is happening?"

"Grace." She felt Isaac take her by the elbow. It was such a familiar feeling that it made her stop in her tracks. "Shouldn't we finish our conversation?" He glanced over his shoulder at the group of men now surrounding them. "Alone."

"I…" she began, still suspiciously eyeing the stack of wood.

"Come with me." He gently pulled her arm. "For just a minute. Please."

Grace gave the workers one last wary glance—as they were now mixing cement—before allowing herself to be led away.

"I'm sorry," Isaac said once they'd walked around to the other side of the house. "This has all been so chaotic, so…"

*"Nontraditional?"* Grace couldn't help finishing for him, then tilting her head to the side.

The corners of Isaac's eyes squinted as if he was holding back a smile. "Nontraditional is the perfect description. And you need to know, Grace, I'd have it no other way." He took a step toward her. "You know that bit of land your father sold?"

"Aye." Grace glanced over her shoulder. "I was just thinking about that."

"He sold it to me."

"You?" She peered at him. "For what?"

He shrugged and gave her one of those silly grins she'd been seeing in her dreams. "I wasn't sure, at first. He'd brought up the possibility of selling it to me that day at the medical clinic when you were outside."

Grace bit her thumbnail. "That was quite a while ago."

"I didn't make an offer on it then, but a few days

ago, when you were away."

She had to think. Isaac had bought her father's land *after* they'd stopped seeing each other? When they were barely speaking?

"*Jah*," he said, nodding, somehow reading her mind.

"But..." She thought further, about that very morning in the car with her father when *Daed* had said he'd known Isaac had already spent his savings. It hadn't been for *Maam*'s surgery, but for the very same land on which she lived.

"It wasn't even difficult to decide to build a house right over there," Isaac added, gesturing toward the back pasture.

"Why did you do that?" Grace couldn't help asking, feeling more confused at the new information, not less.

Suddenly, Isaac lowered his chin, as if unable to look her in the eyes. "Maybe I'm a fool, but I never lost all hope," he said, staring down at his boots. "Every day, I can't help wishing and praying that we'll somehow make amends. That you'll trust in me again."

"Isaac," she whispered, the thrill of optimism making her voice weak.

"I realize it might be awkward, me living so near you, but..." Finally, he lifted his chin and shot her a look she remembered from that night in the barn when he'd held her in his arms. She'd never felt so loved. So safe. "I'm not ready to give up on us, Grace. It's a long shot, I know, but I'm hopeful—I have to be, or else Heaven and Earth make no sense."

Grace felt lightheaded, dizzy on her feet. She tried to speak again, but her heart was in her throat.

"At worst," Isaac continued, "I'll convert my house

to a barn and sell it back to you, if that's what you want."

"And at best?" she managed to whisper as she gazed at him.

Slowly, he lifted one corner of his mouth, setting those hazel eyes upon her. "At best? A home," he said, his voice full of emotion. "Home for me and Sadie, and for one of the barn kittens she's got her eye on." He blinked slowly. "And home for anyone else who'll have me."

"Isaac," she said, eyes flooding with tears while her heart beat strong and steady.

Just as she summoned the strength to reach out to him, he said, "I don't think I fully answered your question about being New Order."

"Oh," Grace said, a bit bewildered at the change of subject. Didn't he want her back? Or was she reading everything wrong once again?

"Do I approve of Amish women holding jobs? Working outside instead of homemaking?" He tapped his chin. "To push the idea even further, would I ever *marry* someone like that?"

Grace heard her breath catch as Isaac took a step forward. She had half a mind to do the same but seemed frozen in place at the word "marry."

"Honestly," he continued, "I never thought I'd be faced with a question like that…until I met you." He pressed his lips together as a little notch formed between his brows, intensity in his hazel eyes. "When I'm with you, it never feels improper or nontraditional. Being with you has brought joy to my life. Even after everything that's happened, I'm not ready to let go of that joy."

Grace saw in his eyes that his words were truthful. Knew without a doubt that it was safe to trust him with her heart.

"Isaac," she said, barely getting his name out before she reached for his hand, squeezing it between both of hers. "You brought me joy, too—I mean *bring*." She smiled. "You *bring* me joy. When I'm with you, I'm never so happy." She looked into his eyes, feeling a rush of relief and then a sweet stirring of warmth in her chest.

"May I hold you?" Isaac asked, opening his arms to her, a pleading tone to his voice.

"Aye," Grace whispered, falling into his arms just as easily as she had the stormy night in the barn. When he wrapped his arms around her, she melted into his chest, pressing her cheek against him, feeling more at home inside his embrace than anywhere else.

"Amazing news about the training farm," he said. "Congratulations again." His words drifted down to her ears as she rested the side of her head against him.

"*Danke*," she simply said, instead of arguing that he should've won the endorsement. Although maybe now there was something she could do about that. After taking in one last inhale of his shirt, she pulled back. "How much begging would I have to do to get you to work for me?"

He chuckled, the sound music to her ears. "Oh, I'm much too expensive." He kissed the tip of her nose, sending a rush of tingles down her arms. "But if you begging me is part of the deal, I might just come for free."

"You're hired." She tightened her grip around him. "What do you think, partner?"

"I love you," he said, looking deep into her eyes.

Grace knew his words were true. Not only did she trust him, but she felt *Gott*'s presence, his loving spirit wrap around them both, bringing her the purest peace.

"I love you, too," she whispered.

He narrowed his eyes. "My sweet Gracie. May I kiss you now?"

She couldn't help her smile from turning into a giggle. *"Jah."*

It was like being in the dim barn with him the night of the storm all over again. But better, for in between sweet kisses, they whispered things to each other Grace had never even dared to dream.

She felt breathless and feminine when they finished. Some of the men from the yard might have gotten an eyeful, but Grace didn't care. All she knew was she stood safely in the arms of the man she loved. The man who loved her back.

"One last thing," Isaac said as if they were in the middle of a conversation.

"Oh heavens," Grace said with a big smile. "What now?"

"What you're saying is…you'll consider living in the new house with me and Sadie someday?"

She rubbed her lips together, longing for another kiss. "You mean, like sometime after this year's wedding season?"

Isaac exhaled a low growl from his chest as he pulled her in tighter. "I'd have you move in with me right now if I could."

"Why, Isaac King." She playfully swatted his chest. "Now who's being nontraditional?"

Just as she was about to press her lips to his, they were suddenly seized upon by Sadie—her dress covered in dirt as if she'd been helping the workers in the pasture. *Or maybe*, Grace couldn't help thinking, *like she's been in the barn with the horses.*

Isaac scooped her up with one arm, keeping the other around Grace. Together they stood under the bright afternoon sunshine.

Grace's heart nearly beat out of her chest with more happiness than she thought her body could hold. She glanced up at Isaac, meeting his gaze, and between Sadie's string of questions, she whispered, "I will."

# EPILOGUE

Isaac's cheeks were beginning to ache from smiling so much. The church service had begun at 8:30 that morning, and the lunch meal of roast chicken, mashed potatoes, and creamed celery had already been cleared from the dozens of long tables set up along the sides and backyard of the Zooks' house. It was nearly two o'clock, and yet their wedding day had only just begun.

"Congratulations," Travis said, shaking Isaac's hand.

"*Danke*," Isaac replied. "And thank you again for coming. I know you're not used to this."

Travis smiled and glanced around, taking in a deep breath. "I've been to my share of big weddings, but I've never witnessed this much neighborly kindness and camaraderie. It's quite an experience. And I've definitely never seen so many different pies in all my life!"

"Well, save room for later. There'll be even more at tonight's dinner."

Travis spoke of Cincinnati and how well the horse was doing at the winter competitions. Isaac was happy to hear that, but it only made his thoughts return to Grace.

*Where's that woman disappeared to?*

She'd been radiant when he'd seen her first thing that morning, wearing a sky-blue dress, starched white apron, and black head covering. The church service seemed to take hours, and his bow tie had felt like it was cutting off all oxygen every time she glanced those blue eyes his way or flashed that dimple she knew made him weak in the knees.

As he greeted another group of guests from Silver Springs, Isaac's heart felt full enough to explode when he remembered kneeling across from her, Bishop Turner reading from the books of Genesis, Judges, and Ruth. The words had been a blur, for all he'd been able to think about was how their day had finally come. Grace would be his forever, and he'd vowed with love, forbearance, and patience to take care of her "as is fitting for a Christian husband."

Isaac was more than ready, right this second, to initiate husbandly privileges with Grace as his wife.

*But where is she?*

Lucas gave him a wink and a nod as he passed by a group of men. Eve, Sarah, and a pack of women came flooding out of the house. It still took Isaac by surprise when he noticed how active his now-mother-in-law had become after only six months of post-surgery rehab. It also continued to amaze him whenever he saw Sarah. His sister-in-law's belly looked ready to pop. She was strong, though, and cheery, and her cheeks glowed—especially when she looked at Amos, the proud father-to-be.

"Have you seen Grace?" Isaac asked, undoing his bow tie.

"Lost her already?" Esther laughed while wiping crumbs off a table. "How clumsy."

"Ha-ha," Isaac chuckled lightheartedly.

"Last I saw her," Sarah said, "she was with Sadie."

That told Isaac everything he needed to know. Though he couldn't believe she'd do this in the middle of their wedding day.

Truth be told, however, he'd never expect less.

"*Danke,*" he said. "Can I help with that?"

"Nay!" Sarah held the stack of dirty dishes she was gathering out of his reach. "Enjoy your day... brother." For a quick moment, they gazed at each other. Isaac couldn't have been any more blessed with his lot of in-laws. Amos had become one of his closest friends. And Sarah, well, he couldn't imagine loving his own sister any better.

After chatting with some of his volunteer firefighter buddies, Isaac was able to sneak off, probably along the same path Grace had earlier.

The sun hung high in the sky. And although it was late October, the weather was still plenty warm. He heard their voices drifting through the autumn air before he saw them...

"Hold it like this. You see? *Jah*—perfect! Now take your time, sweetie."

Isaac couldn't help but stand in place and watch from a distance. Sadie was holding a set of long reins in one hand, turning in a slow circle, as Tangerine—the newest pony to be brought to Zook's Horse Training Farm—trotted a loop in perfect obedience.

"You're doing it," Grace said in delight, clapping her hands and jumping up and down. "I knew you could!"

Isaac chuckled when he noticed her black bonnet was sitting askew on her head. Her white apron had a streak of dirt across it, and that sky-blue dress she'd handmade for her wedding was hiked up and tied in two knots, a pair of faded brown trousers underneath. From that distance, he couldn't see her shoes, but he could only imagine.

"Daddy!" Sadie dropped the rope and dashed over to him. "Did you see? Did you see Tangerine?"

"I did!" Isaac exclaimed as he pulled her up into his arms. "You're getting so good at training. But shouldn't you be at the house? Hannah is surely looking for you."

"Is there pie left?" Sadie asked, her eyes as big as saucers.

"Why don't you go find out."

Sadie looked at her father, but then glanced at Grace. "Can I Grace? I mean, Mommy?"

Grace laughed while pulling off Tangerine's harness. "Of course, *liebling*. We'll practice later, okay?" She patted the horse's rump, encouraging her to run free around the pasture.

"Ew-key!" Sadie gasped in excitement, wiggled out of Isaac arms, and began running up the hill, showing that the bottom of her dress was also hiked up and knotted.

When Grace's blue eyes moved to Isaac, her cheeks glowing with exercise, he wondered if he'd ever been as happy as he was right then.

"Care to explain yourself, Grace Zook?" he said, walking toward her.

"Grace Zook *King*, you mean."

Catching the playful sparkle in her eyes, Isaac had no choice but to reach out and pull her into his arms. "Grace Zook King," he whispered into her ear. "Mmm, I like that."

"You'd better," she whispered back. Her body shook with laughter as he squeezed her extra tight. "Honestly, I meant to have Sadie out here for only a second. Was I missed?"

Isaac smiled down at her, adjusting her *kapp*, then he pressed his lips to her forehead. "Only by me."

"Oh?" Grace blinked a few times, sent a quick glance over one shoulder, then looked up at him. Something in her expression made Isaac's heart skip a beat. "So, no one will notice if I do this…?"

The heat of a campfire erupted in Isaac's chest, but he dared not move a single muscle as his bride slid her palms up his chest, rose onto her toes, wrapped her arms around his neck, and kissed him in a way that made him wonder if he'd ever be able to walk in a straight line again.

"I love you," she whispered. "With all my heart."

Isaac's breaths were mere gasps when he tried to speak.

"Shh." Grace placed a finger over his lips. She kissed him again, gently this time, but enough for Isaac to recall the first time he'd seen her…dirty dress, crooked *kapp*, a smile on her face that would forever be branded on his heart.

How could he have not known—even back then—that this woman was a blessing from *Gott* he'd never be able to repay?

He leaned down to kiss her, his restless fingers digging in to her hips.

"Careful," Grace whispered, gazing up at him. "I don't want you to lose your strength yet. Our lives are just beginning."

# ACKNOWLEDGMENTS

*Danke*: My editor, Stacy Abrams, for encouraging this project when I was completely out of steam; the wonderful team of editors at Entangled Publishing; my gal pals, Nancy, Ginger, and Jen, who keep me going with bread and gelato; my family for their enthusiasm and support; and especially to my husband for his surprising creativity when I've written myself into a plot corner and can't get out. I love you all!

*If you loved* The Amish Cowboy's Homecoming, *you won't want to miss the companion novel, which Shelley Shepard Gray called "simply wonderful!"*

# NEVER *an* AMISH BRIDE

*by Ophelia London*

Everything changed for Esther Miller with the death of her beloved fiancé, Jacob. Even years later, she still struggles with her faith and purpose in the small, tight-knit Amish village of Honey Brook—especially now that her younger sister is getting married. All she wants is to trust in the Lord to help her find peace...but peace is the last thing she gets when Lucas, Jacob's wayward older brother, returns to town.

Lucas Brenneman has been harboring a secret for years—the real reason he never returned from Rumspringa and the truth behind his brother Jacob's death. Honey Brook still calls to him, but he knows his occupation as a physician's assistant must take precedence. With sweet and beautiful Esther he finds a comfort he's never known, and he feels like anything is possible...even forgiveness. But she was Jacob's bride-to-be first. And if she knew the truth, would she ever truly open her heart to him?

*Love may be right around the corner in the heartwarming, sweet, and gentle Pine Creek series from Amity Hope.*

# Pine Creek
# COURTSHIP

After the death of her beloved father, Emma Ziegler just wants to keep her family's maple syrup farm afloat and raise her two young siblings. But when her meddling aunt's first choice of a husband for her turns out to be Emma's last choice—Pine Creek's most notorious bachelor—Emma grows desperate. Her aunt won't listen, no matter how much she tries to tell her the man in no way embodies the Amish values of faith or hard work.

Kind and industrious Levi Bontrager has always wanted to protect his best friend Emma, even after a secret from their youth left them growing apart. Which is why he steps in to claim that Emma cannot wed anyone else, as she is currently courting *him*. Yes, the small lie leaves him feeling guilty, but Levi's hope is that if he can win back the beautiful Emma's trust, he can also win over her heart...for real.

But can a courtship that began just for show ever blossom into a true romance that could save both their futures?

*A pregnant Amish woman discovers the true meaning of Christmas in this inspirational, heartwarming debut—coming soon!*

# CHRISTMAS GRACE

## *by Mindy Steele*

Grace Miller believed herself in love with the charming *Englischer* who eventually broke her heart. Now alone except for the secret life growing inside her, she arrives in the unfamiliar small village of Walnut Ridge, Kentucky, to hide and hopefully gain forgiveness.

She is pleasantly surprised, however, to find a tight-knit, welcoming group who help her heart grow right alongside her belly. And with the holidays around the corner, there's plenty of preparations to occupy her mind. Also occupying her mind? Her strong, protective neighbor, Cullen Graber, the town's blacksmith, who seems intent on not allowing her to ever suffer alone.

Cullen Graber gave up on love after too many losses early in life. He planned to live out his days focusing on his smithy business, yet the beautiful and mysterious Grace refuses to leave his thoughts. But can they open their hearts to God's grace and create a new family together before Grace must return home?